PRAISE FOR THE JIG THE GOBLIN NOVELS:

"In *Goblin Hero*, as in *Goblin Quest*, Hines recognizes that wisdom is most often common sense and that mouthing off to the big guy with the sword is a very bad idea." —Tanya Huff, author of the *Blood* books

"*Goblin Quest* is a fun enjoyable read. Role reversal and gibes at the genre make Jig not only a sympathetic character, but seemingly the only sane one there for the reader to identify with. Of course, if you read this book and drive your spouse into fits of annoyance listening to you snort and giggle at the absurdity the author continually throws at poor Jig, don't blame me. I merely said it was a great book."   —*SFRevu*

"*Goblin Quest* is hilarious. It has a wonderful angle on some classic material that's in the DNA of many of my generation and younger. . . . Jim Hines' Jig is a clever character, in several senses of that term. He's got the RPG warrior mentality nailed to the wall. He's got a lovely sense of plot and pacing. Most of all, he has an excellent sense of fun."

—Jay Lake, author of *Trial of Flowers*

"Once again, Jim C. Hines turns the fantasy world on its ear with this insightfully hilarious look at the traditional cannon fodder of the genre." —greenmanreview.com

continued . . .

JIM C. HINES'

Jig the Goblin Series:

GOBLIN QUEST (Book One)
GOBLIN HERO (Book Two)
GOBLIN WAR (Book Three)

GOBLIN WAR

JIM C. HINES

WITHDRAWN

DAW BOOKS, INC.

DONALD A. WOLLHEIM, FOUNDER

SHEILA E. GILBERT
PUBLISHERS
www.dawbooks.com

First Printing, March 2008
1 2 3 4 5 6 7 8 9

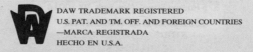

To Jamie

ACKNOWLEDGMENTS

Ask any writer what would happen if they ever got the opportunity to meet one of their characters in real life. Most of the time, the results would be . . . unpleasant. As authors, we aren't very nice to our heroes.

If Jig were given the chance, I'm quite sure he would hide fire-spider eggs in my socks, stick a lizard-fish in my bed, and then feed my remains to the tunnel cats.

He has good reason for hating me, though. I've dragged him through not one, not two, but three different adventures, not to mention a handful of short stories. Jig and I have been through a lot together, and I don't blame him for wanting a bit of payback.

Of course, I wouldn't be the only target of Jig's rage. Oh, no. Once he finished with me, he would probably go after my agent, Steve Mancino. Steve was instrumental in bringing these books to the world, so it's perfectly understandable that Jig would want to slice him up and snack on Steve-topped pizza.

Next I imagine Jig would head to the DAW offices in New York. There he would find targets aplenty, from Sheila Gilbert to Debra Euler to the rest of the DAW family who have helped so much with the goblin books. But given what editors have to deal with on any given day, I imagine they would be more than tough enough to handle a goblin and his fire-spider.

Mel Grant, my cover artist, should also be fine. How could Jig possibly hold a grudge against someone who paints such marvelous goblins?

So Jig would instead go after my beta readers, whose feedback and suggestions for all three books have been invaluable. To Teddi Baer, Catherine Shaffer, Bill Rowland, Heather Poppink, Mike Jasper, Nicole Montgomery, and Anthony Hays, all I can say is I'm sorry.

Lastly, Jig would return for my family. I can't imagine how I would have written these books without the love, encouragement, support, and patience of my wife Amy and my two wonderful children. Here at last Jig's rampage would come to an end, since my daughter would insist on trying to catch Smudge in an old peanut butter jar, and my little boy would steal poor Jig's spectacles, then tackle him.

I love that little goblin, though he would never believe it. It has been a wonderful experience to share that love with all of my readers. Thank you all. I hope you enjoy this third volume in the adventures of Jig Dragonslayer.

Recitation of the Deeds of Jig Dragonslayer
(written by the goblin Relka, Founder of the Children of Shadowstar)

Relka: In the beginning, there was a muckworking runt called Jig.

Goblins: We stole his food and threw rats at him.

Relka: But destiny brought adventurers into our mountain haven. And lo, Jig set forth to combat these so-called heroes.

Goblins: Better him than us.

Relka: It was a battle of great chaos and bloodshed, and Jig did kicketh the human prince right in the rocks.

Goblins: Such should be the fate of all nonbelievers.

Relka: Though he was captured again, Jig was not afraid.

Goblins: Long may his loincloth remain unsoiled.

Relka: Jig led them into darkness, where he slew hobgoblins, the Necromancer, and even the dragon Straum with no more than a broken kitchen knife.

Goblins: Hail the miracle of the wobbly blade.

Relka: Jig returned triumphant, blessed by Tymalous Shadowstar with the gift to heal our wounds, though they be many and often self-inflicted. But lo, some were displeased with Jig's triumphs. The treacherous goblin chief Kralk sent Jig away, and none dared challenge her.

Goblins: For she was big and scary, and carried many weapons.

Relka: Guided by the light of Shadowstar, Jig descended into the mountain. There did he discover a great threat.

Goblins: Stupid pixies!

Relka: Jig and his companions returned to leadeth his fellow goblins in battle, but Kralk refused to believe. She fought, and she fell.

Goblins: Thus did Jig teach a great lesson: Never turn your back on a hobgoblin.

Relka: Jig set out to destroyeth the pixies, but still there were some who did not believe. A single kitchen drudge attempted to steal his glory for herself.

Goblins: And lo, Jig stabbethed you in the gut.

Relka: But Jig Dragonslayer was merciful. Upon his triumphant return from battle, and after drinking too much klak beer, he did heal my wounds, pouring the light and life of the Shadowstar into my very blood.

Goblins: Praise be unto Jig Dragonslayer, high priest of Tymalous Shadowstar. Long may he heal our wounds and fight our foes.

CHAPTER 1

Starlight sparkled in silver mortar as Tymalous Autumnstar ran his fingers over the wall of his temple. The black stone was warm to the touch, constantly changing to record the prayers and gifts of his followers.

Every image and tribute ever created in his honor was here, preserved in the rock. To his right, the blood paintings of the Xantock Warrior Elves shone in the light, still wet after thousands of years. Overhead, the intricate carvings of the Undermountain Dwarf Clan spelled out their long-winded prayers.

The temple had gotten uncomfortably large over the years.

Tiny bells jingled on Autumnstar's sleeve as he touched a starburst a child had drawn in the mud. The ebony stone mimicked her painting so perfectly he could even discern the tiny whorls and loops where her fingertips had pressed the mud. Clumsy hieroglyphs below the picture read Tell gramma I miss her and please send me a puppy.

The painting was two centuries old, and the girl had long since followed her gramma. Autumnstar's forehead wrinkled. He had forgotten to take care of the puppy. That had been right around the start of the war, so he could probably be forgiven an oversight or two, but it still bothered him.

The temple shuddered, as if someone had taken the moon itself and smashed it against Autumnstar's roof.

Autumnstar's movements were slow, almost absent-minded as he raised a silver shield overhead. The second blow crumbled the ceiling to reveal the deeper darkness beyond. Mortar fell in glittering clouds as cracks spread through the walls. Stones shattered against Autumnstar's shield, centuries of worship and idolatry reduced to rubble.

Overhead, the Autumn Star burned red, casting a bloody glow over the remains of the temple. By the time the attack slowed and the dust began to clear, the remnants of the walls came no higher than Autumnstar's knees. He lowered his shield and used one foot to sweep some of the debris to one side. He preferred his home tidy.

The light of the Autumn Star vanished, blocked by the looming form of another god. Noc, a newly empowered death god, bent to touch a fallen shard of rock. The rock dissolved into smoke at his touch.

"Show-off," Autumnstar muttered.

Noc stepped over the broken wall and drew a sword of white light.

"You know," Autumnstar said slowly. "My temple had a door."

Goblin war drums wouldn't be so bad, Jig decided, if the drummers would only stick to a consistent beat.

He squeezed between a clump of pine trees. Snow spilled from the branches, most of it sliding down the back of his cloak. The rest landed in Jig's left ear.

Jig yelped and poked a claw into his ear, digging out the worst of the snow.

"We should stay quiet," Relka said behind him.

With great effort, Jig restrained himself from stabbing his fellow goblin. He wiped his nose on his sleeve and tried to ignore her.

Relka brushed snow from his back. "Don't you like the cloak I gave you? Why don't you use the hood?" She grabbed the hood before Jig could warn her. A moment later, she was cursing and shoving her singed fingers into the snow.

"Because that's where Smudge rides," Jig said, his annoyance vanishing as quickly as it had come. He grinned as he reached back to stroke his pet fire-spider. Smudge was still warm, but he settled down at Jig's touch.

"But you do like the cloak, don't you? I got it from an adventurer last month." Relka sucked nervously on her lower lip, tugging it between the curved fangs of her lower jaw. She did that a lot around Jig. Between that and the bitter cold, her lips were always cracked and bleeding.

Relka was one of the younger goblins, a kitchen drudge who worked with Golaka the chef. Her fangs were small for a goblin, and her face tended to be sweaty and streaked with soot from the cook fires. She had used an old tunnel cat bone to pin a blanket over her clothes for warmth.

Jig fingered the hole in the front of his cloak. Old blood had turned the frayed edges the color of rust where a goblin had gotten in a lucky blow with his spear. Still, even with the hole, at least the cloak was warm. Lavender wasn't exactly Jig's color, and he could have done without the embroidered flowers and vines running along the edges, but he wasn't about to complain. It was *warm*, and even better, the material was highly flame-resistant. Even if it did smell faintly of blood.

"You hate it, don't you?" Relka slumped. Even her wide, pointed ears sagged.

"It's not bad," Jig said grudgingly. "I like the pockets."

Relka beamed. Before she could speak, Jig quickly asked, "Shouldn't you be taking me to Grell instead of fussing about a cloak?"

Relka squeezed past him, close enough for her necklace to tangle in Jig's sleeve. She tried to tug it free, but only managed to jab Jig's arm.

"Sorry," she mumbled, her face turning a brighter shade of blue.

Her necklace was supposed to symbolize her devotion to Jig's god, Tymalous Shadowstar. Rat bones were lashed together to form a crude starburst. Pieces of a broken kitchen knife formed a lightning bolt, the lower tip of which was currently poking Jig's forearm.

Relka's obsession with Jig and Shadowstar had begun when she tried to stab Jig in the back. Instead, Jig had run her through, leaving her with a nasty belly wound while he led the other goblins off to fight pixies. Relka had crawled away to hide, terrified that Jig would return to finish her off.

Which he might have done, if Tymalous Shadowstar hadn't had this strange obsession with mercy and forgiveness. Also Relka made really good snake egg omelettes.

Jig clenched his jaw, driving his fangs into his cheeks as he waited for Relka to free her necklace. What was Grell doing outside in the first place, anyway? During a time of battle, a goblin leader traditionally stayed back where it was safe. Especially when it came to enemies like this.

The attack had begun this morning, and from what Jig had heard from the few goblins who limped back to the lair, this was no simple adventuring party.

"Grell?" He tried to speak loudly enough for the aging chief to hear, while at the same time keeping his voice low to avoid attracting any human attention. What emerged could best be described as "quavering."

"She said she was going to take care of the drummers," Relka said.

Oh. Jig felt a moment's sympathy for the goblin drummers. If they had caused Grell to miss her after-lunch nap, she would be even crankier than usual.

The area immediately around the goblin cave was flat, covered in small pine trees. If you walked directly away from the lair, you could go about fifteen paces before tumbling off a steep, rock-strewn drop-off.

The drummers would have taken the left path, which led along the cliffside and up toward the lake.

The higher they climbed, the more people they could annoy with their drums.

The trees were denser as they approached the river. Their branches seemed determined to drop snow and needles down the back of his cloak. Trampled snow showed where goblin warriors had stormed through in search of humans to fight.

Pools of blue blood showed exactly where the humans had ambushed them. The bulk of the humans were still farther down the mountainside. They must have sent scouts ahead. It was a smart idea. The scouts could watch to see where the goblins were going, then report back to whoever was in charge. If they got the chance to surprise a few goblins, so much the better.

Jig didn't bother searching for the injured goblins. There were no bodies, which meant they had probably followed typical practice and fled like frightened rats. If Jig were smarter, he would be doing the same.

But where had the humans gone?

Relka hurried past before Jig could stop her. He crouched down, waiting for her to be shot or stabbed.

Nothing happened. She was already climbing up along the riverbank, using the shrubs and small trees to pull herself along the rocks. Jig held his breath and crept after her.

"It sounds like they're near the lake," Relka said. She drew a long, wickedly sharp knife. A cooking knife, from the look of it. Hopefully Golaka didn't know Relka had swiped it.

The drums grew louder as they followed the river back to the lake. Jig started to draw his sword, then thought better of it. Given the rocky, snow-covered terrain, he'd only end up tripping over a rock and impaling himself.

They scrambled on hands and knees to the top of a rise bordering the lake. As Jig pulled himself up, he heard the ripping sound of a dying drum, followed by the squealing sound of a dying goblin. He covered his eyes against the sun's glare. Only the edges of the lake were frozen, and the still water at the center created a second sun, reflecting the light into Jig's eyes and blinding him doubly. The amethyst lenses of his spectacles helped, but any relief they brought was balanced by splotches of melted snow. He wiped his sleeve over the lenses, but that only smeared his vision worse.

A short distance ahead, a human in leather and steel armor stood on the edge of the lake, surrounded by fallen goblins. He wore a green tabard with a picture of a giant four-legged boar standing in front of a tower. The animal appeared almost as large as the tower itself, and it held an enormous sword in one paw.

Humans wore strange clothes.

A dent in the human's helmet suggested the goblins had landed at least one good blow before they fell. Of the four goblin bodies scattered across the snow, only one was still moving.

"Oh, no," Jig whispered. The surviving goblin had fallen onto the ice at the lake's edge. She struggled to push herself up on twin canes of yellow-dyed wood. One cane punched through the ice. She fell back with a curse, losing her grip on the cane.

"Come on," said Relka. She started to rise, but Jig dragged her back.

"Humans have weird rules about killing unarmed old women," Jig said. "Some of them do, at least. Grell will be fine."

This human appeared to be one of the "honorable" ones. He kept his sword ready, but didn't try to stop Grell from crawling to the edge of the lake.

"At least you put a stop to that blasted drumming," Grell said. She took another step and her remaining cane slipped.

The human laughed.

"Oh, think this is funny, do you?" Grell rolled over and slammed her cane into the human's leg.

The cane broke. The human laughed even harder.

Jig shook his head. "It's not a good idea to laugh at Grell."

Grell stabbed the broken end of her cane into the

human's thigh, right through the bottom corner of his tabard.

The human staggered back. He reached down with his free hand to rip Grell's cane from his leg.

"We've got to save her!" Relka grabbed Jig's hand and pulled him over the ridge.

They weren't going to make it. With only one cane to support her hunched body, Grell could barely even walk. The human was going to kill her, which would leave the goblins without a chief.

The last time that had happened was close to a year ago, when a hobgoblin named Slash killed the previous chief. The goblins had chosen Jig to take her place.

Jig still had nightmares about his short time as chief. Half of the lair had expected him to solve all of their problems. The other half had been busy plotting to kill him and take his place. Jig wasn't about to let that happen again.

He yanked his sword from its sheath. In the songs and stories, warriors sometimes threw their weapons as a last resort to kill distant enemies. As Relka ran ahead, Jig steadied himself, drew back, and flung his sword as hard as he could.

Either Jig was no warrior, or this wasn't the right kind of weapon for throwing. Probably both. The sword nearly cut off Relka's ear as it spun end over end. She dove into the snow.

The sword curved to the right and bounced harmlessly off a tree, halfway between Jig and the human. A bit of snow sprinkled down from the branches.

Everyone turned to look at Jig . . . who had now thrown away his only weapon.

Relka was busy digging through the snow. She must have dropped her knife when she tried to avoid Jig's sword. Wonderful. With a single throw, Jig had managed to disarm both himself and his companion.

Relka waved at him. "Don't worry! Shadowstar will guide you to victory!"

Jig stared at the limping human. Jig was unarmed,

but the human carried enough weapons for three goblins. He switched his sword to his left hand and drew a knife with his right. He flipped the knife, catching it by the blade, and threw.

The knife spun past Jig's head, close enough for him to hear the whirring sound of its passage. With a loud thunk, the knife buried itself in a tree trunk.

Right. *Warriors* could throw their weapons. Goblins were better off running away.

Jig turned to run. He leaped over the ridge, skidding and flailing his arms for balance. He managed to run a whole three steps before tripping over a tree root. Rocks scraped his knees and hands, and the impact stole his breath. He pushed himself up. Snow smeared his spectacles, rendering them all but useless. He peered over the top of the frames at the blurry figure of the approaching human, who now carried swords in both hands.

That was simply unfair. Two swords against none? Jig squinted. Was that—? It was! The human was carrying Jig's own sword in his off hand.

"For Shadowstar!" Relka waved her knife as she charged to Jig's defense. It was a typical goblin tactic, with typical results. The human stepped to one side. Relka was running too fast to change direction, but she tried anyway, saving her life in the process. She stumbled, dropping her knife again as she fought to recover her balance. The human's follow-up attack missed, and then Relka was face-first in the snow.

"There's no place to run, goblin," the human said. He had faced four goblins, and he wasn't even breathing hard! "Turn around and die like a man."

Now there was a stupid suggestion if Jig had ever heard one. Jig pulled himself to his feet and searched his pockets for weapons. There were at least twenty pockets sewn into the cloak, enough for Jig to carry most of his belongings.

Unfortunately, that was far too many pockets to remember exactly where everything was. He found an old smoked bat wing, an extra pair of socks, some dead wasps he was saving for Smudge . . . hadn't he tucked a knife in here somewhere?

The human twirled both swords. The blades hissed through the air. His hands moved so fast Jig could barely follow, and his swords were all but invisible as they created a web of whirling steel. One limping step at a time the human advanced, bringing those blades closer and closer to Jig.

Jig reached into his hood and grabbed Smudge. For a moment Jig simply stood there, letting the fire-spider's warmth thaw his numb fingers. Then Jig threw him at the human.

Smudge landed on the human's chest and clung there, a blurry spot of black and red in the middle of the human's tabard. He had landed near the head of the beast embroidered on the tabard, like a tiny smoldering hat.

Unfortunately, the tabard gave no indication of bursting into flames. Either Smudge wasn't as frightened as Jig, or else the poor fire-spider was too cold to generate enough heat.

Well, on the bright side, Jig wouldn't have to worry about the other goblins trying to make him chief again.

The human's scream was so unexpected—and so terrifying—that Jig found himself screaming in response.

Both swords fell to the ground as the human grabbed the edges of his tabard and tugged it away from his body. He shook the tabard faster and faster, trying to shake Smudge free. Jig could have told him not to bother. Each of the fire-spider's legs had tiny hairs, like burrs, that let him cling to almost anything.

The human changed tactics. Still screaming, he dropped to his knees and tried to yank the tabard over his head. Unfortunately, he forgot to remove his helmet first.

Slowly Jig walked over to retrieve his sword. The human was still trying to rip the tabard off his helmet when Jig stabbed him.

He wiped his sword as he waited for Smudge to

cool. Apparently all that flapping had been enough to wake Smudge up. The poor spider struggled to climb down off the human. The meandering path of smoldering spider footprints on the tabard was proof of Smudge's dizziness.

Jig stared at the dead human, trying to understand his reaction. You'd think he'd never seen a fire-spider before. Smudge wasn't even the biggest specimen Jig had encountered, being only a little larger than Jig's hand.

Humans were weird.

More shouts made Jig jump. He might have killed one human, but there were plenty more running about, and Jig didn't have enough fire-spiders to fight them all. He cocked his head and twitched his good ear. The other ear had been torn in a fight with another goblin, long ago. Still, a single goblin ear let him hear better than any two-eared human.

From the sound of it, the humans were getting closer.

Jig plucked Smudge from the human and stroked the spider's still-warm thorax before returning him to his hood.

"I knew Shadowstar would bring us victory," Relka said. Blood dripped down her cheek. Her fang had broken the skin when she fell.

"Right," said Jig. "Maybe next time Shadowstar can kill the human, and I'll stay in the lair where it's warm."

Grell appeared to be uninjured, judging by the volume of her cursing as she yanked her remaining cane from the ice. Jig grabbed the human's sword and gave it to her as a substitute. The tip sank deep into the earth, so Jig went back to retrieve the scabbard.

Grell took another step, resting her weight on the sheathed sword. With a grunt of approval, she hobbled over to the human and whacked him with her remaining cane.

"Blasted humans," she said. "Don't they know the dragon's dead? Treasure's all gone."

"What were you doing so far from the lair?" Relka asked.

Jig was more interested in knowing how Grell had made it so far. Grell was the oldest goblin in the lair, with the possible exception of Golaka the chef. But where Golaka had gotten stronger and meaner with age, Grell got smaller and wrinklier, like fruit left out in the sun. Sometimes Jig thought the only thing keeping her going was sheer stubbornness.

Grell began walking toward the lair, wheezing and grunting with each step. "There are too many humans for them to be adventurers. Adventurers are like tunnel cats. A few of them might be able to live and hunt together, but if you add more, they all start biting and clawing and hissing at one another."

Relka cocked her head. "They're not exactly the same, though. When you eat tunnel cats you spend half the time picking fur out of your meal. You don't have that trouble with adventurers. Except dwarves."

Grell jabbed her cane at the human Jig had killed. "There could be a hundred of them. Far too many for us to fight. And a few of the warriors are saying they saw elves."

"That's why you wanted to stop the drumming." Goblins didn't have formalized signals for battle. So long as the drums kept beating, the goblins kept fighting. If the drummers died or ran away, that was the signal for everyone else to do the same.

Jig perked his ears. He only heard one drum now, off to the other side of the lair.

"I sent Trok out to shut that one up." Grell scowled. "Probably should have been more specific about *how* to shut him up."

Jig's skin twitched with every shout and scream. He reached for Grell's elbow to hurry her along, but a rheumy glare made him back down.

"Maybe they're hunting," Relka suggested. "For

food, I mean. There hasn't been as much to eat since the snow came. Humans have to eat too."

"Humans don't eat goblins," Jig said. His stomach clenched at the thought of the things they did eat. Dried fruit and porridge and bread. What little meat they ate had all the flavor cooked out of it. Jig had been a prisoner of human adventurers for only a few days, but it had taken close to a month for his stomach to recover.

The last drum fell silent. After a lingering scream, so did the drummer. Shouts echoed up and down the mountain as the goblins began to retreat.

Jig squeezed through a clump of pine trees and waited, holding the branches out of Grell's way. He could see the lair from here. How bad would it be to let the branches slap Grell to the ground so he could scamper to safety? Smudge was already getting restless in his hood. The cloak was relatively fireproof, but the wisps of Jig's hair weren't.

A trio of limping goblins scurried into the lair up ahead. A fourth followed, hopping on one foot. His other leg bled from the thigh, leaving a bright blue path in the muddy snow.

The cave was partially hidden by a fallen pine. A heavy gate had once blocked the way, but that gate had disappeared a few months back. The hobgoblins had stolen it to build a bigger cage for their trained tunnel cats.

The pine tree didn't block anyone out, but it did hide the lair from casual view. The only drawbacks were the brown needles that tangled into your hair, and the sticky sap that covered your clothes, not to mention the overpowering pine smell. The smell had faded with time, but the tree seemed to have an endless supply of brittle needles with which to torment innocent goblins.

Two more warriors disappeared into the lair before Jig and his companions reached the tree. Jig played with one fang and tried not to let his impatience show as Grell hunched to step inside. Her joints popped, and she wheezed with every step.

Jig could hear the humans shouting as they closed in. Grell was right. There were an awful lot of humans out there.

Trok ran past, knocking Jig into the snow as he tried to get into the lair. He didn't make it. As he squeezed past Grell, she dropped her cane and twisted her claws into Trok's ear. With her other hand, she shook her borrowed sword until the scabbard fell free. "Relka, do you know any good recipes for goblin ear?"

"Four," Relka said. "Do you want something spicy?"

"Spicy food puts me in the privy all night." Grell gave up trying to draw the sword. She clubbed Trok's foot with the partly sheathed weapon. "Of course, I could put him on privy duty as part of his punishment."

Trok was a big goblin. He wore several layers of fur to make himself look even bigger, despite the fact that all of those furs made him sweat something awful. Trok's glistening face twisted into a sneer.

Grell pinched her claws deeper into his ear, drawing spots of blood. Trok yelped and backed down. He rubbed his ear as he waited for Grell to pass beneath the pine tree.

Neither Jig nor Relka received the same courtesy.

The obsidian walls of the tunnel muted the sounds of battle somewhat as Jig finally scurried into the darkness of the mountain. His eyes struggled to adjust. The warmer air had already painted a film of mist onto his spectacles. But no goblin who survived through childhood relied on vision alone. Jig could hear Grell grumbling and stomping her feet for warmth up ahead. A quick sniff assured him that Trok wasn't waiting nearby to take his annoyance out on Jig.

Grell's cane and sword tapped the rock as she moved on. From the sound of it, she was limping even worse than usual. The cold had been hard on her, and she had asked Jig and Braf for healing almost every night for the past month. Jig and Braf were the only two goblins "gifted" with Shadowstar's healing magic. That gift meant they both spent much of their time healing everything from cold-dead toes to rock serpent bites to that nasty case of ear-mold Trok had gotten a few months back.

The last glimmers of sunlight faded behind them, replaced by the comforting yellow-green glow of muck lanterns burning in the distance. Jig splashed through puddles of half-melted snow as he followed Relka and Grell through the main tunnel toward the rounded entryway into the temple of Tymalous Shadowstar.

Glass tiles on the ceiling portrayed the pale god looking down at the goblins. As always, Jig's gaze went to the eyes. Sparkling light burned in the center of those black sockets. No matter where you stood, those eyes always seemed to be watching you.

Once, Jig had painted a blindfold over Shadowstar's face. The god had not been pleased.

The temple was the first cave anyone saw after entering the mountainside. Looking back, Jig probably should have put it somewhere a bit more out of the way. Mud and slush covered the floor where goblin warriors had stomped their boots and brushed themselves off as they passed through. Other warriors stood dripping by the small altar in the corner, where poor Braf struggled to heal them as quickly as he could.

Relka touched her necklace. "Make way for Jig Dragonslayer!"

Grell coughed.

"And Grell," Relka added hastily.

The announcement of Jig's arrival didn't have the effect Relka was hoping for. Instead of spreading out to make room for Jig, the goblins split into two smaller swarms, one of which immediately surrounded Jig, the same as they had done with Braf.

"Why should Jig Dragonslayer provide the healing power of Shadowstar to nonbelievers?" Relka demanded. She wrapped both hands around her bone-and-knife pendant. "How many of you have donned the symbol of— Ouch." She stuck her finger in her mouth. Apparently the knife blades on her necklace were still sharp.

"Everyone back to the lair," Grell snapped. "You think those humans are going to stop once they reach the entrance? Go on."

Slowly the crowd dispersed through the three tunnels on the far side of the temple. All three merged a bit farther on. No doubt there would be further injuries to heal once the goblins reached that junction and fought to go first.

Grell grabbed one goblin as he turned to leave. A bloody gash crossed his scalp. "You don't have pine needles in your hair. How did you manage to get yourself injured without leaving the tunnels?"

"Bat."

"A bat did that to you?"

"No." He pointed to another goblin. "Ruk was trying to hit the bat with his sword, and—"

"I would have got him, too," interrupted Ruk. "But then he flew away."

Grell rubbed her forehead. "Ruk, go up the tunnel and wait by the entrance. Humans don't see well in the dark. They'll be disoriented. Stay there and kill anything that comes in. Anything that's not a goblin, that is."

She smacked him with a cane for good measure.

Ruk left, grinning and jabbing imaginary humans with his sword. Jig watched him go. "Do you really think he'll be able to slow down the humans?"

"Nope," said Grell. "But any idiot who'd slice his own partner is one I won't miss. When he screams, we'll know they've entered the mountain."

Despite the imminent attack from the humans, Jig found himself relaxing as he followed Grell deeper into the dark tunnels. The closer he got to home, the more the smell of muck smoke and Golaka's fried honey-mushrooms overpowered the scent of pine. His boots clopped against the hard stone. He ran one hand over the reddish brown wall, smiling at the familiar rippled feel of the obsidian. The warm air drifting from deep within the mountain helped drive the worst of the numbness from his fingers. Of course, that air also carried the faint smell of hobgoblin cooking, but at least it was warm.

A group of armed goblin warriors crowded near the entrance of the cavern, joking and boasting about what they would do to the humans. These were the same goblins who had shoved past Jig and Grell in their eagerness to flee back to the lair. But now that they were here, every last one shouted tales of triumph and victory, trying to top the rest.

Jig had seen it before. The worst part was that every goblin started to believe what the others were saying. Before long they would be charging back out of the mountain to prove themselves.

Grell solved the problem by jabbing the closest warriors with a cane. "You three go wait in the temple. Ambush anyone who comes in."

Relka shoved past Jig, clearing a path through the remaining warriors. She raised her voice, so her words echoed through the tunnels. "The high priest of Tymalous Shadowstar has returned!"

From the direction of the hobgoblin lair, a faint voice shouted back, "Shut up, you stupid rat eaters!"

"Stupid hobgoblins," Relka muttered. "Why aren't they out there fighting the humans too?"

"Because I sent Braf to ask them for help when the humans first arrived," Grell said.

Relka shook her head. "I don't understand."

"The fool went and told them the truth about how many humans and elves we were fighting. The hobgoblin chief told him. . . ." Grell shook her head. "Well, it doesn't matter. Braf's not flexible enough to do it, at any rate."

Jig hunched his shoulders and followed them into the deep cavern the goblins claimed as their home.

Inside, goblins scampered about like rats with their tails on fire. A group off to the right traded wagers as to how many goblins would die in the fighting. Others squabbled over the belongings of the dead and the almost-dead. Jig's attention went to a skinny goblin girl near the edge of the cavern. She kept her head bowed as she moved, carefully refilling the muck pits and lighting those that had gone out.

A few years ago, that had been Jig's job. The caustic muck could blister skin, the fumes made the whole cavern spin, and woe unto the careless goblin who let a spark land in his muck pot. Still, as smelly and humiliating as muck duty had been, at least it hadn't involved running out into the snow in the middle of a battle. Or fighting dragons and pixies and ogres. Or trying to avoid Relka and her band of fanatics.

Jig wondered if the muckworker would be willing to trade.

Several of Relka's friends were already crowding around Jig. Like Relka, they wore makeshift necklaces to show their devotion to Tymalous Shadowstar. Most were goblins who had been healed by Jig or Braf in the past. Given how the rest of the lair reacted to their endless praise of Jig and Shadowstar, they tended to need healing fairly often.

"Jig, come with me," Grell snapped. She hobbled through the crowd to one of the few doors in the cavern. Fixing wood to rock was tricky, but Golaka the chef made a paste that could be spread on the walls. The mold that grew on the paste clung equally well to stone and wood, enabling the goblins to erect a few crude doors. The chief's cave was the only one with a lock.

Grell grabbed the door with both hands. Goblins everywhere cringed as the wood screeched over the stone floor. Jig reached out to help, but a glare from Grell stopped him.

"I can open my own door, thank you." Eventually she managed to slide the door wide enough to slip inside.

A single muck pit cast a weak green glow over the cluttered space within. A handful of weapons sat beside a batskin mattress filled with dried grasses. Grell wheezed as she lowered herself onto the bed, a complicated process that involved much grunting and repositioning of her canes. Finally she sat back and pulled a blanket of tunnel cat fur over her body.

"Perhaps Jig Dragonslayer should lead the goblins while you rest?" Relka suggested as she dragged the door shut behind her.

Grell opened her eyes. "And perhaps you'd like me to find a new place to store my cane." She reached to the other side of her mattress and grabbed a clay pot. Jig's nose wrinkled at the smell of stale klak beer. "The dragon take this wind and snow. Every time there's a storm, my joints swell up like leeches on an ogre's backside. And I think I did something to my knee out there on the river."

Jig sat beside the bed. He shoved the blanket back and put one hand on her knee. He could feel the joint grinding as Grell straightened her leg, and her kneecap popped beneath his fingers.

No matter how often Jig healed Grell of one ailment or another, nothing seemed to last. Was Shadowstar's magic failing? The other goblins stayed healed. Well, except for Relka's friends. But when you interrupted a warrior's dinner to sing the praises of Tymalous Shadowstar, you had to expect a plate-size bruise on your face.

The warmth of Shadowstar's magic flowed through Jig's fingers, driving away the last of the snow's pain as Jig healed Grell's knee.

I can help you fix the damage she did on the ice, but it won't last. Tymalous Shadowstar, forgotten God of the Autumn Star, sounded strange. His voice was softer than usual.

Why not?

Because she's old, Jig.

But what's doing this to her? Jig glanced around,

frowning as he spotted the klak beer. *Is someone poisoning her?*

No, she's just old.

I know. Everyone knew Grell was old. That's why her skin was all wrinkly, and she had to run to the privy four times a night. *But why is she—*

This is what happens when people get old. Their bodies begin to give out. Don't goblins ever die of old age?

Jig shook his head.

Oh. Right.

The tendons twitched beneath Jig's hand, and Grell gasped. She bent her leg, and this time the kneecap stayed where it was.

"That's a little better," Grell said with a sigh. "Praise Shadowstar."

Jig glanced up at Relka, then bit back a groan. She had taken off her blanket. Her shirt was torn in the middle, revealing the scar where Jig had stabbed and healed her.

In the old days, you would have had hundreds of followers like Relka and her friends, Shadowstar said. *Well, not exactly like her. But it's only natural for them to look up to you and Braf.*

Can't they look up to us from a distance? Jig asked.

Shadowstar laughed, a sound that always reminded Jig of tiny bells. *Be thankful I'm not asking you and the others to perform the solstice dance.*

What's the solstice dance?

Another jingling laugh. *On the first night of autumn, when my star is highest in the sky, you and the others spread your yearly offerings on a great bonfire. The idea was that the smoke would carry your prayers to the stars. Then you dance from sundown to sunrise to celebrate another year of life.*

Jig wasn't much of a dancer, but that didn't sound too bad.

Did I mention that the high priest dances naked? added Shadowstar.

Goblin war cries erupted from the tunnels. Jig twisted around, his ears perked high. The door muffled the noise somewhat, but it sounded like the humans had reached the temple. He hoped Braf had made it away before the humans arrived.

"That idiot Ruk." Grell crawled off the mattress and rummaged through her pile of weapons. "He was supposed to scream before they killed him."

Smudge was squirming about in Jig's hood. Now that they were inside, the cold didn't suppress the fire-spider's heat. Jig grabbed Smudge and dropped him into a pocket in his cloak, one he had lined with leather. Then he stuck his fingers in his mouth. Smudge wasn't hot enough to blister skin, but he was close.

"Shadowstar will protect us," said Relka. "I am not afraid."

Another scream punctuated her words.

"Like he protected that poor fool?" Grell asked.

"If those goblins had truly believed, Shadowstar would have saved them."

"I miss Veka," Jig mumbled. Veka was a distillery worker with delusions of heroism. She had followed Jig around for a while, just like Relka. Veka had dreamed of learning the secrets of magic in order to become a sorceress and a hero.

Jig thought she was mad, but at least Veka had been useful in a fight. Unfortunately, she had left shortly after the battle with the pixies and the ogres, going out into the world to "pursue her destiny."

Jig had never worried about pursuing his destiny. Generally, destiny pursued him. Then it knocked him down and kicked him a few times for good measure.

This time it sounded like destiny planned to bully the entire lair. The humans had already reached the main cavern.

In the past, the goblins would have charged into the tunnels two or three at a time, to be killed at the humans' leisure. These days, they had learned to wait and allow intruders to charge into the lair, where they would be surrounded and outnumbered.

The twang of bowstrings and the shrieks of goblins told Jig how well that tactic was working.

"We should have covered the muck pits," Jig whispered. Humans didn't do well in the dark. Extinguishing the fires might have given the goblins more of an advantage.

"Come on." Relka grabbed Jig's arm and tugged him toward the door. She had her knife ready. "The goblins need their champion!"

"What am I supposed to do?" He pressed his ear to the door. The clank of armor and the clash of weapons had already spread. He heard shouts from the back of the cavern, where goblins were no doubt fighting one another in their eagerness to escape down the garbage crack that led to the lower tunnels.

"What do you think you're doing?" From the opposite side of the cavern, Golaka's outraged shriek was loud enough to make Jig flinch back from the door. A loud clank followed, as if an enormous stirring spoon had dented a soldier's helmet.

"Focus your efforts on that one!" A human's voice. Male, with a slightly nasal tone to it. "Form a line and drive the rest of these vermin back!"

"Clear room for the archers!" This voice was female. At least Jig thought it was. With humans, it could be hard to tell. They all sounded a lot alike, probably because of those tiny mouths and teeth.

An arrow punched through the door in front of Jig's nose. He leaped back so fast his head hit the wall.

"Jig, open the door."

"What?" Jig stared at Grell. How much klak beer had she drunk since they returned?

Grell pulled her blanket up to her chin and settled back. "We face them now and find out what they want, or else we wait until they've slaughtered every last goblin in the lair."

"I like waiting," Jig mumbled.

"Open the door, or else when we get out of this, I'll tell Golaka you've been stealing her fried rat tails."

"So you're the one!" Relka whispered.

"No!" Jig's toes curled in his boots at the thought of the last goblin Golaka had caught stealing her treats. Golaka had turned his ears into a spice pouch. "I mean, it was only a few. Smudge likes them, and—"

The loudest crash yet made the door shiver. Golaka must have flung one of her cauldrons at the attackers.

Grell bared her yellow teeth. "Enough of this. Relka, go tell Golaka—"

Jig shoved the door open a crack. Then another shout from the humans pushed any thought of Golaka from his mind.

"We have the spoon!"

"Oh no," Jig whispered. He peeked past the edge of the door.

The humans stood in a half circle in front of the main entrance. Another group battled Golaka and the other goblins near the kitchen. A ring of humans lay groaning at her feet. Skewers, forks, and other utensils protruded from their bodies.

One of the humans ran back toward the entrance, waving an oversize stirring spoon above his head. Several others shot arrows to stop the goblins from pursuing. One arrow rang as it ricocheted off the iron lid Golaka held in one hand. Another hit her in the arm. More arrows drove her back into the kitchen. Humans with spears pursued, keeping their weapons extended to break any counterattack.

"Where is your chief?" That was the female voice. She stood near the entrance. A tight ring of soldiers blocked her from sight.

The goblins backed away. Seeing Golaka driven to retreat had taken much of the fight out of them. Several pointed toward Jig.

"Him?" The human sounded skeptical.

"No!" Jig yelped. "Not me, her!" He shoved the door wider and pointed to Grell.

Whatever the woman tried to say was overpowered

by screams from the kitchen. Spears clattered to the ground as the humans stumbled out, covered in steaming lizard-fish pudding.

"Forget the chef," the woman shouted. She and about twenty soldiers shoved their way toward Grell's cave.

Jig scurried out of the way as soldiers stepped into the room. One of them smirked as he studied the goblins. "Nothing to worry about, Highness. A runt, a girl, and an old woman."

The woman entered next. She was shorter than the others. Her tabard was black, as was the embroidered crest of that odd beast. Jig could barely see the shine of the thread. The hardened leather of her armor was black as well, reminding Jig of the shine of the lake deeper in the tunnels.

Her sword was thin and sharp, with a blackened guard like a metal basket that covered her entire hand. Even the gem that shone in its pommel was black. Her boots, her belt, her gloves, even her hair . . . it was as if someone had spilled nighttime all over her.

A round helmet—black, of course—left her pale face bare, and something about that sweaty expression seemed familiar.

She glanced at Jig and Relka, then turned to Grell. "I'm supposed to believe one of you leads these monsters?"

"That's right," said Grell. "And you're in charge of this mob?"

"My brother and I, yes. I am Genevieve, daughter of—"

"I don't care." Grell tossed her blanket to one side. In her hands she held a small, cocked crossbow. Before anyone could react, she pulled the trigger. The bolt flew into the woman's neck . . .

. . . and dropped to the ground. A small drop of blood welled up on Genevieve's neck where the point had—barely—penetrated the skin. The blood was surprisingly colorful against her pale skin.

Grell flung the crossbow to the ground. "Stupid, worthless piece of hobgoblin garbage."

One of the soldiers leaped to the bed and pressed a knife to Grell's throat. Another kicked Jig to the ground for good measure. Relka got the same treatment on the other side of the cave.

"Easy there," said Grell. "Cut my throat and you'll never find the antidote."

"Antidote?" Genevieve touched her neck and stared at the smear of blood on her glove.

"I keep that little toy by my bed to discourage younger goblins who think they should be chief," Grell said.

The soldiers stepped aside as Genevieve approached the bed. One slipped out of the cave and ran back toward the tunnels.

Genevieve leveled her blade at Grell's chest. "Give it to me, goblin."

"Tell your people to retreat and leave us alone," Grell said.

Jig glanced at the floor where Grell's crossbow bolt had fallen. With everyone's attention on Grell, he could snatch that bolt and plunge it into Genevieve's back.

And then what? Killing a goblin chief led to chaos. Half of the goblins turned on one another, eager to take the chief's place, while the rest fled to avoid getting drawn into the brawl. But humans weren't like that. They had things like discipline and loyalty, not to mention enough weapons to kill every goblin still in the lair. Killing their leader wouldn't stop them; it would only make them angrier.

"The antidote," Genevieve said. "Or I'll cut off your ears."

"Don't give it to her!" shouted Relka, earning another kick.

Grell sighed and pointed to a small box.

Genevieve grabbed it and wiped crumbs from the top. Inside was a wooden tube, plugged with wax.

Jig had never seen Grell give up that easily. Actually, he had never seen Grell give up at all. He stared at Grell, but her face was pure, wrinkly innocence.

Genevieve uncapped the tube and poured the cloudy liquid down her throat. She coughed and wiped her lips on her wrist. "What a foul concoction."

"So I've been told," Grell said. "I thought about mixing blackberry juice to mask the taste of the poison, but—"

"The taste of the what?" Genevieve stared at the empty tube.

"Poison. That's a mix of rock serpent venom and lizard-fish blood."

Relka snickered.

"You said that was an antidote to the poisoned bolt," Genevieve said.

"Poisoned bolt." Grell rolled her eyes. "You think I'd risk poisoned weapons with this lot?" She lay back and adjusted her blanket. "Call off your army."

"I'll not bargain with goblins."

Grell shrugged. "What about a wager? I'm betting the rock serpent venom will paralyze you before the lizard-fish blood starts to burn holes in your stomach."

"I'll bet a week's worth of dessert that the lizard-fish blood hits first," Relka said brightly.

"Fetch my brother," Genevieve said. "Tell him I've been poisoned, and—"

"Not to worry." The other human leader was already pushing his way into the cave, followed by a pair of elf archers.

Unlike Genevieve, this human wore elven armor: thin scales of magically hardened wood, each one polished until it gleamed like metal. "What's the trouble, Genevieve? Did the goblins turn out to be too much for you? You're not trained for such things, Sister. It's as I was telling Father."

Genevieve sounded bored. "If you'll recall, goblin treachery got the best of Barius, too. And he used to thrash you with ease. Tell me, Theodore, how many times did you run to Mother, crying because Barius had made you clean out the stables with your bare hands, or—"

"Enough," snapped Theodore. His face was bright

red, and he looked like he had completely forgotten about the goblins.

Jig was barely listening. He should have learned by now. No matter how dark and dire the situation, things could always get worse. And they usually did.

No wonder they had known about Golaka's spoon. Prince Barius Wendelson had been one of the adventurers who came to the mountain two years ago in search of the Rod of Creation. He and his fellows had killed the rest of Jig's patrol and dragged Jig deep into the mountain as an unwilling guide.

"Aye, enough indeed." A hefty, black-haired dwarf stepped into the cave. "Let's be getting that garbage out of your sister's blood before I have to go back and tell her folks how a goblin finished off their only daughter."

Jig pressed himself back against the cave wall. *I don't suppose your magic can make me invisible?* he prayed.

The dwarf glanced at the goblins as he moved toward Genevieve. He whirled back around, his mouth round with shock. "Jig?"

I'm afraid not, said Shadowstar.

Jig's shoulders slumped. "Hello, Darnak."

CHAPTER 2

*H*ow many of Autumnstar's companions still fought? Blind Ama had been the first to fall after Noc's betrayal. Whose idea had it been to let a blind god charge into battle, anyway? The old fool had raced straight into Noc's lightning.

And now Noc had come for Autumnstar.

"You've gotten stronger," Autumnstar commented.

Noc's tactics were simple but effective. Lightning struck Tymalous Autumnstar's shield over and over until it glowed from the heat.

The bells on Tymalous Autumnstar's sleeves began to melt. Molten silver dripped over his free hand to splash upon the floor. He winced and raised his hand to his mouth, sucking the singed flesh.

"The two have pronounced sentence upon you and your fellows," Noc said. His voice had gotten deeper, too.

"The two gods of the beginning couldn't even pronounce my name," Autumnstar answered. "They're mindless, so caught up in their own struggles they never even noticed us." The lightning made it difficult to see, but Autumnstar thought he saw Noc shrug.

"The upper gods have pronounced sentence in their stead," Noc admitted. "Now stop interrupting. Entire civilizations once looked to you for guidance and comfort, and you betrayed them. In punishment—"

"We tried to protect them!" Autumnstar dropped to his knees.

The lightning grew brighter. The edges of Autumnstar's shield began to smoke, the god-forged metal boiling away under Noc's assault. Vision was useless in such an onslaught. Closing his eyes, Autumnstar felt the floor for anything he could use to protect himself. His weapon had been lost in the last battle, but surely there was something. . . .

His fingers brushed one of the fallen stones. He traced the familiar impression of the child's starburst.

"As punishment, you and all who turned against our forefathers shall be erased from history. Civilizations shall fall, and civilizations shall rise, but none shall remember your existence. None shall ever again speak their praise to the Autumn Star. None shall whisper your name, begging for comfort in their final hours. You are forgotten, Tymalous Autumnstar."

"And you talk too much." Autumnstar threw the stone as hard as he could. It caught Noc in the chest, knocking him right out of the temple.

In that moment, Tymalous Autumnstar turned and fled like a frightened mortal.

So this was how a rat felt right before Golaka skewered it for lunch.

Everyone was staring at Jig. For the most part, they appeared confused. Except for the elves, who looked bored, and Darnak, who had begun to gnaw his knuckles.

"Sorry," Darnak said, yanking his hand from his mouth. "Bird habit."

Jig hadn't seen Darnak since he had used the Rod of Creation to transform the dwarf into an oversized, ugly bird. As a bird, Darnak had still been able to talk.

Darnak had known the rod was disguised as Golaka's stirring spoon, unknown to anyone in the lair except Jig. He must have instructed Theodore in its use.

Darnak appeared no worse for his time as a bird. His dark hair and beard were a tangled mess, coming well past his thighs. He kept one hand on the wall for balance. Unfortunately, Darnak had already started to chew his other hand again, which meant he had no way to close the oversized blanket which was his only item of clothing.

Apparently Darnak had forgotten to instruct Theodore to create clothes.

"Do you mind?" asked Genevieve.

"Right. Sorry about that." Darnak yanked the blanket tight, so that only the tips of his toes peeked out.

Darnak studied Jig just as closely, taking in the cloak, the spectacles, even Smudge, who had crawled out from Jig's pocket to perch upon his shoulder. "I see you found yourself another spider."

"Not exactly," Jig said. "Smudge was—"

"You know this creature, Darnak?" asked Theodore. He held Golaka's stirring spoon with both hands.

Jig looked longingly at the door, wondering who would kill him first if he tried to flee. Probably one of the elves. Or maybe Grell.

"Jig led us down through the tunnels two years ago. He even saved our lives once or twice." Darnak forced a grin. "Those oversized white worms were a bit of fun, eh?"

Dwarves clearly had a different concept of fun than goblins.

"This was your guide?" Theodore whispered.

Memory was a funny thing. In that moment, Jig remembered Barius and Ryslind so clearly they could have been standing before him. If Grell's room hadn't been so crowded, at any rate.

It was almost funny how Theodore got exactly the same cold, angry expression on his face when he was getting ready to kill you.

Jig braced himself, wondering if he had time to swipe some of Grell's klak beer first.

"Jig ran away when we got to the dragon's cave," Darnak continued. "Never thought to see him again."

"Typical goblin cowardice." Theodore's attention

wandered back to Grell. He tried to give the rod a quick twirl, and accidentally thumped one of his guards with the spoon. The guard scrambled back, tripping in his eagerness to get away.

Jig stared at Darnak, who blinked and turned his head. Darnak knew Jig had killed the princes. Why was he—

"That's a lie," Relka said.

Jig's chest went cold. Relka was too far away for him to stab, so he searched for something to throw at her.

"Jig is no coward," Relka continued. "He killed Straum himself, and then—"

"A goblin killed the dragon?" Theodore looked genuinely amused. "And how exactly did he accomplish such a feat?"

Relka folded her arms, a pose familiar to most goblins who had endured one of her lectures. "According to 'The Song of Jig,' he—"

Jig finally found something to throw. Grell's "poisoned" crossbow bolt bounced off Relka's forehead. She blinked and turned to Jig, her mouth compressed into a pout.

Genevieve coughed and rubbed her neck. "Much as I'd love to spend the afternoon listening to goblin songs, do you think we could cleanse the poison from my body first? If nobody has anything better to do, I mean."

"Right. Poison." Darnak rubbed his hands together, which had the unfortunate effect of loosening his blanket again. He stepped toward Genevieve, moving in a clumsy waddle. No doubt he was still adjusting to being a dwarf again.

"What were you thinking, coming in here before the area was secured? Are you really so eager to make your brother an only child?" Darnak squeezed between the goblins and soldiers until he was close enough to touch Genevieve's hand.

"There were only three goblins." Genevieve's cheeks were red. "Hardly a threat."

"That's the kind of thinking that got your brothers killed," Darnak said. He dug through his beard to retrieve a silver amulet. Either Theodore had restored the tiny silver hammer, or else it had somehow survived Darnak's transformation. "Don't you worry, lass. Poison can be nasty stuff, but it's no match for Earthmaker's magic."

"So can we execute this one now?" Theodore asked, pointing the spoon at Grell.

Genevieve waited for Darnak to finish, then turned to her brother. "Idiot." She took a deep breath. "She's the leader of the goblins. Kill her, and who's going to surrender to us?"

Theodore slammed the spoon onto the edge of Grell's mattress, raising a small puff of dirt. "As leader of these goblins, you will surrender yourselves to us. If you continue to resist, we will kill every last goblin in these awful caves. Your blood will seep into the earth, and your bodies will be left to rot. Not one goblin will be left to—"

"She gets the point," said Genevieve.

"I still say we should kill them all," Theodore muttered. "Father never meant for you to—"

"Father's not here. He charged me with Avery's defense, not you, remember?"

From the fury on Theodore's face, he most certainly did. "Father only allowed you to take command of that ill-gotten town because no self-respecting army would bother to attack it, even if—"

Grell groaned and lay back in her bed. "Would you mind going outside while you argue? I could use a nap. You're welcome to fight your way back in when you're finished."

Genevieve and Theodore glared at one another a while longer. Eventually Theodore huffed and stormed out of the cave, followed by the elves.

"Your strongest goblins will come with us," Genevieve said, turning back to Grell. "The rest will remain here, sealed within the mountain by the power of the rod."

"Why?" Jig asked before he could stop himself. He wasn't sure whether to laugh or cry. He had sealed the mountain himself, back when he first found the rod. Then, on Shadowstar's advice, he had opened the cave again to keep the goblins from stagnating and dying in their isolation. Had he known what would happen, he could have left the cave sealed off and saved everyone a great deal of trouble.

"Part of their orders from the king was to make sure the goblins wouldn't be a threat," Darnak said. "Only two ways to make that happen, and only one way that lets you keep breathing."

Relka cocked her head. "So you came onto our mountain, slaughtered our warriors, broke into our lair, attacked our chef, and stomped into the chief's cave because *we* were a threat to *you*?"

Darnak shrugged.

"Gather your strongest goblins," Genevieve said. "Except for that chef. I get the sense she wouldn't be quite as easy to control."

That was quite the understatement. When nobody responded, Genevieve shrugged. "If you prefer, I can let my brother give the order to kill you all."

"Can't you take the hobgoblins instead?" Jig asked.

"No time," said Darnak. "Besides, hobgoblins are a nasty lot. We were thinking you goblins would be easier to manage."

"A difficult choice, we know," said Genevieve. "For a leader to willingly surrender those under her protection, or to—"

"Make sure you take Trok. That sorry excuse for a warrior keeps trying to poison my beer. Better yet, shove his arse over a cliff." Grell cocked her head. "Will you be passing any cliffs, do you think?"

They took Jig too, even though he was no more a warrior than he was an ogre. As Genevieve and the others were tying up the biggest and the strongest goblins, Theodore seized Jig's arm and tugged him along as well. "We should bring this one. He killed a dragon, after all. Surely he's the mightiest of goblins."

"You are such a child," Genevieve said, even though to Jig's eye she was significantly younger than her brother.

One of the elves looped a thin rope around Jig's neck and twisted a tight knot, adding him to a line of almost forty bound goblins. Jig found himself at the end of the line, directly behind Trok. He tried not to breathe through his nose, but it didn't help. The stench of Trok's sweat-soaked garments was so potent Jig could taste it.

Maybe if he told Genevieve and Theodore the truth about their brothers' deaths, they would kill him quickly and get it over with.

Near the front, Braf leaned out and waved at Jig. Whatever he started to say turned into a loud squawk as a passing elf tugged the rope, yanking him back into line.

"Wait!" Relka hurried out of the cave. She clutched her pendant with one hand. "Where Jig Dragonslayer goes, I go."

The elf glanced at Theodore, who shrugged. Soon Relka was bound behind Jig, close enough for him to smell her breath. Relka had been dipping into Golaka's honey wine again . . . which might explain why she had insisted on following Jig.

The elf took her knife, then grabbed the pendant.

"No!" Relka clawed the elf's wrists, to no avail. A sharp tug to the side choked off Relka's protests, and a quick flick of the knife severed the leather thong.

"You're an idiot," Jig whispered.

"Be not afraid," Relka said. She raised her voice. "Fellow goblins, this is but a trial of our strength. Believe in Shadowstar, and he shall set us free!"

Trok snarled and tugged the rope with both hands, pulling Jig off-balance. Jig lurched into Trok's furs, and then Relka crashed into Jig. Trok reached over Jig's head to punch Relka in the middle of her forehead. "Last I checked, both of Shadowstar's mighty priests were right here tied up with the rest of us."

Jig squirmed out from between them and spat in the snow. Trok's furs were shedding.

"They're going to eat us," Trok muttered. "That's why they wanted the meatiest goblins."

Jig shook his head. "Humans don't eat goblins."

Whatever they were going to do, Jig hoped it happened soon. Anything had to be better than Trok's smell and Relka's babbling.

As if to prove him wrong, Relka began to sing.

> *"My Shadowstar is a glorious star.*
> *He shines upon us day and night.*
> *We are but worms before him.*
> *He guides his goblins from afar,*
> *Forgiving us our every slight.*
> *We are but dung beneath him."*

With a snarl, Trok shoved past Jig, looped the rope around Relka's throat, and hauled her off the ground. Relka kicked and squirmed, then slammed her head back into Trok's chin.

There was little slack in the rope between goblins to begin with, which meant Jig found himself pulled tight against Relka and Trok as they struggled. Relka's heel kept hitting Jig's gut, and every time Trok shifted his weight, his elbow smashed Jig's spectacles against his face.

Where were the guards? Several of the humans were watching, hands on their weapons, but they made no move to intervene. The elves were looking up and down the line, bows ready. As for the other goblins, they mostly appeared relieved. Not that Jig could blame them. Relka's hymns were, in a word, awful. Jig had heard this one several times, and it only got worse, comparing goblins to rotting meat, vomit, and in the penultimate verse, hobgoblins.

Still, she was one of Shadowstar's worshipers, and

the god had funny ideas about protecting Jig's fellow goblins. "Trok, put her down."

"You think just because these idiots worship you, that means you can run around giving me orders?" Watery blue blood trickled down Trok's chin when he spoke.

"No." Jig swallowed and pulled back as far as his bonds would allow. He managed to twist far enough that Trok's elbow hit him in the ear instead of the eye. "You think they're going to cut her body free after you kill her? They think this is a trick, a distraction so the others can escape. Look at the way they're watching the rest of the goblins. Most likely, they'll leave Relka tied up, and we'll have to drag her body along to wherever it is we're going. You might not mind hauling her weight, but I doubt the other goblins will appreciate it."

Low mutters spread through the line, but Trok didn't let go. Relka had turned a deep shade of blue, almost purple, and her kicks were weaker.

"Besides, what do you think Golaka will do when we get back and she finds out you murdered one of her kitchen drudges?" Jig added.

That did it. Trok dropped Relka as if she had sprouted lizard-fish spines.

"Shadowstar's wrath—" Relka coughed and clutched her throat, then tried again. "His wrath will smite you like—"

"Shut up, Relka," said Jig. The wind picked up, spitting snow at the goblins, and Jig shivered. He could feel Smudge burrowing in his pocket.

What did the humans want? Darnak had said they were supposed to make sure the goblins weren't a threat. But if that was all they wanted, why drag the strongest warriors—and Jig—away before sealing the lair?

Whatever it was, Jig was certain he wouldn't like it.

They marched throughout the day, until the sun was little more than a scattering of red-orange light through the trees. At first they had made their way through the trees, crossing back and forth down the rocky, uneven ground of the mountain until the muscles in Jig's legs felt as though they were on fire.

The most tortuous spot so far was a steep slide of loose stone, conveniently hidden by a blanket of snow. Braf had been the first to stumble, but his weight pulled the next goblin off-balance, and soon the entire line was tumbling down the hillside.

Hobgoblins could learn a few things about traps from this place.

Jig had taken some satisfaction in knocking the legs from beneath a few humans as he fell. Unfortunately, they hadn't stopped long enough for him to heal his scrapes. The blood seeping from his elbow kept sticking to his sleeve.

The goblins stayed close to one another as they walked, in part to keep from choking, but also for warmth and reassurance. Jig had never explored more than an hour beyond the lair, and that had been years ago, when he was fleeing from a bully named Porak. Most goblins spent as little time as possible on the surface.

"I hate the outdoors," Jig muttered, shoving his hands into his sleeves for warmth. The sound of the branches humming in the wind conjured images of dragons and worse. The trees here were skeletal, their dead leaves covering the ground to turn it even more treacherous. The clouds drifting overhead made him feel as though the ground were shifting beneath his feet.

The world was simply too *big*. Back home in the lair, there were only so many caves and tunnels to explore. Out here, they could be going anywhere.

Eventually they left the tree-covered stone of the mountainside for a road of frozen mud. Even more armed humans waited here. Most were tending to their horses.

Jig stared at the closest horse. He had never actually seen one before. Oh, adventurers would occasionally have an image of a horse painted on their shield or armor, and once the hunters had brought back most of a horse for dinner. But living, breathing horses were very different.

For one thing, they were a lot bigger. And scarier. The closest had gray fur with white spots. Its eyes were huge, and it bared a row of enormous flat teeth as the goblins limped forth from the trees. It pawed the road, and Jig realized it wore a heavy piece of curved iron on its feet. No doubt to help it crush goblin skulls.

Most of the humans were already climbing onto the horses. Theodore jabbed his heels into his horse's sides, and the horse trotted to the front of the line. The elves followed. They remained on foot, but seemed to have no problem keeping up with the horse.

The goblins were dragged into the middle of the road. Soldiers rode on either side, tugging the reins to keep their horses under control. Those horses were even bigger than tunnel cats! A single one could probably kill and eat half the goblins here.

Now, instead of tripping over tree roots and icy rock, Jig found himself tripping over ruts in the road and frozen horse tracks. The horses also left other less savory signs of their passage. Some of those piles must have been from the journey here, as they were frozen hard as rocks.

Trok had already thrown one at Relka's head.

Jig twitched his ears, trying to restore feeling to the tips. He could hear Theodore joking with one of the elves up ahead, though the wind kept him from making out their words. Genevieve rode behind, along with another group of humans.

A low hooting sound made Jig jump.

"They're going to feed us to the monsters," said one of the goblins.

"I'm doubting the owl would be interested in making a meal of you." Darnak chuckled as he jogged to catch up with the goblins. Thankfully, he had managed to find clothes. His trousers bagged out of the tops of his boots, and his shirttails hung down to his knees.

He had twisted his beard into a rope and tied a knot in the end to keep it out of the way. Staring at Jig, he said, "Keep your mouth shut and do what you're told, and you'll be all right."

Jig nodded. "But why did you tell them—"

"Mouth shut I said." Darnak shook his head and stopped walking, allowing the goblins to draw away. "Ears the size of saucers, and they still don't listen."

The sky was dark by the time Prince Theodore ordered a halt. A yank on the rope punctuated his cry. "We're here!"

By now Jig had lost any sense of distance or direction. Even if he were to escape, he would never be able to find his way back to the lair. Jig pulled to one side, trying to see past the other goblins, but it was no use.

Genevieve rode to join her brother. Her horse was black, naturally, all except a spot of white above its front foot. Its tail flicked like a whip as she passed.

Jig cringed away from that tail, then turned around, trying to get a sense of their surroundings.

Black shadows rose in the distance to either side. The road appeared to run through a wide valley. Jig sniffed, hoping the smell of the air would tell him more. All it told him was that Trok had worked up a good, sour sweat over the course of the day.

The land immediately to either side of the road was flat and clear of trees. Jig squinted at a bulky shape to the left. Could that be a building of some sort? Tall, bulky animals stood in a tight group to one side of the building, letting out an occasional moaning cry.

"Get those goblins out of here," someone yelled. "They're scaring the cows!"

"Welcome to Avery," Darnak said as the line of goblins began to move again. He had made the entire journey on foot, and he kept muttering about how it would have been so much faster with wings.

Up ahead, flickering torches illuminated a wooden wall that rose four times as high as a goblin. There had to be some sort of platform near the top, supporting the soldiers who stood with spears and crossbows. The light of the torches turned them into flickering, ghostly figures. The platform was low enough that only the soldiers' upper torsos could be seen. It was a bit disconcerting, watching all those half-soldiers moving around to point their weapons down at the goblins.

Guards on the ground dragged open a door that was nearly as tall as the entire wall. Theodore and Genevieve were the first through. From where Jig stood, it looked as though they were steering their horses into one another, each one trying to shove the other aside so they could be first into the city.

"What's going to happen to us, Darnak?" Jig asked, wiping his eyes. His vision kept blurring, and his nose wouldn't stop running. The cold had been making his face leak all day, but the problem was even worse here.

"Genevieve means to put you to work," Darnak said. "You'll be helping fortify the town. Be careful. Folks around these parts aren't too fond of goblins."

"Nobody's fond of goblins," Jig said.

"True enough." Darnak's arms twitched as he walked, and he kept shaking his backside. Was he sick? It was only when he shook his head, fluffing out his black hair, that Jig recognized the movements. He had seen birds do the same thing, twitching their wings and shaking their tailfeathers when they were nervous. Darnak had spent far too long as a bird.

But why would he be nervous? Darnak wasn't afraid of anything!

"What about food?" Relka asked.

Farther up the line, Braf twisted around to add, "And a privy?"

"Some blankets would be nice," said another goblin.

"What about a nice hot cup of lichen tea?"

"And maybe some wood for a fire?"

"I'll need a new pair of trousers if you don't give us that privy soon!"

"That's enough," bellowed one of the humans. He

pointed his crossbow at the line, and the goblins fell silent.

Jig blinked, trying to focus on the wall. Rather than the logs or planks Jig had expected, the wall appeared to be made of individual trees, growing so closely together that there was hardly a finger-width of light between them. The branches had been cut away, except for the very top, where they grew together into the bushy platform where the guards watched. And the bark appeared to be *moving*, rustling like a swarm of rats.

Jig sneezed, spraying the back of Trok's furs in the process. Not that anyone would notice.

As they walked closer, Jig realized it wasn't the tree bark that was moving. The trees were covered in drooping yellow flowers. Even the smallest was as large as Jig's hand. He sneezed again as the sickly sweet scent of the flowers overpowered even Trok.

"What is this place?" Relka whispered.

"Used to be an elf town," said Darnak. "There was a bit of a disagreement between the elves and the humans about sixteen or so years back. They eventually hammered out a treaty that gave this valley to King Wendel. It's not all that comfortable for humans, but the land is great for farming. Unnatural, the way elves and plants get along. One of them pisses on a rock, and the next day you've got a sapling. Avery produces twice as many crops as any other town its size. Of course, if you wander into the poison ivy on the south side, you'll pray for a quick death. Vines as thick as your finger. I suspect the elves planted it deliberately, as a going-away present.

"For the most part, the elves stay on their side of the border. But every once in a while, they try to 'recruit' a human to their way of thinking." Darnak scowled at Theodore as he spoke. "Humans are suckers for all that grace and so-called wisdom. Not to mention the hair. As if one of those pointy-eared tree-lovers could grow a proper beard."

Darnak stepped aside as the goblins passed through

the opening. The ground was softer here, covered in
rotting flower petals. The walls were two trees deep.
Thick branches grew together overhead, and a nest of
birds squawked angrily from behind the flowers.

Inside, a wide path of snow-crusted wood chips led
through more living buildings. Everywhere Jig looked,
he saw vines and leaves and flowers of all colors and
shapes. He wiped his nose again and blinked to clear
his vision.

Genevieve dismounted from her horse. "Take them
to the stables for now. Bring food and water. Blankets
as well. I didn't drag these filthy creatures down here
only to have them freeze."

"What about that privy?" Braf stood with his legs
tightly crossed, and his voice was higher than usual.

Genevieve turned away. "Bring a bucket."

Jig had a hard time falling asleep that night. Maybe
it was the fact that nobody had bothered to untie
them, so every time Trok or Relka shifted in their
sleep, Jig choked. Or maybe it was the human food
they had been forced to eat.

The humans had brought two barrels. The first contained hard, green, smelly things called *pickles*. He
had tried to feed some to Smudge, and the fire-spider
grew so hot he nearly burned Jig's hand. The slimy,
hard vegetables smelled a bit like Trok. Hardly an
appetizing aroma.

The other barrel contained grungy brown bulbs with
white shoots sprouting from them like tentacles. The
humans called them *potatoes*, and they were cold,
hard, and tasteless.

Still, after trying a pickle, "tasteless" was a signifi-
cant improvement.

One of the horses snorted and shifted position. That
was the real reason Jig hadn't slept. The goblins
shared the stables with at least thirty horses. Sure, the
horses were penned in their stalls, but Jig doubted
those flimsy gates would stop them.

The dry air coated Jig's mouth and nose, though at

least there were no flowers in here. He and the rest of the goblins huddled together at the far end of the narrow wooden building.

Do you know why we're here? Jig asked.

Shadowstar's answer was anything but helpful. *Probably because it's the only place in town big enough to hold forty goblins.*

"Jig?" Relka's whisper interrupted Jig's retort.

"What is it?"

"Do you think they're going to kill us?"

Jig closed his eyes. "Probably."

"Do you think I'll get to meet Tymalous Shadowstar when I die?"

He didn't answer. If he said no, Relka would spend the rest of the night praying and singing, trying to prove herself worthy. And if Jig said yes, he had no doubt that Relka would immediately provoke Trok into killing her, just to hurry things along.

Eventually exhaustion overpowered fear. Jig didn't sleep comfortably, not with Trok's elbow wedged into his gut and Relka's knees in his back, but he slept.

The clang of bells ripped him from a dream in which elves leaped from the walls to shoot pickle-tipped arrows at Jig and his fellow goblins. Trok leaped to his feet, nearly breaking Jig's neck in the process.

"Everyone out!" The stable door swung open to reveal the shapes of Genevieve and several of her soldiers. The bright sunlight made it impossible to discern anything more.

The horses in their pens bared their huge teeth as the goblins passed. Those round eyes seemed to bore right through Jig's skin. Maybe that was the real reason Genevieve had brought goblins to Avery. They had run out of horse food, and the horses were too smart to settle for pickles or potatoes.

"How are we going to fight them?" Trok whispered.

Jig looked around, trying to see who Trok was talking to. A tug of the rope yanked his attention back to Trok. "Me?"

"You're the dragonslayer, right? You're the one

who fought all those pixies." Trok glanced at Genevieve. "So how are you going to kill this lot?"

Technically, Jig hadn't really killed the dragon. And while he had fought pixies, most of the goblins who had accompanied him in that battle hadn't come back.

"No talking," Genevieve said, saving him from having to come up with a response. She walked along the line, studying each goblin. Behind her, several men handed out more potatoes. Another dipped water from a barrel, offering each goblin a drink. These were no soldiers. They were unarmed, and their wide eyes barely blinked as they watched the goblins.

Other humans watched from windows and doorways. Those who passed walked faster, either staring at the goblins or averting their eyes.

The roads all seemed to stretch out from the center of town, with smaller paths between them. They reminded Jig a bit of branches growing from a tree. Buildings and trees crowded together between the roads. For the most part, the buildings appeared far younger than the trees. Many were wood and stone, though a few seemed to be built into the base of the trees themselves. Those looked like miniature versions of the wall surrounding the town.

A pair of children whispered and pointed from high up in one of the trees. An older man stood in his doorway holding an ax. They were afraid. Were goblins so terrifying? The rope around Jig's neck was clearly visible to anyone.

A rough-shaven man slapped a potato into Jig's hand, and his stomach clenched. He forced himself to take a bite. He picked one of the bitter sprouts from between his teeth. The white sprouts were the only part of the potato with any flavor, but Darnak had mentioned that they were also toxic. It figured.

Genevieve kicked her horse, yanking the reins to lead it back toward the gate. The goblins gagged down the rest of their food as armed guards escorted them out of the city after Genevieve.

There she slid down and drew a knife. Before she

could speak, the horse butted its head into her shoulder, knocking her into the wall. Then it stepped past her and began to chew one of the flowers.

"Stop that." Genevieve reached up to tug the reins, then swore as the horse nipped her arm.

Theodore laughed as he rode his own horse alongside hers. Most of the elves rode behind him. Like the elves, Theodore rode bareback, though he still used reins. "If Windstorm is too much to handle, I'm sure we could find you a more suitable mount. I believe I saw an old mule in one of the farmhouses."

"I believe I see one riding horseback with the elves," Genevieve shot back.

Even their insults brought back memories of Barius and Ryslind.

Genevieve handed the reins to Darnak and stepped to the wall.

"This is steelthorn. It's an elf tree." She wrapped her fingers around the base of a flower, pulling the petals out to expose the brown stem. She placed her knife at the tip of the stem. The flowers must have been tougher than they appeared, because it took several hard tugs to cut through.

She dropped the petals and wiped her hand on her trousers. "Each of you will be given a knife." She tossed hers to the nearest goblin, who immediately tried to cut himself free. When the rope wouldn't budge, he shrugged and lunged at the princess.

An arrow pinned his rear foot to the ground. He screamed as he fell, and the knife dropped into the snow.

Genevieve picked it up. "Use your knife on anything but these flowers, and one of my brother's pet elves will put an arrow through your throat." She pointed to the top of the wall, where a slender figure waved his bow in salute.

"So you captured goblin warriors to fight flowers?" Trok asked.

Genevieve shrugged. "If you prefer, I can find other uses for you. Your bodies could fertilize the fields."

Jig studied the stem where Genevieve had cut away the flower. Thin, reddish-brown leaves had already begun to curl tightly around the stem. Smaller thorns covered the outside of the leaves.

"Every flower must be cut," said Genevieve.

Jig stared at the wall. The flowers in front of him were too many to count, and the wall stretched on to surround an entire town. Not to mention how high they grew.

"A waste of time," Theodore shouted as he rode his horse to the gate. He pulled the Rod of Creation from his belt and held it overhead. He still hadn't bothered to take the metal bowl off the end of the spoon. "I take my leave of you, dear Sister. While you play with your pet goblins, Father and I shall protect our kingdom once and for all."

"And while you play with your rod, dear Brother, I shall restore this city."

Several of the goblins snickered. Theodore pointed the rod at the nearest, but that only caused the goblin to laugh louder.

"That's enough you two." Darnak walked right past the prince's horse, completely unafraid of those enormous hooves. "Teddy, you need to be getting yourself to Skysdale. Your father's expecting you. Genevieve, stop posturing for the goblins and put them to work already."

"You overstep your bounds, dwarf," Theodore said, wrenching at the reins with one hand. Jig watched him closely. If he dropped the rod, Jig could try to grab it, and . . . his shoulders slumped. The rod could only affect one person at a time. He could transform the prince into a worm, and then Genevieve and the humans and elves would all take turns slicing Jig into worm food.

Darnak pulled a slightly wrinkled red fruit from his pocket and held it up for Genevieve's horse. "My oath is to your father, boy." He waved the fruit in the air, and the horse calmed enough to pluck it from Darnak's hand. Darnak chuckled and grabbed a silver flask from another pocket. He took a deep swallow. "Get on with you. Elf steeds or no, you've a long ride ahead of you."

"The dwarf speaks the truth," Theodore shouted. He turned his horse around so he faced the small crowd. "I shall return, good people, with tidings of victory. Sa'illienth é traseth!"

Darnak choked on his drink. "Begging Your Highness' pardon, but are you sure you don't mean sa'illienth é trathess? 'Victory and honor' is the traditional elvish battle cry. Not that there's anything wrong with 'Victory and bacon,' mind you."

"Come my friends," Theodore said, his face red. "Alléia!"

Jig doubted human ears would have picked up Genevieve's muttered, "*Illéia*, you twit."

By the time the sun reached the top of the sky, Jig was ready to collapse. He and the other goblins had spent the entire morning cutting flowers from the wall. As he had guessed, the flowers were tough as leather near the base. His hands were cramped and blistered, and sweat kept dripping onto his spectacles. His nose was too stuffed up to breathe, and he sneezed every time he cut another steelthorn flower.

Their only break from harvesting flowers had come when humans passed out rakes, ordering them to drag the flowers off toward one of the farmhouses. There, some of the petals had been fed to fat, lumbering beasts the men called cows.

Jig paused to wipe his nose and study the wall. They had begun to the left of the gate, and had cleared an area roughly thirty paces wide and one goblin high. Where flowers had grown, shiny thorned spikes now covered the trees. Jig reached out to test one. It was surprisingly hard, considering how the leaves had curled so easily around the stems.

"Have you figured out how to escape yet?" Trok asked.

Jig shook his head. "This used to be an elf town."

He touched another of the spikes. "These are the same color as the armor they wear. I'm betting they'll be hard as metal by tomorrow. And as deadly."

"Let's find out." Before Jig could respond, Trok grabbed the goblin to his right and shoved him into the wall.

The goblin, a warrior named Rakell, screamed and stumbled back. Only a few of the spikes were hard enough to pierce his skin. Puncture wounds in his chest and leg dripped blue. Several more of the spikes had broken away from the tree, leaving oozing wounds in the bark. Jig touched the sap, which was slick as oil. Anyone who tried to climb the wall would either impale themselves, or else the thorns would break away. The sap would cause them to slip and fall.

"What's all this ruckus?" Darnak asked. He and some of the humans were rolling a now-familiar barrel through the snow.

Trok snarled at the sight. "If they try to give me one more pickle, I'm going to beat them all to death with it."

Jig turned back to the wall. A small beetle crawled out of the bark. Jig smashed it with his thumb, then dropped the bug into his pocket for Smudge. At least one of them would eat a decent meal today.

Rakell finally recovered enough to punch Trok in the face. Trok snarled and grabbed Rakell by the throat. Goblins to either side stumbled, their ropes pulling them into the fight. Jig found himself pressed against Trok's furs, close enough to realize that what looked like a death-bite on Rakell's throat was actually Trok whispering to the other goblin.

With a shout, Trok shoved Rakell away, toward Darnak. Rakell raised his knife.

The human who had been helping Darnak with the barrel leaped away. Darnak simply waited.

An arrow buzzed from the top of the wall and punched through Rakell's throat. Darnak plucked the knife from Rakell's hand as he fell. A second goblin flung himself at Darnak, who caught him by the arm.

A quick punch sent the goblin staggering back with one fang missing.

The goblins stopped moving. Darnak tucked Rakell's knife into his belt. "Anyone eager to join this poor wretch?" He nudged Rakell with his foot.

Nobody moved.

"Right," said Darnak. He turned his attention back to the barrel. "Then it's pickles and cheese for lunch."

"What about Rakell?" Relka asked.

"I don't imagine he'll be having much of an appetite," said Darnak. "Or did you mean the ropes? You'll have to wait for the elf to untie him. It takes a special touch to unknot an elven rope."

"No," said Relka. "What are you going to do with the meat?"

Darnak shook his head and muttered, "Goblins."

He and the human passed out the food. The morning's hard work had given Jig enough of an appetite that pickles sounded almost palatable. Almost. Jig accepted a pickle and a rock-hard lump of white cheese.

"Darnak, what is everyone afraid of?" he asked.

The dwarf shook his head. "Earthmaker willing, nothing at all."

Trok crunched into his pickle. "Your princess wouldn't be worried about preparing this wall unless she expected to need it. She's planning for an attack."

Jig turned to stare at the bigger goblin. That was more insightful than he expected, coming from Trok.

Darnak took a steel flask from inside his cloak. "His majesty the king sent Genevieve here at her own request. Restoring Avery is one of her pet projects. There's not a lot for a princess to do around the palace, you understand."

The dwarf's breath alone was enough to make Jig feel tipsy. He didn't remember Darnak drinking so much before. This didn't smell like dwarven ale, though. More like . . . old leaves.

"Theodore talked about tidings of victory," said Jig. "Victory against who?"

"Orcs," said Relka. Everyone turned to stare.

"When you dragged us from the lair, I heard Theodore boasting about how many he'd kill."

"Idiot boy," Darnak muttered, too low for human ears.

Jig and Trok stared at one another. How had Jig not heard about the orcs? Oh, wait, that would have been when Jig had been clutching his ears, wondering if the pain of ripping them off would be better than the pain of Relka's hymns.

"Aye," said Darnak at last. "Not only orcs. Billa the Bloody has got goblins, too. Goblins and orcs and worse. Thousands of monsters, all marching this way. All of them after killing everyone in their path."

"Is Genevieve going to make *us* fight Billa's army?" Jig asked.

"Avery's a poor target." Darnak took another drink, then waved his flask at the distant rise. "We're right on the border of the king's lands, and there's no real strategic advantage to taking the town. The early snowfall would only make things messier for an attacking army. Wendel's men would sweep down from the valley to crush her. Billa's too smart to lead her forces into such a slaughter." He stared at the ground. "In part, Wendel sent his daughter here because it's likely safer than the palace itself. Not that the palace is in any true danger, mind you."

He had barely looked at Jig at all. How odd. Goblins never took their eyes off each other. The instant you stopped paying attention, that was when you'd take a knife to the gut.

"Darnak, what's going to happen to us when we finish the wall?" Jig asked, his voice soft.

"Don't you worry about that." Darnak took another drink, then stood to go.

Jig grabbed his arm. It was like grabbing rock. Two years as a bird hadn't softened Darnak at all. "Tell me."

Darnak sighed and tugged the end of his beard. He glanced back at the town, then nodded. "Aye, you've earned as much." He dug into his shirt and pulled out his tiny silver hammer. He twisted free of Jig's grip, and his own fingers clamped around Jig's arm. Before Jig could break free, Darnak rapped the hammer on his forehead.

Jig yelped. It was as if his skull were a bell that wouldn't stop clanging. He pressed his ears, but the sound came from within.

"Earthmaker's Hammer," Darnak said. He tucked the necklace away, then nodded toward the other goblins. Every last one of them was scowling at Jig, ears flattened against their heads. "It's a minor spell, but useful when you prefer a bit of privacy. They'll hear nothing but the blows of his mighty hammer."

Relka's mouth moved, but Jig couldn't make out the words. Trok said something as well. He started to reach for Darnak, and then Relka pointed back toward the town. Probably reminding Trok of the elf and his bow.

"You have to understand, Jig. King Wendel lost two sons to you goblins." Darnak pulled a tin cup from a pouch at his waist and poured a drink for Jig. "He would have marched his whole army into your tunnels two years ago, but we couldn't find the entrance."

Jig felt a moment's smugness as he sipped his drink. He had been right to seal the entrance after all.

And then he felt nothing but a burning sensation on his tongue. He doubled over, dropping the cup as he coughed and scooped snow into his mouth.

"Elf beer," said Darnak. "Potent stuff, but it tastes like the trees' own piss."

Jig shuddered. His tongue felt as if it had grown a layer of mold. "What's going to happen to us?"

"Wendel decreed that any goblins found anywhere in the kingdom were to be executed on the spot. Genevieve managed to get around that law because she needed the extra muscle, but once the work is finished . . ."

Earthmaker's hammer pounded away as Jig stood there, staring. He wasn't surprised, exactly. Rather, he was more surprised the humans hadn't killed him and the other goblins already. "So if we come into their kingdom, they have permission to hunt and kill us like we're nothing but animals?"

"Well, no." Darnak took another drink. "The king has laws limiting the hunting of animals to certain places and times, and protecting—"

"But we didn't *want* to come into your stupid kingdom! You tied us up and dragged us. You can't kill us for being somewhere we never wanted to be. That's—"

"Easy, Jig." Darnak glanced at the other goblins. By now they had figured out that Darnak and Jig were the source of that awful noise. If it continued much longer, a few arrows wouldn't be enough to stop them from ripping the dwarf apart. "It wouldn't have mattered anyway, lad. That mountain you call home is a part of Wendel's kingdom too."

"Our mountain?" Jig stared.

"Wendel's, according to the treaty he signed with the elves." Darnak pointed to the other side of the valley. "He rules everything up to the top of those hills."

That was too much. "No matter where we go, they'll kill us."

"That's about the size of it. The story of Barius and Ryslind has spread. Everyone knows they were killed by goblins, and they're none to happy about having you on their lands." Darnak pressed the flask into Jig's hand. It was surprisingly heavy. "Forged that flask myself, with Earthmaker's help. You need it more than I do."

Jig nodded.

"You killed Barius and Ryslind, but you also saved our lives. You spared me, and I've not forgotten that. I've done my best to convince Genevieve to be merciful. The real trick is persuading her father. The royal children have skulls of granite, it's true, but they come by that honestly."

"Can't you let us go?"

Darnak shook his head. "I'm sworn to obey. Besides, there's no place to go. Theodore used the rod to seal your lair.''

Jig could have wept. Without the rod, he could never go home again. And Theodore had taken the rod deep into the human kingdom, where everyone would kill Jig as soon as look at him. Though that really wasn't anything new. He was a goblin, after all.

"Grant me time to work on Genevieve," Darnak said. "She's a bit odd, that one, but she's got more control over her passions than her father. A bit too much control, really. Takes after her mother that way. If I can convince her it's in her best interest to keep you goblins alive—"

"Why would it be in her best interest?" Jig asked.

Darnak snorted. "If I knew, I'd be halfway there." He clapped his hands, and the ringing of Earthmaker's Hammer faded, to be replaced by the cursing of angry goblins.

"—with his own beard," Trok was saying.

"What about Jig?" asked another.

"Jig doesn't have a beard," said Braf. Trok and the other goblin both shook their heads.

Darnak raised his voice. "May the gods watch over you, Jig."

"They do," Jig whispered. "But it never seems to help."

I resent that, said Shadowstar.

Jig didn't answer. He turned around, studying the scattered farms, and the woods beyond.

So you plan to run away, do you?

Running away is a proud goblin tradition, Jig said.

So is getting shot by elves.

Jig glanced at Rakell's body, then looked back at the wall. Only one elf, but there were other humans there. Not to mention the soldiers and their spears and swords. The knife he had been given to cut flowers was better than the old kitchen knife he used to carry, but it still wouldn't do much against trained warriors.

"What did the dwarf say?" asked Relka. Trok and the other goblins crowded around him, curiosity overpowering their annoyance.

Jig took a drink from Darnak's flask and forced himself to swallow. "He said we're all going to die."

CHAPTER 3

*F*leeing to the realm of the mortals was a desperate move, but it almost worked.

Almost.

Tymalous Autumnstar had made it halfway across the world before Noc's attack struck him from behind, driving him to the ground. How long ago had it been? The black streaks of lightning that racked his body made it difficult to track the passage of time.

Surely when even the victim had grown bored of the torture, it was time to move on.

The desert sands where Autumnstar lay helpless had been transformed into irregular spikes and blobs of hot glass. Noc could have followed him and finished the job long ago, but to manifest in the real world would make him vulnerable, just as it had with Autumnstar. Noc was being cautious, mindful of another trick. Autumnstar approved, even though he was far too weak for tricks. Every time another streak of blackness shot down upon him, he grew weaker.

Noc was a boring killer. There was no banter, no gloating, nothing but lightning. Was it so much to ask that he at least vary his attacks? Pillars of fire would be a nice change, or maybe the sand could whirl in a blinding storm, each grain ripping at his skin. For a god of death, Noc showed very little imagination.

Between blasts, something tickled Autumnstar's

*awareness. A sand lizard, one of the tiny ancestors of
the dragons, stood at the edge of the glass crater. The
lizard's crest and wings were raised aggressively. He
was probably hoping for a precooked meal.*

*Autumnstar and his fellow gods had often contem-
plated whether they were truly immortal, but not once
had they stopped to consider whether or not they
were edible.*

*Pressure built in the air as Noc readied another as-
sault. Autumnstar closed his eyes and dropped his de-
fenses, gathering what little power he had.*

*Jagged blackness cracked the sky, and then all that
remained was the burned, lifeless body that had been
Tymalous Autumnstar . . . and a lone sand lizard that
scurried away as quickly as its squat little legs would
take him.*

Another goblin died by the time Jig finished his
pickle. This one had managed to loop the rope around
a human's throat.

The human leaned against the pickle barrel, shaking
and touching his ear, as if to assure himself it was still
there. Jig almost felt sorry for him. First a goblin had
nearly killed him, and then an elf had shot an arrow
past his face into that goblin's throat.

On the other hand, this was the human who had
helped Darnak inflict another round of pickles on the
goblins, which did away with Jig's sympathy.

Jig hooked a finger through the rope, tugging it
away from his windpipe. The rope was thin and light,
but not even Trok was strong enough to break it.
Their knives did nothing. Trying to loosen the knot
only resulted in broken claws. The elves could work
the rope as if it were nothing but string. But Jig would
have to cut off his own head to escape the bonds.

He had kept that last thought to himself, not wanting to give the others ideas.

"What's your fire-spider doing?" Relka asked.

Jig stared. Smudge despised the snow, but he had
crept out of Jig's pocket and crawled down to the

ground, climbing onto the edge of the cup Jig had dropped, the one with the elf beer. Apparently the dwarf had forgotten about it.

Six of Smudge's legs clung to the rim and handle. Smudge's head and forelegs disappeared into the cup. "Maybe he's thirsty?"

Back at the lair, fire-spiders would sometimes drink the muck the goblins used to fuel their lanterns and fire pits. The only problem was if an unwary goblin happened to startle one of the spiders in midfeast. On the other hand, Golaka never complained about precooked meat.

Smudge was still drinking. Compared to muck, elf beer might be almost palatable. Better than pickles, at any rate.

"Back to work," shouted one of the humans. He waved his spear at the goblins, then grabbed the end of the rope from the snow. Several of the goblins snarled, but nobody tried to fight.

Jig grabbed the cup and reached in to brush the bristly hair on Smudge's back.

A puff of blue flame shot from the cup, singeing Jig's fingers. Smudge tried to turn around to see who had touched him, and ended up falling headfirst into the cup. Jig squatted long enough to stick his burned hand into the snow.

Smudge looked as sheepish as it was possible for a spider to look. He climbed slowly out of the cup and onto Jig's wrist. There, all eight eyes stared up at Jig. Smudge continued to stare, even as he toppled slowly into the snow. Jig hastily scooped him up with the cup. "How much of that elf beer did you drink?"

Smudge curled his legs to his body. Steam rose from his back.

The humans swapped their knives for rakes, and Jig joined the other goblins in dragging another pile of flowers away from the wall. He carefully returned Smudge to one of the larger pockets in his cloak, tossing the empty cup away.

Jig worked with the other goblins, falling into an

easy rhythm. Rake, then sneeze. Another sweep of the rake, then wipe his nose on his shoulder. If he stayed much longer, these flowers would be the end of him.

The humans directed them to a different farmhouse on the opposite side of the road. From here, Jig could see other humans working on the wall beyond the gate.

Jig slowed his efforts as they neared the farm, raking with one hand.

"No slacking, runt," Trok snarled. To his other side, Relka gave him a curious glance, but said nothing.

With his other hand, Jig reached in to retrieve Darnak's flask. Before he could do anything, Trok snatched it away and unscrewed the top. "You've been holding out on us!"

Jig started to protest, then changed his mind.

"Paugh!" Trok spat. "Tastes like something that came from the wrong end of a carrion-worm!"

Jig fought a grin as he took the flask from Trok, then poured a bit of elf beer onto the rope. He did the same on his other side, then put the flask away and grabbed Smudge.

"Hey, what are you doing?" Trok grabbed Jig's arm. His claws poked right through Jig's sleeve, until it felt as if they were gouging the bone beneath. "If you're going to escape, you're taking me with you."

"I can't," Jig said. Freeing himself would also free Relka, since she was tied to the rope behind him. But that couldn't be helped. And the longer he stayed, the more likely someone would notice. Already the human farmer was walking out with his pitchfork, either to help move the flowers or to protect himself from the goblins, Jig wasn't sure.

"You won't get far with a broken arm, either," said Trok.

Jig tried to tug free, but it was no use. "Fine," he said. "Give me your rope."

There was a choked squawk from the next goblin as Trok pulled his own rope into Jig's reach. Jig poured a bit more beer over the rope, then grabbed Smudge. He wasn't even certain this would work.

He placed Smudge on the rope.

Smudge listed to one side, faster and faster, until he swung down to dangle upside down from the rope. One pair after another, his legs gave way, and he dropped into the snow.

Jig picked him up again. Smudge promptly scrambled up Jig's sleeve and set it on fire.

"Stop that," Jig hissed. He patted himself out, and Smudge fell again. "No more elf beer for you," Jig muttered.

By now, the other goblins had slowed in their efforts so they could watch Jig. They didn't realize what Jig was trying to do, but a drunken fire-spider was more entertaining than anything else they had seen since leaving the lair.

"Make him fall off the rope again," said Braf, grinning.

Jig wrapped his hand in the edge of his cloak and grabbed Smudge from the snow. He took the beer-soaked rope and yanked it down, choking Trok in the process. When he lifted the rope again, it burned with a merry blue flame.

"Smells like burned hair," Trok complained.

Jig said nothing. Next to Trok's own stench, the burning rope was almost pleasant.

Trok grabbed the rope on either side and pulled. The rope snapped. With a triumphant snarl, he flung his rake into the snow.

"Wait," Jig shouted. "We're still tied together!"

Trok began to run, dragging Jig and Relka behind him. Jig barely managed to get Smudge back into his hood. He hoped Smudge didn't set it on fire.

If any of the humans had missed Jig's attempted escape, the cheering of the other goblins took care of that.

"Get past the farmhouse," Jig shouted.

Trok veered away from the farmer and his pitch-fork. The farmer did the same, fleeing in the opposite direction. Jig grinned as he struggled to keep up with Trok and Relka.

He craned his head to look behind. Several humans were running after them. The lead human tripped as a rake flew into his legs. Braf turned to Jig and waved.

The farmer was running back toward the town, shouting. Shouting to the elf on the wall. Jig squinted, trying to see through the smeared lenses of his spectacles.

The elf only needed to shoot one of them. Dragging the dead weight of a dead goblin would slow the other two enough for the humans to catch them. Jig watched as the elf drew an arrow from his quiver.

Jig grabbed the rope on either side of his neck, then lifted both legs from the ground. He fell, and his full weight yanked the rope, choking Relka and Trok. They collapsed on top of him.

Trok swore. "What are you—?"

An arrow thumped into the snow just ahead of them.

"Praise be unto Shadowstar," Relka whispered.

"I don't see Shadowstar down here, dodging elf arrows," Jig muttered. He crawled toward the farmhouse, craning his head to watch the distant figure on the wall. The elf would be mad now. They didn't like to miss. Jig waited, trying to hear over the shouting and his own gasping breath. There it was, the sharp *twang* of another shot.

Jig pulled out Darnak's flask and turned it over, gripping it in front of his throat with both hands.

The impact flung him back into the snow, but by now they were almost to the farmhouse. Trok and Relka hauled him the rest of the way, ducking behind the corner of the building as another arrow buzzed past.

"How did you do that?" Relka asked. She plucked the dented flask from Jig's hands. "It's like you knew exactly where the arrow was going to hit. Did Shadowstar bless your vision so you could see the future?"

Jig shook his head. He was still gagging from being

dragged through the snow. "No self-respecting elf is going to shoot someone in the chest, not if they can make a harder shot to the neck." He glanced at the dented flask and shivered. Darnak made a good flask. This thing was thicker than armor.

"At least I grabbed the arrow," Trok said, grinning. The tip was bent from the impact.

"Good," said Jig. He tugged Trok around. "You can use it to fight the humans with their swords and axes."

Trok's grin disappeared. Goblins weren't the smartest warriors, but even he knew better than to take on armed humans with nothing but a sharp stick. He handed the arrow to Jig.

As soon as Jig recovered enough to stand, they were off again. They made for the trees, keeping the farmhouse between themselves and the elf.

It didn't stop the elf. Arrows continued to arch over the roof, landing disturbingly close. "Unfair," Jig complained as another arrow hissed past his ear.

And then they were shoving past branches and stumbling over roots and low-growing plants. A branch snapped into Jig's face, making him yelp.

Trok grinned. Deliberately, he reached out to bend another branch. Jig ducked, and this one hit Relka instead. Then Trok ran face-first into a tree.

"Concentrate on running away," Jig said. Trok grunted his agreement as he rubbed his jaw.

One of their pursuers shouted, "Their tracks go this way!"

"Tracks?" Relka asked.

Jig looked back. The snow was thinner here, little more than a white crust sprinkled with fallen leaves and pine needles. But even Jig could see where he and his companions had gouged the snow with every step. He kicked the snow, trying to fill in a footprint, but only made things worse.

"Go deeper into the woods," Jig said. "There are more trees, so there's less snow."

According to what Darnak had told him, this was

the human side of the valley, which meant he didn't have to worry about crossing some invisible boundary into elf lands. For once, luck was with him.

On the other hand, fleeing through elf-infested woods would at least have resulted in a quick death.

Jig tugged the rope, leading Trok and Relka to a long cluster of thorn plants. He tore his cloak and scraped his hands on the way through, but hopefully the thorns would slow the humans, too.

"Don't let them escape!" That was Genevieve. Jig cocked his head, aiming his good ear at the sound. He heard hoofbeats, but he guessed she was still at the edge of the woods. He still had trouble judging distances and sounds out here in the open, though.

"She never should have brought those monsters into our town to begin with."

Jig swore under his breath. *That* voice was far closer than Genevieve's. Jig was still thinking like he was back in the lair, assuming the humans would have to follow the same route the goblins had taken. But there were no tunnel walls here, and the humans had spread out. They could send an entire line sweeping through the woods to make sure they didn't miss the runaway goblins. They had probably even avoided those stupid thorns.

He didn't know how many of the humans were soldiers, but it was a good bet they all had better weapons than Jig's lone arrow.

He could hear two sets of footsteps closing in from the left. "Under here," Jig whispered, hurrying toward a small stream. The water was frozen save for a thin trickle in the center. There were fewer trees here, but one was a fat pine with branches sagging to the ground. Jig crawled beneath the branches, then waited while Trok and Relka crowded in behind him. Jig reached out with one hand to smooth the pine needles the best he could.

"Where'd you go, Samuel?" shouted one of the humans.

"Stopped for a rest."

Jig gripped the arrow with both hands. He could see the second human, Samuel. His legs, at least. Samuel had stopped less than a stone's throw from their hiding spot. He rested his weight on a large, double-headed ax.

Trok pressed something cold and scaly into Jig's hand.

"What's that?" Jig whispered, once he regained control of his breathing.

"Pinecone. I thought you could pour more of that elf piss on it and set it on fire, then maybe throw it at the humans."

"You want me to use flaming pinecones against humans and their axes?" Jig barely stopped himself from shoving the pinecone in Trok's ear. Only the knowledge that Trok would probably eat Jig's arm in return stopped him.

"I got the idea from a story. Apparently there was this great wizard, and—"

"And the best he could do was set pinecones on fire?" Jig bit his lip as the humans moved closer.

"Think they took to the stream to hide their tracks?" asked one.

Jig grinned. That was a clever idea. Though knowing his luck, he'd slip on the ice and break his knee.

"Who cares?" said the other, Samuel. "If you ask me, we should cut them all loose. Better yet, take the axes to them. My little girl had nightmares all through the night after seeing those monsters."

"I hear they eat their young." The first human tromped closer.

"Only if they can't get ours," Samuel answered. "And you'd better mind your wife, Virgil. You know how goblins lust after human women."

Jig glanced at Trok, who grimaced. How could any self-respecting goblin be attracted to a human female and her tiny ears? Not to mention their flat teeth and pasty skin.

"Genevieve's mad, bringing them here. Who knows

what kind of disease they're carrying? My cousin Frederik knew a man whose sister's husband got his arm scratched by a goblin. The wound spread, and they had to take his arm at the shoulder."

Diseases? Well, there was that toenail fungus Jig had been fighting. Shadowstar's magic helped, but the yellow gunk kept coming back. He didn't think the humans could catch that, though.

"I hear if they bite you, you turn into one of them."

Samuel smacked his companion on the arm. "That's wolfmen, you idiot."

"Doesn't matter. I'm not losing my arm to some stinking goblin."

Jig hoped that was merely a figure of speech. If the humans could smell Trok from there, the goblins were as good as dead.

"Forget this." Samuel cupped his hands to his mouth and shouted, "No sign of the goblins. We're heading back."

Jig couldn't believe it. Even as the humans turned and hurried back through the woods, he kept peeking around, waiting for an elf to pop out of a tree and shoot them.

"Why are they leaving?" Relka whispered.

Jig thought back to what Darnak had said. "They're afraid of us." These weren't heroes or adventurers. They were ordinary humans, and they had probably never seen a goblin in their lives before Genevieve dragged them all to Avery.

It was like the stories the goblins used to tell about the Necromancer. Even though no goblin before Jig had seen the Necromancer and survived, they still told tales frightening enough to make children cry.

In the Necromancer's case, most of those tales had turned out to be true, but that was beside the point. The humans were afraid of them!

"What do we do now?" Relka asked. "Go back to the lair and rescue Grell and the others?"

"We can't," Jig said. "Theodore used the rod to

seal the lair." Not to mention he wasn't sure how to find his way back. The woods and mountains were all so big. *Could you lead us to the lair?*

Probably, said Tymalous Shadowstar. *Where you'll be killed by whatever guards Theodore left behind. Or if he left the lair unguarded, you can sit around and starve to death.*

"What's wrong with him?" Trok poked Jig in the neck.

"Stop that," said Relka. "He's talking to Tymalous Shadowstar. You can tell, because his eyes cross a little, and sometimes he drools."

You'll need help to save your people, Jig Dragonslayer.

Jig wiped his mouth. *You mean Billa and her army of orcs and goblins. They could help us fight the humans.*

Shadowstar hesitated. *This goes beyond the humans, Jig. Not once in my memory have orcs and goblins come together like this. An army of monsters . . . something is wrong. Do you remember when I warned you about the pixies?*

I remember that you nearly got me killed!

This is worse.

Maybe this was why gods stayed on another plane of existence. If they stayed here in the mortal world, their followers would be too tempted to punch them in the face. *Of course it is. I don't suppose you'd be willing to tell me exactly what you're worried about?*

I would if I knew, said Shadowstar.

I hate you, you know.

Shadowstar didn't answer.

Jig waited to make sure he could no longer hear the humans' voices, then crawled out from beneath the tree. "Come on," he muttered. "We can follow the stream, and—"

Jig stopped. Far downstream, Genevieve sat on her horse, staring at them. She looked as startled as he felt. Even as Jig watched, she kicked her horse into motion. So much for humans being scared of goblins.

He handed the arrow back to Trok, then pulled out Darnak's half-empty flask. With shaking hands, he poured the remaining beer over the pinecone.

"I thought you said that was a stupid idea," Trok said.

"It is." Jig dropped the flask, twisted around, and snatched Smudge from his hood. He poked Smudge with the tip of the pinecone.

Nothing happened. Smudge had fallen asleep.

Genevieve had her sword pointed toward them as she charged. Toward Jig in particular.

"Wake up, you stupid spider!" Jig blew in Smudge's face. The fire-spider stirred. He took several tentative steps, then fell off the edge of Jig's hand. He dropped slowly, suspended by a silken line that ran from his backside to Jig's palm.

Jig thrust the pinecone into Smudge's face. The pinecone burst into flames. So did the line of web. Smudge plopped into the snow, and Jig threw the pinecone as hard as he could.

He was aiming for Genevieve's cloak, but he had thrown too low. The pinecone was going to hit the horse instead.

The horse reared back on his hind legs, and Genevieve tumbled to the ground.

Jig sucked on his hand. Smudge's web had burned swiftly, like any fire-spider web. Jig could already see a nasty blister where the line had stuck to his skin.

Genevieve tried to stand, then yelled and clutched her knee. She toppled onto her side, one hand holding her knee, the other reaching for her sword.

Trok was already dragging Jig and Relka toward the princess. He extended his arrow like a lance. Jig wondered if he had learned the tactic from watching Genevieve's people kill goblins the same way.

Genevieve reached her sword. A single swipe of her blade snapped the arrow in half, and then Jig was wondering whether Trok's body was bulky enough to stop the backswing from hitting Jig, too.

Trok leaped back. Genevieve stretched far enough

to slice his arm, but the effort overbalanced her. She yelled again, and tumbled slowly into the snow. This time she didn't get back up.

Trok studied the broken arrow. Genevieve's sword had cut cleanly through the wood, leaving a nasty point. With a shrug, Trok raised it overhead like a knife.

Jig grabbed the rope and pulled him back.

"What are you doing?" Trok said, gasping for air. He turned the broken arrow toward Jig.

"She's faking to lure you close enough to kill." Jig pointed to her hand. "See? She's still holding her sword. And she fell with her good leg bent, so she could push off and run you through."

"How did you know?" asked Relka.

Genevieve turned her head. "Yes, how *did* you know?"

"I fall down a lot," said Jig. "I've never landed as softly or comfortably as you did."

Trok grinned. "Great. Jig, help me throw Relka at her."

"What?" Relka yelped.

"Genevieve will stab her, but by the time she gets her sword free of Relka's body, I can kill her with my fangs and arrow."

To his shock, Relka merely nodded. "If it helps to protect Shadowstar's chosen." She closed her eyes. "May Shadowstar guide your fangs."

"Who?" Genevieve sat back, shaking her head. "Never mind. Kill me, and every goblin at Avery will be executed."

Trok grinned, showing off his fangs. "But we won't be at Avery." He started to shove Relka at Genevieve.

"Wait." Jig braced himself, yanking her back by the rope. "Princess, we can either kill each other, or else you can let us go and limp back to town. Darnak can fix your leg."

"If my brother were here, he would sooner die than bargain with a goblin."

"Your brother is an idiot," Jig snapped.

Genevieve tilted her head. "True enough."

"And what would your parents say if they lost another child to the goblins?"

"My mother would weep. Father would probably say something along the lines of 'I told you so.' And then he'd spend the next month in mourning, wearing nothing but black and talking more about his dead daughter than he did in all the time she was alive." Still, Genevieve nodded, conceding the point. Goblins paid no attention to parentage, but such things were important to humans and other surface dwellers. "He hates black."

"*You* wear black," Relka pointed out.

Genevieve almost smiled. "It annoys my father."

"Give us your dagger," said Jig. He glanced at Relka and Trok, then added, "And tell us where to find Billa's army."

Genevieve switched her sword to her left hand, pulling her knife with her right. A flick of her wrist sent the knife into the ground at Jig's feet.

Jig clenched his teeth, hoping nobody had heard his frightened squeak. He grabbed the knife and sliced back and forth on the rope.

"Did you really guide my brothers through the mountain?"

The knife slipped. Genevieve kept a sharp blade. Not sharp enough to cut elf rope, but more than enough to slice deep into goblin flesh. Jig could barely feel the cut on his hand, despite the blood. "They didn't give me much of a choice."

"No, they wouldn't." Genevieve shook her head. "To get so close . . . to actually find the Rod of Creation, only to fall to goblins."

"Well, there were a lot of goblins." Jig glared at Relka, silently begging her to keep her mouth shut.

"Did they fight well?"

"Sure. Dead goblins everywhere. It took months to clean up the mess." Jig cut himself again, in almost exactly the same spot. A few more tries, and he should be able to completely sever his own thumb.

"Elf ropes," Genevieve said. "The knife will never get through them."

"It doesn't matter. Smudge can do it once he's sober." Jig pointed to the sheath on Genevieve's belt. "Could I have that, too? It's awfully hard to carry a knife otherwise."

Genevieve shook her head as she tossed him the sheath. "Billa is on her way to Pottersville. Follow the road to the west for five days, keeping to the base of the mountains." She studied the goblins. "Make that a week."

"We're taking your horse, too," said Trok.

"What?" Jig didn't know who said it first, him or Genevieve. He stared at the horse, which had wandered a short distance away to munch a sad, half-frozen fern. Was it his imagination, or was the horse watching him? The horse's tail twitched like a whip. "We'd be safer on foot."

"Horses are faster," Trok argued. "It's big enough to carry us all. We could ride in comfort, like the humans." He stared off into the distance. "An ax in one hand, a spear in the other, cutting down anyone who dared stand in my way. Anyone I missed, my warhorse would trample into the earth."

"Warhorse?" Genevieve glanced at the horse. "Windstorm?" Her face tightened. It almost looked like she was trying not to laugh. "Only if you swear to take proper care of him."

"We don't need a horse," Jig said. "We can—"

Trok grabbed the rope around Jig's neck, choking Jig and Relka with one tug. "Come on. You two go around and distract him. I'll sneak up and grab the reins."

Genevieve grinned and moved out of the way. "Windstorm can be a little stubborn. If he won't run, all you have to do is dig those claws into his ear and twist."

Trok was right about at least one thing. Windstorm did speed their progress. Not in the way Trok had imagined, perhaps. . . .

"He's running back to the road," Relka called. Jig groaned. His stomach had already begun to cramp from all of the running.

"Don't let him turn back toward the town." Trok threw a rock at Windstorm's head. He missed, but the horse snorted and veered away. They were actually making better time than Jig had hoped, running after the horse.

Windstorm had crossed into a farmer's abandoned field, which was overgrown with dry, withered vines. Dead, half frozen orange gourds the size of Trok's head were scattered about like hobgoblin traps. No matter how closely Jig watched, he kept tripping over the rotting things. The toe of his boot was stained orange from the last one he had kicked. Why would the humans work so hard to grow these things, only to abandon them?

Cold flakes tickled his face, spotting his vision. He glanced at the sky, remembering what he had heard back at Avery. Snow had come early this year. Maybe they hadn't meant to leave their plants to die.

"Try to get in front of him!" Trok crossed Jig's path, trying to get behind the horse. "Keep him distracted while I sneak up and grab the reins."

Windstorm stopped to munch the plants at the edge of the field. Either that or he was playing with them, giving them the chance to catch up before darting off again. Just as he had waited for Jig to finish burning through their ropes before running away. Jig was starting to think horses were even smarter than he had realized. This one clearly intended to defeat his goblin foes by running until they passed out, at which point Windstorm could consume their unconscious bodies at his leisure.

Relka stepped into the road and raised her hands. "In the name of Jig Dragonslayer and his glorious god Tymalous Shadowstar, I command you to halt!"

Windstorm flicked his tail and began to relieve himself.

Trok crept up behind the horse. As Windstorm finished, Trok lunged. His fingers closed around the reins. "I caught him!"

Jig winced, waiting for Windstorm to bite Trok's nose off or smash his skull with one of those huge, iron-shod hooves. But Windstorm only snorted.

"Help me into the seat," Trok said.

Slowly Jig moved closer to the horse. Maybe Windstorm was waiting until all three goblins were close enough to kill.

"I think the humans called it a saddle," Relka said.

Humans climbed into the saddles by putting one foot in the metal loop on the side and swinging their bodies up onto the horses' backs. But humans had longer legs than goblins.

Trok solved the problem by punching Relka in the gut with his free hand. She dropped to her hands and knees, and Trok put one foot on her back. Pushing himself up, he managed to swing his other foot into the metal loop.

Windstorm trotted a few more steps to eat another bit of snow-covered plant. Trok tried valiantly to hold on, but there was only so far his legs could stretch. He squealed and fell onto the ground, still clutching the reins with both hands.

Relka's fury slowly eased, giving way to amusement as they watched Trok dragged through the snow, flopping about like a broken toy.

Trok tried to pull himself up and punch Windstorm in the head. But he had to release the reins to swing. In the time it took to recover his balance, Windstorm trotted easily out of reach.

"Stupid horse," Trok shouted.

Relka glanced at Jig. "I'm starting to see why the princess let us take him."

This time, Trok threw himself onto the saddle before Windstorm could move away. Trok scrambled to hold on, kicking his leg around and gripping the saddle with both hands. He straightened, and his triumphant grin faded. In his haste, he had managed to seat himself backward.

"Aw, pixie farts," Trok said.

Before he could straighten himself out, Windstorm reared back on his hind legs. Trok tumbled into the snow and dirt.

Windstorm's whinny sounded a lot like laughter.

Goblins like Trok lived by making sure everyone else was afraid of them. When that fear faded, he did whatever it took to restore it. Apparently that went for horses too. Trok snarled and grabbed the front of Windstorm's saddle. With his other hand, he stretched up to grab the horse's ear.

"Wait," said Jig. "I don't know if you should—"

Windstorm squealed.

"Ha! Think you can best a goblin warrior, do you?" The horse slammed his head into Trok's chest. Given the size of Windstorm's head, Trok flew back as if he had been punched by an ogre. Windstorm snorted, then reached down to nip Trok's ear.

"Make him let go!" Trok screamed, but Windstorm had already released him. Jig didn't blame him. If Trok tasted as foul as he smelled, Jig would have rather eaten plants too.

Trok grabbed his bloody ear with one hand. His other clenched into a fist.

"Trok, wait."

"What is it, runt?" Trok pulled out his broken arrow. "You think you get to give the orders, just because you got lucky with those pixies?"

"And the dragon," Relka said. "And the Necromancer. Don't forget the old chief, Kralk. And the hobgoblins. Also, he's the one who saved you from taking Genevieve's sword through the belly. Personally, if Jig Dragonslayer told me to wait, I'd listen."

Jig stepped back. From the look on Trok's face, the only thing stopping Trok from killing them all was that he couldn't make up his mind who to kill first.

"There are probably still some humans out looking for us," Jig said. He was tempted to let Trok and Windstorm work things out. But Trok would be more useful as an angry goblin warrior than as a blue smear of slush in some farmer's field. "We'll need your help if we're going to make it to Billa's army."

"Why?" asked Relka.

"Because there are a lot more humans out there." Jig took a deep breath, never taking his eyes off of Trok's weapon. "Look, even if you do manage to ride him, we—"

Trok snarled.

"I mean *when*! When you ride him. Well, it's still going to take a few days to get to Billa's army, right?"

"I suppose," said Trok. "What does that have to do with anything?"

"Well, none of us brought any food."

Slowly both Trok and Relka turned toward Windstorm. . . .

CHAPTER 4

Autumnstar stretched his wings on the broad stone, basking in the sun's warmth. It had taken a few years to adjust to his new body, but all in all, being a sand lizard wasn't too bad. Though he doubted he'd ever get used to eating bugs.

After seven days of smoked horse meat, Relka and Trok were beginning to look tasty. Jig was certain they were having similar thoughts about him.

He was almost sure Relka wouldn't murder him in his sleep, and Trok seemed more annoyed by Relka than Jig, so he would probably kill her first. That would give Jig time to flee. And Relka was the only one who knew how to cook, which was likely the reason Trok hadn't already strangled her. If Trok's frustration ever outweighed his need for a good meal, Relka was in trouble.

For the past few nights, Jig had taken to sleeping with Smudge in his hand. Hopefully his burning fingers would wake him up if the humans found them, or if either of the other goblins tried anything. He debated again whether he would be better off running away. He couldn't decide whether the protection of having two additional goblins around was worth the threat of having two additional goblins around.

"I still say we should have killed the human," Trok

said as they crossed another bridge. The first time Jig saw a human bridge, he had been convinced it was magical. How else could an arch of stone hold together with nothing beneath it?

Now he merely groaned. Another bridge meant another treacherous crossing over icy wooden planks stretched between those unnatural arches. There was no railing or wall, only a row of taller stones to either side. The stones were gray and white, with dying grass and moss growing in the cracks. Beneath them, mud turned the thread of flowing water a strange reddish-brown color.

"She attacked our lair, and you just let her go. Besides, the human lied to us," Trok continued. "We've crossed half the world, and I've seen no sign of Pottersville or any army."

"We'll find it," Relka said. She coughed and spat to clear her throat, then sang:

> *"I walk through darkness and through cold.*
> *Tym gives me strength. He walks beside me.*
> *When I was hungry and alone.*
> *Tym gave us food. Windstorm was yummy!*
> *Trok wiped himself with toxic leaves.*
> *Jig's magic caused the itch to flee."*

Jig had been trying so hard to forget the leaves incident, too.

A hard-packed ball of snow and ice hit Relka in the face. "Next time it'll be a rock," Trok said. From the expression on Trok's face, he would definitely be killing Relka first.

"If we had killed Genevieve, the rest of the humans would still be chasing us," Jig said. Though he understood Trok's feelings, not to mention his hunger. How many times did they have to fight humans and pixies and everything else until they all just left the goblins alone?

He glanced down at the icy river as he crossed the bridge. Glinting yellow eyes stared up at him.

"Who are you?"

The voice sounded more female than male, if you could get past the growling and the snapping of her jaws. Jig had never seen such a creature. She was slightly shorter than a goblin, with a long face that reminded him of a wolf or dog.

Her armor was . . . unique. She appeared to have taken a heavy blanket and cut holes for her head and arms. Scraps of metal were fastened to every part of the blanket. Rusty metal rings decorated the hem, jingling when she moved. Bits of twine secured enormous iron hinges to her shoulders. A rusted key, a bit of old chain, and several of those crescent-shaped bars Windstorm had worn on his hooves all clanked together on her chest.

Bristly brown fur covered her exposed skin. She carried a short spear, which she jabbed in Jig's direction. The gesture was less intimidating than it might have been, thanks to the fish still flopping on the end of the spear.

Trok was the first to react. He grabbed Jig by the arm and flung him off the bridge at the creature.

Jig twisted, trying to avoid the spear. The creature did the same, presumably to protect her fish.

His shoulder hit first, slamming into her chest and stamping a key-shaped bruise into his shoulder. They crashed to the ground together, and then the creature's feet shoved Jig back into the stream. Jig ducked as the creature swung her spear back and forth. She scrambled back to the riverbank, where she threw back her head and yipped.

Trok jumped down and tried to grab the spear. She dodged and smashed the shaft against his knuckles. As Trok howled, she swung the other end, smacking him in the face with her fish.

"Take that, smelly goblin!" She did a triumphant dance, never taking her eyes from the goblins. In the distance, Jig could hear other yips and howls. Whatever this thing was, she wasn't alone.

"Wait," Jig said. "Darnak said Billa had put together an army of monsters. Goblins and orcs and worse. This thing is probably from that army."

Trok scowled. "This thing is supposed to be worse than a goblin?"

At the same time, the creature growled and bared an impressive number of sharp teeth. "Kobold! Stupid goblins."

"Can you take us to Billa?" Jig asked.

The dog-woman—the *kobold*—tilted her head to one side. "First you pay me. Then I let you go find Billa's army."

"What?" Trok yelled. "Why should we pay a mangy dog like you?"

Relka tapped his arm and pointed. Jig counted eight more kobolds—with eight more spears—running toward the bridge.

"What kind of payment?" Jig asked.

"Metal." As her companions arrived, she straightened and said, "Metal for everyone."

The rest of the kobolds jangled to a halt, pointing their weapons at the goblins. One wore a helmet made from an old pot. Another had armor made entirely of tarnished copper coins with square holes in the centers. A third wore a suit of arrowheads, with the metal points sticking out like animal spines. His fellow kobolds gave him a wide berth.

"What's going on, Hessafa?" asked the spiny one.

Hessafa pointed her spear and said, "Smelly goblins won't pay."

Jig could feel Smudge stirring in his hood. The firespider wasn't giving off the searing heat of imminent death, but that could be because of the cold.

Nine armed kobolds against three goblins. Jig still had the knife he had taken from Genevieve, and Trok had his stick. But the kobolds were all armed and wearing armor . . . such as it was.

Jig made his way to the edge of the ice. "That's not true!"

"So the smelly goblins *will* pay?" Hessafa asked.

"We did pay." Jig stepped to the side, out of reach

of her spear. "We paid her lots of metal. Coins and nails and a dwarf shield She didn't want to share!" He pointed back at the road. "She buried it in the snow so she could keep it all for herself!"

"Lies!" Hessafa shouted. But the other kobolds had begun to mutter to one another.

"Lots of shiny metal," Jig said. "Iron and copper and steel and brass."

"Where?" demanded a fat male. The butt of his spear was studded with rusty metal fishhooks.

"Back on the other side of the bridge. She made us close our eyes, so I don't know exactly where she buried it."

"*Hessafa* knows," said a kobold who wore a shovel blade for a breastplate.

"That's right," said Jig, trying to look surprised. "Hessafa does know. She could show you."

"No!" Hessafa shouted. "Smelly goblins lie!"

But it was too late. Hessafa yipped and snarled as the other kobolds dragged her across the stream.

"Come on," Jig said. The kobolds had to have been nearby to respond so quickly. He glanced over his shoulder, wondering what they would do to Hessafa. Would they believe her when she couldn't lead them to her stolen metal, or would they try to pound the truth out of her?

And then he crested a low hill, and all thought of Hessafa vanished. They had reached Pottersville.

Pottersville was built on the intersection of several roads, as well as that annoying river. One road led off toward the mountains to the north. Another bridged the stream and disappeared up into what Darnak had said were elf lands.

As with the town of Avery, Pottersville was surrounded by a low wall. From the look of things, it hadn't done much to protect the town.

Whole sections were ripped down, with figures moving in and out like bugs. Big bugs, with swords and axes and spears. To the right of the smashed gate where the road passed through the wall, goblins swarmed over abandoned farmhouses. There had to be hundreds of goblins down there. Some worked to load barrels and other bundles onto wagons. Others chased after a group of fluffy gray animals who had apparently escaped from inside a battered wooden fence.

The kobolds had taken over the other side of the road. Small groups of kobolds crept along the edge of the woods. Hunting for food? Or perhaps they were guarding against human survivors who might come back for revenge.

"What are those?" Relka pointed to where huge, long-limbed creatures with rubbery green skin chopped a fallen section of wall into individual logs.

"Trolls," said Jig. He hadn't seen one since his involuntary quest a few years ago. There had been a few trolls living down in the lower caverns with Straum the dragon back then. As far as Jig could tell, they had been eaten by the ogres.

Being uneaten, these trolls were better off than the ones back home, but not by much. As far as Jig could tell, they were prisoners. They were chained together by metal collars, a bit like the goblins had been back at Avery.

"And those monsters guarding them must be orcs," Relka said.

The orcs wore dingy metal breastplates and shields, all painted a dull black. Or maybe they were just dirty. Either way, Genevieve would have appreciated their sense of style.

"Look at them," Trok whispered, his tone very similar to Relka's when she talked about Tymalous Shadowstar. "They're so tough, the cold doesn't even bother them!"

Most of the orcs kept their muscular arms bare. Though when Jig squinted through his spectacles, he could see a few shivering as they marched through the broken gate. And they did march quite close together, presumably for warmth. It was still an impressive sight.

Jig wondered if the grayish tinge of their skin was their natural coloring or an effect of the cold.

His breath caught as he glimpsed more orcs within the town walls. Between the kobolds and the goblins and the orcs, there had to be thousands of monsters gathered here. Strong monsters. Warriors and fighters who would have no problem defeating Genevieve's little band of soldiers. All Jig had to do was persuade them to help.

As he watched, one of the goblins snuck away from the others to relieve himself on a rather out-of-place tree with thick, bare branches. The tree shivered, sprinkling snow. Then, before the goblin could react, the tree stomped him into the earth.

"First rule," Jig said, his throat dry. "Don't pee on the trees."

"Right." For once, Trok spoke without his usual bluster.

Jig watched as the tree wiped its . . . foot in the mud, then wrapped several branches around the remains of the goblin. It lifted the goblin, bent back until the body nearly touched the ground behind it, and then snapped straight. From the trajectory, the goblin landed somewhere near the back wall of the town.

Maybe this hadn't been such a great idea. For goblins, safety lay in numbers. Billa's army had sounded like the safest place to hide.

Back at the lair, Jig had always been able to disappear into the background. Well, up until everyone found out about that healing trick. But nobody here knew he could do that.

He glanced at Relka and sighed. Even if he asked Trok to cut out Relka's tongue right now, he would never blend in here. He was scrawnier than any goblin in sight. A part of him wanted nothing more than to flee and hide.

One of the goblins broke away from the others and jogged up the road. Toward them. Waving a sword in the air. "What are you worms doing away from your regiment? If Oakbottom catches you, he'll toss you all! He's still convinced he can clear the far wall if he finds a light enough goblin."

"Who are you calling worms?" Trok still carried his sharpened stick, and he jabbed it at the approaching goblin.

Jig and Relka glanced at each other and took a quiet step back, leaving Trok to his fate.

"Threatening a superior officer is grounds for summary execution." The approaching goblin was smaller than Trok, but his sword made up for any difference in size. His left ear was gone, sliced off at the scalp, and he was missing two fingers on his left hand. He wore a simple helmet of hammered metal, shaped like a bowl with large crescents cut on either side for the ears. Given this goblin's handicap, his helmet listed a bit to one side.

He pulled out a flattened stack of stained, rat-chewed pages and waved them under Trok's nose. "Regulations also give the condemned soldier a choice. Would you rather I force feed you your own weapon or toss you to the trolls?"

"We're not soldiers," Jig squeaked. "The humans attacked our lair, but we escaped, and—"

"You mean you're here to enlist?" The goblin's entire demeanor changed in an instant, as if the word "enlist" were a magical spell. "A wonderful choice. You won't regret it, I can promise you that. I'm Gratz. Corporal in the army of Billa the Bloody."

He sheathed his sword and hurried over to clap Trok's shoulder. The move was so unexpected that Trok didn't even stab Gratz. "Joining Billa was the best choice I ever made. Changed my life. Come on, I'll take you to Silverfang."

"Silverfang?" asked Relka.

"One of Billa's lieutenants," said Gratz. "He's in charge of the whole goblin regiment. He'll be the one to decide whether you're fit to join us."

"What if he decides we're not?" asked Jig. He

doubted Trok had much to worry about, and even Relka was bigger and stronger than Jig. But the more Jig saw of this army, the more out of place he felt.

Gratz studied Jig closely, and his forehead wrinkled. "Don't you worry," he said, though his cheerful confidence had disappeared. "Silverfang will find a use for you, one way or another."

Somehow Jig wasn't reassured. He glanced behind, wondering if it was too late to flee.

The angry yaps of the returning kobolds answered that question.

"Right," said Jig. "The sooner we get to Silverfang, the better!"

Growing up, Jig had learned to avoid the warriors whenever possible. The warriors were the goblins most eager to prove themselves. For some reason, proving themselves always seemed to involve tormenting Jig. Whether it was dropping rats in his muck pail or locking him in the garbage pit, they all took their frustrations out on Jig.

So he had learned to watch for the signs. If a band of adventurers slaughtered some goblins in passing, Jig would hide in the nursery or the distillery for a few days. If Golaka blackened a warrior's eye for trying to steal a toad dumpling from her kitchen, Jig would do his best to stay on the opposite side of the lair, along with the rest of the weaker goblins.

Here in Billa's army, there were no weaker goblins. Only Jig. He tried not to make eye contact, but he could feel them staring as he followed Gratz toward the walls of Pottersville. Slitted eyes peered out from crude tents. Mud-covered goblins working down by the river paused to look. Farther on, a line of goblins stopped stabbing stacks of hay to watch Jig. Why they were attacking hay was beyond Jig's comprehension, but better hay than him.

Beside him, Trok was grinning and pointing and babbling like a child. "When can I get an ax like that?" he asked. "And that shield with the big spikes on the edge. I want one of those, too. And that helmet with the animal horns on the sides."

"One thing at a time," said Gratz. "Recruits start off with standard arms and armor. Regulations give you the right to claim better equipment from the enemy. Or from the bodies of your fellow goblins. Just make sure they're dead first." He pointed toward the wall, where several wide planks of wood had been lashed together and propped up to create a makeshift cave. "First you talk to Silverfang."

They passed a small cook fire, where two goblins were roasting one of the fluffy gray animals.

Relka stopped. "That's not right."

"What do you mean?" asked Gratz.

"They're not even saving the blood. How are they supposed to make the gravy?"

Gratz laughed. "Gravy? With this lot, you're lucky to know where the meat ends and the bones begin."

As if to prove his point, the spit holding the animal broke and fell into the fire. Both goblins immediately began to shout at one another. Neither bothered to try to get the meat out of the fire. The smell of burned fur made Jig's eyes water.

"That's enough!" Both of the would-be chefs jumped. Neither one made a sound as the biggest, meanest-looking goblin Jig had ever seen ducked out of the wooden cave.

"Lieutenant Silverfang, sir," Gratz snapped, his body stiffening.

A scar on the left side of Silverfang's face twisted his mouth into a grimace. His left fang had been re-placed with a round steel spike, apparently held in place by the three small pins protruding from his jaw. He wore black plates of metal for armor, like the orcs Jig had seen in the town, and on his back he carried a curved sword that was almost as long as Jig was tall.

Silverfang's heavy boots crunched through frozen mud. His sword slid free, and both chefs closed their eyes. Silverfang thrust his sword into the burning animal. With a grunt, he hauled it into the air and flung it to one side, nearly hitting another goblin. He turned to jab a thick finger at the nearer of the two chefs. "Fetch another goat. Ruin this one and I'll make you eat the coals."

He beckoned the other chef closer, then grabbed him by the shirt. A whimper slipped from the goblin's lips.

Turning that huge sword with one hand, Silverfang wiped the blade on the goblin's collar. When he let go, the poor goblin fell on his backside in his eagerness to scramble away.

Silverfang turned to Gratz. "Fresh meat?"

"They want to enlist," said Gratz.

Silverfang came closer. His left eye was cloudy and oozed blue-black crud from the corner. He fixed the right on Trok. He grunted, then turned to study Relka. This time, his grunt sounded amused. He poked Relka's shoulder hard enough to knock her back a step.

Finally he turned to Jig.

"*You* want to join Billa's army?" He chuckled. "You're not even worth feeding to the kobolds."

Relka had done nothing when Silverfang poked her. But now she stepped in front of Jig, standing so close she could have bitten Silverfang's nose.

"That's Jig Dragonslayer. He's smarter and stronger than any warrior in your—"

Silverfang punched her in the jaw. She landed on the ground, spitting blood.

"Stronger than me?" Silverfang asked.

Jig thought about the knife tucked through his belt. Should he kill himself and get it over with, or would it be better to stab Relka first?

Silverfang stabbed his sword into the ground. With one claw, he traced the scar on his face. "A dwarf's ax did that. Took my tooth and my eye with one swing, and still I bested him. He forged this tooth before I tossed him to the wolves." He raised his voice. "Gather round, men. Let the little dragonslayer show off *his* battle scars."

"My what?" Jig tried to back away. He bumped into another goblin who had come up behind him. Jig turned to find himself ringed by goblin warriors, most of whom shared Silverfang's disdainful smirk.

"Your scars," said Gratz. "To prove your experience and worth as a warrior. It's how we measure the experience of new recruits. Regulations even allow you to enlist at a higher rank, if your scars meet certain criteria."

Silverfang rolled his eyes.

"Jig *is* a warrior." Relka still sat on the ground where she had fallen.

"But wouldn't the best warrior be the one who didn't get stabbed?" Jig asked.

Utter silence told him exactly how big a mistake those words had been. He cringed as he turned back to Silverfang, who was rubbing the huge scar on his face. "I didn't mean *you're* not a good warrior. I only—"

"Show us your scars, or I'll give you some," said Silverfang.

Scars. Right. Jig's hand shook as he pushed back his sleeve. "That's a sword cut from a few years ago," he said, pointing to a nasty gash on his forearm. He didn't think anyone needed to know it was self-inflicted.

He pulled off his cloak. The cold wind made him shiver even harder. Tugging down the shoulder of his shirt, he pointed to a small hard circle of pale skin. "That's from a wizard's arrow." He turned around to show them the matching spot on his back, beside the shoulder blade.

By now the goblins had stopped laughing.

Jig tugged his shirt up. "I can't reach it, but there's another stab wound in my back, below the ribs." He reached to touch the wrinkled scar on his ear. "I tore that in a fight with another goblin, years ago."

He wondered if he should include the various burns Smudge had inflicted over the years.

"How did a runt like you survive all that?" Gratz

asked. Silverfang scowled, and Gratz's face went pale. "Sorry, sir. Didn't mean to speak out of turn. Won't happen again. My apologies. I'll make sure—"

"Gratz talks too much," Silverfang said. "But he has a point." He grabbed Jig by the shoulder and spun him around, poking the arrow scar. "Most of this lot would have curled up and died from a wound like this."

"That's nothing!" Trok shouted. "A tunnel cat clawed half my leg off once." He yanked his trousers down to his knees, revealing a row of scars crossing his thigh. "I still killed that beast with my bare hands."

Relka snickered. "I was in the kitchen when you brought that 'beast' in for Golaka. It was so old there was barely any meat. It was missing most of its teeth, not to mention a leg." She sat up on the ground and pulled up her shirt, revealing the scar in the middle of her belly. "My wound was given to me by Jig Dragonslayer himself, for daring to challenge him. Not by some crippled old beast who gummed my leg a few times."

"You shut up!" Trok drew back his leg to kick her.

Silverfang was faster. He punched Trok in the side of the head, knocking him to the ground beside Relka. Silverfang flexed his fingers. "Next one of you who acts up gets the sword. Got it?" He turned back to Jig. "If the best warrior is the one who doesn't get stabbed, I guess you're one lousy warrior."

"Definitely," Jig said.

"And I suppose you expect me to believe her nonsense about you slaying a dragon?" Silverfang asked.

For once, Jig managed to keep his mouth shut. He doubted there was anything he could say that wouldn't infuriate Silverfang even further.

"So does he qualify for enlistment at a higher rank?" Gratz asked.

Silverfang closed his eyes. His fingers tightened around the hilt of his sword, and every goblin backed away.

"First they ought to prove themselves, don't you

think?" Silverfang turned to Gratz. "Take them to the wolf pens."

The sound of goblins wagering on their survival did nothing to calm Jig as he followed Gratz through the camp. Nor did Trok's babbling about Silverfang and the army.

"Can you imagine if we had a chief like him?" Trok was saying. "We'd chase those hobgoblins right out of our mountain! The humans and elves wouldn't dare set foot in our territory." He paused to spit. His blood was bright blue against the snow. "Did you see how fast he hit me?"

"Do you think we could get him to do it again?" Relka muttered.

Gratz grinned. "I was the same way when Billa came to our lair. All those goblins and orcs, and even the kobolds. We had been living near a dwarven copper mine. They mostly left us alone unless we ventured near their tunnels. Those tunnels used to be ours, but the dwarves ran us off." He punched the air with both hands. "The dwarves didn't stand a chance against Billa the Bloody. They'll never set foot in our territory again!"

Relka grinned at Jig. "Ask him about our lair."

"Me? Why can't you— Oh, never mind." Jig turned to Gratz. "The humans attacked our lair. They used magic to seal the entrance. Do you think Billa could beat them?"

"Nothing can stop Billa the Bloody," Gratz said. He sounded as earnest as Relka when she talked about Shadowstar. "Armies, magic, even the gods."

Cocky little goblin, isn't he? Shadowstar asked.

"Unfortunately," Gratz went on, "regulations prohibit me from sharing our marching orders until Silverfang accepts you into his regiment."

"What regulations?" Trok asked. "What are you talking about?"

Gratz beamed and pulled out the folded pages he had shown them before. "I've written down everything

Billa and her lieutenants have ordered since I joined up with her. Rules, punishments, every order from how to use your shield in combat to the best way to clean your fangs. These pages right here are what turn us into the most dangerous army in the world."

"Where are we going?" asked Relka.

"You get to clean up after the wolves." Gratz pointed. Up ahead, the walking tree they had seen before was lifting logs into place to reinforce what appeared to be a long, roofless building outside the wall. Oakbottom, Gratz had called him. The tree's branches creaked loudly as he worked. He had no joints, but the branches appeared to bend more where they forked into smaller branches. Jig saw no sign of eyes or a mouth, but the tree could clearly see what he was doing.

"That's enough, Oakbottom," Gratz shouted. "Silverfang wants these three to feed the wolves today." He turned to Trok. "Normally Oakbottom cleans the pens. He's strong enough to take care of himself, and the wolves don't like the taste of wood. Oakbottom tends to the wolves, and in exchange, Billa lets him toss as many humans as he likes when we go to war. Goblins and kobolds too, if anyone falls out of formation. It's the one thing he actually seems to enjoy."

The tree tromped off, his roots digging deep, muddy grooves in the earth.

Gratz gathered up shovels and buckets from the base of the wall. "Say, did you really face a dragon?"

"Sort of," Jig said. "I faced him, and then he smashed me into a wall. How big are these wolves?"

"Compared to a dragon, they're not so bad," Gratz said. "I've been riding for close to a year now, you know. A goblin warrior on one of these wolves can take out a human on horseback."

Jig glanced at Trok, who was practically drooling at the idea. Actually, he *was* drooling, but that was mostly due to his swollen lip.

"And Silverfang wants us to clean up after them?" Relka asked.

Jig could hear snarls and the snapping of jaws coming from behind the walls. The nearest wall shook as something huge slammed into it. Snow and dirt sprinkled from the top of the wall.

"Does Silverfang make everyone do this before they can join?" Jig asked.

"Only the ones he doesn't like." Gratz frowned as he led them around to an iron-clad door. It looked like the door and wall had been ripped out of another building, then carried here. Probably by that walking tree. Ropes and planks secured the mismatched sections of wall. "He made me do it, actually."

The walls shook again, making Jig jump. Smudge was already uncomfortably warm in his pocket. "How did you survive?"

"Don't know that I should say." Gratz scratched his ear, then shrugged. "But there's nothing in the regulations against it. There were three of us, just like you lot. I stabbed the others in the back, pushed them in, and then shoveled out the pens while the wolves were eating."

A typical goblin solution. Jig could see Trok nodding his approval. Both Jig and Relka moved away from him.

Gratz pressed his face to the crack at the edge of the door. "They're beautiful animals. Take a look."

Trok practically shoved him to the ground in his haste to see. "They're enormous! Those things could toss a tunnel cat about like a toy! Do we get to choose which one we ride? When can we take them into battle?"

Jig moved to another corner of the pen. The walls were tightly secured with loops of thick rope, but a bit of light still shone through. He pressed one eye to the gap.

He had to grab the ropes to keep from falling. His legs had simply gone numb. Which was the only thing preventing him from running away as fast as he could.

The beasts inside the pen were the size of small ponies. Jig counted fourteen in all. To these creatures,

a goblin would be little more than a rat to a tunnel
cat. Their teeth were the size of his thumbs, and they
had an awful lot of them. Bristly brown fur covered
their bodies. The fur stood straight up on their necks
and backs, except where it was covered by heavy
leather harnesses.

One turned to snarl at Jig. Long tufts of fur dangled
from the tips of the wolf's ears, an effect that might
have been comical on another creature. Like one that
wasn't currently gnawing on an arm.

Any snow or plants here had long since been trampled into the mud. Red-brown earth was caked onto
their legs and fur. Looking at the slick mess of mud
and worse, Jig doubted he would be able to take two
steps without slipping.

"The big one is named Bastard," Gratz shouted.
"He's the pack leader."

Jig had no trouble picking Bastard out of the pack.
He would be the one who had wandered over to casu-
ally lock his jaws around the throat of the one with
the arm. The arm dropped to the mud, and Bastard
snatched it up.

Wolf discipline had a lot in common with the goblin kind.

"The one rolling around in the back is Smelly,"
Gratz continued. "Nobody rides him unless all the
other wolves are taken. The one with the patchy fur
is Fungus. Ugly is the girl whose food Bastard just
swiped. The one with the scarred muzzle and missing
eye. She tried to steal Bastard's food once. Not
smart."

Jig barely listened as Gratz named the other wolves.
You're one of the forgotten gods, right? he asked
silently.

That's right. We were cursed after—

And now Braf and I are your only real followers?
Jig continued.

*What can I say? Anyone's standards will slip a bit
after a few thousand years of solitude.*

It wasn't easy to shout inside your own mind, but

Jig managed. *So if we goblins are all you have, why aren't you working harder to keep us from being eaten by wolves?*

I'm a little busy here, Jig. Fight your own wolves.

The abruptness of Shadowstar's response left Jig too stunned to reply, and then Gratz was dumping shovels and buckets in front of the gate. "Make sure they don't get out of the pen. Silverfang gets really mad when the wolves escape. They gorge themselves on whoever's closest, and then they're too stuffed to fight for at least three days."

Relka was the first to move, picking up a battered shovel and walking toward the gate. "I'm not afraid. Shadowstar watches over me."

And laughs, Jig added.

Only sometimes.

"They do their business near the back," Gratz said. "That spot where Smelly keeps rolling." He handed shovels to Jig and Trok.

Jig took the shovel with both hands and slammed it into the back of Gratz's head, knocking him face-first into the door. He bounced back and collapsed in the snow, groaning and holding his nose.

"Ha!" said Trok. "Good thinking, Jig!" He grabbed the bar holding the door shut. "Come here, wolves. Snack time!"

"Tymalous Shadowstar frowns upon the murder of our fellow goblins." Relka tried to push Trok aside, but he barely noticed.

"I'm not the one killing him," Trok said. "Shadowstar can talk it out with the wolves."

"Maybe we could feed them one of those goats instead." Relka turned to Jig. "Does Shadowstar say anything about killing goats?"

"I don't think so." Jig grabbed Gratz's sword and glanced around. A few other goblins were watching them, but nobody tried to interfere.

"Hey, that's right! He told us we were allowed to loot the dead," said Trok, seizing Gratz's helmet. "What else does he have worth taking?"

"I don't think he's dead yet, but. . . ." Relka shrugged and started tugging at Gratz's boots.

"Wait," said Jig. Relka backed away. "Trok, stop."

"Why, did you want the belt?" Trok glanced at Jig. "I don't think it will fit you."

Jig shook his head. If Silverfang were like other goblin leaders, this wouldn't be the last time he tried to feed Jig to the wolves. Next time Jig might not have the chance to whack his captor with a shovel.

There had to be a better way to control the wolves. The goblins couldn't feed someone to the wolves every time they mounted up for battle. Well, they could, but it would be awfully messy, and it probably wasn't a good idea to keep feeding them goblins. Not if you didn't want them to start seeing goblins as meals instead of riders.

Jig knelt beside Gratz and poked him a few times until he groaned. "You're one of their riders. How do you keep them from eating you?"

Gratz reached up to touch his fang, which was loose from his collision with the gate. "According to the manual, as a prisoner I'm required to give you only my name and rank. You already know all that, so I don't have to tell you anything."

"Fine." Jig stood. "I'll open the door. Trok, you throw him through."

"Of course, the manual also says that as victors, you're entitled to any spoils," Gratz said hastily. "Like that blue sack dangling from my belt."

Trok held the belt while Jig slid the sack free. The smell of old meat and blood made his eyes water. He reached in and pulled out what felt like a rock wrapped in leather. Something sharp jabbed his palm. He turned the object over to see a thick, yellow-green toenail.

"Troll toes," Gratz said, struggling to sit up. "The wolves love them. And trolls heal quick. You can get ten toes a week from the healthy ones."

There had to be thirty or forty toes in there. Jig stepped toward the pen and tossed one over the wall.

Snarling broke out even before the toe hit the ground. Jig peeked through the crack in the doorframe as the wolves lunged for the toe. Bastard bit another wolf on the rump, and suddenly he was alone. He dropped to the ground and began to gnaw the toe.

"Order them to sit," Gratz said. "Now that they know you've got toes, they should obey. Make sure to reward them all when you're done. They'll remember if you don't."

Before Jig could move, Trok shoved him out of the way and yanked open the door. Bastard leaped to his feet and snarled.

"Sit!" Trok shouted. The wolves obeyed, and Trok laughed. "It works!"

Gratz sat up and rubbed his head. "Go on, then. The sooner you start shoveling, the sooner you'll be done."

Relka was already following Trok into the pen. Jig stared at his shovel. How did he know the wolves weren't just waiting until all three goblins were within reach?

"I told you Shadowstar would protect his followers," Relka said. "And Trok, too." She didn't sound as happy about that part.

Jig tucked Gratz's sword through his belt, gritted his teeth, and stepped through the doorway. Shadowstar wasn't the one walking past hungry wolves to clean up six varieties of filth. No, he was busy with more important matters.

Maybe I just trusted you to take care of this one on your own, Jig.

Jig reached the back and stabbed his shovel into the nearest pile. A crunching sound startled him, and his feet slipped. He landed on his side, looking back at the wolves. Bastard had gone back to playing with his troll toe, cracking the tiny bones in his jaw.

Relka began to sing as she shoveled.

> *"The wolves of war are drawing near.*
> *They want only to eat him.*

He shovels their filth with no fear.
He trusts his god to guard him.
Their furious howls he will not hear.
He trusts his god to save him.
He falls and gets scat in his ear.
He trusts his god to wash him."

Jig threw the contents of his shovel at her. He missed, but it was enough to shut her up. He heard divine chuckling in his mind.

I like her, Shadowstar said.

Eventually they shoveled the entire mess into buckets, to be dragged into the woods and dumped. It still wasn't as bad as privy duty back at the lair on those nights when Golaka made extra-spicy bat skewers.

Jig made sure to feed troll toes to all of the wolves. He dropped a few into his pocket, thinking they might make a good snack for Smudge. He shut and barred the door behind him just as Silverfang arrived.

Silverfang stared. "What are all three of you doing still alive? Haven't you cleaned those pens yet?"

Trok pointed to the buckets.

Silverfang went so far as to sniff the contents. He turned back to Jig. "You just cost me one of my good knives, runt. I had a bet with Gratz that there'd be nothing left of you but a few bones and scraps of that elf-ugly cloak." He bent to pull a knife from his boot, then slapped it into Gratz's hand.

"So now are we part of your army?" Jig asked.

Silverfang's face twisted as if he had choked on a troll toe, but he nodded. "Gratz, take them to get weapons and armor. And take your sword back from the runt. The orcs want us to send out a few more hunting parties to find those blasted elves that have been harassing our flanks."

"Elves?" Gratz looked surprised. "What are they doing in human lands, sir?"

"Who cares? They've been snooping and killing Billa's officers for the last day or so with their damned bows. She wants them dealt with."

They were going to hunt elves? Jig wondered if Silverfang would let him stay here with the wolves instead.

"What about our lair?" Relka asked. "Our warriors are imprisoned at Avery, and—"

Silverfang grabbed the front of her apron with one hand. He twisted the material so tight she could barely breathe, then lifted her off the ground. "You're a part of Billa's army now. I said to get weapons and armor. The next time you run your mouth instead of obeying, I'll eat your face." He opened his mouth, and the tip of his steel fang dented the skin beneath her jaw. All he had to do was let go, and Relka would be impaled.

He tossed Relka to the ground and walked away. Jig prayed she wouldn't say anything stupid, but for once she kept her mouth shut.

Gratz had pulled out his parchment and an ink-stained quill. "Running your mouth instead of obeying," he mumbled. "Punishable by having your face eaten." He tucked the regulations back into his shirt. "Come on, let's get your equipment. And don't worry too much about Silverfang. He's much more likely to just turn you over to Oakbottom. I think he's lost his taste for goblin, to tell you the truth."

Jig wasn't worried about Silverfang. He and the others were being sent to hunt *elves*. Jig suspected he would be dead long before either Silverfang or Oakbottom had the chance to kill him.

CHAPTER 5

*A*utumnstar watched from behind a clay pot of pickled rattlesnake eggs as a wrinkled woman with spider silk hair set a trap for him.

"Blasted sand lizards," she muttered, scooping a pile of dumplings into a clay bowl. "I was cooking that rabbit for my daughter's birthday feast." She set the bowl on a mat of woven leaves. Furniture was a luxury in the desert, where trees were scarce. Benches, shelves, and even beds were carved from the sandstone of the great cliff city . . . which probably explained the woman's leathery skin.

Autumnstar belched softly, wrinkling his snout at the aftertaste of overcooked rabbit. He crept closer to the edge of the shelf, watching as the woman slipped a string noose in among the dumplings. Her name was Anisah, and her traps had kept Autumnstar's life interesting for many years now. His followers had long forgotten him, and Anisah was the closest thing he had to a companion . . . even if she was always trying to lure him into a basin of sticky resin or brain him with a rock.

He felt no guilt about the rabbit. He had seen Anisah's daughter, and she could afford to miss a few meals.

Autumnstar crossed his front legs and settled his chin on his feet, staring out the open window. Even his enemies had forgotten him. He had sensed nothing from Noc since their battle in the desert, and Noc was not a *patient god. If Noc thought Autumnstar had survived, he would have hunted him down years ago.*

Wet coughs drew Autumnstar's attention back to Anisah. She was on her knees, doubled over as she hacked and struggled for breath. Flecks of blood and saliva sprayed the dumplings. A single look told him she wouldn't survive. Anisah's time was nearly over. She would be frightened and hurting.

Autumnstar climbed over the edge of the shelf, his claws finding easy purchase in the sandstone. Clinging to the edge, he spread his wings for balance and prepared to jump.

Noc may have taken away his followers, but he was still the God of the Autumn Star. For thousands of years he had brought comfort to the elderly and the infirm as their lives faded into darkness. Noc would have to send him back to the void before Autumnstar would give that up.

Anisah's coughs were growing weaker. Her hands pressed the floor, and her arms trembled.

Autumnstar glided to the ground, then scurried past spilled dumplings until he reached her side. He hadn't dared use his powers since fleeing Noc, for fear of being noticed. But he couldn't turn his back on suffering. He might not be powerful enough to stop death, but he could ease its sting. He spread his wings and reached out to touch her arm with his claws.

Nothing happened.

Rather, something did happen, but it wasn't what he had intended. Withered fingers clamped around Autumnstar's long neck.

"Got you at last," Anisah wheezed. For a dying old woman, she had a very strong grip. "This must be the gods' reward for a pious life."

Her last act before dying was to smash Tymalous Autumnstar's small body into the floor.

The town walls—what was left of them—rattled in the wind as Gratz led the goblins through a jagged gap. Jig wasn't sure what he had expected. Smoldering ruins, perhaps. A mob of orcs scrounging through the remains.

Instead, for the most part, the buildings inside were undamaged. Most were various shades of red, brown, and orange. As they passed, Jig saw that mud had been layered onto the wooden structures to give them their coloration. He half-expected to see humans peeking out the doors, as they had done back in Avery.

Gratz noticed him staring, and grinned. "Most of the humans had already fled by the time we arrived. They're scared of us, Jig. We haven't fought a true battle in over a month. Though Billa says we'll see real combat soon enough."

Jig and his companions were the only goblins in sight. Only orcs lived inside the walls. Everywhere Jig looked, he saw orcs hurrying between the thatch-roofed buildings or working to repair a broken wagon or hauling bundles of chopped wood.

This was Jig's first time seeing orcs up close. Their gray skin was bumpy, with a greenish tinge. Their flattened noses reminded Jig a little of boar snouts. Many of the orcs had scarred faces, though the scars were too precise to be battle wounds. The one carrying pots out of a home had three short lines running up the cheeks. Another who was hauling a wagon full of blankets had a broken line over her eyebrow. They all seemed to have a single scar beneath their noses as well.

"Tribal scars," Gratz said. "Each tribe of orcs has its own pattern. But they'll all have that scar on the nose. That's Billa's scar. All the orcs wear it to mark their loyalty."

"They let Billa cut their faces?" Jig asked.

Gratz shook his head. "They're orcs. They do it themselves." He gestured to another orc who was carrying a bundle of spears. Most of the orc's nose was missing. "Sometimes they get a little carried away."

"We don't have to do that, do we?" Jig asked, trying not to stare.

"No scars until you become an officer. Even then, only the orcs of Billa's tribe receive extra facial scars to mark their ranks. The rest of us get different marks, on our arms." Gratz actually sounded disappointed. He pointed to a pair of orcs standing guard in front of a building with swirls of darker mud blended onto the walls. Pot shards hung from one corner of the roof, clinking in the wind.

The orcs watched them approach. Neither said a word. Jig wondered how close the goblins could come before being cut down by those huge, double-headed axes.

"I need weapons and armor for these three," Gratz said. "Lieutenant Silverfang's orders."

One of the orcs grunted and disappeared into the building. Jig stared in wonder. Back home the guards would have been playing a game of Roaches or drinking stolen klak beer. Here they were actually *guarding*. The remaining orc was like a statue, barely blinking as she stared at the goblins. Though a statue wouldn't have had pimpled skin on her arms from the cold.

"How many of them freeze to death?" Jig whispered, staring at the muscles on those bare arms.

"A handful each week," said Gratz. He didn't bother to lower his voice. "They believe an orc who isn't strong enough to survive doesn't deserve to survive."

Jig could only imagine what they thought of him. Of all the goblins and kobolds, actually. How did they feel, traveling with so many "weaker" monsters?

The first orc returned carrying an armload of leather and steel, which he dumped into the snow.

"What's this?" Trok said, picking up one of the swords. If it could even be called a sword. The blade was a simple length of rusty steel, sharpened on one side. There was no crossguard. Twine held a bit of padding around the end for a handle. "Why can't I get an ax like yours?"

Relka grabbed a suit of armor. Heavy pads of leather were sewn together to form a crude breastplate. She stared at the various straps which connected it to smaller pads. "Could I get a suit without an arrow hole? One that doesn't smell like blood?"

The orcs ignored her.

Jig picked up a helmet, a simple bowl of metal like Gratz wore. He placed it on his head, then yanked it off. "They're freezing!"

"Put it on," Gratz snapped. "That helmet is your best friend. Not only can it save your life, but it also serves as a stool, a pillow, and a bowl for your meals. I know one fellow who uses it as a backup chamber pot, but I wouldn't recommend that."

Judging from the smell, this one had been used to serve a stew of mold and fetid meat. The edge of the helmet pressed down on the earpieces of Jig's spectacles.

Jig grabbed another suit of armor. Relka was having little luck with hers. Jig turned the armor about, then glanced at Gratz, trying to guess how everything fit together. If he put his head through the straps at the top, then those heavy pads would fall across his shoulders. . . .

The shoulder pads came nearly to his elbows, and the bottom of the breastplate brushed his thighs when he tried to walk. He pulled out the hood of his cloak, transferring Smudge there so the armor wouldn't squish the poor spider. No matter how tightly he tied the armor's straps, he still felt like a dried seed rattling around in a pod.

"A little large, but it should do," said Gratz.

"Why do they bother guarding this garbage?" Trok asked.

Gratz drew his own sword, which was far nicer than Trok's. Without a word, he swung the edge of the blade into Jig's stomach.

Jig staggered back. Why hadn't he taken a sword, too? He tried to grab his knife, but he had donned the armor over his cloak and belt, so this involved sticking his hand inside the breastplate.

"That's why," Gratz said. "You wear your armor at

all times, follow orders, and you might actually survive your first battle."

Before Jig could respond, a second blow slammed into his back. This one knocked him face-first into the snow by the orcs' feet. He rolled over to see Trok grinning down at him.

"Hey, this is fun!" Trok raised his sword again, and then Relka slammed her own sword into his side.

"Watch it," Trok snapped. "You almost hit my arm." He thrust the blunt tip of his weapon into Relka's gut, and she doubled over.

"That's enough," Gratz shouted. "One of the first rules states that if you strike a fellow soldier, Billa gets her choice of your ear, your eye, or your hand." He reached up to rub his own missing ear. "It's how she keeps discipline. And believe me, you don't want to be drawing her attention."

"Does that mean Silverfang can't really kill me?" Jig asked hopefully.

"Oh, it's different when it's an officer doing the killing," Gratz said. "Silverfang could kill every last one of us, if he felt the urge. But then who would clean the wolf pens?" He laughed loud and hard at his little joke as he grabbed Jig's wrist and hauled him from the ground. "Now come on. We've got elves to hunt."

Jig picked up the remaining sword. The weapon was horribly balanced, like someone had strapped heavy rocks to the end of a stick. Testing the edge on his cloak, he decided rocks on a stick might actually be a better weapon.

Once they were away from the orcs, Gratz glanced around and said, "Billa brought along some orc smiths who make those swords. I think they deliberately blunt the edge. It's harder for new recruits to rebel when they're spending all their free time trying to hone their weapons."

That made sense. Unfortunately, it also meant Jig would be hunting elves with nothing more than a metal stick for a weapon.

Relka stopped so abruptly Jig bumped into her. "What's that?"

The building she pointed to was covered in large tiles. The doors had been ripped away, revealing an enormous brick oven at the rear of the building. The mouth glowed orange, and Jig could feel the heat from here. He moved closer, raising his hands to the warmth.

"Humans call it a kiln," Gratz said. "They use it to make pots and such. I'm told this town's famous for it. I think the orc smiths tried using it as a forge, but they couldn't get it hot enough." He kicked a broken shard near the doorway. "The walls broke almost as easily as the pottery. I don't understand why Billa chose this place as a target. No real fighting, and no tactical value that I can see. But that's why I'm only a corporal, eh?"

Relka didn't appear to have heard a word of it. "I could bake two bodies at a time. Three if they were dwarves. Golaka's oven is full of cracks, but this one . . . do you realize how much faster I could cook? We have to get one for the lair, Jig!"

"Maybe we should figure out how to get into our lair first," Jig pointed out.

Trok stomped another bit of pottery. "It doesn't sound like Silverfang's interested in helping us."

"You're welcome to complain," Gratz said. "You wouldn't be the first. Back when Billa first brought the orc tribes together, they didn't get along at all. They were stabbing each other every time you turned around. So Billa ordered that anyone who couldn't resolve their own problems should come to see her."

"And that worked?" Jig asked.

"They say that first day there had to be thirty orcs lined up at her tent. Billa marched out, took one look, and ordered them all butchered for breakfast. Things have been a lot calmer ever since. Still, if you catch her in a good mood, she might listen." Gratz continued toward the walls, leaving the goblins little choice but to follow. Jig didn't want to know what the punishment would be for fresh recruits found wandering through the town.

Gratz waved to a small group gathered by the gate. "Oh, good, they're ready for us."

The shabby weapons and armor were similar to Jig's own, but it was the kobold who caught his attention.

"Hessafa?"

"Kobolds aren't worth much in a fight," Gratz said. "But they're fast little things, and the best trackers in this goblin's army. They're not too fond of goblins, though. Being assigned to help us is punishment among the kobolds. I wonder what this one did to get herself into trouble."

Hessafa's lips pulled back, showing off her teeth. Her yellow eyes never blinked. Jig wasn't sure how to read kobold expressions, but he suspected it was a very good thing that Billa's law prohibited her soldiers from killing each other.

"Kobold, make sure you stay at least ten paces ahead of us, as spelled out in procedures," Gratz shouted. He turned to check the other goblins. "The rest of you spread out far enough that your weapons can't touch if you start swinging. Keep your ears up and your eyes wide. Elves are tricky bastards, but we'll find them."

"Only one elf," said Hessafa. "This way."

Jig kept his arms spread for balance. Hessafa had insisted on taking them over the frozen swamp. Dead trees and brown weeds jutted through the ice all around them, like an enormous version of the spiked pits the hobgoblins built back home.

Jig's boots were soaked from breaking through the thin ice, and most of the goblins had slipped and fallen at least once. Hessafa seemed determined to lead them through every pool of mud, filth, and foul-smelling slime she could find, while somehow avoiding them all herself.

"You can really track the elf through the swamps?" Jig asked.

"Hard to track elf over smelly goblin, but elf stink

is here. Always trust scent, goblin." She sniffed the air and bared her teeth. "Scent goes this way."

"Up those icy, bramble-covered rocks?" asked Trok.

Hessafa's yips sounded suspiciously like laughter. "Goblin skin is so fragile. Try not to bleed too much. Spoils the scent."

The sun was low, nearly touching the horizon. Jig's stomach gurgled. They had already missed dinner. How much longer did Gratz plan to hunt this elf? "Why would an elf be sneaking around here anyway?"

"Hard to say." Gratz scratched the scarred nub of his ear. "Normally, elves stick to themselves. They look at humans like short-lived savages. Kind of how humans see us, actually."

"No, I mean why here?" Jig asked. "What good can a few elves do against an entire army?"

They're scouts," Gratz said. "They shot a few arrows, killed an officer or two here and there, but mostly they're spying. It takes time to move an army. They want to know what we're doing and when we do it. If you can anticipate your enemy's actions, you can crush them."

"What *are* we doing?" Trok asked.

"We're changing things." Gratz's voice was soft, but his eyes were afire. "You said those humans attacked your lair. Well, Billa the Bloody is going to make sure no surface-dweller ever threatens us again!"

He drew his sword and shook it overhead. "It started a few years back, when Billa led her tribe against the trolls. She drove those trolls right out of their mountains. The trolls had nowhere else to go, so they started lurking about human villages, raiding their farms for food,

"Naturally, the humans didn't take kindly to this. Trolls, orcs, goblins, it's all the same to them. They began hiring adventurers to come into the mountains. They paid gold for every orc ear or troll head. So Billa summoned the other orc tribes, slew those who wouldn't follow her, and led the rest into battle."

He picked up a handful of snow. "They say the gods themselves were on her side that day. Snow blinded their soldiers. The wind fouled their arrows. Billa the Bloody sent those surface-dwellers fleeing for their lives. Everywhere she goes, she draws new monsters into her army. She plans to conquer every last inch of this land."

He crunched the snow into a ball and ate it. "At least, that was the plan. Turns out this land is a bit bigger than anyone realized."

Jig studied the other goblins. Trok was in heaven, beaming as he jabbed his sword at imaginary humans. Relka was fingering her necklace—when had she found time to make a new one?—and smiling to herself. Even Jig had to admit Billa's plan was appealing. Drive the surface dwellers back once and for all. No more adventurers sneaking in to the mountain to kill goblins and hunt treasure. No more humans and elves dragging goblins off as slaves. After all these years, they would be *safe*.

Was that why Shadowstar had sent him here? So Billa could protect them once and for all?

Not exactly, Shadowstar said. *The danger isn't from the humans and elves.*

Billa and her orcs? Jig guessed.

No. Something else.

Jig tugged his ears, using the pain to distract him from his frustration. *Is it too late for me to start worshiping a different god? One who isn't so vague with his warnings? Maybe one who will tell me to stay in the lair where it's safe, and eat hot rat stew and drink warm klak beer all day?*

You want Rionisus Yelloweyes, God of Revelry. But I don't think he'd be interested in goblin worshipers. Shadowstar paused. *Jig, you and the other goblins are my window to your world. In my prime, with worshipers throughout the world, I probably would have been strong enough to sense exactly what threat you faced. But now . . . I'm sorry.*

"How much farther?" Trok asked. "I want to kill an elf!"

"Quiet, smelly goblin." Hessafa dropped to all fours, pressing her nose to the rock. They had finally left the swamps, climbing into a rocky, lightly wooded area. Now if they could only leave the stench of the swamp as well. Unfortunately, Jig and every other goblin was caked in the stuff.

"It is elves?" Trok asked.

"Quiet means no talking." She crept forward, sniffing hard. A clump of snow balanced atop her nose when she next looked up. She sneezed and spat. "Elf scent. Smells like fruit and flowers. Better than goblin stink, though."

"So what do your regulations say about stabbing our tracker in the back?" Relka asked.

"They're vague," Gratz said.

Hessafa continued to mutter to herself as she scrambled up the rocky earth. "First goblins lie to kobolds, saying Hessafa stole metal. Then kobolds punish me by making me track for stupid goblins! Elf this way."

"Where?" asked one of the other goblins. An instant later he lurched back, slamming into the goblin behind him. An elven arrow pinned the two goblins together.

"There!" Hessafa dove to the ground. "Hessafa tracked elf. Goblins go kill it now!"

Jig could see the elf standing halfway up a snow-covered tree. He balanced easily on a branch, not even disturbing the snow as he nocked another arrow.

"Down!" Gratz shouted. He needn't have bothered. The other goblins were already scrambling for cover, hiding behind trees and rocks and each other. There wasn't much cover on the rough hillside. The trees were sparse and thin.

The elf's second shot pinned a goblin's exposed ear to the earth.

Gratz was actually smiling as he glanced at the other

goblins. His voice was loud enough to carry over the frightened screams. "Regulations say the best attack formation for a small group like ours is the Grab-and-Squeeze. Spread out like a giant hand, then everyone closes in at once. As commander, I'm the middle finger, so I'll charge up the center."

He jabbed his sword at the other goblins. "You three are the thumb and pointer. To my left. Jig, you and the kobold are the little finger. You head to the right. Now go!"

The goblins spread apart, obeying without thinking. Had they been thinking, Jig was sure they would have run the other way. But even he had jolted into motion at Gratz's sharp tone.

Hessafa threw her short spear as she ran. The elf twisted easily out of the way, but at least he couldn't shoot anyone and dodge at the same time. Trok stooped to grab a rock, then threw it without breaking stride.

The elf caught it. With a crooked smile, he threw it back.

Trok ducked his head. The rock that would have crushed his face instead rang off of his helmet. Trok staggered and toppled into the snow. Even from here Jig could see the dent in the top of his helmet.

By now the remaining goblins had almost reached the elf. Still smiling, the elf stepped back from his branch, dropping lightly into the snow. He used his bow to parry the nearest goblin's attack, then whirled, putting himself behind the goblin. A kick to the backside launched the goblin straight into the tree. The sound of skull hitting wood reminded Jig of the war drums back home.

Gratz and Relka reached the elf next, and both attacked at once. The elf tossed his bow into the air, where it hooked neatly over one of the branches. He caught Relka's wrist and twisted her arm so her sword pressed her neck. Had the blade been sharper, it would have cut her throat. The elf pressed harder, then grimaced in disgust. He slammed his elbow into

Relka's temple, knocking her to the ground, and then Gratz swung his sword down onto the elf's bare wrist.

Nothing happened. Gratz tried again, and this time the elf caught the blade and yanked it from his hand.

Jig stopped running. He looked at Hessafa, who had started to follow him up the hill. Both took a tentative step back.

Another goblin screamed as he charged the elf, sword swinging. Jig wasn't sure if he was screaming to try to intimidate the elf, or because he still had an arrow dangling from his ear. Either way, the elf barely blinked as he parried the attack with his arm, then used Gratz's sword to run the goblin through. The body tumbled down the hill toward Jig's feet.

Dull or not, that blow should have shattered the elf's arm. And Gratz's weapon was certainly better than anything the others carried. Yet the elf hadn't even flinched as he grabbed Gratz's blade.

"Elf magic?" Hessafa whispered.

"No, this magic is worse." He recognized this elf now. This was one of Theodore's companions. Theodore must have used the Rod of Creation to strengthen the elf's skin, turning it tough as armor. The elf flexed his arms, stretching as though he had just awakened from a pleasant nap, then retrieved his bow from the branches.

"Run?" Hessafa asked.

Jig didn't move. They couldn't run fast enough to escape an elven archer. *Is this the part where we all die?*

No, said Shadowstar. *Well, it's not the danger I've been sensing, at any rate. That danger is magical and widespread. This one should be quick and efficient.*

Jig lay flat, hiding behind a tree and the dead goblin with the arrow in his ear. The upper edge of his armor pressed into his throat, cutting off his breath, but it didn't matter. He was too scared to breathe anyway.

Hessafa crouched beside him. He could see the elf approaching.

Why didn't goblins ever get the magical armor and

the enchanted weapons and the— Wait. Jig reached out to yank the elf's arrow from the dead goblin's ear. If Theodore had used the rod to strengthen the elves, would he have done the same to their weapons? Jig brushed a finger over the arrowhead, grinning as a dot of blood appeared. The tip was so sharp he hadn't even felt the cut.

I don't suppose you could distract him for me? Jig asked.

There's one thing I could try, said Shadowstar. *I haven't done it in several thousand years, and it probably wouldn't work, but—*

Jig would have laughed if his throat hadn't been so tight. *A magic elf is about to snap me in half. Try it!*

Stand up.

Jig cradled the arrow in both hands. *What?*

Warmth rushed through Jig's body. The sensation was similar to what he experienced when he used his healing magic. But where the healing magic was concentrated in his hands, this bubbled up from his chest and spread outward. And while healing magic usually warmed his hands, this felt as though he had swallowed a fire-spider.

Rise, Jig Dragonslayer. Rise, and tell your kobold friend to close her eyes.

Why?

Shadowstar sighed. *Because if you don't, the elf is going to kill you.*

"Cover your eyes, Hessafa," Jig said. Hessafa buried her face in the snow. Jig wasn't sure if she was obeying his instructions, or if she just didn't want to see the elf kill her. Not that it mattered.

Smudge scurried out of Jig's hood and leaped off of his shoulder, a single line of silk slowing his fall. Snow melted beneath the spider's body, and he disappeared as he scrambled toward the shelter of the tree. Smart spider.

Jig stood. The elf was almost within reach. Would he shoot Jig with his bow and arrow? Break Jig's neck with one hand? Use Jig as a club to beat Hessafa to death? There were so many possibilities.

The elf hesitated. His skin and armor had a reddish tinge. So did the snow. Jig glanced behind, but the sky had only begun to take on the orange hue of the sunset.

The red light grew brighter and brighter. Blinking didn't help. In fact, it made the glare worse. The light was coming from Jig's own skin, including the inside of his eyelids.

The light didn't bother Jig too much, but the elf was squinting. Jig raised his arrow. If he could attack while the elf was distracted—

Wait.

Jig stared at his hands. Red fire danced over his fingers. Curls of flame danced out from his skin, spitting wisps of fire into the air. *You're turning me into a fire-spider?*

A fire-spider? This is the Light of the Autumn Star! The divine mark of my champions! Well, a mild version of it, anyway. Still, the universe hasn't seen this aura of power in thousands of years!

The light brightened faster now, painting everything the color of human blood.

Hessafa whimpered. The elf moved quick as thought. An arrow buried itself in the tree in front of the kobold.

The elf had *missed*. The light must have blinded him. Already the elf had begun to retreat.

Jig stepped closer.

An arrow tore through Jig's armor. And through Jig. He could see the hole where it had entered the armor. He could feel a matching hole in the back, though this one was wet with blood.

It cut your side and grazed a rib. You'll live. Shadowstar hesitated. *Unless he shoots you again, I mean.*

Jig clamped his jaw, trying not to whimper. Even blind, elves were dangerous archers. There were no fancy throat shots here. The elf was shooting for Jig's chest. A handspan to the left, and he would have taken Jig in the heart.

Stupid snow. Jig couldn't move without his boot crunching loud enough for even a human to hear. Tears streamed down his cheek from the pain. He held his breath. The elf had to realize Jig hadn't fallen. He should have fallen down and pretended to die. Then when the elf came closer, Jig could have stabbed him.

Either that, or the elf would have put a few more arrows into him to be safe. *I don't suppose you can do anything about his hearing?*

Sorry. I wasn't even sure I could still do the Light of the Autumn Star anymore. What did you think? Pretty impressive, isn't it?

The creak of wood drew Jig's attention back to the elf and his bow. He held the string steady at the side of his face, listening. Jig's chest hurt from holding his breath, but he didn't dare exhale. He could throw the arrow to distract the elf, but throwing away his only decent weapon wasn't much of a plan.

Behind him Hessafa craned her head and howled. Jig flinched and flattened his ears against the sound. Another arrow buried itself in the tree, but Jig could barely hear the impact over the echo of Hessafa's cry.

He stared at the arrow. If *he* couldn't hear . . . Jig leaped forward and stabbed his own stolen arrow into the elf's chest.

The elf dropped his bow. Both hands touched the arrow. He squinted at Jig, and his expression was one of mild puzzlement. Slowly he toppled back into the snow.

Jig's whole body sagged with relief. Terror must have helped block the pain, but now that his terror was fading, the hole in his side felt as though it were on fire. Jig reacted by screaming and clutching the wound with both hands.

Hessafa scurried out from behind her tree. She retrieved her spear and prodded the elf. "Killed by noisy goblin. How?" Her fur bristled as she turned to point her spear at Jig. "More magic?"

"No, it—" Jig clenched his jaw. His breath hissed past his fangs. *Would you mind helping me?*

What? Oh, sorry.

Jig gasped with relief as the skin along his side began to heal. Eventually he managed to stand. He grabbed the hem of his cloak from beneath his armor and tried to wipe the snow from his spectacles, but between the snow, swamp muck, and various colors of blood, his cloak was a complete disaster. Albeit a colorful one. He ended up cleaning the lenses on the sleeve of the elf's shirt instead.

He checked Relka next. She would have a nasty bruise on her head, but she should live. Trok was snoring, so Jig figured he was okay. So was Gratz. His arm was broken from when the elf had tossed him aside, but that could wait until Jig checked the others. Of the two goblins who had been pinned by the same arrow, the one in back still lived. Barely. Jig managed to keep him alive as he pulled the arrow free, then did his best to heal the wounds.

By the time he finished, Jig was exhausted and covered in goblin blood. But only two of his companions had died.

"First you catch on fire, then you kill the magic elf. Now you heal stupid goblins." Hessafa was still staring, her fur making her head appear comically large. Her teeth were bared, and her eyes wide. "What are you, goblin?"

Don't tell her, Shadowstar said.

I don't want to. Can you imagine what it would sound like if she and Relka started singing together? But how am I supposed to explain catching on fire in the middle of a battle, not to mention—

Jig, you're not going to like this.

Jig closed his eyes. If Shadowstar was bothering to warn him, the news had to be truly unpleasant.

When I placed the mantle of my star upon you, something noticed.

The mantle of your star? Oh, you mean the light. Jig stiffened as the rest of that sank in. *What noticed? Are there other elves out here?*

They didn't notice you, Jig. They noticed me.

From Shadowstar's tone, this was a bad thing. Yet Jig couldn't help feeling relieved. For once, the unimaginably scary monster wasn't after him!

That's true, but anything searching for me is going to find you as well. Don't tell her anything, Jig. Don't tell anyone until I learn more.

So much for relief.

"What are you?" Hessafa asked again.

Jig glanced at the other goblins. Gratz was groaning, and Relka had begun to stir. "Hessafa, I didn't kill the elf."

"Kobolds not stupid. I saw!"

Jig shook his head. "You killed her."

"Elf attacked stupid goblins. Hessafa hid. Then you—"

"Think what the stupid goblins will say when you explain how you saved them," Jig said. "How you snuck up and stabbed that elf with his own arrow. The kobolds sent you with us because they're mad at you. Imagine how they'll react when you tell them you killed the elf."

Hessafa hesitated, glancing at the elf, then back at Jig. She straightened. "*Hessafa* killed elf!"

"Did I hear that mutt right? A kobold killed an elf scout?" Gratz's voice was hoarse but firm. He sat up and rotated his arm. "Huh. I could have sworn I heard bone crack."

Jig glanced around, searching the hillside and the trees. Shadows had begun to stretch as the sun sank lower.

Trok was the next to recover. He groaned and climbed to his feet, brushing snow from his furs. His ears perked when he saw the body. "Hey, fresh elf!"

"No eating." Gratz rubbed his arm again. "The last thing we need is for an entire squadron to come down with the runs from raw elf."

"Who said anything about eating him raw?" Trok asked. He jabbed a finger at Relka. "She's a cook!"

Their brief argument ended when Trok realized his knife wouldn't pierce the elf's skin. They might be able to cook the elf, but they had no way to eat him.

Even though Jig's stomach gurgled at the thought of roast elf, he was just as happy to move on. Cooking the elf meant more time alone in the woods, with wild animals and magically armored elves and whatever was hunting Tymalous Shadowstar.

What could possibly hunt a god?

Generally, nothing but another god, said Shadowstar.

As Jig followed Gratz and the others back toward Billa's army, he tried very hard not to think about that. He failed.

Do you remember what Darnak said, back when he first told you about me? Shadowstar asked as they crossed through the swamp.

Jig could feel Smudge rustling in his hood. Was he sensing Jig's nervousness, or was Shadowstar's hunter already closing in on them?

They had been deep in the tunnels of the mountain. Jig had seen Darnak's own healing powers and had asked about the gods. Darnak had been delighted to have an audience, and he had talked until Jig's ears were literally numb. *He mentioned you were one of the fifteen Forgotten Gods, and said something about a war.*

The War of Shadows. Bells rang sharply, which Jig had come to recognize as a sound of annoyance. *Stupid name, I know. I'd bet anything Noc was the one who thought it up. It suits his sense of melodrama. Still, it's simpler than "The Folly of Fifteen Gods Who Thought They Could Challenge the Two."*

That would be difficult to work into a song, Jig agreed.

The realm of the gods is a convoluted place, Jig. At the end of the war, vast stretches of that realm were cast into shadow and darkness. The fifteen rebellious gods were destroyed, their homes eradicated.

All fifteen? Jig repeated. Including Tymalous Shadowstar. *They thought you were dead.*

I nearly was. I've kept quiet since then. None of the magic I've used should have drawn the attention of another god. Not unless they were already searching for me.

Jig shivered. The evening had grown colder, and his breath clouded in the air. *I thought gods were supposed to be immortal.*

Some of us are more immortal than others.

Jig glanced at Relka. What would she say if she knew? For most of a year, she had praised Tymalous Shadowstar to anyone who would listen, and many who wouldn't. She sang about his strength and wisdom. But what Shadowstar had revealed made him sound less like an all-powerful god and more like . . . well, like a goblin. A goblin among gods, hiding and afraid.

I resent that. I'm far better looking than any goblin.

Jig ignored that. *Do you know which god is hunting you?* And, more importantly, would that god bother with Shadowstar's goblin followers?

I have my suspicions. Noc ascended to the role of death god during the war. He earned the name God-slayer. I trust you can figure out why?

"Weapons ready, men," Gratz barked, drawing Jig's attention back to this world. "Jig, Hessafa, spread out to either side. Stay out of sight. Flanking formation."

"What does that mean?" Jig asked.

"It means you get your scrawny arse out of sight and wait for orders. If this is another elf trick, you and Hessafa attack from either side."

Jig hurried away, crouching down in the swamp and barely noticing the stench. A part of him wanted to keep on running. Nobody would bother to follow a lone goblin runt.

But where would he run? Even if he managed to avoid elf scouts and Billa's warriors, he didn't know how to hide from a vindictive death god. Though he would probably freeze to death long before that became a problem. He squatted in the snow and tried to keep his teeth from chattering too loudly.

"Gratz, is that you?" The voice was Silverfang's. What was he doing out here? Jig peeked through the trees.

Silverfang sat astride Bastard, clutching the wolf's ropes in both hands. Bastard snarled and tugged his head. Silverfang leaned down and punched him in the head, after which Bastard settled down. Two other wolf-riders waited to either side.

"We were on our way back," Gratz said. "We found and killed an elf scout."

"I see you lost the runt." Silverfang looked pleased.

"No, sir. Jig, Hessafa, get back here!"

Jig stomped his feet as he walked. His toes were starting to go numb. That couldn't be good.

"Stupid goblins," Hessafa muttered. "First go hide. Then come back. Can't make up their minds."

"Corporal Gratz, report," Silverfang said, his voice strange. He wasn't yelling, exactly. He sounded like he wasn't sure whether or not to be angry. "Exactly what happened when you fought this elf?"

"He had some kind of magical protection," Gratz said. He hesitated, then grudgingly added, "The kobold finished him off."

"That's right!" Hessafa raised her spear. "Hessafa killed him. Goblins just fell down a lot."

"Is that so?" Silverfang scowled at Gratz. *There* was the anger. "You let a useless kobold fight your battle?"

"We used the Grab-and-Squeeze formation," Gratz said. "Just like regulations say. We goblins did the bulk of the fighting, wearing the elf down so the kobold could—"

"Save it." Silverfang smiled. "You can explain it to the orcs. It seems Billa herself would like to ask you a few questions about your little battle."

CHAPTER 6

~~~✦~~~

*T*ymalous Autumnstar dug his front claws into the sandstone and slid his broken body across the floor. His rear legs and tail were limp and lifeless. From the feel—rather, the lack of feeling past his wings— Anisah had snapped his spine. Fortunately, it was difficult to truly kill a god.

Not so difficult to smash one senseless, as it turned out.

Finally he reached the wall, where various pots and sacks provided shadows and shelter. He squeezed behind a stack of fleshy cactus leaves. Hopefully nobody would need the pungent, needle-covered leaves for tonight's meal. Anyone who found Autumnstar here would either toss him into the pot for dinner or break his neck to put him out of his misery.

His tongue flicked out, smelling the cool night air. He rested his head against the barrel and looked out at Anisah's body.

Well, at least she had died smiling. Even if Autumnstar hadn't planned to comfort her in quite that fashion.

What had gone wrong? Healing a mortal body needed only the tiniest pinch of magic. He should have had no trouble easing Anisah's pain. Or fixing his own crushed spine, for that matter.

He closed his eyes, fighting off fear as he peered

beyond the stone walls of the city. Surely the gods weren't still hunting him after all this time. A quick peek into the realm of the divine shouldn't draw any notice. Priests did it all the time, using purely mortal magic. And sometimes a particular type of mushroom.

He braced himself as his surroundings appeared to fade, but nothing more happened. Autumnstar rested his head on a cactus leaf and tried to relax.

It was strange to see the stars from down here. The constellations were recognizable, but altered. Tarvha the Trapper was much skinnier from this angle. The Three-Headed Dragon appeared to have his leftmost head wedged in a very improbable location. Then again, dragons were quite flexible.

He turned, trying to orient himself. A half-moon hovered over the eastern horizon, which meant The Guardian should be to his right. The Guardian looked like a potbellied dwarf from here. Autumnstar followed the tip of The Guardian's nose, toward—

"It's gone," he whispered. He searched again, making sure the oddly distorted constellations hadn't tricked him, but there was no mistake. Before, a lone star had burned red in the sky between The Guardian and Elsa the Drunk. Now there was nothing.

No, not nothing. He squinted, trying to make out a spot of darkness that was somehow blacker than the surrounding space. A point in the sky that seemed to absorb the light of nearby stars.

He should have guessed. Noc was nothing if not dramatic. No doubt the death of the Autumn Star had been a great spectacle, seen by gods and mortals throughout the universe.

"I hope you burned your eyebrows off," Autumnstar muttered.

A circle of orcs waited at the edge of the swamps. Jig counted at least eight, though there could have been more in back.

They stood with swords and axes ready. How much time did they spend polishing their blades, to get them

to shine like that? And had they deliberately positioned themselves so their weapons would best reflect
the moonlight?

Intentional or not, it worked. Jig didn't even realize
he had slowed down until one of the other goblins
bumped into him.

"Say nothing unless Billa talks to you," Gratz whispered. "Don't make any sudden moves, either. If one
of those orcs decides you're a threat, you'll be dead
before you can spit."

Jig pulled his cloak tight, tucking his hands into his
armpits. His fingers felt numb, as if the blood had
frozen. Even the inside of his nostrils felt like they
were coated in a thin layer of ice. He stared longingly
at Trok's furs, then gave a tentative sniff. Cold as it
was, the icy breeze couldn't completely kill Trok's
stench.

Silverfang pulled Bastard to a halt a few paces away
from the lead orcs. The wolf snarled, but the orcs
didn't so much as blink.

Billa was awfully confident, to come with so few
guards. Sure, any one of those orcs could probably kill
every goblin here, but with enough goblins and
wolves, there was always the chance one would get
lucky. Most of the goblins were new recruits. How did
Billa know there wouldn't be trouble?

"General," Silverfang said, bowing his head.

The frontmost orcs stepped to either side, revealing
Billa the Bloody.

Jig's first thought was that Billa looked awfully
skinny for an orc. Her skin was paler, too. Her hair
was a dirty white, pulled into a thick, snarled rope at
the top of her head. Despite the white hair, she appeared quite young. Her face was unwrinkled, marred
only by the tribal scar on her nose and a sprinkling
of pimples on her forehead.

She wore a cape of white horsehair over her armor.
Like the rest of the orcs, her arms were bare, but she
didn't appear to notice the cold. Her skin wasn't pim-

pled like the others, nor did her face have the same flushed appearance.

She chewed her thumbnail as she contemplated the goblins. The rest of her nails were bitten raw.

Jig would have sworn the air got colder when she turned to look at him. Even the wolves backed away as her gaze swept them. She spat a bit of nail into the snow. One hand brushed the hilt of her sword.

"What happened tonight?" Her voice was softer than Jig expected.

Gratz cleared his throat. "We found and killed one elf, sir."

"Good. Who killed it?"

Gratz made a face like he had bitten into a fried rat, only to have it bite him back. "Her," he said, pointing to Hessafa. One of the orcs snickered.

Billa chewed her lower lip as she studied the kobold. "You killed an elf scout?"

Hessafa glanced at Jig, then grinned. "Goblins fight stupid. Hessafa killed elf."

"Nothing stupid about the Grab-and-Squeeze formation," Gratz muttered.

Billa drew her sword. Gratz squeaked once and was silent.

No wonder Billa hadn't worried about a few goblins and their wolves. With a sword like that, she could kill—

A god, said Shadowstar.

Most of the blade was a cloudy gray, rippled like sand on the shore of the underground lake back home. The edges were clear as glass. Fog rose from the surface, and frost soon covered the blade from hilt to tip. Cold spread from the sword like stink from Trok, so powerful Jig might as well have been standing naked in the snow.

So it isn't Noc after all, Shadowstar said absently. *This could be bad.*

Jig snorted, then tensed, hoping nobody had noticed. *What's worse than a god of death hunting us?*

"So I'm to believe a kobold summoned the power of Tymalous Autumnstar to help her overcome this elf?" Billa asked, her voice still mild.

For an instant, Jig felt hope. *You're Tymalous Shadowstar. Maybe she's confused you with some other god?*

Isa, Shadowstar whispered. *I thought she was dead.*

"Tymalous who?" Hessafa glanced at Jig again before asking, "Is that another stupid goblin?"

So who is Isa? Jig demanded.

Another goddess. She created that sword during the war. For Billa to carry it means Isa has taken her as her champion.

Billa stepped toward Jig. "Tell me what you know of Tymalous Autumnstar, little goblin. Lie to me, and I'll cut out your tongue."

Relka stepped forward. "Jig is—"

Silverfang punched her in the head. "No speaking out of turn!"

Jig gave silent thanks for Silverfang and his temper. Relka would get them all killed if she didn't keep her mouth shut. "I've never heard that name before," Jig said.

Too late he wondered if Billa could read his thoughts. No . . . if she could, Jig would already be dead. He tried to imagine how an innocent goblin would act. Terrified, most likely. Jig could do that.

"She probably means Tymalous Shadowstar," Trok said.

Silverfang drew back a fist, but Billa held up her hand, and he hesitated.

"Tymalous Shadowstar?" Billa stepped toward him, leaving Jig to shiver uncontrollably from cold and fear. "Tell me where you heard that name."

Trok folded his arms. "If I do, will you make me a wolf-rider?"

Gratz started to say something about regulations and orders, but Silverfang was faster. He reached for Trok, bellowing, "I'm going to rip off your arm and—"

"Yes," said Billa. "Tell me what I want to know, and Silverfang will make you one of his wolf-riders."

Silverfang's scowl wrinkled his face so badly his metal tooth pricked the skin beneath his eye. A drop of blue blood trailed down his cheek like a tear. But he said only, "Yes, sir."

Even if Jig could have stopped shaking, there was nowhere to run. The wolves would be on him in a single leap, assuming Billa didn't simply run him through with that sword. He stared at Trok, waiting for him to condemn Jig to death.

"You want her," Trok said. He nudged Relka with his foot, then reached down to grab the new pendant she had made.

Relka groaned and tried to take it back.

"She won't shut up about Tymalous Shadowstar," said Trok. "You should hear the hymns."

His feral grin made his motivation obvious. He might not know why Billa was asking about Shadowstar, but anything that rid him of Relka's presence was a good thing. As a bonus, he would get to be a wolf-rider and keep Jig around to heal whatever injuries he might suffer . . . up until Relka opened her mouth and told Billa the truth.

"She's not—" Jig swallowed and tried again. "Relka's not the one you want."

"Is that so?" asked Billa, turning that frigid glare on him once more. Trok looked angry too, but he was a minor worry compared to Billa.

"You want Shadowstar's priest." He blurted it out quickly, before his sense of self-preservation could render him mute. "A goblin named Braf. Relka might have prayed to Shadowstar while we were fighting the elf, but Braf is his one and only true priest."

Come to think of it, Relka probably had prayed to Shadowstar during the fighting. Jig wouldn't be surprised if she prayed for Shadowstar's blessing every time she washed a pot or cooked an omelette.

She does. Why do you think they taste so good?

"Go on," Billa said.

"Braf cast spells for his followers. He put them on those necklaces. But he's not very good with magic." That last part was true, if nothing else. Braf had trouble concentrating on what he was doing. Jig still remembered the time Braf tried to heal one of the kitchen workers Golaka had stabbed for swiping firespider eggs. Braf had pressed two fingers into the wound, guiding Shadowstar's magic deep into the goblin's body. Jig found him there hours later, having healed the wound with his fingers still inside.

With a grimace, Jig said, "Relka must have used that magic to try to help her during the fight." He shrugged. "I didn't notice anything. Shadowstar never struck me as being a very helpful god."

Billa took the necklace from Trok and studied it closely. "What happened to Braf?"

"He died," Jig said quickly. "When Princess Genevieve attacked our lair."

"Champions of a god aren't so easy to kill." Billa waved at Relka. "Take her." Two of her orcs hauled Relka upright. "Prepare your goblins, Silverfang. We march tonight."

"Tonight?" Silverfang cleared his throat. "Begging your pardon, but I've got two squads out with boot rot, and we haven't finished—"

"Leave them." Billa glanced at another of the orcs. "Spread the word. We march through the night."

Relka's feet dragged through the mud and snow as the orcs hauled her away. She watched Jig the whole time, hardly even blinking.

Billa sheathed her sword. "And give this goblin a wolf," she added, waving a hand at Trok.

Now what? asked Shadowstar.

Jig's shoulders slumped. *I was hoping you would tell me.*

Goblin drums beat out a steady rhythm as Billa's army marched up the road. At first Jig had been delighted to hear drums actually pounding in unison. Such a nice change from the cacophony of battle back at the lair. Row after row of goblins, all marching in step. Not one knew where they were going, but that didn't seem to matter. What mattered was staying in line and not drawing Oakbottom's attention.

The walking tree wandered through the ranks, his bare branches lashing out like whips at anyone who faltered. As far as Jig could tell, he never actually stepped on anyone. The base of his trunk split into four "legs," each one ending in a long mess of gnarled roots. He walked slowly, but with his size, he could take one step for every five of Jig's and still keep up. And his branches were long enough to strike seven lines ahead or behind, as the goblin next to Jig had learned earlier. The poor fellow was still limping.

As one of the newest, and presumably one of the most expendable recruits, Jig found himself near the front line. A group of orcs on horseback led the way, followed closely by the goblin wolf-riders. Trok rode Smelly, which seemed a perfect match. To either side of the main column, small groups of kobolds jogged along, presumably searching the woods for ambushes.

He glanced behind, still amazed at the sheer size of Billa's army. They filled the road and much of the land to either side. Billa and most of her orcs were toward the rear, followed by troll-drawn wagons. Presumably Relka was back there as well, assuming Billa hadn't killed her.

She's alive, said Shadowstar. *Frightened and exhausted, but alive.*

She hadn't told Billa about Jig, either, judging from the fact that Jig was also still alive. *What does Isa want with you? Who is she? What happened to Noc?*

Isa was Goddess of the Winter Winds.

That would explain the cold. If Jig had to face another god, couldn't it have been a god of warm, comfy breezes?

She was also my wife.

Jig stopped walking. Goblins behind him cursed and swore as they collided with one another. Jig hunched his shoulders against a punch to the back that sent him staggering. He hurried to catch up with the rest of his line, hoping Oakbottom hadn't noticed.

Your wife? he repeated. Goblins didn't mate for life, but he knew surface-dwellers had different habits. Habits apparently shared by the gods. *I don't understand. Shouldn't you be happy to see her then?*

I'm glad she's alive, Shadowstar said, though he sounded less than certain. *I'll be happier when I know why she's hunting me.*

Another goblin crashed into Jig as a small brawl erupted behind him. He tried to hurry away, but the formation was too tight. He had no place to go.

That didn't stop Oakbottom. He kicked goblins aside like pebbles in a tunnel. Branches shot out, hauling goblins into the air. Jig counted eight goblins, all squirming and kicking and helpless as bugs in a spiderweb.

"Most of you are new to Billa's army," Oakbottom said. He had no mouth or face that Jig could see, though the thick branches concealed much of his trunk. Many of his words were punctuated by a sound like boards clapping together. "So most of you probably don't know the punishment for brawling on duty."

More branches wrapped around one of the goblins, and the great tree spun in a quick circle. The goblin flew in a long arc over the rest of the formation and into the darkness beyond. His scream faded with distance, then cut off abruptly.

"Now you know," Oakbottom shouted. He tossed the rest of the goblins to the ground, where they scrambled back into line.

A short distance ahead, Gratz chuckled. "That ought to keep things quiet for a few days." He glanced back at Jig and lowered his voice. "Oakbottom's a very angry tree. Doesn't like anyone, but he's especially mad at humans. Makes him a great asset during battle, and he's good for discipline."

"Why would a tree hate humans?" Jig asked.

Gratz winced. "Not so loud."

It was too late. Oakbottom was already stepping

toward Jig. Despite the lack of visible ears, Oakbottom could hear as well as any goblin.

"You think you blood-sacks are the only ones to be abused by the humans?" Oakbottom asked.

"Here he goes again," one of the other goblins whispered.

"When I was little more than a sapling, there was a little boy who used to visit me," Oakbottom said. "Every day he came. He would swing from my branches. He slept in the shade against my trunk. Sometimes he shot stones at squirrels and birds with his little sling. I loved that little boy. We were happy."

"What happened?" Jig asked.

"Time passed, and the boy grew older. He stopped visiting as often. But one day he returned. He had fallen in love, and he wanted to make his girl a gift. So I told him, 'Take my leaves and branches and weave a beautiful headband.' And so he did.

"He came back a year later. He and this girl were to marry, and he wished to build a great bonfire to celebrate. So I said, 'Cut more of my branches and dry them for your bonfire.' And so he did. Soon I saw smoke in the distance as they celebrated and danced.

"Seasons passed, and I thought the boy had forgotten me. Then one day he returned, carrying an ax. He said to me, 'Old friend, my wife is pregnant, and there is no space in my father's home for a baby. Give me your wood so I can build a house.' "

Oakbottom shuddered as he walked. "He slammed that ax into my trunk. You can still see the scar. And so I did what any self-respecting tree would have done. I ripped the ax out of his hands and gave him a taste of his own blade."

"He's been killing humans ever since," Gratz said. "Naturally Dilla made him an officer. He doesn't like to be called sir, though."

"Trees don't concern themselves with ranks and titles," Oakbottom said. "Give me the sun on my leaves, damp earth beneath my roots, and humans to throw, and I will be happy."

"Hear, hear!" Gratz shouted. The other goblins joined in.

Lovely company you're keeping these days, Shadowstar commented.

Jig didn't answer. He would have gladly listened to a hundred such stories. Marching was dull, mindless activity, which meant he had far too much time to worry.

Where was Billa taking them? What would happen if Relka told the truth about Jig? Were the goblins back at Avery still alive? When would they stop to pee?

The wind blew harder, freezing the tips of Jig's ears. He pulled up his hood and transferred Smudge into a small pouch at his waist. *If Isa is a goddess of winter and snow and cold, does that mean it's not likely to warm up any time soon?*

No, said Shadowstar. *And the stronger she gets, the colder you'll be.*

It figured.

Three days later, Jig barely even heard the beating of the drums. The quick double-beat that signaled a halt hardly registered. He bumped into another goblin, then mumbled an apology.

Every part of him slumped. For the past three days, he had trudged along, staring at the boots of the goblin in front of him. He knew every blemish of the wet leather, every loose stitch, even the frayed threads hanging from the bottom of the goblin's trousers.

He rubbed the front of his thighs and hissed from the pain. His legs had banged the hard lower edge of his armor so many times he felt like his thighs would be permanently dented.

"Sleep with your weapons ready," Gratz shouted. "We're getting close."

Other goblins had already begun to drop, curling up in the middle of the road and shoving one another for space. Gratz and Oakbottom walked through the ranks, kicking them awake.

"You know the drill, you lazy bastards," Gratz said.

"Sleep in your armor and you'll be too stiff to move, come dawn. Any goblin who's too sore to keep up gets tossed."

Jig dropped his helmet onto the road, flexed his fingers, and fumbled with the straps of his armor. His hands were little more than blocks of ice. The buckles refused to move, and the straps slipped through his fingers. After four tries, he was ready to draw his knife and cut away the armor. He would have done it, but he suspected that would violate one of Gratz's precious regulations.

Finally he lay down on his stomach and pointed his arms overhead. Feeling like a fool, he wriggled backward.

He lost a bit of skin from his ears and nose, but he managed to squeeze out of the oversize armor. Pressing his back against the armor, he drew his knees to his chest and rested his head on the road. He kept one hand on his sword and closed his eyes.

He heard voices in the distance. Silverfang was shouting at the wolf-riders to take care of their mounts. Poor Trok. How long would he be awake, caring for Smelly?

Elsewhere, Oakbottom lashed a group of kobolds awake, sending them out to keep watch.

The rest of Gratz's squadron fell asleep fast, all of them exhausted. Jig soon found himself squeezed into a mass of snoring, squirming, farting goblins. It reminded him a bit of home. And at least he was warm.

Jig giggled quietly, a sure sign of exhaustion or terror. Maybe both. But the more he thought about it, the funnier his situation became. If it weren't for a forgotten goddess who was hunting for him, this would have been the safest Jig had ever been. Surrounded by goblin warriors, he was well-protected from adventurers and armies and anything else . . . short of the gods, of course. And Billa's rules protected him from those same goblin warriors.

No wonder Billa had amassed such a following. Her army provided security. Security and hope.

Shadowstar didn't even know why Isa was hunting him. Maybe she just missed her husband.

And maybe Braf will stop picking his nose with his fangs, but I wouldn't put money on it.

Jig rolled onto his back. Smudge scurried out from beneath his neck, climbing onto his chest. Jig absently rubbed the spider with one finger as he stared up at the night sky. The sight of the clouds drifting past the stars gave him vertigo, and he clenched his eyes shut. *How do you know? Not about Braf, but that Isa is dangerous?*

It would be easier to show you, said Shadowstar.

That's all right, Jig said hastily. *I don't need to see—*

The ground beneath him seemed to give way, as if Jig had plunged into an endless pit. He squealed and flailed about.

Open your eyes, Jig.

Brilliant sunlight made him squint. Moments later he was leaping out of the way as a sea of dwarves charged past, waving axes and hammers and shouting in a language he didn't recognize. Though the dwarves didn't appear to notice him, he somehow managed to avoid being trampled into the grass.

When the footfalls had faded into the distance, he opened his eyes and squinted to block the worst of the sun.

"We have *not* lost!"

He turned around to see . . . Jig wasn't sure how to describe her. She reminded him of a dwarf, only taller. A giant dwarf? Clearly his mind was still delusional from fatigue.

She was taller than most humans, but her broad shoulders and stocky build reminded him of Darnak without the beard. Her armor and helmet shone like glass, and in one hand she held a sword of ice. The same sword Jig had seen in Billa's hand that evening.

"Isa?" Jig guessed.

"Have you lost your wits as well as your courage?" Isa spat in disgust. Even though it felt like late summer or early autumn, the spittle froze before it touched the ground.

The jingle of tiny bells warned him Shadowstar was near. He turned, but saw no sign of the forgotten god. Silver hair drifted in front of his eyes, and—

Jig stopped moving. He had never had hair this long, even before Smudge came along. Jig reached to touch his scalp, and the bells jingled again. He wore a loose shirt of cool black material, striped with silver bells. Tymalous Shadowstar's shirt. And Shadowstar's hair on his head. He reached for his ears, and tried to bite back his dismay at the puny, misshapen things he found there.

"It's you who've lost your mind, Isa," Jig said. His chest tightened with fear. Had he just insulted a goddess? "Wait, I didn't mean to say that!"

Relax. This happened thousands of years before you were born. Nothing you say or do can change the outcome.

Ah. This was a stupid god trick. *Couldn't you just tell me how it happened?*

This is more effective. It's also more fun to watch. Now relax and enjoy being me.

Isa pointed. Across a field, the dwarves were attacking men mounted on giant serpents. "Old Sethina sided with the two over us. Perhaps she'll reconsider when her precious snake lovers have been wiped out."

The snake lovers were putting up quite a fight. The serpents' scales were strong enough to turn most blows, and like the rock serpents Jig knew from back home, they struck too fast to dodge. Unlike those serpents, these were large enough to take an entire dwarf in their jaws.

Jig wondered briefly how the men remained in their saddles. Or how they stopped the saddles from sliding down the snakes' scaly bodies, for that matter. Magic, he guessed. Probably the same magic that kept the riders from throwing up as the snakes slithered and struck.

Twenty dwarves fell for every snake that died, but there were enough dwarves to defeat twice this number. The dwarves fought without fear, driven by Isa's magic.

And how did Jig know that?

"Ama is dead," Jig said. He had no clue who Ama might be, but the words continued to pour forth. "Noc has betrayed us. Even now, Ipsep flees to his temple in the black lake, and Talla the Merciful weeps over the loss of her sister. We've lost, Isa."

"Then we will make them pay for their victory." Isa pointed her sword over the field, to where the last of the snakes were falling. "Beginning with Noc. My dwarves will march into the very halls of death, and there they will—"

"Die." Jig interrupted. His terror had begun to fade. He still wasn't completely sure what was happening, but Isa hadn't killed him yet, and that was a good sign. But now he felt himself growing angry. Not the loud, frightened anger of a goblin, but the deep fury of a god. Anger powerful enough to wipe out every dwarf on that field, if he chose to unleash it. Instead, he—or Shadowstar—turned to face Isa. "You're serious. You're going to send mortals to face a god in his home. Every last one of your followers will die, Isa."

Isa shrugged. "They'll take some of Noc's protectors with them. Death is inevitable, dear Autumnstar. You of all beings should know that."

Jig felt himself grinning. "And you of all gods should know better than to push me." His vision flashed. Isa shielded her face from the red light pouring from Jig's eyes. Across the field, those dwarves who survived began to age. From this distance, the dwarves appeared no larger than his thumbnail, but Jig could see them all clearly as his magic took effect. Tough, sunbeaten skin wrinkled. Gray spread through hair and beards. Joints grew stiff, and old injuries began to ache.

"Stop!"

Isa's scream made Jig want to disappear, but instead he shook his head.

"You would kill them yourself?" Isa shouted

"They're not dead, just old," Jig said. "Too old to fight. They'd make it three steps into Noc's temple before half of them lost bladder control. But they're dwarves. They should live at least another century. Longer than they would if they continued to follow you."

Isa drew back her sword. Jig whimpered, even as he raised his left arm. A silver disk appeared on his forearm, absorbing Isa's attack with ease. Isa struck twice more, ringing the bells on Jig's sleeve but doing no real harm.

"Where can I get a shield like this?" Jig whispered.

Noc melted it a few years after this battle, when he came to kill me. Sorry.

Isa backed away. "You're a coward," she whispered. "You're afraid to face Noc." Her next blow came so suddenly that Jig barely raised his shield in time to deflect it. The force knocked him to the ground, but Isa didn't bother to follow up her advantage.

Moments later, Jig was alone, grimacing as he rubbed his arm.

Now do you understand why she makes me nervous?

His chest burned. Was this another of Isa's attacks? Fire seemed out of character for her. Jig opened his eyes just as Smudge raced over his face, jumping down into his hood.

There was an orc staring down at him. Scars split the orc's eyebrows, and his breath smelled like kobold. The orc grabbed Jig's fang.

With a squawk, Jig was yanked to his feet. The orc kicked his way through the groaning, snoring goblins, dragging Jig to the edge of the group. Jig was almost positive he recognized this orc as one of the guards who had been with Billa.

"Billa wants to know exactly what we'll be facing

when we reach your lair," said the orc. "What's the size and makeup of this force that attacked you?"

"Well, Darnak's a dwarf, so he's pretty small," Jig said, rubbing his eyes. "Genevieve is average height for a human, but she's skinny." He stared. "Wait, did you say we were going to our lair?"

"What numbers will we face when we arrive at your lair?" The orc spoke slowly, like Jig was an addle-brained child.

"I don't know." Jig rubbed his eyes and adjusted his spectacles. "The humans sealed the entrance. The only way in is to get the Rod of Creation back from—"

"Never question the power of Billa the Bloody or Isa of the Winter Winds." A halfhearted punch to the chest drove the orc's point home and knocked Jig onto his back. "How many goblins did they leave in the lair?"

"A few hundred," Jig guessed. He started to sit up, then thought better of it. If he stayed on the ground, the orc couldn't reach to hit him. "All but the strongest warriors were sealed inside. The rest were taken away to Avery."

"So what are you doing here?" The orc snorted and shook his head. "What else lives in this mountain of yours?"

"Hobgoblins, mostly," Jig said. "There used to be ogres and a dragon, but we killed the dragon and then the pixies came and wiped out the ogres. We killed the pixies too, and—"

The orc leaned down. "Pixies? Goblins killing a dragon? Didn't your commander tell you there was no drinking in Billa's army?"

Jig said nothing. The orc hauled him upright and shoved him back toward the other goblins. Jig picked his way back, trying not to step on his fellow soldiers. The orc headed to the front, presumably to interrogate Trok.

Jig settled back down on the cold earth, but this time, he was unable to sleep. In the moonlight, he could just make out the shape of the mountains. Billa was bringing him home.

Why?

Billa's army believed she would lead them to victory, protecting them from the surface-dwellers once and for all. Jig remembered how Isa had been ready to send her dwarves to their death, all so she would have the chance to slay her enemy.

Now Isa had a new army.

Jig just hoped he and Shadowstar weren't her new enemy.

CHAPTER 7

The worst part about losing the power to heal was that he couldn't heal himself either. Fortunately, Anisah's daughter Hana found his broken body. After cooing over Autumnstar for close to an hour, she had decided he was the reincarnation of her mother's spirit.

Hana had never struck Autumnstar as being overly bright.

Without his star, Tymalous Autumnstar's power was almost as limited as a mortal's. Even more than his temple, the Autumn Star had been both the symbol and the source of his power. But he was still a god. His willpower alone was enough to keep the sand lizard alive, and over time, this body would heal.

For more than a year, Hana carried him around in a woven sling, feeding him beetles and ants and whatever other insects she could catch. His bones knit, the torn membrane of his wings sealed itself, and he regained the use of his tail and rear legs . . . though Hana still insisted on wrapping tiny diapers around his backside.

There was something profoundly wrong about a god being forced to wear a diaper. Had Autumnstar been a vengeful sort, he would have conserved his power for some serious smiting.

Instead he found himself slipping into lethargy. It

would be so easy to let go, to allow his awareness to dissipate into this body and truly become a sand lizard. His star was gone, and he would be killed if he ever tried to retake his place among the gods. Here he was warm and comfortable and safe.

But one day Hana would grow sick or old. He might have enough strength to help her, but then what? Wait another ten years until he was powerful enough to help another person? Turn his back on the rest of the sick and the dying, the old and the weak, and all those who needed his protection?

He tested his legs, digging his tiny claws into his sling and stretching. His back arched, and his wings fluttered. He jumped free, spreading his wings as he glided toward the floor. He fell faster than expected. Hana's incessant feeding had left him a bit heavier than before.

Before he could recover his balance, Hana snatched him by the neck. Autumnstar coughed and squirmed as she dropped him back into his sling. She held him in place as she hurried back to her room, where she looped a length of goat wool around his neck.

"I have to take care of you, Mother," Hana said. She started to tie the leash to the strap of her sling. "Don't you remember what happened last time? If I let you go, you'll get yourself crushed or eaten or lost, and you'll never find your way back to me."

Autumnstar bit her thumb.

He scurried out the door and raced up the wall, hiding atop the overhang of the roof. Hana followed, her shouts muffled as she sucked her bleeding thumb.

Autumnstar snorted. Served her right for trying to leash a god.

They marched for two more days. Sheer exhaustion numbed Jig's fear. By this time, he would have happily cut Trok's throat for the chance to ride a wolf. Terrifying as the wolves were, Jig was almost willing to risk being eaten if it meant he wouldn't have to walk anymore. His feet were so blistered he was amazed his boots hadn't burst at the seams. His legs were numb, and his ill-fitting armor had rubbed bloody streaks along his neck and shoulders.

Then on the morning of the fifth day, as Jig was scarfing down a breakfast of goat meat and warm milk, he spotted Trok hobbling into the woods to water the trees. He walked bow-legged, and even from here Jig could hear him yelp when he adjusted his trousers. On second thought, maybe marching on foot wasn't so bad. Painful as Jig's blisters and sores were, others had injuries that were far worse. All Jig knew was that he wasn't about to heal *those* wounds.

"Hurry it up," Silverfang shouted. He still rode Bastard, and he held Trok's wolf by the ropes. Trok ran back, his face tight with pain. Silverfang tossed Trok the ropes and turned to face the goblins. "We march double time today!"

Jig gulped down the last of his meat, dropping a bit into his hood for Smudge. He turned to Gratz. "What's double time?"

Gratz grinned. "You'll see."

The drums began to pound a quick, sharp rhythm. Apparently "double time" meant hurrying along at an awkward pace that was too quick to be a proper walk, but not quite fast enough to be a jog.

It was certainly a more efficient pace. Normally it took Jig most of the morning before his stomach began to cramp and the muscles in his thighs knotted. Marching at double time, he reached that same level of pain before they were even out of sight of last night's camp. By the time the sun was overhead, he was about ready to cut out his stomach with his sword. He probably would have done it too, if his stupid armor hadn't been in the way.

The ground was steeper today. Roots and saplings fought to reclaim the edges of the road. Those soldiers unfortunate enough to be at the edges of the formation were constantly stumbling and cursing as they fought to keep up.

Three thunderous drumbeats signaled a halt. Jig

turned around, standing on his toes to see past the other goblins. A group of orcs rode through the trees, toward the front of the lines. He recognized Billa by her white cape. Relka rode with her. Her eyes were squeezed shut, and her hands were tied. She looked like a child, squeezed onto the front of the saddle with Billa.

"The temple is nearby," Billa shouted. "Silverfang, bring your goblins."

Jig blinked. He had thought they were going back to the lair. What temple—?

Mine, said Shadowstar. *She must have sensed it.*

What would happen when she realized she couldn't get into the mountain to reach the temple? Jig stared longingly up the mountainside, wondering how the remaining goblins had fared since he left. They had survived for over a year the first time Jig sealed the entrance. They should be fine. Why, even now Golaka was probably preparing stuffed snakeskins and lizard-fish pudding.

Jig's mouth watered, and a bit of drool slipped past one of his fangs.

Silverfang turned Bastard in a tight circle. "Gratz, your squadron's with me. The rest of you take a break, but anyone who falls asleep had better pray I feed you to the wolves. At least they'll be quick!"

Jig and the rest of Gratz's squadron groaned. Behind them, goblins collapsed to the ground, leaning against one another for support.

Silverfang tugged Bastard's ropes and shouted, "March!" Bastard trotted after the orcs, and the rest of the wolf-riders fell in behind him.

Trok cursed as Smelly lunged away from the pack, teeth bared as he charged the closest of the horses. Trok yanked the ropes, fighting to get his wolf under control, but Smelly ignored him.

Silverfang threw a rock. No, not a rock. One of those troll toes. It flew past Smelly, who skidded to a halt. His front paws shoveled snow as he dug after the toe. "Next time you lose control of your mount, it's

your toes I'll be feeding him," Silverfang said as he
rode past.

Jig adjusted his helmet as he and the other goblins
jogged up the mountainside after the wolves. His
armor bounced with every step, deepening already-
painful bruises.

They kept up that pace for what seemed like years,
until Jig began to worry that his feet and legs would
simply snap away from his body like twigs. Finally the
horses and wolves slowed near a half-frozen stream.

"Gratz, take your men up the mountainside and
scout around." Silverfang grinned. "If you find anything, scream really loud before they kill you."

Jig glanced behind, surprised at how far they had
climbed. When he turned back, he realized he knew
this place. Farther upstream was where he and Relka
had come to rescue Grell from a human soldier a few
weeks back. He was home!

"Spread out," said Gratz. "Weapons ready."

Jig tugged his sword free. The leather wrapping on
the hilt did little to protect him from the cold metal,
and he switched the sword from one hand to the other
as he walked. His other hand he shoved into his cloak
pocket, petting Smudge for warmth.

The snow had hidden most evidence of battle, but
here and there Jig still saw signs of the humans' attack.
A spear stood point-first in the snow. At first, Jig mis-
took it for a sapling. Farther along, a bluebird perched
on an arrow embedded in a tree. The bird chirped
and fluffed its chest, apparently trying to mate with
the bright-colored fletching.

What Jig didn't see was any hint of humans or elves.
Genevieve had taken her goblin slaves down to Avery,
while Theodore and his elves ran off to join the king
and await Billa's army. How long would it take them
to discover Billa had chosen an alternate path? An
army of monsters was hardly subtle.

"Jig!" Gratz's sharp whisper made Jig jump.
"You're on point. Take us to this lair of yours."

Jig's chest tightened as he crept past the others toward the small clearing up ahead.

"Everyone else hold back," Gratz said. "Regulations say the best way to spring traps and ambushes is with a single scout. Be ready."

That made sense. One goblin would spring the trap, and then the rest could rush in. It was a great strategy for everyone except the poor scout. But Smudge was still relatively cool, and Jig heard nothing but the eager whispers of his fellow goblins. He crept forward, ears held high, until he reached the entrance. What remained of the entrance, at any rate.

Before, a fallen pine had sheltered the entrance, blocking the wind and hiding the cave from casual view.

Theodore must have used the Rod of Creation on the tree. The flat, brown needles now stretched in all directions, even into the rock of the cave. They were as wide as Jig's claws, and the edges appeared sharper than Jig's own sword. Smudge might be able to creep through the cracks between those tight-woven needles, but no goblin would fit. Not without first being chopped into spider-size pieces.

He decided to keep that last thought to himself, lest Gratz or Silverfang start to get ideas.

He would have given anything to be able to crawl through the tree and retreat to his lair. He wanted to be home, not stuck in the cold, waiting for Billa and her goddess to discover who he was.

This is your fault, he muttered. Shadowstar didn't argue.

"Is the lair secure?" Gratz called.

"Yes." It was more than secure. He rapped his sword against one of the needles. The needles bent slightly, like good steel, but when he tried to push them further, they sprang back.

Gratz shouted down the mountainside, then waved for the other goblins to join Jig. The orcs and wolf-riders had left their mounts a short distance below.

Jig stepped as far to the side as he could to make way for Billa and her orcs. And Relka. Relka's bound hands clutched her pendant tight.

Billa scowled at the tree. "Cut it away," she said.

Orcs raced to obey. Goblins raced to get out of the way of the orcs. Swords and axes crashed against the tree, to no avail. Like the elf scout Jig had fought, the tree was hardened by the Rod of Creation. Indestructible, save for magic.

Billa shoved Relka into the snow and drew her sword. "I know you're here, Autumnstar. You can't hide from me forever."

Billa chopped her sword onto the branches. The magically strengthened branches snapped as though they were dead and rotted. A few more swings, and Billa had cleared away enough of the tree for her to slip inside. She grabbed Relka by the arm.

"Nobody comes into this cave, friend or foe," said Billa. Her orcs grunted and took up positions to either side of the cave.

Relka had time for one frightened look at Jig, and then Billa dragged her into the darkness.

"This is boring," Trok muttered, not for the first time. Silverfang had taken several of the goblins down to tend the wolves. The rest were supposed to help the orcs guard the cave, a duty made more difficult by the orcs' determination to kill anyone who came too close.

Trok was sitting beneath a tree, rubbing a stone over the flat tip of his sword to sharpen it. He raised the sword high, holding it by the blade so the tip pointed down at his boots. He let go, and the sword buried itself in the snow and dirt, a finger's width from his right foot. "It's not right, leaving us out here to freeze. This is *our* lair. Why should Billa get it all to herself?"

Jig didn't answer. Billa had opened the lair! All he had to do was wait until everyone left, and he could return home. He stared at the orcs guarding the cave. Would anyone notice if Jig slipped away to hide?

An angry scream echoed from inside the tunnels.

"On second thought," Trok said, "Billa seems to know what she's doing."

"That was Relka," Jig said.

"*Was* being the important word." Trok yanked his sword from the ground and began sliding the stone along the edge. "With the warriors gone, who do you think will end up eating the rest of the goblins? Tunnel cats or the hobgoblins? My bet's on the hobgoblins. The yellow-skinned sneaks are probably raiding the kitchens even now."

"I doubt it," Jig said. "They'd have to get past Golaka to do that."

Jig, you have to go in there.

What? Jig glanced at the cave. *Didn't you hear that scream? And what about all of those orcs guarding the cave?*

Billa is in the temple, Shadowstar said. *She's going to kill Relka unless I manifest before her.*

So manifest!

There was a long silence. *Billa carries Isa's sword. That weapon could kill even me, Jig.*

Then I'm pretty sure it would kill me, too!

Trok punched him in the shoulder. "You're doing that thing where you stare and mumble to yourself again. It's creepy."

Jig bit his lip to keep from mumbling. *She's your wife, not mine.*

Jig, now that Billa has entered my temple, I can hear Isa whispering to her. She means to kill me if I don't help her. I'm not strong enough to fight another god.

So help her! Jig sat in the snow as he realized what Shadowstar was saying. *You're afraid.*

So are you, said Shadowstar.

Well, yes. I'm a goblin.

Relka screamed again. She sounded more angry than afraid.

Wait, I thought Isa wanted to kill you. Now she wants your help? Jig asked.

She wants me to help her kill Noc.

Jig's head was starting to ache. *Didn't you say Noc was the one who betrayed you? If she has a way to kill him, why wouldn't you help?*

It's more complicated than that.

Jig wasn't surprised in the least. Gods were supremely talented when it came to complicating things. Most of the non-goblin races were, come to think of it.

He's my son.

But why can't you help Isa kill him?

Shadowstar's sigh rang through Jig's skull. *Why did it have to be goblins?* Without waiting for an answer, he said, *Imagine if Billa told you she would destroy you unless you helped her to kill Smudge.*

Jig scooped Smudge out of his pocket and shielded him in both hands. *Why would Billa want to hurt my fire-spider?*

Don't make me smite you. Another divine sigh, and then, *I don't expect you to understand, Jig. But I can't let Isa kill my son.*

Wouldn't he be Isa's son too? Jig asked.

Shadowstar paused. *No. That's another reason Isa isn't too happy with me. Jig, whether you understand or not, I need you to do this. I can't help her kill Noc, and I can't let her sacrifice one of my followers in my own temple.*

Save Relka. From an orc and a god. Tymalous Shadowstar was afraid to go into that cave, but he expected Jig to go in?

You swore an oath to me, Jig Dragonslayer. There was no room for argument in his tone. This was Shadowstar at his most serious. *Relka believes in me. She believes in you. You can do this.*

Jig stared at the orcs standing around the cave. He closed his eyes as another shout tore out of the darkness. *No.*

The answering silence spooked him more than anything Shadowstar could have said.

If I go in there, Billa will kill two of your followers instead of only one. How is that better?

Still Shadowstar said nothing.

Noc is a death god, Jig said. *Why does he need our help against Isa, anyway?*

Noc doesn't know we survived. Even a goblin can kill a larger foe if that foe doesn't realize the goblin is there.

Jig shook his head. *Isa and Billa know I'm here. So do those orcs guarding the cave.*

Be not afraid, Shadowstar whispered.

And like that, Jig wasn't. The knot in his gut relaxed. The tension in his shoulders loosened. He stopped cringing every time Relka shouted. *What did you do?*

"You're still mumbling, runt," Trok said. He grabbed Jig's arm. "It's weird."

Jig punched Trok in the jaw.

Trok stumbled back, eyes wide. The bigger goblin looked more stunned than anything. That wouldn't last, though. As soon as Trok recovered, he would snap Jig like a stick.

Jig knew what Trok would do to him, and he didn't care. He didn't *want* to die, but he wasn't afraid, either. He stared at Trok and said, "I don't like being called runt."

Trok didn't move. "What happened to you?"

"Shadowstar." Jig rubbed his hand. Next time he would have to remember to punch something softer. Jaws were too solid. *You took my fear away.*

It's one of my gifts.

Had Tymalous Shadowstar been present, Jig would have punched him, too. Fear was what kept goblins alive! It didn't always stop them from running into stupid situations, but it helped. Which was presumably why Shadowstar had done this. To make Jig charge in like an idiot to rescue Relka.

What if I don't? Jig asked.

Then I'll hit you with the Light of the Autumn Star again. How long do you think it will take for Isa to

*sense that and send Billa out to get you. At least if you
sneak in, you get the element of surprise.*

True enough. Jig turned to Trok, who was still staring at him. Jig knew he should be afraid, but even
knowing Trok was angry enough to kill him did nothing. It didn't help matters that Trok looked so goofy
when he got mad. His eyes were all squinty, and his
nostrils flapped with every breath. Jig fought the urge
to reach up and pinch his nose.

"If a god ever decides to talk to you, the best thing
you can do is pretend you don't hear him." Jig
grabbed Trok's arm and tugged him toward the orcs.
"We have to save Relka."

Trok's anger disappeared, replaced by laughter.
"Why would we do that?"

"Because if you don't, I'll pull out my sword and
cut your throat." Jig reconsidered the state of his
weapon. "Or I'll bludgeon you to death with it."

Trok laughed even harder, until he started to cough.
"Try it, runt."

Jig didn't bother to draw his weapon. He simply
spun, smashing the sheathed blade into Trok's knee.
Trok yelped and fell. A few other goblins glanced
their way, then went back to whatever they were
doing.

"I told you not to call me that," Jig said. "Now one
of two things is going to happen. Either I kill you, in
which case you're dead. Or else I'll try and fail, and
you'll kill me."

"Let's find out," Trok snarled.

Jig pointed to where Gratz and Silverfang were yelling at another goblin who had been so careless as to
get himself bitten by one of the wolves. "Kill another
soldier in Billa's army, and they'll feed you to the
wolves. Either way, you die."

Of course, the same was true for Jig. But Trok
hadn't had his fear sucked out of his ears by a cowardly god.

Trok nodded slowly. "I'll help you."

Jig turned around. He suspected he would be dead

very soon, but in the meantime, living without fear
was kind of fun. He took a single step, only to have
Trok yank him back by his cloak.

"*If* you support me as goblin chief once this is
over," Trok finished.

Jig stared. "Grell is chief. She'd have us both for
dinner if I tried to make you chief in her place."

"Grell won't live forever." Trok spun his sword in
a lazy circle. "The goblins look up to you. They listen
to you. If you tell them I should be the next chief,
they'll believe you."

There had been a time, years ago, when Jig would
have thought Trok was the perfect choice to be chief.
The job had always gone to the biggest, meanest goblin, the one who could kill all challengers. And then
Jig had helped kill the previous chief, and suddenly a
nearsighted runt was in charge of the entire lair. Jig
wasn't crazy, so he had surrendered power as soon as
he possibly could, turning the job over to Grell . . .
who had turned out to be the best chief Jig could
remember.

She wasn't strong. She wasn't loud. She rarely bothered to kill anyone. People obeyed her not because
she threatened them, but because she was *Grell*. She
kept her enemies busy killing one another instead of
trying to kill her. It was a trick Jig really wanted to
learn someday.

Trok wasn't stupid, but he was a warrior. What kind
of chief would he be? More importantly, what would
he do to Jig once he took power? If Jig helped make
Trok chief, it followed that Jig could take that away
as well. The smart thing would be for Trok to immediately slit Jig's throat.

On the other hand, since both of them would probably die trying to save Relka, none of it made any
difference anyway. "Fine. You'll be chief. Now go distract those orcs."

"How am I supposed to do that?"

Jig tugged Trok's sword from his hand. To his
amazement, Trok didn't try to fight him. How had Jig

ever been scared of him? Jig marched over to the orcs, stopping just out of reach of their weapons. "Do any of you know how to play Toe Stub?"

The orcs stared. Jig could see their eagerness. Just a few more steps, and they would have an excuse to kill a goblin.

Jig turned back to Trok. "See? I told you they'd be too afraid to play."

That got one orc's attention. "Afraid of a goblin game?"

Jig slapped the sword back into Trok's hand. "Trok here was the best Toe Stub player in our whole lair." That wasn't saying much, considering Jig had just made up the game. "But I made a bet that he couldn't beat a real orc warrior."

By now several other goblins had approached. They whispered and pointed, and Jig heard at least one wager being made.

Trok leaned down to Jig and said, "Toe Stub?"

"Watch," said Jig. "Trok holds the sword by the blade and drops it. The winner is whoever gets the blade the closest to their foot without cutting off a toe. If you get scared and yank your foot away, you lose."

"Give me that," said the orc. He grabbed Trok's sword.

Trok started to smile. "You have to hold it so the tip is at least as high as your face."

The orc dropped the sword. It plunged into the dirt, a good distance from his foot. He cursed and clutched his hand.

"A typical beginner's mistake," Trok said, chuckling as he eased into the deception. He picked up his sword and said, "You have to yank your hand back quickly, or else you'll slice your fingers."

Jig grinned and backed away. His luck appeared to be changing. Neither the orcs nor the goblins paid him any attention.

Of course, since his apparent good fortune was giving him the means to slip into the tunnels to confront an orc and her god-forged sword, perhaps his luck hadn't changed after all.

Jig crept through the darkness with one hand on the tunnel wall. Frost coated the obsidian, numbing his fingers. Up ahead, he heard a sound like smashing glass, followed by another angry shout.

"I'll kill you!" Relka's voice was hoarse. "I'll puree your ears for the toddlers. I'll use your bones to make soup! I'll—"

"Will you please shut up?" Billa snapped. "How does your god put up with all of this babbling?"

Orange light told Jig he was close, as did the steadily increasing warmth coming from Smudge. Jig reached back to rub Smudge's thorax. Smudge clung to Jig's finger with his forelegs until Jig tugged free. Jig might not be able to feel fear, but his fire-spider certainly could.

He stepped to the end of the tunnel and peered into the temple. What was left of it. The little stone altar had been shattered. Of the glass mosaic on the ceiling, only a few tiles still clung to the rock. The rest lay scattered on the floor.

Relka sat amid the remains of the altar, her knees hugged to her chest. Billa stood beside her, a lit torch in her left hand. In her right she clutched Isa's sword.

Was it Jig's imagination, or did the torch's flames actually bend away from the sword? Even fire feared the touch of that blade.

"Shadowstar will crush you for this." Relka spat at Billa's feet. "He'll destroy you. You think he fears your little army?"

From Jig's angle, he could see Billa roll her eyes. "*Please* can I kill her?" Jig didn't hear an answer, but he saw Billa's shoulders slump. "What if I just cut out her tongue?"

Relka laughed. "Go ahead and kill me. I would be honored to die a martyr for Tymalous Shadowstar."

Go now, Jig.

Jig didn't move. He wasn't afraid, but he saw no need to charge out and die on that sword, either. *I don't want to be a martyr.*

Isa will sense your presence soon anyway.

Jig gritted his teeth and stepped into the temple. He didn't bother to draw his sword. What good would it do? He cleared his throat and said, "Shadowstar says if you kill her—or me!—he'll collapse the entire temple and crush us all." Actually that wasn't a bad plan.

"What are you doing here, goblin?" Billa snapped.

Relka's grin shone with triumph. "That's Jig Dragonslayer, high priest of Tymalous Shadowstar. He's here to kill you, orc."

"You? You're the priest?" Billa stared. "Seriously?"

"We can't all have magic swords and armies." Jig glanced around. Three other tunnels led away from the far side of the temple. A pair of goblins lay dead in the rightmost tunnel. They appeared to be two of Golaka's kitchen workers. They must have been sent to investigate all the shouting and destruction. Each one had been stabbed through the torso, but there was hardly any blood.

Jig crept closer, keeping Billa in his sight as he knelt to study the bodies. Blue ice crusted the wounds on the two goblins. Billa's blade had frozen their blood. It made for a much cleaner corpse than Jig was used to. Most nights he had to wipe up the blood of the wounded before heading back to the lair. If all goblins would do him the courtesy of getting stabbed with magically cold weapons, he could cut his cleaning time in half.

"Does your god speak to you?" Billa asked.

Jig groaned. "Usually at the worst times."

"Isa was so excited when she first realized Autumnstar—I mean, Shadowstar—was still alive." Billa sat down and jabbed her sword at Relka. "She was as bad as this one. Gave me a headache like you wouldn't believe. Whenever she's riled, it's like my whole skull freezes."

Jig nodded in sympathy. "Shadowstar wears tiny bells all over his clothes. Sometimes it takes days for my ears to stop ringing."

Billa chuckled. "After we first conquered the trolls, the orcs held a feast to celebrate. I overindulged on the wine, and had to retreat into the snow. There I am, in the middle of spewing an entire bottle back to the earth, and Isa pipes up to talk about tactics for the next battle."

"Shadowstar once made me heal a hobgoblin's backside," Jig said, his voice mild.

Billa shuddered. "You win."

"Do the other orcs sing hymns about you?" Jig asked, glancing at Relka. He knew he was supposed to be saving Relka, and maybe killing Billa too, but this was the first time he had ever found someone who understood what it was like having a god in your head. There was Braf, of course, but Braf wasn't much of a conversationalist.

"They used to," said Billa. "Growing up, I had horribly dry skin, and my nose was always bleeding. That's where they came up with the name Billa the Bloody." She glanced around, then sang,

> *"Billa the bloody-nosed orc,*
> *armed with Isa's magic blade,*
> *led her people to battle.*
> *Soon the trolls were sore afraid.*
>
> *Billa the bloody-nosed orc*
> *triumphed over every foe.*
> *None may stand against her.*
> *Forever shall her nostrils flow!"*

Billa coughed to clear her throat. She actually appeared to be blushing. "I cut out the tongue of the first orc to sing that song within earshot. They don't sing it anymore." She rubbed a finger beneath her nose. "This cold weather makes it even worse."

"My hymns are better," Relka muttered.

Billa straightened. "So has Tymalous Shadowstar agreed to help us? Imagine their power—*our* power— once they're free of Noc's curse. With Shadowstar and Isa working together, we can summon Noc and destroy him." She jabbed her sword into the air, then cocked her head. "I wonder what god tastes like."

"Noc's a god of death. He's probably poisonous." Jig stepped away from the bodies. They were beyond his help anyway. "How will you summon him?"

"Death," Billa said simply. "The gods aren't like us, Jig." Strange to hear Billa the Bloody addressing him as an equal. "They can't act against their natures. Isa summons the winds because she must. Just like Noc must attend when the death is widespread enough to warrant his attention."

Jig glanced at the entrance. "I don't see why you need me or Shadowstar."

"Even gods can grow lonely," Billa said. "I think Isa misses him. And Autumnstar—sorry. *Shadowstar* has the power to calm and comfort. He can lull Noc's suspicions, dulling his reflexes and giving me the chance to strike. He can do the same with the rest of the gods, easing their wrath. It's one of his gifts, to calm people's passions."

Or their fear. "He wants you to free Relka first."

Billa turned around. A touch of her blade severed Relka's bonds.

"Let me have your torch," Jig said. "Shadowstar's magic should be able to heal your nose so it doesn't bleed anymore."

The orc's eyes widened. "You can do that?"

"It wouldn't be the first nose I've healed." Jig took the torch and circled Billa, studying her nose and positioning himself closer to Relka. He smelled burning cloth—right, that would be Smudge searing the hood of Jig's cloak. If Shadowstar hadn't worked his magic on Jig, he would probably be just as terrified as the spider.

With his free hand, Jig reached up to touch Billa's nose. Her skin was cool to the touch, especially the rough, pale scar. Old blood crusted the edges of her nostrils.

I'm willing to help you heal her, Shadowstar said. *But I won't join Isa. I can't.*

Shut up. Shadowstar had taken Jig's fear, but that only left more room for anger. Showdowstar wouldn't allow them to kill Noc, but he was perfectly willing to let Jig risk his own life. After all, Jig was only a goblin.

That's not—

I said shut up. Jig shoved the flaming torch into Billa's face.

Billa screamed and staggered back. She swung wildly with her sword, but Jig had already leaped away. As hard as he could, he hurled the torch down the right-hand tunnel.

The temple went dark.

Jig dropped to his hands and knees and grabbed Relka's leg. He dragged her away from the altar, toward the central tunnel. "Come on," Jig said, loud enough for Billa to hear. He tried to make himself sound afraid. All his life, he had fought to keep his voice from squeaking. Now thanks to Shadowstar, he had to force it. "If we can make it to the lake, we'll be safe."

He took a few steps into the tunnel, then shoved Relka against the wall and pressed a hand over her mouth. One of her fangs dug into the fleshy part of his palm, but he barely felt it.

He twisted his good ear back toward the temple and Billa's pained whimpering. Her footsteps crunched on stone and glass. Would she run after the torch? Or would she try to follow Jig and Relka into the darkness? If so, she had a one-in-three chance of bumping right into them.

The smart thing for her to do was to retreat. She could bring her kobolds to track Jig, and orcs to finish them off. But Billa was angry and hurting, and if Jig wasn't mistaken, hitting her in the face had caused her nose to start bleeding. She wouldn't be thinking clearly.

"Run away, little goblin," Billa whispered. She grunted as she tripped over the two dead goblins. She was going after the torch. "I'll feed your eyes to the wolves when I find you."

Jig waited until her footsteps faded, then hurried back through the temple, pulling Relka along behind him. He hoped Billa did find her way to the lake. Maybe the poisonous lizard-fish would take care of things for him.

"I knew you'd save me," Relka whispered.

"I didn't have much of a choice." Jig dragged her toward the entrance. He hoped Trok was still there. If the orcs had gone back to watching the cave, Jig was dead.

He squinted as they neared the light of the outside world. The crack of steel on stone made him jump. One of the orcs howled.

"Ha!" Trok shouted. "A half-sever. I win again!"

Jig peeked out to see orcs and goblins gathered in a circle. Trok picked up his sword. "I can beat that with my off-hand. Double or nothing." His sword scraped the edge of his boot when it landed.

"It's not fair," complained the orc who was sitting in the snow, clutching his bloody foot. "Goblins are closer to the ground than we are."

"No welshing," Trok shouted. "Play or forfeit." The other goblins joined in, taunting and jeering.

"Come on," Jig whispered. He took Relka's hand and led her out of the cave. One of the orcs glanced up and spotted them, but he didn't say anything. He probably thought they were just another pair of goblin soldiers come to watch the game.

Jig and Relka had just reached the cover of the trees when another orc screamed. Jig glanced back to see him tugging his sword from his foot while the goblins laughed.

"I win again," Trok cried. "Pay up, orc."

"I am *not* running naked to the river and back," the wounded orc protested.

"We went double or nothing," Trok said. "You're going twice!"

"Hurry," Jig said. Before he had to add the sight of a naked orc to his list of nightmares.

"I'm not afraid," said Relka. "Shadowstar watches over us."

Jig's jaw tightened, but he said nothing.

CHAPTER 8

*A*utumnstar traveled with no real destination. With his star gone and his temple destroyed, he was forced to hoard his power like a mortal wizard.

Everywhere he went, he felt people calling. The pain, the fear of death, they whispered to him, begging for comfort and solace. He couldn't do much to help them, but neither could he ignore them. He wandered from a battlefield to the collapsed tunnels of a gnomish silver mine, from a village buried by early winter storms to a flooded town on the other side of the world. Always he watched for signs of Noc or the other gods. It would be safer to do nothing, but Autumnstar could no more turn his back on suffering than he could steal back his star.

One day he found himself drawn to an old man curled in a ball near a small pond, a day's march from the nearest village. He had been cast forth to die. This time Autumnstar needed no magic. The man was not afraid, nor did he appear to be in excessive pain. The village had too little food, and this man had accepted death in order to ease his family's burden.

Autumnstar folded his wings and rested his head on the man's thigh. The rough scales startled the man at first, but slowly he relaxed. His fingers scratched Autumnstar's neck, tentatively at first.

"I hope you mean to wait until after I die to eat me,"

*he said, his voice hoarse. His smile revealed a few yellow
teeth. "Sorry there's not much meat on these old bones."*

*A black scavenger bird circled low, landing in the
grass nearby. Autumnstar raised his head and spread
his wings. With a screech, the bird flew away.*

"Thanks."

*Autumnstar's tail quivered. He hopped away from
the old man and sniffed the air. He smelled pond scum
and goose crap, a dead fish rotting in the mud . . . and
another god.*

*Autumnstar hissed and turned to flee, but then his
reason caught up with his instincts. If Noc had found
him, he would already be dead.*

*He crept toward the water. Was this what had drawn
him here? The power was familiar, though it had been
ages since Autumnstar had encountered another god.
Weak and frightened, the presence reminded Autumnstar a little of himself.*

*His wings fluttered with excitement. Could one of his
companions have survived? Noc was powerful, but he
was also arrogant and more than a little lazy. Autumnstar had escaped. Why not others?*

*Water lapped his toes. He stretched his neck, squint-
ing to see past the reflected sunlight on the surface.*

*Black-shelled fingers clamped around his neck and
dragged him down.*

*And that's what he got for trusting reason over
instinct.*

Gut-twisting nausea combined with the damp sweat
breaking out over Jig's body told him Shadowstar's
magic had worn off.

"Where are we going?" Relka asked once they were
out of sight of the orcs.

"I don't know." He hadn't really planned that far
ahead. Running was good, so he did that. He hadn't
figured out how to get past the rest of the goblins.
Nor had he thought about how to avoid the rest of
Billa's army, waiting farther down the mountain.

But he had thought about what Billa would do if

she caught up with him. Given the choice, Jig would rather face the army.

The sound of Billa's voice helped him run even faster. "I ordered you to stand guard," Billa yelled. "Not to play games with goblins."

A strangled scream made Jig whimper. He kind of hoped Trok wasn't the one Billa had chosen to make an example of.

"Did anyone else come out of this cave?" Billa yelled. Jig tensed, but whatever answer she received only added to her frustration. "Tell Silverfang to send these useless goblins out to form a perimeter around the lair. Don't let anyone past. You, fetch a team of kobolds and send them in after me."

Kobolds tracked by scent. They would quickly realize Jig and Relka hadn't gone down any of the tunnels.

Jig shoved through another pine tree and emerged onto a wide ledge of stone. This spot was a common meeting point for hunters. From here, he could see much of the land sloping out below. An animal trail led higher into the mountain, toward a pond which was probably frozen over by now.

He turned back as another thought struck. Widespread death . . . what if Billa simply slaughtered the rest of the goblins in the lair to summon Noc?

Not likely, said Shadowstar. *The goblins know their lair. Most would escape into the lower tunnels. To summon Noc, she'll need something much bigger.*

Something like another army. King Wendel's army. She didn't want to defeat Wendel. She wanted to cause as much death to both sides as she possibly could.

"Avery," Jig whispered. "Darnak said Billa was too smart to lead her forces into such a slaughter."

Well, that settled that. Jig turned to climb higher into the mountain, as far from Avery as he could possibly get.

You have to warn them, Jig.

Jig's fists tightened. *You mean I have to protect your son. Even if it kills me.*

If you're afraid, I could—

"No!" Jig flushed.

"What's wrong?" Relka asked.

"Shadowstar wants us to go back to Avery and stop Billa."

Relka touched her necklace. "I warned her that Shadowstar's wrath would be terrible." She grabbed Jig's hand and tugged him toward the edge of the ledge. Her fingers were rough and callused from working in the kitchens. "We'll get there faster if we go this way."

Jig peered at the slope of fallen stone, made all the more treacherous by the snow. "We'll die faster, too."

"You said Shadowstar wanted us to go to Avery." Relka released Jig's hand and stepped off of the ledge.

Jig watched her struggle to control her fall. For the most part, she kept herself in a sitting position, sliding down the rocks. "I'm not healing those scrapes," he muttered.

"Come on!" Relka said.

Jig shook his head. She didn't even question why they had to go to Avery. Jig could have said Shadowstar wanted her to march back to the lair and kick Billa in the backside, and she would have done it.

Hm . . . it *would* slow Billa down.

"Hey!"

Jig spun to see a pair of goblins running up the trail, weapons drawn. Right. Jig sat on the edge, moved Smudge into one of the front cloak pockets, and hopped down after Relka.

He slid on his back, legs flailing in the air. His armor absorbed the worst of the damage, but his helmet clattered away after the second bounce.

His leg hit a pine sapling, spinning him around. He glimpsed the goblins standing at the ledge, laughing and pointing. Then Relka caught him by the wrist, presumably to slow him down.

Instead she overbalanced and fell across his legs. The goblins above laughed harder as Jig and Relka slid a short distance farther before thudding into a boulder. Then their laughter stopped. Presumably they had remembered they were supposed to chase after Jig and Relka.

Jig grinned and hauled Relka to her feet. "Come on."

"What are we doing?" Relka asked.

"Trust me."

The guards shouted a challenge, and then Jig heard curses and the clatter of stone. Jig kept fleeing, letting the downhill slope of the mountainside add speed to his steps, until he felt like he wasn't running so much as falling.

His cloak snagged on a tree branch. The branch snapped, but the tug threw him off-balance. He twisted as he fell, hitting the snow hard with one shoulder and sliding a good distance. Relka skidded to a halt and grabbed his arm. She pulled him up and started to run.

"Don't bother," Jig said. The delay had cost them their lead. The goblin guards waved their swords in the air as they charged.

Jig folded his arms and tried to catch his breath. This would never work if he was panting too hard to speak. He thought about Silverfang, remembering the loud, angry bark of his voice, like he was just dying for an excuse to eat you. Which was probably true.

The guards spread to either side. What had Gratz called it? Flanking. It was a good maneuver, making sure Jig couldn't focus on one of the guards without exposing his back to the other.

"Off for a romp in the snow?" asked the guard on the right.

"This runt's a bit small, girl," said his partner. "How about I show you what a real goblin—"

"A real goblin?" Jig snapped. "You?" He straightened his back and brushed snow from his cloak, trying to remember what it had been like to feel no fear. "You're a disgrace. What's wrong with you two?"

The goblins glanced at one another, clearly confused. Jig hadn't drawn his sword, and he wasn't trying to run away. "Us? What's wrong with you?"

"What were your orders?" Jig raised his voice. "Your orders, goblins."

"To guard the perimeter of the lair."

Jig pointed up the mountainside. "That lair? That perimeter? The one missing two of its guards, so that any elf who felt like assassinating Billa the Bloody could slip right through the gap you left when you came charging after us? Is *that* the perimeter you're supposed to be guarding?"

The goblins glanced at each other. "Well—"

"Well, *sir!*" Jig snapped. "What if I was a decoy for an ambush?" He stepped toward the closer of the two goblins, shoving the guard's sword to one side with his bare hand. His gritted his teeth and clenched his hand. Just his luck, to run into one of the goblins who kept his blade sharp. "What if the humans had paid me to lead you here so that their archers could kill you?" He pointed to a random tree, and both goblins leaped back in alarm.

"But you were running away, and—"

"And you followed," said Jig. He lowered his voice. "Save your excuses for Silverfang. I'm sure he'll be very interested to hear how you were busy propositioning this girl instead of obeying his orders."

He tugged the guard's sword out of his hand, then rapped the flat of the blade against the second guard's skull. "If you're lucky, he'll feed only one of you to the wolves. Knowing Silverfang, he'll choose whoever is slowest to get back."

The goblins fled. Jig waited until they were gone from sight, then turned to Relka. He meant to pass her the extra sword, but he was shaking so hard he dropped it in the snow.

"That was incredible," Relka whispered.

"Thanks," said Jig. Then he threw up on her boots.

Jig finished shoving his armor beneath a bush, then stretched his arms overhead. Without the weight of all that leather, he felt as if he could leap as high as the treetops. Better still, he could walk without the armor rubbing his limbs to the bones.

He tightened his belt and repositioned the sword back over his hip. He had given Relka his own sword, keeping the one he had taken from the goblin guard for himself. It was still junk, but at least it was sharp junk.

"Why didn't you stay to fight Billa?" Relka asked as they resumed walking.

"Because *my* god didn't give me a magic sword," Jig said. "The only weapon I had is that sword in your hand, and it's not sharp enough to cut wind."

"She was in your temple," Relka said. She jogged alongside him, staying just out of sight of the road below. "You're the high priest of Tymalous Shadowstar. You're stronger than she is."

She made it sound like such a simple fact, like she was telling him snow was cold or dragons were dangerous or hobgoblin cooking tasted like rat droppings.

The howl of wolves interrupted them before Jig could tell her exactly what he thought of Tymalous Shadowstar. Jig slowed, wondering if he should go back for his armor. Not that the leather would do much against angry wolves.

"Have faith." Relka turned around and raised her sword. "We are servants of a great god."

"So let him fight the wolves," Jig muttered as he searched for shelter. A cave, a cliff they could climb, anyplace the wolves might not be able to follow. But this far down from the lair, the ground was disgustingly gentle. He glanced at a tree. He doubted wolves could climb, but they could surround the tree and wait for him to come down. More likely, the goblins would pelt him with rocks, or maybe just cut down the tree with Jig and Relka in it.

Jig pulled out his sword just as the first of the wolves came into view. Silverfang yanked the ropes, pulling Bastard to a halt as the rest of the wolf-riders joined him. It looked like Billa had sent all fourteen of

Silverfang's wolf-riders after Jig, including Trok, who struggled to keep Smelly under control.

"I knew you were trouble," Silverfang shouted.

His sword was much larger than Jig's. When he charged, the wolf's speed would probably give him the strength to cut clean through Jig and Relka both. At least it would be a quick death.

"The runt is mine." Silverfang grinned and kicked Bastard in the sides. The wolf began to trot toward Jig.

Jig backed away. He fumbled with his cloak. Which pocket had Smudge crawled into? Bad enough Jig was about to be wolf food. Smudge didn't need to die too. He didn't know how long Smudge would survive outside in the cold, but it had to be longer than he would with Jig. Where was the stupid spider hiding?

He plunged his hand into another pocket, and his breath caught.

"What is it?" Relka asked.

Jig handed his sword to her.

He couldn't tell who howled first, Silverfang or Bastard. The two of them harmonized quite well together, actually. The wolf's huge paws flung dirt and snow into the air behind him. They ran like a single creature, half wolf, half angry goblin, and the only question was whether the wolf's teeth or the goblin's sword would kill Jig first.

Relka leaped in front of Jig, waving both swords in the air. It might have been an impressive sight, if she hadn't managed to clank the blades together, knocking one of the swords from her hand. Undeterred, she gripped the other with both hands and shouted, "Prepare to face the wrath of Tymalous Shadowstar!"

Jig kicked her in the back of the knees, knocking her down. Bastard and Silverfang were almost on top of him. He pulled the large troll toe from his pocket and waved it overhead. He saw Silverfang's eyes widen as he realized what Jig held.

"Bastard," Jig shouted. "Sit!" He threw the toe at Bastard's face.

The giant wolf tried to obey. He reared and twisted, snapping at the toe even as he tried to settle his hindquarters. He might have managed, if not for Silverfang roped to his back. Jig had seen tunnel cats manage similar midair twists to snatch a bat or bird from the air. But with an armed, armored goblin tied to his back, Bastard had no chance.

Jig pulled Relka out of the way as Silverfang's weight dragged Bastard off-balance. The wolf twisted sideways in the air, his legs flailing and kicking. His jaws closed around the toe, and then Silverfang's shoulder struck the ground. Bastard slammed down on his side, bounced, and barely missed sliding into a tree. The giant wolf staggered to his feet and shook, spraying snow and mud and goblin blood in all directions. He took a single step, then spun and tried to bite Silverfang's leg.

"Behold the fate of all who challenge Jig Dragonslayer," Relka shouted.

The other goblins appeared unimpressed. They spread out in a formation Jig didn't recognize. He decided to call it the "Make sure every wolf gets a bite of Jig" formation.

Slowly it dawned on Jig that Silverfang wasn't moving. At least not under his own power. Bastard continued to snarl and snap at Silverfang's left arm. Silverfang slumped more and more to the side. His right hand was tangled in the reins, and his weight caused them to dig cruelly into Bastard's jaws, driving him in tighter and tighter circles.

One of the goblins laughed. Jig was fairly certain it was Trok.

Bastard appeared to have forgotten all about the troll toe. His eyes were wide, and foam sprayed from his jaws. Jig could see where the rope harness cut into his mouth and throat. His teeth clacked together, but he couldn't quite reach Silverfang.

One of the goblins threw a chunk of ice at Bastard's nose, spurring him into even faster circles.

"None of that!" Gratz pointed his sword at the

other goblin. "A named wolf is as much a soldier in Billa's army as you. We came out here to do a job. Let's kill these two and be done with it."

"Wait!" Jig squeaked. "Silverfang ordered you to let *him* kill me!"

"Silverfang's dead."

"Are you sure?" Jig glanced behind. Bastard had planted his front paws together, swiveling the rest of his body around in circles. Silverfang's arm dragged through the snow, his battered body showing no sign of life. "What if he's just unconscious? If you kill me, you're disobeying an order. What's the penalty for that?"

Pain seared Jig's belly. Oh, *there* was Smudge. Jig tried to grab Smudge from his pocket, but he was too late. The terrified fire-spider burned completely through the fabric and dropped into the snow. He tunneled beneath the surface, leaving a line of melted snow to mark his progress toward a cluster of tree roots.

"Fair enough," Gratz said. He pointed his sword at Jig. "Close in. Drive him toward Bastard and Silverfang. They'll finish him off one way or another."

The goblins spurred their wolves forward. Turning around, Jig shouted, "Bastard, sit!"

Bastard ignored him, spraying snow and dirt in Jig's face as he spun. The other goblins moved closer. Jig could see them fighting to keep their wolves under control. Several were actually drooling at the prospect of sinking their teeth into Jig. So were the wolves, for that matter.

Bastard's tail flicked Jig's leg in passing. Stupid wolf. Bastard's tongue flopped from the side of his mouth, and his mouth sprayed spit and blood.

Relka waved her sword at the nearest goblins, who laughed. One wolf lunged at her. She backed away, bumping into Jig and knocking him off-balance, directly into Bastard's path.

Jig plunged his hands into his pockets, searching for more troll toes, and then the full weight of Bastard's rump collided with Jig's hip. It wasn't as bad as being hit by a dragon's tail, but it was close. Huge paws trampled Jig's side. Why had he thrown away his armor? He covered his head as Silverfang's body bounced past.

Jig grabbed Silverfang's arm with both hands and clung with all his strength. His added weight barely even slowed Bastard down.

The world spun past. If Jig hadn't already thrown up once today, the whirling would have cost him the contents of his stomach for certain. He tried to pull himself up onto Bastard's back, but it was all he could do to hang on. The goblins were laughing even louder, and Relka . . . was she *singing* again?

Jig slid one hand onto Silverfang's belt, trying to get to the front of the wolf. Silverfang tilted even further, spurring Bastard to increase his speed. Jig braced his foot beneath Silverfang's chin and tried to push himself up onto Bastard's back. Something tugged him back. Turning his head, Jig saw his cloak caught on Silverfang's steel tooth.

He pulled harder, and the cloth tore. Jig swung his other foot over Bastard's back. His fingers twisted into the sweat-matted fur.

Help me heal Bastard's mouth, Jig said. *If I can calm him down, maybe he won't eat me.*

That might not be a good idea, Shadowstar said. *We don't know whether Isa can sense that kind of magic.*

If Bastard eats me, you'll have to rely on Braf to stop Billa the Bloody.

Jig's fingers warmed. He reached out, his fingers brushing the edge of Bastard's jaws. Snapping teeth nearly took Jig's fingers. He tried again, directing Shadowstar's magic into Bastard's torn skin.

Gradually the wolf slowed. His tongue lolled, and he stopped trying to eat Jig's hand. Those huge ribs bellowed beneath Jig as Bastard gasped for breath. Jig reached down to draw his knife. He stretched forward, using the knife left-handed to saw Silverfang free of the harness. Both Jig and Silverfang slid to the ground.

Bastard moaned, a sound that reminded Jig of the wind back home as it passed over the entrance to the lair. He tried to walk, but his head kept twitching, and he staggered like a drunken goblin. He managed one sideways step before toppling over onto Jig and Silverfang.

Silverfang's body protected Jig from the worst of Bastard's weight. He continued to heal Bastard's mouth and neck. The sooner Bastard recovered, the sooner he might get off of Jig. Bloody bristles of fur tickled his palm. Bastard panted, dripping warm drool over Jig's wrist.

Eventually Bastard climbed to his feet, took a few tentative steps, then sneezed three times. Relka hurried over to grab Jig's arm.

"Good . . . wolf," Jig gasped.

Relka hauled him upright, then turned to glare at the other goblins. "Who will be next to challenge the champion of Tymalous Shadowstar?"

The so-called champion of Tymalous Shadowstar promptly fell down again, where he clutched his head with both hands and waited for the woods to stop spinning.

"I told you he'd survive," Trok said to another of the wolf-riders. "Come on, pay up." Jig looked over to see Trok trading his old weapon for a gleaming two-handed broadsword.

"He'll be dead by sundown," the other goblin muttered with a glare at Jig.

"Want to wager on that, too?" Trok asked. "Those are some nice boots you're wearing."

Bastard walked back to Jig. He still wobbled a bit, but he seemed to have recovered from the dizziness faster than Jig. Or maybe this was just an advantage to having four feet. Not that it made any difference. Even if Jig could have stood, he wasn't fast enough to outrun a wolf.

Bastard shoved his head into Jig's side and licked his hand.

Gratz cleared his throat. "With Silverfang dead, I

hereby assume command of this unit. Seize the prisoners."

Several goblins hopped down from their wolves and advanced, weapons ready.

Gratz jabbed a finger at one goblin after another. "Trok, you and Dimak tie Silverfang's body onto Bastard's back. We'll—"

Bastard's snarl cut off the rest of Gratz's orders. The goblins who had moved toward Jig leaped away.

"Even the wolves recognize the greatness of Jig Dragonslayer and Tymalous Shadowstar," Relka said.

Gratz dug into a pouch and pulled out a wrinkled troll toe. He tossed it into the air.

Bastard bounded up to catch it, knocking Jig back into the snow.

"Good wolf," Gratz said. He pointed at Jig. "Kill!"

Bastard lay down and crunched his toe. Gratz squirmed on his wolf. Trok chuckled.

"Look out!" Relka pointed to Dimak, who was struggling to cock a small crossbow.

Jig put his hands on Bastard's damp fur. Slowly he swung one leg over the wolf's back. He lay down, flattening his body against Bastard's, then looked over at Dimak. "Be careful. If you shoot Bastard by mistake, you might make him angry."

"Shoot him," Gratz shouted. "That's an order!"

Dimak stared at Bastard, then tossed his crossbow to Gratz. "You shoot him."

Gratz's face turned a darker shade of blue. "This is mutiny! Billa the Bloody will crush your skull with her bare hands for this. It's right here in the regulations."

Jig had no doubt that was true. But Billa the Bloody wasn't here right now. Bastard was. And Bastard was bigger than any other wolf in the pack. Jig cleared his throat. "Billa the Bloody can only punish you for crimes she knows about."

Slowly, Dimak and the other goblins turned toward Gratz.

Gratz backed his wolf away. He pointed the crossbow at one goblin, then another. "Stay back. I'm a corporal in the army of Billa the Bloody, and acting commander of this unit!"

"And that's a big, angry wolf," Trok said, pointing at Bastard.

Gratz pulled the trigger. The bolt slammed into the side of the nearest goblin. Instead of intimidating the rest of the goblins, the attack only seemed to solidify their rebellion. In part, no doubt, because Gratz didn't have another crossbow bolt. He tossed the crossbow down and pulled out his sword.

"Wait," Jig said. To his surprise, they obeyed.

"What are you doing?" Relka whispered.

"I have no idea." Jig started to speak, then dug his fingers into Bastard's fur as the wolf stood. Jig had never realized how tall the wolves were. Relka's head was now level with his waist. He swallowed and said, "Corporal Gratz, what do regulations say about surrendering to an enemy?"

Gratz frowned. "I don't think that particular situation has ever come up."

"Then there's nothing in the regulations to stop you from surrendering to me before Bastard eats you?" Jig asked.

Shaking his head, Gratz said, "Any soldier who quits fighting is to be executed on the spot by his commanding officer."

"You mean that commanding officer?" Jig pointed to Silverfang's body. "It's your choice, Gratz. Surrender, or I order Bastard to eat you."

Gratz's lips moved as he turned around. He appeared to be counting the other goblins. "Right. I hereby surrender command of this squadron to Jig," Gratz said. He lowered his voice. "According to regulations, this means you receive a field promotion to the rank of lieutenant, with all the inherent responsibilities and—"

"Fine," Jig said. "Now put your sword away before Bastard decides you're a threat."

Gratz flung his sword into the snow. His hand barely trembled as he snapped a quick salute. "Orders, sir?"

Jig glanced around. Trok was laughing at him. The other goblins appeared skeptical at best. Aside from Relka, naturally. She was beaming and mumbling to herself, no doubt composing another hymn. Jig dreaded to think what she would rhyme with "lieutenant."

Gratz cleared his throat. "Sir?"

Jig was tempted to order them all to return to Billa's army. But with Jig gone, Gratz would probably resume command and come after him again.

Stalling for time, he turned to Relka. "This is my second-in-command." Since Relka was probably the only one here who wouldn't happily murder Jig to take his place, she was the safest choice.

Relka grinned. "So they have to obey me now, right?"

"That's right, sir," said Gratz.

Relka's claw stabbed at Trok like a spear. "Sing."

"What?"

Relka's smile was pure evil. "I like to listen to music. Sing 'The Song of Jig' for me, soldier."

Trok started to draw his sword.

"Are you disobeying an order, goblin?" Gratz shouted. He hopped down from his wolf and grabbed his own weapon. "Shall I cut out his tongue, sir?"

Jig shook his head in disbelief. Gratz was serious. Moments before he had been determined to kill Jig himself. Now he was ready to kill anyone who disobeyed him. Or Relka. If Jig had ordered him to eat his own leg, Gratz would even now be marching over to Relka to borrow a fork.

Jig tucked that idea away for later. For now . . . "Tie up the wolves. Relka, they'll probably be hungry, so why don't you feed Silverfang to them? Gratz, help them make a new harness for Bastard."

The goblins scurried to obey. Jig rubbed his fang nervously as he watched them work. How long could he keep up this charade? He was no leader. Sooner or later the discipline Billa and Silverfang had pounded into them would wear off, and they would go back to being goblins. He wondered if that would happen before or after Billa sent her orcs to find out what had happened to Silverfang.

Jig's good ear twitched, following Relka's footsteps as she approached. He had done the same thing a year ago, back in the lair. He remembered the sound of her footsteps, the cold of his own sweat dripping down his sides as he waited for Relka to try to kill him.

If Jig had known where he would end up, he probably would have let Relka go ahead and stab him in the back.

"The wolves are fed," Relka said. She sounded almost perky. Jig wanted to punch her. "We had leftover Silverfang, but I wasn't sure whether you'd want to take the time to prepare the meat properly."

Jig shook his head. Back home, the tunnels and caves restricted the flow of smoke. Out here in the open, it would be a clear signal to anyone searching for him. And since pretty much everyone wanted him dead, a fire was a very bad idea. So was eating Silverfang raw, of course, but Jig would rather risk knotted bowels than whatever death Billa had planned for him.

"Billa was supposed to drive the surface dwellers away forever." Jig's throat tightened. No more adventurers slaughtering their way through the lair. No more princes and princesses dragging goblins away to build their stupid walls. No more quests and fighting and fleeing for his life.

Instead, Billa was just using them. At least when Princess Genevieve used the goblins, she was honest about it. She didn't pretend she was trying to help anyone. She simply tied them up and dragged them to Avery. Nor did she pretend she wouldn't kill every last goblin if they gave her a reason.

"I believed in her." He stared at Relka's pendant. Jig had been every bit as much of an idiot as Relka. "Shadowstar is afraid of Isa," he said. He wasn't sure why he had blurted it out.

Relka stiffened. "What do you mean?"

"He could have manifested in his temple to protect you, but he knows Billa could kill him. So he sent me instead. He'd rather let me die than risk himself. He used me. Just like everyone else." Jig waited, watching to see how she would react.

Suddenly Relka's face broke into a smile. "This is a test, isn't it? You want to know how strong my faith is, so you know whether or not you can rely on me for the trials ahead."

Jig wondered if Shadowstar's magic could heal whatever was wrong with Relka's brain. "Trials? Shadowstar wants me to go to Avery and stop Billa the Bloody!"

"The life of a champion is not an easy one," Relka said.

"Not easy? I just shoved a torch into Billa's face. She's going to send her entire army after me, and when they catch me, they're going to—"

"You've got an army too," Relka said, pointing back at the wolf-riders.

Jig's mouth stayed open, but he had run out of words. Nothing he could say would shake Relka's faith. She fully expected him to save Avery, defeat Billa and her goddess, and save all goblinkind.

Jig stood and brushed snow from his legs and backside. *Why couldn't you have chosen Relka? She would love to be a priest of Shadowstar, running around fighting pixies and orcs and doing all of your dirty work.*

If I remember correctly, you sought me out, said Shadowstar.

Jig didn't have an answer to that, either.

If it's what you truly want, I'll leave you alone, Jig. Do this thing for me, and I'll never disturb you again.

Wait, Jig said quickly. Lose the ability to heal himself and the other goblins? Jig shuddered, remembering the long list of war scars he had displayed for Silverfang. Without Shadowstar, most of those injuries would have killed him. *That's not what I meant.*

Of course. Shadowstar sounded amused.

Right. Billa was probably starting to wonder about her wolf-riders. Soon she would send more troops out to find them. Jig turned around . . . which way was Avery, from here?

Follow the road to the east.

To Avery, then.

"We need to warn Princess Genevieve what she's facing," Jig said. "The humans think they're fighting a regular army of monsters, an army that wants to win. Billa doesn't care about beating humans. She wants her army to die, and she wants to take as many humans with them as they can."

"I'll tell the others to get the wolves ready." With that, Relka turned to go.

"Thanks," said Jig.

Relka hesitated. "Do you think the humans will listen to you?"

The king had ordered all goblins killed on sight. Jig's last encounter with Genevieve wouldn't have encouraged her to change that order. "Not really, no."

CHAPTER 9

Tymalous Autumstar squirmed to break free as the black-shelled arm dragged him deeper into the water. He twisted his long neck about until he saw his attacker.

"Ipsep? Is that you?"

The former sea god looked awful. Pale cracks lined his shell, most of which was covered in algae and mussels. His thick green hair had fallen out or wilted; what remained was little more than brown tufts of seaweed stuck to his scalp.

"You betrayed us, Autumnstar," said Ipsep. "You abandoned us."

*"*Noc *betrayed us." He bit down on Ipsep's finger. Autumnstar's teeth were useless against the armor of Ipsep's shell. All he got for his trouble was a mouthful of seaweed and one angry snail.*

"You were the first to give up when Noc turned against us. You're a coward." Ipsep tightened both hands around Autumnstar's neck and shoved him deeper into the water. "You left us to be killed, or worse, to be forgotten."

Autumnstar didn't argue. Even if he hadn't been drowning, there was nothing he could say. Ipsep was right. He had turned his back on the war.

Ipsep stumbled, and his grip loosened. Instantly, Au-

tumnstar twisted free. His wings thrust him to the surface, where he gasped for breath.

The old man Autumnstar had comforted stood knee-deep in the pond. As Autumnstar watched, he threw another stone at Ipsep.

The first attack had startled the god. This time Ipsep hardly appeared to notice as the rock bounced off his shell.

Autumnstar threw himself on Ipsep's back, digging his claws into the cracks of his shell, but it wasn't enough. Ipsep's fingers clacked together. The old man shouted in fear as he was drawn deeper into the pond.

Ipsep turned his attention back to Autumnstar. Clawed fingers reached around to sever the tip of Autumnstar's tail. Ipsep's other hand caught him by the wing. Autumnstar's claws broke as he was pulled away from Ipsep's back.

Autumnstar stopped fighting. He had never been much of a warrior anyway. Even during the war, in the midst of battle, he had barely been able to stop himself from throwing down his weapons and comforting the wounded and the dying.

Ipsep was both, and he didn't even know it. Only rage kept his despair at bay, and even in a god, rage couldn't last forever. Especially once Tymalous Autumnstar began to soothe that rage.

"They've forgotten us, Autumnstar," said Ipsep. Already his voice was softer. "The mortals don't even remember our names."

"Rest, old friend," Autumnstar whispered. "Be at peace."

"Peace." Ipsep waded deeper into the water, pulling Autumnstar with him. "An eternity of cowering in the shadows, waiting for them to find us. What kind of peace is that?"

Autumnstar clung tighter, pouring what little power he had into the other god. Most gods would barely have noticed his feeble efforts, but Ipsep was as weak as Autumnstar.

Soon Ipsep sank beneath the surface and disappeared. Slumbering or dead, Autumnstar couldn't say.

He struggled to swim to his would-be rescuer. How long had the old man been submerged? Autumnstar's left wing was crushed and useless. His blood flowed into the pond with every desperate stroke.

By the time he touched the body, he knew it was too late. Autumnstar had spent most of his hoarded power in his fight with Ipsep. Even had he been strong enough to heal the body, the soul had already fled.

"Thank you," he whispered.

Moments later, Tymalous Autumnstar climbed out of the pond, took a single step, and fell flat on his face. He rolled over, examining his new body and wondering how long it would take to get used to having only two legs again.

Jig should have known better. Gratz was a goblin, and goblins didn't take kindly to losing their commands. Especially not to an upstart runt like Jig. But Jig had been so busy being afraid of humans and gods and everything else that he had forgotten to be afraid of his fellow goblins.

The knife in Gratz's hand was short and straight. Barely long enough to pierce Jig's heart, though if Gratz was smart, he'd go for the throat instead.

Gratz had intercepted him after Relka went back to ready the wolves. The other goblins were too far away to help. Nor would Jig have expected them to. This was his own fault. He should have killed Gratz. Failing that, he should have made sure Gratz was disarmed and bound. Gratz had snuck up on him as though he were a deaf human.

Jig backed away, one hand reaching for his sword. Could he draw it before Gratz pounced? Probably not. "Don't regulations say anything about drawing a knife on a superior officer?"

Gratz blinked. "What, this? Oh, no, sir. I was only going to offer to cut your officer's scar."

"Officer's scar?" Jig stared, trying to understand.

"Now that you're a lieutenant and all that, you'll be wanting the scar of rank to show everyone. Six cuts to the right forearm." He frowned as he studied Jig more closely. "You're skinny, so I'll have to cut small. . . ."

"No."

"But you're an officer now." Gratz smiled wistfully as he looked at the knife. "I remember the day old Silverfang gave me my first scar of rank. Couldn't use that arm for a month."

"No!"

Gratz looked hurt. "It's not that bad, sir. The actual designs are sort of pretty." He yanked down part of his shirt to reveal a patch of dark blue scars below the shoulder. A single zigzag, with two diagonal lines cut through the center. Tiny angular cuts dotted the right side of the mark. "General's scars are even better. There's a double circle around the whole thing."

Jig! Shadowstar sounded shaken. *You can't let him carve that mark on you.*

I'm not the smartest goblin in the world, but I had figured that much out on my own.

You don't understand, said Shadowstar. *Those scars are how Billa plans to kill everyone.*

Jig waited a long time before following Gratz back to the group. He sat for so long that Smudge crawled out and nipped him on the ear, just to make sure he was still alive. Jig winced and tugged the fire-spider from his ear.

"They're spells," Jig whispered to Smudge. Every officer in Billa's army carried a spell upon his or her shoulder. Shadowstar wasn't sure exactly what the spell would do, but he thought it powerful enough to kill everyone within ten paces. If Billa waited until her army was locked in battle with the humans and elves, she could destroy them all with a single command.

You have to go back, Shadowstar said.

With a numbness only partly due to the cold, Jig

pushed himself up and trudged toward the rest of his "army." As he returned to the group, they stared at him with the same expression the wolves wore when they saw fresh meat. They all had to know it was only a matter of time before Billa caught up with him. Jig was a walking corpse.

What they didn't realize was that the same was true for them all. And if Jig told them what Billa truly planned, one of two things would happen. Either they wouldn't believe him, and Gratz would quote some regulation against letting madmen command the troops.

Or else they would believe him. Jig suspected that would be even worse. Whatever self-control and discipline Billa had trained into them would shatter, turning them back into an unruly mob. A very angry mob.

Jig had never done well with mobs.

"We have a choice to make," Jig said. His voice cracked, and several goblins smirked. He cleared his throat. "We can return to Billa's army and rejoin the others. Go back to being soldiers in Billa's war." He began to pace, more to keep his feet warm than for dramatic effect. "*Billa's* army. *Billa's* war. Do you think anyone will remember the goblins, once this war is over?"

The smirks faded slightly.

"Billa sent you to capture me," Jig said. "But where's the glory in dragging a half-blind goblin runt back to be killed? You think anyone will sing songs about that? How fourteen wolf-riders triumphed over a pair of runaways?"

He saw Trok nodding. Hopefully the other goblins were of similar minds.

"You know what's going to happen to me," Jig said. "Billa wants me dead, right?"

The goblins shifted uncomfortably. Honesty was an unfamiliar tactic to most of them.

"Well, that's fine," Jig said, raising his voice. "But first I say we show her what goblins can do. We'll show Billa and her orcs. We'll show the humans. We'll show them all—"

The goblins cheered. What was the matter with them? Jig hadn't finished yet. Were they so eager to prove themselves? They didn't even know what they were cheering for!

He pointed down toward the road. "There's a human town up that road. They've taken—"

A whisper from Shadowstar broke his rhythm. He sighed and pointed in the other direction. "They've taken the warriors from our lair. I say we free them all and capture another town for Billa the Bloody! By the time we're through, everyone will be singing about our triumph at the Battle of Avery!"

More cheers. Were all goblins mad?

From what I've seen— Shadowstar began.

Shut up.

Gratz stepped forward. It was all Jig could do to stop himself from flinching away. If Billa suspected Jig was here, all she had to do was trigger that spell on Gratz's arm.

"Begging your pardon, sir," said Gratz. "But it's against regulations for us to engage an enemy force without orders, unless that force attacks first or —"

"Trok," Jig yelled. "The next time Gratz contradicts my orders, you have permission to feed him to the wolves."

Trok grinned. "Yes, sir!"

Jig pointed to a few random goblins. "Clean up this mess. The rest of you, finish getting the wolves ready."

He watched in amazement as they obeyed. Couldn't they see how desperate Jig was? That he was making this up as he went, and that every last one of them would likely die if they actually attacked Avery?

They're goblins, said Shadowstar. *I've grown rather fond of you us a race, but you're not so good at thinking things through.*

You're right, said Jig. *Otherwise I would have known better than to get involved with gods.*

*   *   *

"I've changed my mind," Jig said, staring at Bastard. They had rigged a new harness, mostly by tying extra knots in the old one. "The rest of you go ahead and capture Avery. I'll catch up."

"Don't be afraid." Trok yanked Smelly's ropes, and the wolf padded over to stand beside Jig and Bastard. "These beasts are magnificent!"

Bastard lowered his head and butted Jig onto the ground.

"See?" Trok said. "He likes you."

"He still has a bit of Silverfang stuck in his teeth," Jig mumbled. Bad enough the wolf could snap him in half with one chomp, but now every time he looked at Bastard, he saw Silverfang. A single stumble, and Jig would end up the same way. Silverfang's remains hadn't been pretty. "Well tenderized" was the phrase Relka had used.

Whose stupid idea had it been to put goblins on wolfback, anyway? The hobgoblins trained their tunnel cats, but no hobgoblin was mad enough to try to ride one.

"He's definitely fixated on you," Gratz said. "You'd best mount him soon, to show him who's boss. Otherwise, you're small enough he might decide to carry you like a pup instead."

"What does that mean?" Jig asked.

"Whenever the pups wander too far away, the adult goes and picks them up by the scruff of the neck." Gratz grabbed his own neck to demonstrate. "The pups have loose, thick skin at the neck to protect them. You and me, well. . . ."

Jig reached out to touch the leather-and-rope harness circling Bastard's chest and neck. Holding the harness with both hands, he slipped one foot into the small noose on the side.

"Not that way," Trok said. "Not unless you want to ride to Avery with your face in Bastard's—"

"Thanks." Jig switched feet. The wolf was so tall that simply sliding his foot into the rope stretched Jig's thighs uncomfortably far. He bounced on his toes, trying to get enough of a jump to throw his other leg over the wolf's back. Finally he managed to haul himself up.

"Well, I guess you'll learn," Gratz said. "Right. Your turn." He gestured to Relka.

"What?" Jig asked.

"The commander's mate rides with him."

"The commander's what?" Jig yelled.

Trok was laughing so hard he sprayed spit over Smelly's back.

Gratz's face, by contrast, was expressionless. "I thought, with the way she looks up to you and talks about you. . . ."

Jig started to argue, but it wasn't like he had much choice. Relka had to ride with someone, and Bastard was the biggest wolf.

Jig clenched his jaw and waited as Relka scrambled up behind him. Gratz tied extra ropes around her legs and waist, cinching her tight against Jig's back.

Smudge scrambled out of Jig's hood barely in time to avoid being squished. He settled down in Bastard's neck fur.

Relka's arms tightened around Jig's chest. "I'm ready."

Jig glared at Gratz. If the other goblin so much as smirked, Jig was going to order Bastard to eat him. But Gratz only grunted and returned to his own wolf. He climbed up, tightened his harness, and waited.

Oh, right. They were waiting for Jig. Bastard was the pack leader, and Jig was in command. Jig leaned down. "Come on, Bastard."

Trok chuckled again.

"Kick him in the sides to start him moving," Gratz said. "Tug the ropes to one side or the other and squeeze with your knees to turn. Pull back to slow him down or stop. If you want him angry, you can reach out and pluck his whiskers. Riles him into a frenzy."

"Kick him," Jig repeated. Gratz was crazy. Jig had

survived this long precisely because he *didn't* run around kicking huge wolves that could eat his head in one bite.

Trok kicked Smelly, then tugged his ropes to guide the wolf in a tight circle. "Nothing to it."

Jig grabbed the ropes with both hands and gave them a light pull. Bastard pulled back, ripping the ropes from his fingers. Jig tried again, his face hot.

"Don't forget to kick," Relka said. Before Jig could answer, she slammed her heels into Bastard's ribs.

Bastard went from a standstill to a sprint so fast Jig's head snapped backward into Relka's jaw. The other wolves raced after them. Jig glanced back to see Trok waving one hand in the air and laughing like an idiot. Trok's hand hit a low branch, dropping snow onto the next wolf-rider.

"To Avery!" Relka shouted.

To Avery. Now all Jig had to do was figure out what to do once they arrived . . .

By the time Jig spotted the outlying farms of Avery, he was starting to wish he had let Billa kill him.

The insides of his legs were damp with sweat. Bastard's sweat or his own, he wasn't sure. But sweaty trousers were the least of his problems. These oversize wolves also had oversize backbones, and their gait was more than a little bumpy. He wouldn't be able to sit down again for days.

His back, and presumably Relka's front, were also soaked with sweat. Her necklace jabbed him between the shoulder blades, and she kept trying to rest her chin on his shoulder, which meant her hair tickled his ear.

The only one who seemed to be enjoying the ride was Smudge. He had climbed up onto Bastard's head, where he stood as tall as he could, the wind brushing his bristly fur.

"We're almost there," Relka said.

"I know." Jig tugged the ropes and tried to squeeze with his legs. Bastard turned. "Wrong knee," Jig muttered, pressing hard with the other leg. Slowly he steered Bastard toward the trees and tried to remember how to stop. He glanced at Trok, who was tugging Smelly's reins. That's right. Jig pulled hard, and Bastard came to a grudging halt.

Falling snow had streaked Jig's spectacles, but when he looked through the trees, he could still make out the wall surrounding Avery.

Jig fumbled with the harness, trying to escape. Relka freed herself first, sliding easily over Bastard's rump. Jig stared at the mess of ropes and knots. Which ones held him in place, and which were part of the hasty repairs to the harness?

Eventually Jig gave up and drew his knife. He freed himself in short order, though he ended up with a loop of rope still tied around one leg. Ignoring it for now, he turned to study his . . . his troops.

The wolves weren't even breathing very hard. For the most part, the goblins appeared eager to charge the town. Their weapons were ready, and they were joking and bantering the way goblins always did before they ran into battle and got killed.

Gratz was the exception. He had already dismounted and now sat on the ground, tugging off his boots.

"What are you doing?" Jig asked, his other problems momentarily forgotten.

"Reg . . . regulations, sir." Gratz shivered hard as the first boot slid free. "After any sustained ride, soldiers are advised to dry off. Prevents fungus and other . . . nasty things."

To Jig's horror, once Gratz was barefoot, he then began to unbuckle his belt.

"No time," Jig said quickly. "We'll dry ourselves in Avery, in front of a warm fire."

That earned a few quiet cheers. Jig turned back to the town. The gate was closed. The elf atop the wall would pick off half his goblins before they even reached the gate. "What do regulations say about attacking a town like this?"

"With a large force, you can cut them off from supplies and reinforcements and wait for them to surrender," Gratz said.

Jig glanced at his goblins. "What about smaller forces?"

"Try to gain the walls, or break down the gate," Gratz said as he rubbed his toes. "Either way, for an attack against a walled town, you're looking at about a ten-to-one casualty ratio. That means for every one of them we kill, they'll probably kill ten of us."

"Wait, what was that?" Jig turned back to Gratz. "We have fifteen goblins. You're saying we'd kill one or two humans before they wipe us all out?"

Gratz beamed. "You catch on quick! Of course that elf on the wall bumps the numbers closer to fifteen-to-one."

The other goblins had grown quiet.

"And our attacking force is made up of goblins," Gratz added. "That makes it more like twenty-to-one."

"But we have Jig Dragonslayer," Relka said. "Champion of Tymalous Shadowstar. Slayer of Straum the dragon and the Necromancer. Vanquisher of the pixie queen. Rider of Bastard. Companion of Smudge. Your regulations know nothing of Jig."

"Unless he's also the Deflector of Arrows and the Breaker of Gates, we're still going to die before we kill a single human," Trok said.

"No back talk," snapped Gratz. "I'm sure our commander has a plan."

Trok smirked as he turned to Jig. "Well, sir? What's your plan?"

Right. A plan. Jig covered his eyes against the sun, studying the goblins working near the gate. They had cleared the flowers from the lower section of the wall, and now they worked on ladders to reach the higher flowers. A single elf watched from above, bow in one hand. It looked like the same elf who had shot at them before. A few armed humans stood by the gate. They mostly appeared to be watching the goblins.

"Princess Genevieve is the key to taking Avery,"

Jig said. "We need to capture her alive." If she was anything like the rest of her family, she would die before she surrendered to goblins, but they didn't know that. Jig only needed a few minutes to talk to her, to force her to listen.

Though if she was anything like the rest of her family, she probably wasn't very big on listening, either.

"We need more troops," Jig decided. "Genevieve dragged at least forty goblin warriors away to Avery. It looks like at least twenty of them are still alive."

"How do we free them without getting killed?" another goblin asked.

Jig closed his eyes. *Tell Braf we're here.*

He waited while Shadowstar relayed the message. Moments later, one of the goblins on the ladders turned around and cupped his hands over his eyes. Jig squinted through his spectacles, trying to be certain that was Braf. Then the goblin waved and nearly fell off his ladder.

"How did you do that?" whispered Gratz.

Jig sighed. *Shadowstar, would you please smite Braf before he alerts the elf and everyone else that we're here?*

Braf jumped like he had been stabbed, then quickly turned back to the wall.

Thank you. Jig stepped closer to the edge of the woods. *Braf, we need to capture Princess Genevieve. We need her help to stop Billa the Bloody.*

Why do we want to stop Billa? Shadowstar did a decent job of conveying the slow, deceptively stupid tone of Braf's voice. Jig wondered what Braf heard. Was Shadowstar mimicking Jig's voice as well?

Because she plans to kill everyone, said Jig. *Goblins, humans, it doesn't matter. She wants us all dead. Also because Shadowstar said so.* Jig studied the goblin prisoners. They would still be tied together, which limited what they could do. They had their knives, but the human weapons were far better. Not to mention that elf on the wall. *How often does Genevieve leave the city?*

A few times each day, Braf said. *She's always there when they drag us in and out of town. Mornings are the worst. It's still dark and cold, and nobody wants to come out and work. Nights are bad too. Also midmorning, when you've been working a while and have to use the privy, but you know it's a long time until lunch. Afternoons are pretty lousy. There aren't any good times, really.*

Genevieve? Jig prodded.

Oh. Right. She and Darnak go for walks in the evenings sometimes, too.

"You're planning to use bound prisoners to help us fight?" Trok asked.

As if the unbound goblins Jig had brought were much of a threat. "They're going to be our distraction." He raised his voice. "We wait until evening. Genevieve will be outside the walls. The prisoners will draw the attention of the guards. When that happens, we attack. No matter what else happens, we have to capture Genevieve."

"Brilliant," said Relka.

No, brilliant would have been running deeper into the tunnels when Genevieve first attacked their lair, and staying there until this whole thing was over. Or minding his own business when Billa dragged Relka into the temple. Really, could anyone but a goblin have managed to pick a fight with *both sides* in a war?

Jig?

What is it? Jig couldn't quite tell whether it was Braf or Shadowstar talking.

Hold on . . . I just got a thorn in my ear.

Braf, then. Jig peered out of the woods, trying to pick Braf out of the group. There he was, clawing at his left ear. How had he managed to . . . on second thought, Jig didn't want to know.

Jig, it would be a lot easier to distract the guards if we weren't tied up.

I'm sure it would. Jig stared at the walls. *It would also be easier if Genevieve ordered her warriors to*

*cook themselves for dinner. But I don't know how to
make that happen, do you?*

*Well, we're about ready to haul another load of
flowers out to the farms,* Braf said. *The guards are
watching for goblins who try to escape. But they probably wouldn't notice someone who joined us. Then you
could use Smudge to burn through some of our ropes
while we worked.*

Jig forgot sometimes that Braf only pretended to be
stupid. Probably because he did such an amazing job
of pretending.

Slowly Jig started to smile. The best part of Braf's
plan was that it would save him from having to ride
Bastard again. He turned to the other goblins. "Relka,
I'm leaving you in charge. You'll know when to attack.
Try to be as quiet as you can. The closer you can get
before they notice you, the less time they'll have to
react. Remember, we have to capture Genevieve
alive."

"I won't fail you." Relka saluted with every bit as
much sincerity and stiffness as Gratz.

Jig tried not to laugh. She was worried about failing
him? He was the one sending goblins into battle
against humans.

The loop of rope from Bastard's harness finally
slipped down from Jig's ankle. He kicked it to Trok.
"Someone needs to fix Bastard's harness again," he said.

"What will you be doing?" Trok asked, his voice
gruff with suspicion.

Jig stared at the mounds of flowers. "Trying not
to sneeze."

Brown stalks tickled Jig's face as he crept through
the field. He squinted, wiping his face as he watched
the goblins climbing down from their ladders. Behind
him, sunlight turned the snow-covered hills and mountains a fiery orange. He saw no sign of his wolf-riders,
which was good. Hopefully, the elf couldn't see
them either.

He jogged the rest of the way to the edge of the field, then stopped. Not only could he see the flower petals piled up beside the farmhouse, he could smell them. His vision blurred, and his nose began to drip. He covered the lower part of his face with his cloak. Smudge crept around Jig's neck and perched on his shoulder.

Holding his breath, Jig ran to the pile and lay down behind it, out of sight of the wall. If anyone had seen him, he was dead. Though at least then he wouldn't have to keep inhaling flower perfume. He pulled his hood over his head and tried to breathe as little as possible.

A tiny spider crept out from beneath the flowers, drawn by the warmth of Jig's body.

Smudge pounced. A quick burst of heat cooked the tiny spider, and then Smudge was retreating back to the warmth of Jig's hood, carrying his meal in his forelegs. Jig felt strangely sympathetic for the smaller spider.

His ear twitched as the goblins left the wall, trudging toward the farmhouse. Jig rubbed his eyes and peered around the side of the pile. That elf was watching the goblins closely now. This was the best opportunity for them to run off, so he would have an arrow ready to discourage them. After Jig's escape, he doubted the elf's pride would allow anyone else to take a single suspicious step.

As if the goblins would have cooperated long enough to escape. They had no way to cut the rope around their necks, which meant they would have to run together. Goblins rarely did anything together.

No, that wasn't true. *Billa's* goblins worked together. They marched as one, fought as one, and if Billa and Isa had their way, they would die as one.

The scritch of rakes signaled the arrival of the prisoners. Jig waited until they had all reached the pile, then darted into line behind Braf.

"Jig!" Braf grinned. So did the other goblins, to Jig's surprise.

"Braf told us he was talking to you," said one. He shrugged. "I figured all that human food had rotted his brain."

"So, how are you going to get us out of here?" asked another.

"Wait, before you free us, can you do something about these blisters on my hands?"

"And my feet are killing me!"

"Quiet," Jig snapped. He glanced at the wall. The elf was still watching them. Had he noticed anything? Probably not, since Jig was still arrow-free. He concentrated on looking like another miserable prisoner. Keeping his voice low, he said, "Once I cut everyone free, you're going to distract the guards."

"Us?" The goblins' grins began to fade. "We're supposed to fight armed humans?"

"And an elf," Braf said, ever helpful.

"Only until my . . . my army attacks." Jig braced himself, but the other goblins didn't even smirk. To his shock, they actually sounded reassured.

Jig sniffled and sneezed and did his best to help with the flowers. By the time they started back, he was about ready to cut off his own nose to stop it from dripping.

Jig bit the rope as they walked, clutching it in his fangs so that, from a distance, he might appear to be tied up with the rest. When they reached the wall, he climbed up the ladder after Braf. The goblin tied behind him crowded uncomfortably close, but hopefully he wouldn't have to stay here for long.

The goblin below climbed up another rung. His breath heated Jig's neck. Jig tried not to think about the fact that every one of these goblins carried a knife.

They wouldn't stab him in the back now. Not while they still needed him to cut them free.

After that, well, anyone who turned his back on another goblin deserved what he got.

Jig set Smudge on the rope. This time, unaffected by elf beer, Smudge clung easily to the thin rope. He turned around and stared up at Jig.

"Go on," Jig said. He poked a finger at Smudge's face, driving him back a few steps.

"What's wrong?" asked Braf.

"He's not scared enough."

Jig cringed as soon as the words escaped his mouth. But before he could take them back, Braf shrugged and tried to stab Smudge with his knife.

He missed, but the knife jabbed Jig's cloak in passing. Smudge scurried back toward Jig, the rope smoldering where he walked. But then he jumped onto Jig's throat.

"Well, he's hot enough to burn," Jig said through gritted teeth. He tried to catch Smudge, but the fire-spider had already darted toward one of his pockets.

Holding the ladder with one hand, he reached into his cloak, trying to figure out which pocket— "Oh, no."

"What's wrong?" asked the goblin below him.

Jig tried to stop the explosive sneeze building in his skull. He failed. The sneeze shook the ladder. He gasped for breath, which only earned him another mouthful of flower smell. He sneezed again, and his hand slipped from the rung.

The next thing he knew, he was on the ground, sandwiched between Braf and the other goblins. From the pained shouts, a few of those goblins had fallen on their knives.

"Hey, what's going on down there?" Atop the wall, the elf gestured with his longbow.

Jig tried to burrow deeper into the pile of goblins, but they were already sorting themselves out.

Where was the rope? He had lost it when he fell. One of his fangs was loose. No doubt the rope had tugged it before snapping out of his mouth. Could the elf see that he wasn't tied up?

"You in the lavender cloak. What are you doing?"

"Purple, not lavender," Jig muttered. One of the humans near the gate was hurrying away, presumably to fetch more guards.

Jig didn't move. He didn't have to. The other gob-

lins had already backed as far from Jig as their ropes
would allow.

"Where did you come from?" the elf asked. "How
did—"

A rock hit the elf in the middle of the forehead.
He grunted, staggered forward, then slowly toppled
over the edge of the wall. Apparently Prince Theodore
hadn't remembered to strengthen this elf before he
and the others left.

Jig turned around. "Thanks, Braf."

Braf picked up another rock. "I've wanted to do
that for days!" His vicious grin was a reminder that
Braf had been a warrior long before he was a priest.

Jig ran toward the elf. He kicked the bow as far
away as he could. The elf wasn't moving, but Jig didn't
mean to take any chances. He knelt and grabbed the
knife from the elf's belt.

Forged from a single curved piece of gray metal,
the knife was light as air. The unstained wooden handle was warm to the touch. He tested the edge on the
elf, then grinned. "Braf, come here!"

Braf hurried toward Jig, dragging goblins behind
him. A single swipe with the elf's knife cut Braf free.

Jig managed to free four more goblins before the
first of the guards arrived.

"Use your rakes," Jig shouted. "Knives are no good
against swords and spears."

A crossbow bolt buried itself in the ground beside
Jig. Atop the wall, several more humans leaned over
the edge, searching for targets.

Jig started to flee, then changed his mind and ran to
the base of the wall. He couldn't get too close without
impaling himself on the spikes growing from the trees,
but the humans would have to lean out awfully far to
shoot him. They were shouting for reinforcement, and
he could hear horses thundering out through the gate.
"Stay close to the wall," he yelled. "Make them
chase us!"

The farther the goblins fled, the longer the gates
would stay open. If the wolf-riders were fast enough,

they might still manage to get into the city and capture Genevieve.

Jig tried to follow the other goblins, but tripped over the elf. The goblins, being goblins, kept right on going, leaving him to be killed. He started to rise, but there was no way he could catch up with the others.

Jig snagged a broken crossbow bolt from the ground and clenched it in his armpit. Hopefully, anyone who passed would assume he was dead. If they didn't, he would be soon enough.

He turned his head slightly as movement from the woods caught his eye. He had never realized how quickly those wolves could move. Already the lead goblins were halfway to Avery. As far as he could tell, the humans hadn't yet noticed.

Several horses pounded past, the thudding of their hooves a startling contrast to the silence of the wolves. Jig held his breath, but nobody paid him any attention. Humans on foot followed. Some appeared to be guards, while others were ordinary men with axes and spears. No doubt everyone who had resented the intrusion of goblins into their town was taking this opportunity to express their unhappiness.

"It's an ambush!" The voice was familiar, and far closer than Jig preferred. Genevieve stood with her sword drawn, pointing toward the wolves. Jig held his breath and hoped she wouldn't notice him.

An arrow or crossbow bolt arched from the wall, hitting one of the wolves. Wolf and goblin tumbled into the snow, and neither one got up again.

"Everyone back inside," Genevieve shouted. "Forget the prisoners! Archers, concentrate on those wolves!"

Jig clenched his jaw. Genevieve had spotted them too soon. They wouldn't reach her before she got her people back inside the gate. Humans rushed past, their rage turned to panic at the sight of the wolves.

"That goes for you too, Ginny!" Darnak's voice, closer to the gate. "We can pick them off from atop the walls."

So much for Jig and his army. His first attempt at

tactics and strategy had fallen apart before his goblins even had the chance to draw their weapons. Genevieve would reach safety, and then they would kill every one of the goblins at their leisure.

Unless someone stopped her.

"I hate this," Jig said as he got up and ran after Genevieve. She moved at a relatively slow pace, all of her attention on the wolves.

Standing at the gate, Darnak was the first to notice Jig. "Princess, 'ware the goblin!"

He was too late and too far away. Genevieve started to turn, and then Jig pounced. He landed on Genevieve's back and clung with one hand. With his other, he pressed his stolen knife to Genevieve's neck.

"Tell your people to stop fighting, Princess!" He had done it! He had captured—

Genevieve grabbed his wrist and twisted the knife away from her neck. Her elbow thudded into Jig's side. The knife fell. Genevieve's free hand snaked up to grab Jig's ear, and then he was flying over her shoulder to slam into the ground.

Genevieve's own knife appeared in her hand. "I know you. You're the runt who helped steal my horse!" She knelt and placed the tip of her knife on Jig's chest. "Jig, wasn't it?"

Oh, dung.

Darnak ran toward them, his heavy boots clomping through the snow. "Princess, forget the goblin and get inside!"

Jig held his breath, waiting for Genevieve to kill him.

A snarling wall of fur shot over Jig, and Genevieve disappeared.

"Ginny!" Darnak raised his war club overhead and charged.

Ignoring the pounding in his head, Jig rolled onto his side. Genevieve lay pinned beneath Bastard's front paws, her knife lost. Bastard looked from Darnak to the princess and back, as if he couldn't decide whether to eat her before he killed Darnak or after.

"Bastard, down!" Jig yelled. Bastard turned, his head cocked in confusion.

Jig lay back down, fumbling through his pockets. He had only a single troll toe left. He threw it to the wolf. "Sit!"

Bastard obeyed. Genevieve had time for one panicked squeal before disappearing beneath Bastard's backside. Only her legs still protruded, kicking furiously.

"Let her go, Jig." Darnak stopped between Jig and Bastard. "I've no mind to fight you."

Bastard growled again. The other wolf-riders spread around Jig and Darnak, forming a ring of teeth and claws and swords. Darnak didn't seem to notice.

Jig glanced at the wall. Several humans stood with crossbows ready. They were watching Darnak, waiting for his order.

"I can't let you kill her," Darnak said. "Not Ginny."

"I don't want to kill her," said Jig.

"So what is it you're wanting, then?" Darnak lowered his club. "If you've come to free your goblins, so be it. Take them and be gone."

Jig waved the other goblins back. They obeyed, though Trok had to tug Smelly's reins several times to get the wolf to turn away.

He couldn't tell Darnak the truth. Not here. No matter how softly Jig spoke, goblin ears would hear. "If she surrenders, we won't kill anyone else."

Darnak turned in a slow circle. Most of the guards had retreated through the gates, following Genevieve's orders. Darnak was alone, surrounded by goblins. Normally, Jig still would have given Darnak the advantage, but even Darnak couldn't fight all of those wolves.

"You planned this, did you?" Darnak asked.

"Well, this isn't exactly what I planned."

Darnak actually laughed. "Every field commander knows that feeling."

Jig kept his eye on that club. Darnak might not be

able to fight everyone, but he could certainly kill Jig before the wolves got him.

"Let Genevieve go." Darnak tossed his war club to the ground in front of Jig. He turned and waved both hands at the men on the wall. "Lower your weapons, men."

Goblins would have shot anyway, out of spite. But the humans obeyed.

"Bastard—" Jig hesitated. Was there a command to make a wolf get up off of a human?

Gratz cleared his throat. "Perhaps a 'Ready' command, sir?"

"Bastard, ready!"

Bastard stood and bared his fangs, head low. Genevieve coughed and crawled out from beneath him. Her normally bored expression was twisted into one of utter horror. When she spotted Jig, her hands clenched into fists. She spat fur and searched the ground for a weapon.

"Easy, lass," Darnak said.

"That wolf," Genevieve gasped. "He *sat on me!*"

Darnak chuckled, then coughed to cover the sound. "It's over."

If only Darnak were right. Jig looked around, confused. "What happened to Relka?"

Trok pointed toward the woods. Jig spotted Relka limping through the snow, her sword dragging from one hand.

"What happened to her?"

"She insisted on riding Bastard in your place. When Bastard saw you were in trouble, he took off like a tunnel cat with his tail on fire. Relka tumbled right off." Trok gave an innocent shrug. "Seems like *someone* missed a few ropes when he mended Bastard's harness."

CHAPTER 10

Tymalous Autumnstar upended the clay mug, finishing off the last few swallows of . . . he wasn't sure, actually. From the taste, it could have been anything from gnomish beer to fermented leopard urine. He belched and ordered another.

"Haven't you had enough, Grandfather?" The middle-aged man behind the bar sounded simultaneously impressed and annoyed. Amber earrings dangled from his ears, marking him as an acolyte of Rionisus Yelloweyes. For the right price, he could arrange all manner of mortal pleasures. So long as he contributed a good portion of his profits to the temple, the emperor's men couldn't touch him.

"Have I had enough?" Autumnstar repeated, adding the empty mug to the collection in front of him. "My followers are long gone. My star has disappeared from the night sky. Most of my companions are dead. Any who survive seem determined to kill me. And not one of you remembers my name. Do you think I've had enough?"

"More than enough. I think it's time—"

"My name is Tymalous Autumnstar." He leaned back, settling into one of the enormous pillows that littered the floor like giant colored animal droppings. There were no chairs in Yelloweyes' taverns. The bar was formed from overlapping slabs of green shale, running along the walls at knee height. "Repeat it back to

me, and I'll pay you ten times the value of these drinks. If not, you pour me another and leave the bottle."

The bartender sat down and clapped Autumnstar's back, not unkindly. "Can you hear yourself? Followers and stolen stars? Go home and sleep it off."

Autumnstar smiled. "My name." Though he hadn't raised his voice, the few patrons in the tavern fell silent. "Repeat it."

"Sure thing, grandfather," the bartender said, humoring him. And then he frowned. "Could you say that name again?"

"Tymalous Autumnstar." He waited while the bartender stammered a second time. In the edge of his vision, he saw one person raise his hand in the sign of the alligator, warding off evil magic.

Eventually the bartender turned and reached for a bottle.

As it turned out, conquering a town was the easy part. Controlling it was another matter altogether. Thirty-five goblins and fourteen wolves couldn't hope to hold a town of this size for long. Both Genevieve and Jig knew it. Which would explain that small smile on Genevieve's face as she stared at him.

Or maybe she was simply imagining all of the ways she could kill Jig once she escaped. Even though he had her weapons and she was tied up, Jig still felt as though he were standing before a dragon, waiting to be eaten.

"We need to talk," Jig said.

Genevieve kept on smiling.

"Aye," said Darnak. "Preferably somewhere other than the middle of the street."

Jig agreed completely, but so far, he hadn't managed to go more than three steps without someone accosting him for orders. Speaking of which. . . .

"The wolves are hungry, sir," Gratz said as he ran up to Jig. A few of the wolf-riders came with him. "They made short work of that dead elf, but they're still growling. Are you sure we can't feed them a prisoner? There are so many humans, they won't notice just one. I'll make sure it's a wounded one, and—"

"No," said Jig. "Talk to Braf. The humans must have food stored somewhere. Wait . . . where did you put the wolves, anyway?"

"That big building down the road. The one with the trees with red leaves."

"Blood oaks," said Genevieve. She snickered. "You put those beasts in the mayor's house."

"It was the sturdiest place I could find," said Gratz. "Last I saw, the wolves were ripping up the tapestries for bedding."

"Poor Detwiler," said Genevieve, a nasty edge to her tone. "Serves him right for fleeing like a coward when he heard about Billa's army."

"Well, if he comes back, he'll want to wash out his closet before he uses it again. I'd throw out the bedcovers, too." Gratz glanced at Jig and added, "Smelly's been rolling again."

Trok and a handful of warriors jogged down the road. "We've finished locking up the soldiers," Trok said, shoving past Gratz. He grinned and added, "We put them in the stables. The doors are barred, and we've got goblins watching the windows."

"What about the townspeople?" Jig asked.

"So far they've kept to themselves. Most of them retreated into that big church and locked the doors." Trok glanced at Gratz. "They're afraid we're going to feed them to the wolves."

Good enough. Jig started to turn back to Genevieve and Darnak.

"So when do we burn the stable?" Trok asked. "Relka says if we throw the right kind of wood into the fire, the smoke will flavor the meat, and—"

Jig groaned. "Nobody is allowed to kill anyone!" he shouted. "Any goblin who disobeys will be executed."

Gratz's forehead wrinkled. "Wouldn't whoever carried out the execution be disobeying your order to not kill anyone, then?"

"If we let them live, they're only going to escape," Trok said. "You know how humans are."

"I'll deal with that later," Jig snapped.

"To think that *he* defeated us," Genevieve whispered.

Darnak chuckled. "Your mother would say it's the gods' way of teaching us humility."

"What do we do now, sir?" Gratz asked. "Now that we've taken the town, I mean. This should be enough to earn Billa's forgiveness. Would you like me to send a messenger back—"

"No!" Jig swallowed and tried again. "No." That was better. He sounded more like a goblin again, and less like a panicked bird. "First . . . first I have to interrogate the prisoners."

"Billa would at least let us eat the dwarf," someone said. Jig searched the crowd, but he couldn't identify the speaker.

"We don't have to kill anyone," Trok added. "We could take an arm here, a leg there. Humans can survive that, can't they?"

"We're not eating the prisoners!" Jig said. Not if he wanted to convince Genevieve to listen. He started to say more, then broke off as Relka ran up and whispered in his ear. Jig sighed. "We're not eating any *more* prisoners."

From the looks on their faces, this was not how a goblin leader kept control of his men. They had fought and won, and now Jig was denying them the chance to celebrate. How long could he keep it up before he went from leader to lunch?

"All of the goblin prisoners are hereby recruited into our army!" he announced. That earned even more muttering, which he had expected. None of the former prisoners would know what this meant, and his wolf-riders looked annoyed that these strangers were now a part of their army. But Jig wasn't finished yet.

"Everyone who rode with me today is hereby promoted to—" His mind went blank. What was a good rank? Gratz was a corporal, and he had said Jig was a lieutenant. "To . . . to captain?"

That earned cheers and shouts, so Jig assumed it was a good rank. But Gratz was shaking his head. "You can't promote everyone. That's too many captains. You have to work your way up through the ranks, and—"

"Are you saying you don't want your promotion, Captain Gratz?"

Gratz licked his lips. "Actually, regulations say that a commander away from Billa's army does have the right to issue field promotions."

"Good." Jig grinned. "Captain Trok, you're responsible for keeping the new recruits in line. Nobody eats the prisoners."

Trok scowled. He knew what Jig had done, but he wasn't protesting. Good enough.

Jig wiped his nose and eyes on his sleeve. His head felt like one of Golaka's stuffed rats. Stupid elves and their flowers and trees. So many roads and buildings and alleyways . . . how did humans find their way around this place? He turned to Genevieve and asked, "Where can we go to talk? I mean, so I can interrogate you."

She pointed to a thick grove of ivy-covered trees to the left of the gate. The dark, knifelike leaves of the vines turned the trees purple. "How about there? It's as peaceful a spot as any."

Jig hesitated. "What is it?"

Genevieve's face was hard to read. "A graveyard." She stepped off of the road, into the snow. "I thought you might like to see where I'll be leaving you when this is over."

Gratz drew his sword. "Threatening an officer of Billa's army is grounds for—"

"Shut up and come with me, Gratz. Relka, go fetch Braf and bring him to the grove." Braf and Relka were the only two goblins in Avery who might be able to hear the truth without immediately killing him. Jig walked toward the trees. "Well? Are you coming or not?"

As soon as Jig stepped past the first trees, the air grew warmer. Not warm enough to thaw his nose and fingers, but the snow underfoot changed to mud and earth, and the air was still.

"Every one of these trees was planted in the body of a fallen elf," Genevieve commented, grabbing a branch and swinging back and forth. "Some of them are centuries old."

"The elves feed their dead to the trees?" Relka asked, staring up at the branches.

"Oakbottom would love it," said Gratz.

"Who?" Braf stared, confused.

Jig sat down in the dirt, trying to find a spot where his legs didn't touch the roots of the elf trees.

"Would you like to be buried there?" Genevieve asked. "I'll do it myself, once my father arrives."

"Wait," Jig said. "Your father's army is coming here?"

Genevieve rolled her eyes, triggering flashbacks to Jig's time with her brother. "We know Billa's army is headed this way. If not for this cursed weather, my father would have intercepted her already. But the passes are blocked. He won't arrive for several days. But we will retake Avery, and when we do—"

Jig lowered his voice. "Billa doesn't *want* this town."

Whatever Genevieve had been expecting, that wasn't it. She looked almost offended. "Why wouldn't she want Avery?"

That list could have kept Jig talking for the rest of the night. Instead Jig turned to Darnak. "If you don't help me, everyone is going to die. Humans and goblins both."

"What are you saying, lad?" Darnak asked.

Jig scooted to the left, trying to watch everyone at once. The goblins appeared puzzled. Genevieve looked annoyed.

"So you captured Avery so that we could help you?" she asked.

Darnak shook his head. "Easy, Princess. Jig's no fool. He saved our lives, mine and your brothers', when we fell into a hobgoblin trap."

"No doubt to save his own worthless skin," Genevieve said.

"No doubt," Darnak agreed. "But that doesn't make the saving any less real." He glanced at the other goblins, then back at Jig. Clearly he had noticed Jig's own wariness. "It's not like we'll be any worse off for listening to what he has to say."

"Unless he plans to torture us for information," Genevieve muttered.

Gratz brightened, and he reached into his cloak to grab his regulations. "I wrote down lots of different techniques. Um . . . we don't have a catapult, so that one won't work. We'd need Oakbottom's help for this one." He blinked and looked around. "Does anyone have a horseshoe?"

Jig took a deep breath. He didn't have time for this. "Captain Gratz, give me your sword."

"Yes, sir." Gratz grinned as he handed the weapon to Jig. Genevieve and Darnak tensed, like they were preparing to leap up and wrest the weapon away. Which was what usually happened when goblins took prisoners. Taking prisoners was the easy part. Keeping them was much trickier. Far better to toss them in the cookpot and be done with it. No prisoner had ever escaped after being eaten.

"Your knife too." Jig waited while Gratz obeyed. He took the knife and handed it off to Braf. "Now take off your shirt."

"Huh?" Gratz blinked. "I mean, huh, sir?"

"Your shirt." Jig glanced at the princess. She still reminded him of a tunnel cat about to pounce, but her curiosity had been piqued.

Gratz stripped off his armor, then pulled off his shirt. He shivered in the cold.

Genevieve made a face like she had eaten something sour. "So this is your plan? To overwhelm us with the horror of goblin nudity?" She touched her fingers to her forehead. "I salute you. A devious plan, and one which has certainly sapped my morale."

"Darnak, look at the scar on Gratz's arm," Jig said.

Darnak glanced at Gratz. "If you're asking me to heal him, those cuts are far too old to—"

"I could heal him," Jig snapped. "Just look at the marks. They're magic."

"What do you mean, you could heal him?" Darnak asked.

"Darnak, please." Jig pointed to Gratz's arm.

"I don't understand, sir." Gratz turned around. "Silverfang marked me himself, when he promoted me." He rubbed his arm.

With a shrug, Darnak grabbed Gratz. Caterpillar brows scrunched together. "These almost look like runes." He yanked Gratz closer, nearly dislocating the goblin's shoulder. "Come over here by the light so I can see better."

Jig followed, as did Genevieve.

"The penmanship is pretty sloppy," Darnak muttered. "Could be a coincidence, I suppose. People are always claiming to see mystic runes and holy images in everything from clouds to sticky buns. Now that I think on it, Princess, wasn't it one of your brothers who came running out of the privy, screaming how Tallis Van's visage had appeared in—"

"Is it magic or not?" Genevieve snapped.

"Could be, though how a goblin wound up with magic runes on his arm is beyond me," Darnak said. He pinched the outer edge of the scar, and Gratz yelped. "The skin is cold to the touch."

"He's half-naked in the middle of winter," Genevieve pointed out. "What is this magic supposed to do, anyway?"

"I'm not sure," Jig admitted. "Something bad. Something powerful enough to kill everyone in this grove, including Gratz."

"Some sort of suicide spell?" Darnak asked. "To

prevent a captured soldier from giving away vital information? There's an assassin's cult that does something similar, but I wouldn't have thought goblins would have the courage to use such magic."

Gratz was looking more and more confused. He yanked free of Darnak's grip and turned to Jig. "Why are you telling them this, sir? Silverfang was no wizard. This is my scar of rank. All the officers have them."

"How many?" Jig asked.

Gratz tilted his head. "Well, you need at least two officers for every squadron. So at least fifty on the goblin side. Probably even more among the kobolds and orcs."

Jig turned his attention to Genevieve. "Imagine what will happen when your father's army arrives. Billa's forces will already be here, positioned in the valley. His men will drive through our lines, fighting deeper and deeper toward the heart of Billa's army."

"Hey now," Gratz said. "Don't underestimate Billa's forces, sir. We can—"

"Shut up, Gratz," Jig said. "Whatever magic Billa carved into her soldiers, I'm betting she can trigger it all at once. Hundreds of spells, killing men and monsters both."

"Ridiculous," said Darnak. "Such a strategy would still kill more of her own troops than her enemies. She might be victorious, but she'd find herself standing in a field of death."

"That's what she wants." Jig glanced at the other goblins. Relka was rapt, drinking in Jig's every word. Not that Relka's attention meant much. Jig could have been discussing various colors of toe fungus, and she would have listened just as hard.

Braf was nodding to himself. Shadowstar was probably filling him in. Gratz looked angry. Jig took a cautious step away from him, then said, "That's the only way Billa can summon Noc."

Silence. Eventually Darnak coughed and said, "The death god?"

Jig nodded so hard his spectacles slipped down his

nose. "Everything she's done has been part of a plan to summon and kill Noc. The only reason she gathered her army is so she could sacrifice them to—"

"That's a lie!" Gratz shouted. A flare of heat from Smudge gave Jig a moment's warning as Gratz attacked.

He made it a single step before Darnak grabbed him by the back of the trousers, halting him in place. Gratz spun and struck Darnak in the chin.

Darnak frowned. Gratz clutched his fist. And then Darnak tossed Gratz headfirst into one of the trees, hard enough that snow drifted from the branches.

He rubbed his jaw. "Not bad, for a goblin. So what were you saying about Noc, then?"

"When Billa kills everyone, the death will summon Noc to the valley. She's going to use Isa's sword to—"

"Isa?" Genevieve interrupted.

"Goddess of the Winter Winds," Jig said.

"Winter winds, eh?" Darnak twirled a finger through his beard. "That might account for the nasty weather we've had lately. And what would this goddess' name be?"

Jig stared. "Isa. She was one of the Forgotten Gods of the War of Shadows. Like Tymalous Shadowstar."

"Like who?" Darnak asked.

Jig didn't answer. Darnak was the one who had first told him about Shadowstar. What was wrong with him?

"I'm more interested in this so-called goddess Billa means to free," Genevieve said. "What's her name?"

"Isa!" Jig said.

The princess nodded. Darnak cocked his head. "I'm sorry, but I'm having a bit of trouble here. Could you say that name one more time?"

Braf snickered. "I think you broke them."

You could stay here all day, and they'll never remember, Shadowstar said. *Our names slip from their minds the instant they're spoken. You could carve my name into his skin and he'd still forget.*

Jig shook his head. *Darnak was the one who told me about you, back in the tunnels. How could he—*

I nudged his mind a bit. Shadowstar gave Jig no time to process that revelation and its implications. *It's the curse Noc laid upon us.*

So that nobody could ever remember your names?

Shadowstar chuckled. *Nobody civilized.*

Oh. Civilized. Like humans and dwarves and elves. What a peculiar curse.

Noc was trying to sound haughty and profound, Shadowstar said. *I didn't discover the loophole in his phrasing for centuries. Apparently Isa found it sooner, since she's had time to build up an entire army.*

Jig turned his attention back to his captives. "Call her Winter."

"Winter, eh?" Darnak frowned. "I thought you said her name was. . . . Well, smell my socks. It's right on the tip of my tongue."

"The gods have many names," Jig said loftily. "As you of all people should know."

"True enough," said Darnak. "Why, Earthmaker alone has well over twenty names. To the dwarves up north, he's known as Old Ironballs, from the time when he was bathing in—"

"There will be time for tales of Earthmaker later," Genevieve said quickly. "Darnak, is the goblin telling the truth?"

Darnak touched the silver hammer pendant hanging from his neck. "Truth magic is tricky stuff, but Jig believes what he's saying."

"Could it work?" she asked. "If Billa slaughtered her own army as well as ours, could she summon a death god?"

"Possibly." Darnak clenched a fist around his hammer. "Noc is a cold, distant god, but the gods are bound by laws, just like us. More than us, really. Laws of men can be broken, but the laws of the universe. . . . If Billa the Bloody does this right, Noc will have no choice but to appear. I wouldn't want to be standing nearby, but if Billa has some way to kill a god. . . ."

Braf stopped in the middle of picking his nose. "If

Noc is a death god, why doesn't he stop Billa before she can summon him?"

Relka reached over and gently plucked Braf's hand away from his face.

Shadowstar's laughter rang softly in Jig's mind. *It turns out that Noc and his fellow gods consider themselves civilized.*

Jig snorted as he realized what that meant. *Noc cursed himself into forgetting you?*

Really poor phrasing on his part. Of course, it's not like I could run into Ux's fiery domain and kick him in one of his asses. They can *remember us, but it's a distant memory. For mortals, it would be like your very first memories: broken and vague.*

Jig's first memory was of one of the other toddlers sinking sharp baby fangs into his leg. There was nothing vague about that one. "Billa is . . . hidden," he said. He wasn't about to try to explain the curse of the Forgotten Gods to people who wouldn't remember half of what he said.

"Hidden," Genevieve repeated. "From the gods."

"That's right."

"So how exactly do you plan to stop her, goblin?"

"I hadn't really planned that far ahead." Jig plucked Smudge out of his hood and ran a fingertip over the spider's fuzzy back. "Maybe your brother could use the Rod of Creation to transform her into a rock or something."

"Or a fish," Relka suggested.

Genevieve's face had gone still. "Even if I believed you, my father would sooner die than accept the help of a goblin."

"Aye, but your father's not the one charged with protecting this town and these people," Darnak said.

"That's true," said Genevieve. "Which is why he'll send Theodore, just as the goblin suggests. And then he'll disown me."

Darnak chuckled. "Lass, if he didn't disown you for setting his throne on fire, he'll not disown you for this."

Angry shouts from outside the grove made the other goblins jump. Not Jig, though. To be honest, he was a bit surprised it had taken so long.

"What's going on?" Relka asked.

"That would be the humans," Jig said. "The soldiers are breaking out of their prison and wrestling weapons away from the goblin guards. The rest of the humans have probably joined them. They'll be running about with their shovels and axes and pitchforks to overthrow their goblin oppressors."

"We've only been oppressing them for an hour," Braf protested.

Jig ignored him. Every monster knew better than to try to imprison surface-dwellers. They always escaped. That was simply the way these things worked. No sooner had you thrown them in a cave than they were bursting free, carrying dead goblins as shields and slaying everyone in their path with stolen weapons.

"Send word to your father," Jig said. "You don't have to tell him the idea came from a goblin. Isn't saving everyone's lives more important than your father's pride?" He bit his lip. King Wendel was the father of Barius and Ryslind, which made that a very stupid question.

Genevieve didn't answer. The shouts outside were drawing closer.

Braf glanced around. "Should we do something?"

"Probably." Jig leaned against a tree, still holding Smudge. He stiffened and moved away an instant later, remembering what those trees were.

"Darnak said you were their guide," Genevieve said, her voice oddly soft. She looked at Jig in a way that made him want to squirm into the dirt and hide. "You escaped. Just like you escaped from me before. Tell me, did you humiliate my brothers the way you've humiliated me?"

Jig dug his claws into his palms to keep himself from shouting. "I'm trying to save you! And us. Mostly us, really."

"Take it easy, lass," said Darnak. "This is hardly the time for—"

"My father gave Avery to me because it was worthless," said Genevieve. "Too close to the elves. Poor strategic location. An incompetent coward of a mayor. Now, thanks to this goblin, he'll take it away and give it to my equally incompetent brother."

"Theodore and his elves are nothing to laugh at," Darnak said. "I've never understood his fixation with the tree-lovers, but they've turned him into quite the warrior."

"Barius was a warrior," Genevieve said. "As was Ryslind, in his way. Yet they fell to the goblins, just as I did. And both times, this goblin was there." She stared up at the trees. "Tell me, Jig. Did you lead that ambush as well, or did you simply lure my brothers into the trap?"

Distracted by shouting from the streets, Jig didn't realize what she was saying until it was too late. He was too far away to stop Braf from blurting out—

"What trap?" asked Braf, turning to Jig. "I thought you killed them with the rod."

Darnak closed his eyes. Relka walked over and punched Braf in the gut.

"Thanks, Relka," Jig whispered.

"You did, didn't you?" Genevieve shook her head. "I didn't really believe it. How did those idiots let you get your hands on the rod?"

Jig's fingers crept to his sword, but so far, Genevieve wasn't making any hostile moves. She actually looked more amused than anything else. Amused and tired.

"You lied to me, Darnak." Genevieve shook. Her face was wet, and she made no sound, but it almost looked like she was laughing.

Relka glanced over her shoulder. "You definitely broke her."

"No, he didn't." Genevieve hugged her knees to her chest. Darnak moved toward her, but she waved him away. "Everyone talks about how my brothers were killed by goblin warriors," she said, wiping her face. "But *him*? He defeated Barius and Ryslind both? He's the one who turned Darnak into that hideous bird?"

She stared at Jig. "You had the rod, and you gave it back to your chef. Why?"

Jig shrugged. "If I kept it, the other goblins would just kill me and take it. I have a hard enough time holding on to my boots." Slowly Jig released his grip on his sword. He set Smudge on his shoulder. The fire-spider was warm, but not hot enough to burn.

"Why didn't you tell us the truth, Darnak?" Genevieve asked.

Darnak shrugged. "Knowing you lot, you'd have all killed yourselves from shame, and then I'd be out of a job."

Hearing that made Jig wish Darnak *had* told them. It would have saved Jig a great deal of trouble.

Darnak clapped a hand on Genevieve's shoulder. "Your brothers died because they were cruel, short-sighted, petty men. I'd not say as much to your father, but it's the truth. I loved them like my own sons, but had they been mine, I'd have boxed some sense into their skulls."

Braf tapped Jig's shoulder. "Is she going to try to kill you or not?"

"I don't know," said Jig.

"If Barius or Ryslind were here, they'd stab this goblin, slaughter the rest, and charge into battle against Billa," Darnak said. "And if Jig's right, they'd get themselves and everyone else killed in the process."

"My father would—"

"Your father's the one who raised his sons to be jackasses," Darnak interrupted. "What would your mother do, were she here?"

Genevieve's mouth quirked. "You mean before or after she lit your beard on fire for lying to us?"

"I just got this beard back," Darnak said, grabbing

his beard in both hands. "Anyone comes near it, and they'll be tasting Earthmaker's wrath."

"She would work to save lives," Genevieve said.

Darnak nodded. "The king left your upbringing to your mother, which means you actually had a chance to learn a little common sense. Whether or not you choose to use it is another matter. But I swore an oath to Earthmaker himself that I'd serve your family, and that means not letting you wipe yourselves out through your own bloody stubbornness." Darnak hesitated, then added, "With all due respect, Your Highness."

"Of course," Genevieve said dryly. She stood and looked at Jig for a long time. "He's so small."

"Begging Your Highness' pardon," Darnak said. "But some of us view our small stature as an asset. There's an advantage to presenting less of a target."

"Darnak, order our people to stand down," Genevieve said. "Tell the soldiers to fall back and wait for orders. Everyone else . . . should leave Avery tonight. They can take the northwest road toward Jasper Valley. If the goblin is right, Billa shouldn't bother to pursue them."

Jig was too stunned that she hadn't killed him yet to really understand what was happening. "Does that mean we can leave too?"

"Oh no, little goblin." Genevieve's grin was enough to make Smudge sear black spots onto the shoulder of Jig's cloak. "You conquered Avery. As ruler of this town, it's your duty to stay and defend it. To the death, if necessary."

CHAPTER 11

~~~~~~~~~~

*T*he sloped paving stones around the temple were designed to draw people toward the entrance, where a woman in dark red robes stood waiting. The outline of her silver-trimmed mask suggested a skull.

The domed temple was taller than the surrounding buildings. The arched entryway made those who passed through look like children. Bits of metal had been mixed into the mortar between the stones, causing them to sparkle in the sunlight. "He stole that from me," Autumnstar muttered.

A marble path inside descended to a blazing fire in the middle of the building. Black smoke rose from the top of the temple, the deathpath of whoever's funeral they celebrated today. The smoke was said to guide the soul to the star of Noc.

"My star," Autumnstar muttered. He had stood outside since before the ceremony, watching, trying to decide what to do. Finally, he turned to the priestess. "The masks are a bit much, don't you think?"

"My mask?" She touched one bony cheek.

"Robes the color of blood. Skull masks." Upon closer inspection, the masks appeared to be painted clay. Heavy, hot, and uncomfortable.

"Our garments are a sign of respect. The masks are a reminder that death walks among us." Her voice held the certainty of youth.

The fire turned those within the temple to shadows. Autumnstar could see several acolytes tossing damp straw onto the fire, sending up new plumes of black smoke. Those nearest the fire did their best to smother their coughs. "Do you think Noc would mind if you wore trousers? A loose shawl, maybe? With a nice hat to protect you from the sun."

She drew a deep breath, visibly trying to compose herself, then extended a hand in a well-practiced gesture of welcome. "Most people come to worship in the twilight of their years. Perhaps you've felt the breath of Noc, heard his whispered call? Many choose to donate to the temple, in the hope of turning Noc's eye from their—"

Autumnstar dug a square coin from his purse and pressed it into her palm. "I hate to break it to you, but the breath of Noc always smelled of fish. He spent too much time eating seafood with Ipsep."

Even through the mask, Autumnstar could see the priestess struggling with his words. He grinned and stepped closer to the entrance. Being careful not to cross the threshold, he pointed to a series of carvings on the inside of the arch. "Tell me, who is this poor creature here? The one writhing in agony beneath Noc's lightning."

"Ah, the challenges." *The priestess straightened her robes, clearly relieved to be discussing something familiar.* "During the War of Shadows, Noc faced fifteen challenges before conquering death itself. Here he throws down one of the demons sent to—"

"War of Shadows?" *Autumnstar shook his head in disbelief.* "Is that what they're calling it?"

"Named after the demons who attacked from the darkness."

"Demons, eh?" *Autumnstar ran his fingers over the carving.* "Awfully handsome, for a demon. The nose is a bit off, though. Does anyone know the poor creature's name?"

"When Noc slew the demons, he erased their names from the scrolls of—"

"He slew them all, did he?" Autumnstar grimaced. *"Whoever carved this got Noc wrong. His ears stick out like paddles from a boat. You'll see when you look upon him."*

Autumnstar stared at the fire. A part of him wanted nothing more than to pass through that archway, to take the single step that would place him within Noc's domain. Revealing himself to Noc would put an end to centuries of weariness and solitude. Not to mention giving the priests and worshipers quite the show. But now that he was here, he couldn't bring himself to take that final step.

Other acolytes lurked around the edge of the temple, rushing to and fro without a sound. Autumnstar leaned in to watch as one collected a donation from a little girl and her mother, then disappeared into the shadows by the wall.

"Be not afraid." In what was clearly meant to be a helpful gesture, one intended to aid an old man in conquering his fear, the priestess took Autumnstar's arm and pulled him toward the arch.

Autumnstar twisted, but his aged body wasn't fast enough. He was already off-balance, and the priestess was strong and determined.

Autumnstar stumbled into Noc's temple.

They found the goblins trapped behind what Jig guessed was a bakery, judging from the foul smell of bread. Jig couldn't see his goblins through the humans, but he could hear their cries, both frightened and defiant.

The closest humans were armed with shovels, pitchforks, axes, and other makeshift weapons. They followed a young man in a leather apron, holding an enormous hammer in each hand.

"It's always the blacksmiths," Genevieve said, shaking her head. "Something about working at the forge all day melts their brains, makes them dream about being heroes."

Darnak stood in the middle of the crowd, bellowing, "Stand down, all of you!"

The blacksmith was the first to respond. "Let us finish them!"

"You want to prove yourself, you're welcome to try that hammer against me." Darnak folded his arms and waited. The others backed away to give him space. "Otherwise, you'd best be obeying the orders of your princess."

The smith lowered his hammer. One of the goblins promptly attacked, and the smith smashed his arm.

"Lower your weapons," Jig yelled, his voice pitifully weak compared to Darnak's. Now that the humans had spread out, he could see a line of soldiers on the other side of the goblins. The blacksmith must have sent someone to free them from the stables.

"Those of you who wish to stay can do so," Genevieve said. The humans fell silent when they realized who was speaking. "You can join me on the walls of Avery, to defend this town against Billa the Bloody and her army. Given the thousands of monsters Billa commands, I will need every last man willing to bear arms to help protect our fair town. You there, you hold your shovel like a warrior. Clearly you would be an asset to—"

The man in question dropped his shovel. "Sorry, Highness. I've got the gout." He limped a few steps and shrugged.

A goblin warrior grinned and started to lunge at him, only to fall squealing when Trok stabbed him in the leg. Trok stepped on the other goblin's ear, pinning him to the ground for good measure. "Your commander said to lower your weapons."

"I don't understand," said the goblin, struggling in vain to pull his ear out from beneath Trok's boot. This was Dimak, one of the wolf-riders. "I thought we were taking this town for Billa! Now we're working with the humans?"

Tell Braf to bring Gratz out. Jig turned to Genevieve and whispered, "If they don't believe me, order your people to kill them."

"You would kill your own warriors?" Genevieve asked.

"Better than letting them kill me."

Gratz shivered and squirmed as Braf and Relka dragged him up the road. He was still bare-chested. His face was bruised and bloody from being thrown into a tree.

Jig took a deep breath. He was fairly sure the goblins from his lair would listen to him, even if they didn't believe what he said. The wolf-riders from Billa's army could be harder to convince. But this was the best chance he was likely to get. "Billa the Bloody plans to betray us."

"Don't listen to that traitorous runt," Gratz yelled. "Follow him, and you'll be every bit as guilty of mutiny as he is! Billa will have your heads on spears. She'll eat your livers, every last one of you!"

"That's a lot of liver," Braf said. He tugged Gratz around.

"And don't call Jig a runt," Relka added, smacking Gratz's head.

Jig pointed to the scar on Gratz's arm. "Those are runes. They're part of a larger spell. Billa means to use magic to kill the goblins. The kobolds too, probably."

"Why would Billa kill her own soldiers?" To Jig's surprise, the question came from one of the humans, not a goblin.

"Because she's an orc, and we're only goblins." Jig's words sounded harsh and bitter, even to his own ears. "Do you really believe Billa cares what happens to us?"

Low, angry muttering spread through the goblins. Angry at Billa, or at Jig? He couldn't tell.

"Billa has led us to one victory after another," Gratz said.

"Her victories," shouted Relka. "And who does she send to take the brunt of those battles?"

"Goblins!"

Jig thought about the marching formation on the road. Any attack would have decimated the front lines—the goblins—leaving most of the orcs well-protected. "I'm tired of being used," Jig said. He hoped Shadowstar was listening too. "Anyone who wants to keep fighting for Billa the Bloody, pick up your weapons and have at it. The rest of you, put away your swords."

Nobody made any move to attack the humans. More importantly, nobody tried to attack Jig.

"They believed you," Genevieve said, her voice quiet. "What did you do to earn such trust from goblins?"

Jig shook his head. "Trust had nothing to do with it. They're outnumbered and surrounded. Goblins will believe just about anything if it keeps them alive."

Jig hunched his shoulders and tried not to look at anyone as he followed Genevieve and Darnak deeper into Avery. Humans glared at him from the windows. Other humans were already hurrying through town, their belongings bundled on their backs or dragging behind on crude sleds.

They came to an intersection of roads and paths, coming together like threads in the middle of a spider's web. Triangular gardens filled the spaces between the roads. A single tree grew in each garden, the branches twining together overhead to provide a bit of shelter from the snow. Even with most of the leaves fallen from the branches, the trees were large enough to provide a makeshift roof.

Unfortunately, the trees were also full of birds. Instead of being crusted with snow, the ground was now layered in fallen leaves and bird droppings.

"Elfhawks," Darnak said. "Back when Avery belonged to the elves, they raised their messenger birds here. When the elves left, the birds remained. They're none too fond of humans, for the most part. A lot like elves, really. Over the years, they've gotten a bit out of control."

The hawks were as blue as the sky. Black markings along the chest and face made them look as though they were wearing tiny masks, or maybe spectacles. As Jig watched, two hawks hopped from the branches and swooped toward a family dragging their sled along the road. They snatched a carelessly bound rabbit from the sled. By the time the family reacted, the hawks had already carried their prize back to the tree.

"They're brilliant hunters," Genevieve said. "But they're even better thieves. They're also the fastest things in the sky, short of a dragon. Smart, too, which means they're the perfect messenger."

Darnak sat down in the middle of the road and pulled out a sheet of parchment. He dug through his pack until he found a pot of ink and a quill. He uncapped the quill and penned a quick message, then handed quill and parchment to Genevieve, who signed it.

Genevieve rolled the message into a tube. She glanced at Jig. "I need a strip of your cloak."

"What?" Jig stepped back.

"The birds are trained by color. Different ribbons signify different destinations. My father's color is purple. Normally we use silk ribbons, but the birds got in through a window and stole them all last week." She pointed toward the top of one tree, where the most colorful nest Jig had ever seen sat amid the branches.

Darnak was already slicing a strip from the bottom of Jig's cloak. He gave it to Genevieve, who tied a tight loop around the parchment, then knotted a larger loop in the rest of the material.

"How do the hawks carry—" Jig began.

Genevieve held out the message so the loop hung down. Instantly, four of the closest hawks dove into the air. Three veered away, and the fourth shot past. His head fit neatly through the loop, ripping the message from Genevieve's grasp.

Jig could feel Smudge burrowing deeper into his pocket

The hawk was already shrinking in the distance, the message hanging from its makeshift necklace.

"He won't stop until he reaches my father," Genevieve said.

"Good," said Jig. Relief made him dizzy. Prince Theodore would bring the rod and stop Billa, Noc would be safe, and Jig would finally be able to go home again.

Genevieve turned to Darnak. "Close the east and west gates. Post double guards on the north and south. I want men on the walls as well."

"What?" Jig stepped back. "I thought Theodore was going to come stop her."

"Billa is too close, lad," said Darnak. He unstrapped his pack and pulled out a long leather tube. "It will be easier to show you with some maps."

With that, he unhooked his cloak and laid it on the road. He then began spreading out sheet after sheet of parchment, weighing the corners with fallen sticks, the ink pot, a dagger, and anything else he could find.

Each map was a work of art. Darnak's own art, judging from the way he puffed up as he unrolled each one. It was a miracle he didn't burst his shirt.

"Hey, that looks like a goblin," Jig said, pointing to a tiny blue figure painted among the mountains. Jig squinted through his spectacles, trying to comprehend the mess of colors and lines and tiny notes, all written in Darnak's painstakingly perfect handwriting.

"Your lair," Genevieve said.

Once the map was secure, Darnak pulled a wooden box from his pack. He opened it to reveal a collection of tiny metal figures. He plucked out a blue-painted goblin, which he set down by a star marked AVERY. He set two armored soldiers beside the blue goblin. The three figures completely blocked out Avery. "Call it about a hundred or so fighters, all told."

"Is this really the best time to be playing with toys?" Jig asked.

Genevieve smirked. Darnak looked indignant.

"They're not toys. They're tools. Markers. Very valuable for visualizing tactics and strategy."

Jig picked up the goblin figurine. "Why did you paint blood on his fangs?"

"Give me that." Darnak snatched the goblin back and slammed it into place. "Now the rest of Billa's army followed you up to the lair, right?" He pulled out several thin stone blocks, each with the number 1,000 carved into the top. The sides were painted with various monsters. Darnak stacked four of them by the lair.

"King Wendel and Theodore will be coming from the capital." More blocks went down on the other side of the mountains, along with two more tiny metal figures. One wore a gold-painted crown, the other a silver crown. "He should be about here when he receives our message."

To Jig's eye, the armies looked equally matched, and equally distant from the tiny force at Avery.

"Even in good weather, it would take an extra day for Theodore's men to get through the pass," Darnak said, pointing to the mountains.

"Assuming he believes me." Genevieve stared at the map. "Knowing my father, he'll toss my warning aside as the frightened nonsense of a naive child."

"We'll mine that vein when we come to it," said Darnak. "Jig, do you have any guess when Billa would have left the lair?"

Jig shook his head. "She might not even know I escaped yet."

She knows, said Shadowstar. *Isa knows. They're hunting us even now, Jig. I've done my best to protect you, but she's stronger than I am.*

Jig swallowed and said, "But she's probably on her way.

Darnak tugged his beard. "She'll have an easy march up the road." He moved Billa's blocks toward Avery. His jostling knocked the goblin figurine onto its back. Jig hoped that wasn't an omen. "Billa could be here as soon as tonight."

Darnak moved the silver-crowned figure through

the mountains, muttering to himself. "Teddy's fast, no question. And his elves can run over the snow like it's good, solid earth, even if they look like fancy-prance twits when they do it."

"We can hold Avery," Genevieve whispered. "Billa has no heavy siege equipment, from our last reports. Avery's walls are strong. The gates are reinforced with elf magic. We only need to stop her for a day, maybe two."

"You couldn't even stop me." Jig glanced at Genevieve's face, then scooted out of reach of her sword. "What about the southern side of the valley? Won't the elves—"

Genevieve shook her head. "The elves will do nothing unless Billa violates their borders. My mother negotiated a treaty with them years ago. No elf can set foot in human lands without permission."

Jig stared at the map. "So give them permission!"

"First you'd have to convince my father," said Genevieve. "He already thinks they're trying to steal his son."

She set the two human figurines in front of Avery. "We'll post our men on the walls." She reached for the goblin. "Your goblins will need to work on the walls, cutting the last of the steelthorn. We should be able to finish— What is it now?"

"I don't understand." Jig studied the map more closely. "What goblins?"

"Your goblins," Darnak said. "They're not much, but they've done a nice job preparing the wall. We won't be tying them up this time, of course."

"Wait, you think they're still here?" Darnak and Genevieve had been standing right there when Jig told the goblins about Billa's betrayal. They heard him tell everyone what was coming, but they still expected the goblins to be here? "They're probably in the woods by now, running away as fast as they can."

Genevieve frowned at Jig. "*You're* still here."

Jig said nothing. Where could he go to hide from a goddess?

"What about that one?" Darnak asked, pointing up the road. "She didn't flee either."

Jig didn't even bother to look. He knew who it had to be. The one goblin he would prefer had abandoned him.

"I brought this for you," Relka said, handing him a hard, brown roll with bits of burned leaves on top. "They say it's an elf biscuit. I'd have made you a real elf biscuit, but they wouldn't let me near their stoves. Also, we don't have any fresh elf."

Jig took a quick bite of the biscuit, which tasted about how he would have expected. If this was what elves ate, no wonder they were so skinny.

Darnak sighed. "Without the rest of those blue-skinned nuisances, we'll need to spread our men even thinner to watch the walls."

"Where are the goblins going to go?" asked Relka, staring at the map.

Jig, Darnak, and Genevieve all turned to stare.

"They haven't run away yet?" Jig asked.

"Most of them are resting in the stables." Relka shrugged. "I guess they got used to it. The straw is warmer than the caves back home, and—"

"They're *resting*?"

"Well, you didn't order them to do anything else," Relka pointed out.

Jig searched for something to say, but the words wouldn't come. The wolf-riders had spent enough time in Billa's army that they might have lost their sense of self-preservation, but why would the goblins from the lair still be here? Unless their minds had been dulled by eating too many pickles.

"Come on," said Darnak, rolling up his maps. "We'd best be getting back. Leaving your soldiers with nothing to do is a recipe for bloodshed, as any commander should know."

As if goblins ever needed an excuse for more bloodshed.

Genevieve was the first to spot the smoke. She broke into a run, leaving the others struggling to catch up.

They arrived to find the goblins gathered around a small fire in the middle of the road. Several humans stood nearby, looking . . . nauseated.

Trok turned around when he heard them approaching. "General Jig!"

The other goblins cheered. The humans tensed and reached for their weapons. In the distance, the wolves broke into howls.

"Dimak," Trok snapped. "I thought I ordered you to feed those beasts."

Dimak hunched his shoulders. "Sorry, sir." He grabbed something from the fire, then turned and fled toward the source of the howling.

"What's he going to feed them?" Jig asked. He glanced at the uneaten elf biscuit in his hand, but trying to feed such a thing to wolves would only enrage them further.

"Grappok and I had a bit of trouble deciding who should be in charge, with you and Relka both gone." Trok flexed his arm, and Jig saw two bloody fang marks at the shoulder. "I won."

"I don't understand," Jig said. Despite his nervousness, he found himself edging closer to the cook fire. The air had grown colder, until his fingers seemed to burn from the wind. "Wait, why did you call me general? And what are you still doing here? I thought you'd have left the city by now."

"It seemed only right to promote you," said Trok. "Seeing how this is officially your army, not Billa's."

"We're going to teach Billa the Bloody a lesson about goblins," somebody said. The others cheered.

"But she has thousands of monsters," Jig said. "She'll slaughter every one of you."

"See?" said the same goblin. "General Jig, he tells it like it is! No lies from this one."

They cheered yet again, idiots to the last.

Jig grabbed Trok's arm and dragged him away from the others. "This is madness." Jig kept his voice low, pitched so nobody else would overhear. "You've seen Billa's army. I can understand humans making a suicidal stand. They're stupid that way. But we're goblins. We survive by running away when we're outnumbered. Or when we're evenly matched. Or anytime we don't have a twenty-to-one advantage, really."

"You stayed," Trok said.

"I'm stupid too. And I can't run away, because Isa would—"

"You're not stupid," Trok said, shaking his head. "You're a whiny, puny, irritating little runt. But you're not stupid."

"Oh, no?" Jig pointed in the general direction of the gate. "Weren't you there when I led everyone against Genevieve's soldiers? A handful of wolf-riders against an entire city?"

"Shut up, sir." Trok glanced at the other goblins. "You think we haven't been talking about you? How any one of us could break you with our bare hands? How Porak used to dangle you over the garbage crack by your legs, or slip bat guano into your drink when you weren't looking?"

"Wait. Porak did what?" And here Jig hadn't thought anything could ruin his appetite more than that elf biscuit.

"I was there the day you came back from slaying Straum," said Trok. "I remember how those adventurers followed you. You led them away from the lair and beat them all by yourself. I remember how you helped everyone fight off those pixies and their ogre slaves, too. I was one of the goblins you sent to help the hobgoblins fight the ogres. I figured we were all dead, and I'd rather die quickly, smashed by an ogre's club, than face the nastiness those pixies were dealing out. Blasted bugs and their magic. But you, you went down there and killed every last one of them."

He grabbed the biscuit from Jig's hand and tossed it into the snow. "You're the one who helped me and Relka escape from this lot," he said, pointing toward Genevieve. "You got us away and found Billa. Then, when she turned out to be a conniving, backstabbing orc, you escaped again. You killed Silverfang, and then you came back here and took an entire town away from the humans."

"They took it back," Jig said.

"Doesn't matter." Trok spat. "I'm not as smart as you, and I know it. But I like to fight. We all do. We're warriors, Jig. It's what we do. And we like to win. That doesn't happen too often when you're a goblin."

That was true enough.

"You're a pathetic excuse for a warrior, hardly worth killing, even for the food. But you're clever. If you're staying, so are we. Even if we lose, it should be a great fight." Trok grinned. "Besides, if you stay here all alone and get yourself killed, who's going to make me chief when Grell dies?"

He dug his claws into Jig's arm and dragged him back toward the fire. "Now hurry up and get your share of Grappok."

Jig shivered in the darkness of the stables. He pulled his blanket tighter over his head, tucking his ears in for warmth. Even if he hadn't been too scared to sleep, the snoring of the other goblins would have kept him awake. How many hours had he lain here staring into the darkness and trying not to think about what was to come? He was almost grateful when Darnak opened the door and whispered, "Jig? Genevieve's wanting to see you."

Jig's teeth chattered. "It's about Billa, isn't it? She's coming."

Darnak was little more than a silhouette, but Jig could see him tilting his head to one side like a bird. "Now, how would you be knowing that?"

"The cold. It's getting worse."

"Aye. Something unnatural in that wind." Darnak waited while Jig gathered his blanket and retrieved Smudge from the tiny web he had woven at the base of the wall.

Outside, lanterns flickered by the gate. Even as Jig watched, one of the lanterns died, extinguished by the wind. "Where are we going?"

Darnak pointed.

"Oh, no." Whereas the outer wall was covered in thorns and a few scattered flowers, the interior was formed of a different kind of tree, covered in smooth, slippery bark. But the tree Darnak indicated was wider than the rest, with some sort of lichen growing on it. The brown disks were spaced evenly to the ground, each one large enough for a man's foot.

"Don't worry about it," Darnak said. He planted a boot on the lowest shelf of lichen, grabbed a higher one, and pulled himself up. "Took me weeks to get used to this place." He shook his head. "Sticking a dwarf up a tree is a violation of nature, like expecting fish to fly and build nests."

Fear dried Jig's mouth and throat. Though that was better than his nose, which was frozen on the inside from the cold. If the lichen could support Darnak's weight, with all his armor and everything he carried in that pack, surely it would hold Jig.

Unless Darnak's weight weakened it. Jig looked back at the stables. "Are you sure Genevieve doesn't want to come down here instead?"

"Don't make me carry you," said Darnak.

Gritting his teeth, Jig grabbed the lowest lichen and hauled himself after the dwarf.

The wind was even stronger atop the wall than it was below. Jig would have been blown clear off if Darnak hadn't seized his wrist.

Genevieve stood nearby, blankets and furs protecting her from the cold. There were no lights.

"Did you enjoy your rest, goblin?" Genevieve asked.

"No." Jig clung to Darnak's hand as he took his first step. The platform was nothing but sticks and leaves, woven tightly together. There were enough gaps to allow the snow to slip through, but the branches were still wet and slippery. They creaked and moved under his weight. "I miss my lair."

Darnak chuckled.

The top of the wall was wide enough for two people to stand side by side, though it required both people to stand closer to the edges than Jig liked. Waist-high railings ran along either side of the platform. Jig crouched against the inner railing. The branches and leaves were woven tightly enough to block the worst of the wind. A thick vine ran horizontally along the top, a railing of sorts. Jig gripped it with both hands and tried not to move.

His ears perked. He could just make out the sound of drums in the distance.

"Are the gates scaled?" Genevieve asked.

Darnak nodded. "We didn't have time to finish preparing the steelthorn, but the lower portion is clear. Nobody's going to be after climbing these walls. The trees might not be as strong as dwarf stone, but they'll do."

Genevieve glanced back at Jig. "Billa's army is coming."

"He knows," said Darnak.

Jig took a deep breath, then lurched across the platform to the outer railing. Staring out at Billa's army, he wondered if it would be better to simply fling himself off the wall and be done with it.

Torches and lanterns burned like tiny fireflies, stretching back along the road as far as Jig could see. Was it his imagination, or had Billa's army grown since Jig fled? Maybe it just seemed larger compared to the paltry numbers here inside the town walls. His ears twitched with each beat of the war drums.

Genevieve pressed a wooden tube to her eye. "Goblins march in the front of the column. She has kobolds scouting ahead and to either side."

"What is that?" Jig asked, pointing to the tube.

"The lenses provide a closer view of our foe," said Genevieve. She barely even blinked as she stared out at the approaching army. "Goblin, how will your men react in the face of this threat? Do you trust them to obey orders and do their duty?"

Jig stared at her. "They're goblins, remember?"

Genevieve sighed. "Billa seems to have no problem controlling her troops. Perhaps the goblins need a stronger leader."

Jig agreed completely, but the disdain in her voice made his hands clench. "Do you know how Billa raised such a large army, Princess?" Jig asked. "She told them . . . she told *us* that if we joined her, we'd never have to worry about people like you or your brothers again."

Genevieve started to say something, then bit her lip and turned back toward the approaching monsters. "We'll have to hold them for at least a day. Darnak, get every available archer to the walls. Nobody attacks until I give the order. Our arrows and quarrels are too limited. Goblin, rouse your men. Position them along the wall in pairs."

Jig didn't move. "And what will you do with us when this is over?"

"I'll figure it out then. Assuming any of us survive." She raised the scope to her eye again. "None of the reports said anything about winged creatures in Billa's army."

Jig rubbed his spectacles on his cloak. Given the condition of his cloak, that wasn't much of an improvement. But by the time he hooked the frames back over his ears, he could make out dark shapes against the moonlit clouds.

"Dragons?" Darnak guessed. Jig edged closer to the ladder.

"The wings are the wrong shape," Genevieve said. "And the tails are more birdlike than serpentine."

"They're coming from the north," Darnak said. "If Billa sent a force through the mountains, our scouts would have known."

"Those are elfhawks," Genevieve said softly. The hand holding the scope dropped to her side. "They carry men upon their backs."

"Theodore."

Genevieve's lips twisted into a sour expression. "He must have used the rod on those birds."

As bad as it had been riding Bastard, the mere idea of riding a giant elfhawk made Jig dizzy. He grabbed the railing for balance as he watched the birds approach. He could see the shapes of the riders, each one bent low against bird's neck.

The first rider drew a sword that burned with orange fire. Why didn't goblins ever get the magical weapons? The rider raised his weapon in salute as he circled toward the wall. Prince Theodore, Jig guessed. He couldn't discern the rider's features, but he doubted the prince's pride would allow anyone else to lead.

" 'Ware the goblin!" Theodore shouted. His hawk swooped toward the wall.

No, not toward the wall. Toward Jig. Talons the size of Jig's foot reached out.

Jig screamed and leaped away, barely avoiding the prince's magical sword.

Unfortunately, Jig's desperate leap took him to the gap in the railing. He tried to twist around, to catch the lichen ladder and stop his fall.

He missed.

CHAPTER 12

~~~~~◆~~~~~

*T*he priest in the middle of the temple missed a beat
as Tymalous Autumnstar fell. He lay sprawled on
the worn tile floor, waiting for Noc's response. Would
it be the lightning again, or had Noc developed new
skills since their last battle? Autumnstar was betting on
the lightning. Noc had never been the most creative of
the gods. Hopefully Noc wouldn't incinerate too many
of his followers in the process.

"Are you hurt?" The young priestess knelt beside
him and touched his arm. She had stripped off her
mask, and her brown face revealed both her youth and
her terror. No doubt there were rules against assaulting
the elderly. "Forgive me. I only wanted to help you
face your fear."

Autumnstar peeked around the temple as the chant-
ing resumed. Noc *was* present, as much as any god ever
was in a temple. But Autumnstar couldn't sense any
change in the death god's attention.

"Isn't that why you came?" the priestess asked. "To
prepare yourself for death?"

Autumnstar pushed himself to his feet. "I came
because . . . because I'm tired." Tired of being alone.
Tired of living as a mortal. Tired of being afraid.

Giddiness knotted his chest. For him to step into this
temple was like walking up to Noc and punching him

in the nose. Yet Autumnstar sensed nothing. "Noc doesn't see me."

"All come to Noc's domain," the priestess said, her voice stern. "Your time is written on the scrolls."

"Noc erased my name from the scrolls," Autumnstar whispered, remembering what the priestess had said before. He started to laugh. "He cursed us, sentenced us to be forgotten . . . and now he doesn't remember me."

People turned to stare. The priest in the center of the temple stopped again. The priestess tried to take Autumnstar's arm and pull him back outside, but he tugged free.

"I'm right here, Noc!" Centuries of hiding, all for nothing. He was invisible. Tears and laughter mixed, until he was gasping for breath.

The shadows shifted as the acolytes ran toward him. Autumnstar hadn't even noticed them lurking in the dark corners. He raced down the aisle, past rows of stunned worshipers, until he reached the center of the temple. He dodged the high priest and climbed onto the edge of the fire pit. "Tymalous Autumnstar lives!"

The fire flared higher, even as the air chilled.

"Whoops." Autumnstar bit his lip. Perhaps that last defiant shout had been a little too much. He gingerly lowered himself from the pit and allowed the acolytes to grab his arms.

Halfway out of the temple, he turned to the priestess. "This body has served me for more than a hundred years. Take care of it. The coins in my pouch should make up for any disturbance I've caused."

The acolytes caught his body as it fell, but Tymalous Autumnstar was already gone. He would have to remember not to flaunt his survival. Noc's curse hadn't blinded him completely. Like Noc's own acolytes, Tymalous Autumnstar would have to keep to the shadows.

The sound of bells was muted as he stepped through the broken doorway of his ruined temple. Tymalous Autumnstar—Tymalous Shadowstar—was home!

*   *   *

Jig's left nostril was on fire.

The first thing he saw when he opened his eyes was Smudge's fuzzy backside. Four of the spider's legs clung to the edges of Jig's spectacles. Smudge reached out again, searing Jig's nose with one of his forelegs.

"Stop that," Jig mumbled. Smudge backed away. Had he been trying to rouse Jig, or simply checking to see if he was safe to eat?

"Jig!"

He tilted his head to see Darnak and Genevieve climbing down the wall. Prince Theodore was already on the ground.

Why was it that every time Jig faced a prince, he ended up flat on his back? He started to sit up, then gasped. His knee felt like someone had smashed it with a rock.

"Easy, lad," Darnak said. "You're lucky you didn't land on your head! A fall like that can be fatal."

"Goblins have thick skulls," Jig said. He reached down to touch his knee. All he learned was that his shoulder was in equally bad shape. He lay back, grabbing his shoulder with his other hand and drawing on Shadowstar's healing magic. His jaw clenched. The pain of rebuilding a joint was bad enough, but couldn't Shadowstar do something about the popping sounds coming from his shoulder?

"Stand aside, Darnak," Theodore demanded, waving that burning sword in the air. He strode toward Jig, and his eyes widened. "By the First Oak, there are more!"

Jig's ear swiveled, tracking the footsteps of approaching goblins. "What did you do to Jig?" Relka yelled.

"Everyone calm down," Darnak shouted. His voice made Jig think of a mountain cracking. Darnak hurried to put himself between Jig and the prince. "They're not your enemy, Theodore."

"They're goblins," Theodore said.

"They're deserters from Billa's army." Genevieve

moved to stand beside Darnak. "Jig risked his life to bring warning of Billa's plans. Plans that your scouts failed to uncover."

"And you believed them?"

Genevieve hesitated only briefly. "Darnak's magic showed him to be telling the truth. And Billa *is* coming to Avery. Really, Theodore. Haven't you more important things to do than wag your elven blade at our allies?".

Jig tested his arm, wondering when he had been promoted to *ally*.

"But they're goblins," Theodore said again, as if Genevieve had somehow overlooked the blue skin and big ears and fangs.

"Forgive the interruption, Prince, but you're looking a bit changed from the last time we spoke," said Darnak.

Jig blinked. He hadn't noticed before. Atop the wall, he had been more concerned with avoiding the bird's claws and the prince's sword. He squinted through his snow-flecked spectacles.

"The Rod of Creation is a gift," Theodore said. He pointed to the top of the wall, where huge elfhawks perched. "How else could I have reached Avery in time to save you all from Billa's wrath?"

"And the ears?" Darnak asked.

Theodore tossed his hair—which was far longer and lighter than before—back over his shoulder. He ran his fingertips over the sharp lines of his pointed ears and smiled. "The rod has helped me to become my true self."

"Eighteen years I helped raise the whelp," Darnak muttered. "Changed his diapers, forged his first sword, even called upon the power of Earthmaker to clear up those pimples. *Four years* of pimples. And he turns himself into an *elf*."

The prince ignored him and patted his belt. The tip of a wooden stick protruded from a purple scabbard. He sheathed his sword on his opposite hip. "I strengthened our armor, our weapons, even the skin of our bodies."

Theodore combed his fingers through his flowing hair. "Even elven hair is superior to our own. I've flown nonstop since we received your message, and look! Nary a tangle!" He grimaced and said, "Though it does tend to flick in one's eyes. I'll have to braid it before we attack. So tell me, dear Sister, would you like me to do something about that nose of yours?"

"I have a better idea," Genevieve said, perfectly calm. "Why don't you take that rod and—"

"All that power, and you couldn't even give yourself a decent beard," Darnak snapped.

Before Theodore could respond, Genevieve asked, "What did the king say about all this? Our father isn't terribly fond of magic these days. Or of elves, for that matter."

Theodore flushed. "I haven't exactly told him. But, Sister, look at me! I'm stronger than before. Faster." He drew the Rod of Creation and raised it overhead. Jig tried to scoot away, but the effort made his knee feel like tiny dwarves were pounding it with great big hammers. "The goblins had all this within their grasp. They too could have transformed themselves into something great, had they only known what it was they had."

"But then we wouldn't have been goblins," Jig said.

Theodore turned and stared. Jig got the impression he had completely forgotten about the goblin's presence. "Such shortsightedness will be the downfall of your race, goblin."

He whistled, and two of the giant elfhawks swooped down to land beside him. The rest of Theodore's elves simply jumped from the wall. They landed easily in the snow, showing no sign of strain or worry about a drop that had nearly killed Jig. Stupid elves.

The two elfhawks were heavily laden with weapons and armor. One of the elves began distributing wooden shields and helmets to the rest.

"Billa is a bloody fool." Theodore grinned at his own wit. "My elves and I shall soar down and destroy her. When our father's army arrives, they will find Billa's forces in chaos."

"There's a mite bit more to this battle than meets the eye, lad," said Darnak. "Billa has magic of her own, and—"

"Billa is an orc," Theodore said. "Barely better than a goblin."

"She's an orc who has raised an army," Genevieve said. "An orc who has marched freely through our land, terrorizing our people and—"

"You worry too much, Sister." Theodore grinned. "You did well to summon me, but now your worries are over. Run along and prepare a suitable meal for me and my friends. A victory breakfast, to celebrate our triumph. Something hot." He slapped his stomach.

Genevieve's fingers twitched over her sword, but she stopped herself. "Father charged me with the protection of Avery. I should—"

"And a marvelous job you've done," Theodore said. "Your people are fled, and your town is infested with goblins. Father will be thrilled."

Genevieve's face turned a deeper shade of red. Darnak placed a hand on her forearm.

"Have your men gather food for our hawks as well," Theodore said, turning away. "Perhaps you could feed the goblins to them and solve two problems at once."

Genevieve waited until they were out of earshot, then turned to Relka. "Someone said you were some sort of chef."

Relka nodded.

"And what meal would you recommend for a prince, goblin?"

Relka rubbed her chin. "My favorite is charred rat with klak sauce, garnished in black-edge mushrooms. The tails are especially good."

Genevieve's lips tightened into a smile. "What are you waiting for? Prince Theodore has requested a meal. I imagine you'll find plenty of rats raiding the granary."

*   *   *

Jig and the other goblins stood by the edge of the road, watching Theodore and his elves mount their hawks. Many of the hawks had perched on the rooftops, forcing their elves to scale the buildings. Not that this slowed the elves down at all.

"If they fail, I've got dibs on the dark meat," Trok said softly.

Jig ignored him. Theodore had the Rod of Creation. All he had to do was reach Billa and transform her into something harmless. Billa was the only one who could set off the spells carved into her goblin and kobold officers. With her dead. . . .

His shoulders slumped. With Billa dead, the humans would have an easy time of it. Wendel's army would arrive in a day or so to drive the monsters back into the caves and tunnels. For those who survived, everything would return to the way it had been.

Billa had the support of a goddess, but she was no goddess herself. Jig had seen the power of that rod. Prince Theodore wouldn't have to come within range of Billa's magical sword. He could swoop down, transforming Billa and her friends at will, or at least until he got tired. The rod could take a lot out of whoever wielded it.

As far as Jig knew, Billa had no flying monsters. Arrows and stones would do little against Theodore's magically hardened armor. Jig still remembered the way ordinary weapons had bounced away from that elf scout in the woods.

So why was Jig still here when he should be getting as far from Avery as he could?

He couldn't concentrate. He flattened his ears against the sound of the wolves. Ever since the hawks had swooped in, the blasted things hadn't stopped yowling. And then there was Billa's army. Thousands of monsters, all shouting and jeering and beating their armor as they approached Avery.

It's part of their strategy. They're trying to unnerve you, Shadowstar said.

"It's working!" Jig pulled up the hood of his cloak. The wind promptly blew it from his head. Yanking it back, Jig turned to scowl at the hawks. Theodore had climbed onto his hawk, tucking his legs beneath the wings and waving to the human soldiers. He made an impressive figure, illuminated by the rising sun.

"Circle a few times to gain some height," Darnak was saying. "The higher you fly, the faster your dive. Don't spend a lot of time hovering before you attack. Hovering takes too much energy, and you don't want to tire the hawks. And—"

The hawk spread its wings and shrieked loudly enough to overpower even the wolves. It took a few quick steps, then slammed its wings, launching itself into the air. The other hawks followed, hopping from the rooftops and causing goblins to scream and dive out of the way.

Darnak hurried after them, still shouting bird advice as he climbed the wall.

Jig continued to pace as he watched the hawks fly away. Something squished beneath his foot. His boot slid out from beneath him, and he waved his arms to keep from falling. His knee twinged with pain. Apparently he hadn't done a perfect job of healing the joint.

He glanced down to see another of the "gifts" Theodore's elfhawks had deposited throughout Avery. Giant birds meant giant droppings. Jig groaned and hobbled over to scrape the boot on a nearby house.

"It could be worse," said Relka as she hurried toward him. She pointed to one of the goblins who had thrown himself to the ground.

Jig grimaced. "Somebody get him a rag. And weren't you supposed to be preparing a meal for Prince Theodore?"

"I was," Relka said. "That's why I came." She held out a blackened rat. "I thought you might like a taste."

Jig snatched the rat from her hand. The meat was still warm, and he gobbled it down, surprised at how hungry he was. When had he last eaten? He forced

himself to slow down, ripping off a bit of tail for
Smudge.

Smudge flattened himself to Jig's cloak, clinging
with six legs while he reached for the meat with his
forelegs. Jig turned his back to the wind, blocking the
worst of it. Even with all those extra legs, the wind
could still rip Smudge from his shoulder and fling the
poor fire-spider—

"Oh, no." Jig's stomach knotted. He shoved both
Smudge and the rat into a pocket and spun toward
the wall. The elfhawks were already gone. Humans
cheered them on from atop the wall.

"What's wrong?" Relka asked.

Jig ran toward the wall. "Darnak! Genevieve! You
have to stop the prince!" The wind swept his words
away.

Cursing, Jig scrambled up the lichen shelves of the
wall as fast as he could. The walkway was crowded
with humans, all staring out at Billa's army. Jig shoved
past them until he spotted Darnak. The dwarf stood
atop his backpack, still watching the hawks. Genevieve
was with him, her face stone. She held one of those
elven scopes to her eye, watching Theodore's progress.

"Darnak, you have to call them back!" Jig shouted.

Genevieve snorted. "Even if he were close enough
to hear, my brothers have never been fond of others
telling them what to do. And I certainly can't imagine
Theodore would take orders from a goblin."

Jig squeezed his way between them and stood up
on his toes. The front edge of Billa's army had reached
the distant fields. Goblins and kobolds spread to either
side. Some loosed arrows and threw spears, but their
attacks had no effect on Theodore's hawks. A few of
the humans cheered as those same missiles fell back
down upon the monsters' heads.

Several of the elves drew swords that glowed like
Theodore's. Jig had half expected them to start firing
arrows back at the monsters, but apparently not even
an elf could aim a longbow and steer a giant hawk at
the same time.

"Billa's going to kill your brother if he doesn't turn back," said Jig.

Suddenly Jig had everyone's attention.

"What did you say?" asked Genevieve.

"It's Isa," Jig said.

Darnak frowned. "Who?"

Jig wanted to punch him. "The goddess Billa worships. *Goddess of the Winter Winds.*"

Darnak was the first to understand. He spun, nearly falling off his backpack. "Every last man into the field *now*! We have to—"

"Too late," Genevieve said.

Jig clung to the railing with both hands as a burst of frigid air fought to throw him down. In the valley, the elfhawks were flung to the ground as if they had been struck by a giant. They landed near the front of the orc lines. Some of the elves leaped down to fight. Others tried to urge their hawks into the air.

Beside Jig, Darnak leaned into the wind, his arms quivering as though he too were fighting to fly. Jig squatted to retrieve Genevieve's scope.

"It doesn't work," he complained.

Darnak reached over, swapped ends, and pressed the scope back into Jig's hand, all without looking away from the hawks.

This time when Jig looked through the scope, it was as if he stood on one of the farmhouse roofs, close enough to reach over and touch Theodore and his battered elves. That they had survived the crash at all was amazing, but none looked ready for battle.

The orcs cleared a circle as Billa strode toward them. The closest elves drew their glowing swords. The hammering of the wind robbed the elves of their usual grace. Billa, on the other hand, seemed untouched by the wind, which was completely unfair. And her sword had no trouble cutting through the elves' magical armor.

"Use the rod, you daft boy," Darnak shouted. "Use the bloody rod, damn you!"

As if he could hear Darnak's voice, Theodore

pulled the Rod of Creation from its sheath and pointed it at Billa.

Billa swung her sword.

"Earthmaker preserve us," Darnak whispered.

The Rod of Creation was the most powerful magical artifact Jig had ever seen. Which admittedly wasn't saying a lot. But Jig had seen what the rod could do. Created by Ellnorein, one of the greatest wizards in history, the rod had the power to create dragons and destroy mountains. For thousands of years, songs had praised its godlike magic.

Billa's sword sheared it in two as if it were nothing more than a rotted stick. A second blow, and Theodore fell. Billa stepped back, allowing her orcs to swarm over Theodore and his elves. Blue feathers as tall as a man swirled in the wind. A few of the elf-hawks fought their way free, wings pounding hard enough to knock their attackers back.

"Theodore," Genevieve whispered.

Billa turned toward the wall, seeming to look right at Jig.

Jig yelped and flung the scope away. He started to shove his way back to the ladder, but a gust of wind drove him to his knees.

He pressed his back to the railing for protection. Those nearest Jig crouched low, battered by the wind. Most of them were still pressed against the other railing, watching the prince's failed attack. So Jig was the first to notice as the snow swirled together, flakes clinging to one another until the shape before him began to resemble a tall, fluffy woman.

Get out of there, Jig.

How? Jig asked. *It's between me and the ladder!*

That's not an it, said Shadowstar. *That's Isa.*

Jig had already recognized her from the vision Shadowstar had shared. The snow packed tighter and tighter, forming ever-finer details. Isa's exposed skin turned clear as any stream. Icy fingers flexed and stretched. She appeared to wear a tight gown of snow, far too low-cut for this weather. The snow clung to her bulky form like silk.

"Hello, Jig." She glanced at Darnak, then turned her head to take in the rest of the humans gathered on the wall. Flakes of snow fell from her hair, reminding him a little of Braf. Braf had developed a nasty scalp condition lately, and even Shadowstar's magic was having trouble curing him.

Jig scooted to the side and tugged Darnak's jacket.

"Not now," Darnak said softly. The wind whipped his beard as he stared out at the field. His face was wet with tears.

Jig grabbed his beard and tugged hard.

"Eh? What's—" Darnak spun. "What in the name of Earthmaker's singed beard is that?"

Isa spread her arms, and the temperature dropped still further, until Jig had to close his mouth to keep his spit from freezing. He flattened his ears, then reached into his cloak to check on Smudge. The fire-spider was curled into a tight, fuzzy ball, and he wasn't moving. Jig cupped him in both hands and held him close to his chest.

"I am Isa of the Winter Winds. I am the Frost Maiden. It was I who first summoned the snows of the north, and it was I who banished them again at the end of winter."

"What did she say her name was?" Genevieve asked.

Isa sighed, sending a puff of frost from her mouth. "Never mind."

She's crazy, Shadowstar whispered. *Even a limited manifestation like this uses a great deal of magic. She could draw Noc's attention before she's ready.*

"I wanted to give you and your god one more chance to join me." Isa smiled at Jig, though the effect of those gleaming icy teeth was less than reassuring. She crouched beside Jig. "Billa would prefer I freeze the blood in your veins and bring you to her as a frozen dessert, naturally."

Darnak thrust Jig to the floor and gripped his war club with both hands. "For Theodore!" he shouted, and swung his club at Isa's head.

The metal-studded wood shattered. Isa reached up to brush a bit of snow and wood from her shoulder.

An arrow ricocheted from Isa's neck. She waved her hand, and the wind flung three of Genevieve's archers from the wall.

Between the fallen humans and Darnak's broken club, only an idiot would continue to attack. Jig turned expectantly to Genevieve. But the princess was smarter than her brothers. Though she had her sword drawn, she didn't try to use it. With her other hand, she gripped the inner railing. "I am Genevieve Wendelson, Princess of Adenkar. I presume you're the goddess who murdered my brother."

"Billa murdered your brother," Isa said. "I just gave her the weapon to do it."

Isa turned her back on the princess and bent toward Jig. Her breath frosted the lenses of his spectacles. "Wouldn't you like to be on the winning side this time, Tymalous? You could be a true god once again. Your name would be sung throughout the world."

Until the rest of the gods showed up to destroy us, Shadowstar muttered. He sounded wistful.

"Whatever our differences, we belong together, Tymalous. Don't tell me you haven't thought about me." She reached up to stroke Jig's ear.

Jig didn't know whether Isa was going to kill him or kiss him. Nor did he know which frightened him more. Kissing a goddess of ice . . . he remembered what had happened after the first snowfall, a month or so back. One of the goblins had dared Braf to lick a steel shield that had been left out in the cold. Even after Shadowstar healed his tongue, Braf had talked with a lisp for several days. Jig had no desire to freeze his lips to a goddess.

Actually it's kind of fun, said Shadowstar. *The trick is to—*

I don't want to know!

Jig cracked his fingers to check on Smudge. The fire-spider cringed at the cold, tightening his mandibles. Faint flares sparked from his bristles as he struggled to warm himself. The poor spider couldn't take much more of this. Neither could Jig, for that matter.

Genevieve's cloak dropped over Isa's head. "Darnak, now!"

Darnak leaped to help the princess. They yanked Genevieve's cloak, trying to drag Isa over the edge of the wall.

It was a good plan. Being formed of ice and snow, Isa should have slid easily across the platform. Maybe her feet had frozen to the branches beneath. Or maybe she was just heavy. Either way, she didn't budge. One hand ripped the cloak away and tossed it to the wind. The other shot out, grasping Genevieve by the throat.

Even as she choked Genevieve, she continued to talk to Jig in that gentle, terrifying voice. "You could be God of the Autumn Star once again, bringing comfort and peace to your worshipers. It's what you are." She stood, hauling Genevieve into the air. Darnak picked up Genevieve's dropped sword and slammed it into Isa's arm, with no effect.

Tymalous Shadowstar sighed. *She doesn't miss me. She needs me. Once Noc is dead and his curse ended, the other gods will remember her. She can't hope to fight them all. Her only chance is to plead for peace. My power could influence things in her favor.*

To Jig, he almost sounded disappointed.

"Well?" Isa asked.

Tell her . . . Shadowstar paused. *Tell her that what I am requires me to protect my son. Just as what she is requires her to be a heartless, frigid—*

"He says he'll think about it," Jig said.

Fog snorted from her nostrils. "Indeed." Faster than Jig could follow, she grabbed him by the throat. Smudge grew hot enough to singe Jig's palms. "Perhaps I can encourage him to make up his mind."

Darnak slammed his shoulder into Isa's side. She

scowled, but fortunately for Darnak, she was out of arms. Otherwise she probably would have tossed him off the wall.

"Sorry about this, Smudge," Jig whispered. While Isa's attention was on Darnak, Jig closed his hand around Smudge and reached out until the fire-spider was directly over Isa's head.

In that instant, as Smudge figured out what Jig was about to do, the fire-spider burned hotter than Jig had ever known. With a hiss of pain, Jig dropped Smudge into Isa's hair.

Steam shot from the top of Isa's head. Her eyes widened. She tossed Jig and Genevieve aside. She reached up to swat her hair, but Smudge had already melted down into her head. Isa's eyes crossed as Smudge sank behind her face. Jig could see Smudge scrambling to climb out, but all he accomplished was to widen the icy pit in Isa's head.

"Cursed goblins," Isa said. Water dripped from the corners of her mouth. "Billa will—"

At that point, Smudge reached the neck, and Isa collapsed. The wind died down, and the biting chill began to ease a bit.

Is she dead? Jig asked.

It takes a lot more than a frightened fire-spider to kill a god.

Isa toppled over, nearly smashing Darnak's toes. Darnak was helping Genevieve to her feet. Jig crouched over Isa's body, watching as Smudge dug his way out of the back of her neck. Still steaming, he scurried up Jig's leg, where he sank his mandibles right through Jig's trousers, biting his thigh.

Jig clenched his teeth and tried not to scream.

With that, Smudge crawled back into his pocket on the inside of Jig's cloak.

When Jig climbed down from the wall, he found a group of goblins waiting for him. Trok, Relka, and Braf stood near the front.

" 'Ware the ice!" Darnak shouted from the wall.

Jig leaped away as Darnak and one of the humans tossed the remains of Isa's manifestation onto the street. She shattered like glass, scattering shards of ice in all directions.

"What was that?" Trok asked.

"Nothing," Jig said. The last thing he wanted to do was admit that Billa the Bloody really had a goddess on her side.

Sure, but so do you, Shadowstar said.

Can you control the weather and manifest in Billa's army and start throwing her people around like toys?

Braf shifted his spear to his left hand. With his right, he picked up a glistening ice finger and sucked on the end. "Is it all over? What did the prince turn Billa into?"

A broken shriek made Jig jump. One of the elf-hawks flew overhead, blood trailing from its chest. Another perched atop the wall, where an elf was climbing down from its back. Falling from its back, really.

The first hawk flew straight for the huge trees in the center of town. Jig could hear squawks of protest from the smaller birds.

"He didn't turn her into anything, did he?" Relka asked.

"Billa killed the prince," Genevieve said as she descended the ladder. She rubbed her throat, then turned to stare at Jig. "How does an orc come to command such power?"

"She's the champion of a god," Jig said. "A mean, scary god." He watched as a stray dog darted from the side of the road to snatch a chunk of ice. The dog trotted away, crunching merrily on a bare foot.

"You fought Billa before." Genevieve tilted her head as she studied Jig. Red marks circled her neck where Isa had squeezed. "And now you've stopped . . . what was her name again? No matter. You saved my life."

"I saved *my* life," Jig said. "Smudge did the hard part."

Genevieve actually smiled at that. "Perhaps I should send your spider out to fight Billa."

From the wall, Darnak leaned out to yell, "Princess! We've got a hawk from your father and a kobold from Billa."

Genevieve waved him back. "Goblin, you—"

"Jig," Relka said. "His name is Jig Dragonslayer."

Genevieve's jaw tightened, but she nodded. "Jig. I didn't believe your companion when he said you killed my brothers. Now I do."

Jig stepped back, one hand moving toward his dagger. Genevieve's smile was a dangerous one. Her expression reminded him of Grell. Grell always smiled like that right before she gave Jig a particularly nasty duty.

"My father has decreed that all goblins be killed on sight," Genevieve said. "For murdering Prince Barius and Prince Ryslind, you are to be drawn and quartered."

"Drawn and quartered?" Jig glanced at the other goblins, who looked as confused as he felt. A few had drawn weapons, sensing the threat even if they didn't understand it. Shadowstar whispered briefly in Jig's mind, explaining the phrase in graphic detail. Jig's legs went soft, and he sat down in the snow. "Oh."

"I will spare your life," Genevieve continued. "If you slay Billa the Bloody for me."

Relka laughed. "You think Jig Dragonslayer fears your threats, human?"

Jig said nothing. Genevieve wasn't as frightening as Billa or Isa, but Genevieve was much closer. He was fairly certain his goblins could overpower her. But what would that accomplish, other than to turn the rest of the humans against him? Billa and Isa were still out there, and Isa was probably quite annoyed at Jig for melting her head.

"Why me?" Jig asked.

"Billa and her goddess want you." Genevieve nudged a bit of Isa with her foot. "You could get close to her."

"Sure I could," Jig agreed. "Billa has to get close to me so she can feed my eyes to the wolves!"

Tell her to spare all of the goblins, Shadowstar said.
What?

*Tell her you'll face Billa, but only if she convinces
her father to let your people live in peace.*

What about letting me live? Jig asked. *In peace or
otherwise?*

I'll be with you.

Why does that not make me feel any better?

Still, Jig wasn't exactly in a position to argue. "If I
fight Billa, you humans have to leave us alone.
Forever."

"That choice is my father's, not mine," Genevieve
said. "But I'll do what I can."

Jig blinked. Where was the angry pride, the humilia-
tion at having to deal with a lowly goblin? She had
agreed far too easily. "And I want a new sword,"
Jig said.

"Done."

"And maybe something to eat that isn't pickled?"

Genevieve's lip quirked. "Anything else, gob—?"
She glanced at Relka. "Jig."

"I'll think about it and let you know."

"Very well." Genevieve turned toward the wall.
"I'll return shortly. I look forward to hearing your
plan." With that, she hurried back to the ladder and
climbed up to talk to Darnak.

Jig stood and tested his legs. The knees still felt a
bit wobbly, and his thigh throbbed where Smudge had
bitten him, but he didn't collapse.

"So now what?" asked Braf.

Jig rubbed his thigh. "That's a good question." All
he wanted was to run away, but there was no place
to run. The gates were likely to be guarded, and if he
climbed over the walls, he would have to deal with
that blasted steelthorn on the way down. Not to mention that Billa would never stop hunting him. Between
Isa sniffing after Shadowstar and the kobolds following Jig's trail, there was no place he could go where
he would be safe.

That's not quite true, Shadowstar said.

What do you mean?

It's time for you to become a champion of Tymalous Shadowstar.

Wait, you mean you were serious? Jig sat back down. *You really want me to fight Billa?*

You fought her before, and you won.

I ran away before she could kill me, Jig said. *It's not the same thing. And I don't think she's going to let me shove another torch in her face.*

I'll help you.

How? By making me stupid again? Jig shook his head. *No, thanks. I can get myself killed without your help.*

I didn't make you stupid, Shadowstar said. *I made you unafraid.*

Same thing, Jig muttered.

Very well, Jig. I hoped it wouldn't come to this.

Come to what?

Shadowstar's silence was far more unnerving than anything the god might have said.

"He's mumbling to himself again," Trok said.

The only response came from Braf, who asked, "Are you sure?"

"Yes, I'm sure," Trok said. "Can't you see his lips moving?"

"Oh. Well, if you say so." Braf blinked, and it slowly occurred to Jig that he hadn't actually been talking to Trok. His bleary eyes focused on Jig. "I'm sorry about this, Jig."

"Sorry about what?"

A burst of heat from Smudge was Jig's only warning. And then Braf slammed the butt of his spear into Jig's head.

CHAPTER 13

*E*ven to a god, the universe was a place of mystery. The realm of the gods was an extension of the gods themselves, a universe built on grudging consensus, constantly evolving with the whims of its inhabitants.

Tymalous Shadowstar stared up at Noc's star, burning black in the sky. The dark flames swallowed the light . . . even light from within. Certainly Noc would never think to search inside his own star. Even if he did, the odds of discovering the second, smaller star burning inside his own were slim at best.

Shadowstar's temple was equally well-hidden, built within the black realm of Xapthlux, the Sleeping God. Shadowstar would have to leave before Xapthlux awakened, but since that wasn't ordained to happen for another fifty thousand years, he didn't let it worry him too much.

He didn't worry about anything, really. Over the centuries, his power began to return. From time to time he reached out, spreading what little comfort he could without drawing the attention of the gods. Beyond that, he mostly slept. And cleaned. Xapthlux's domain was a dusty place.

He wasn't sure what had awakened him this time. Looking around, he sighed and plucked a rag from the nothingness.

A distant voice tore through his chest like a sword.

The bells of his garments betrayed his nerves as he tried to calm himself. The call had been so weak. A stammering, lisping excuse for a prayer, but after so many years of silence. . . .

"I think it says Tymalous Autumnstar." The speaker was a spindly blue creature with crooked fangs—a goblin, from the look of him. He sat in a hot cave, squinting at a yellowed tome. "It's hard to read. That human bled all over the cover."

"That book was supposed to go to the chief." A much larger goblin waddled over, brandishing a huge stirring spoon. Her other hand clutched her swollen belly. "Though why he can't use lichen when he visits the privy is beyond me."

The first goblin peered out of the cave. "He'll need half the book, the way he's gobbling down that adventurer." He laughed. "Golaka, look at how—"

"Get up!" Golaka knocked the book from his hand. "Bad enough you did this to me," she said, touching her belly. "If you're going to stay here, you're going to help! Otherwise you can go back to the distillery and play in your muck."

"I carved that adventurer and served him to the warriors, didn't I? Besides, I want to know how they made it all the way to Straum's lair and survived. Can you imagine if we had magic like that? This one would have escaped too if he hadn't succumbed to those lizard-fish stings in his leg. Imagine it, Golaka. If we could get their weapons and their magic, we could drive the hobgoblins back. We could fight off the adventurers. We could—"

Golaka dropped her spoon. "Did you say lizard-fish stings?" She grabbed the smaller goblin by the arms and hauled him upright.

"It looked like lizard-fish stings. A row of bloody holes that wouldn't scab over. But I'm not sure. I don't see too well, remember?"

"You mean you fed poisoned meat to the chief and his warriors!" Golaka shouted.

The smaller goblin paled. Outside, someone shouted,

"Where is that miserable runt Jarik? His food's making the chief sick!"

Eyes wide, Jarik twisted free of Golaka's grip. He spun, reaching for a bread knife that lay next to a jug. Then he changed his mind and grabbed the jug instead.

"Klak beer for everyone!" he shouted. As the first angry goblin burst into the cave, Jarik shoved the jug into his hands. "Golaka's finest beer for our finest warriors!"

It was a good attempt, and it almost worked. By the time the lizard-fish poison killed the chief, most of the warriors were too drunk to care.

Unfortunately, drunken goblins were violent goblins, and when poor Jarik ran out of klak beer, the results weren't pretty.

Shadowstar sighed as he watched Golaka carry the bloodstained book to the privy. "Tymalous Autumnstar, huh?" she muttered. "Stupid name."

Shadowstar sat down on the edge of his temple, his legs dangling in nothingness.

They remembered him!

These weak, violent, uncivilized goblins could remember his name. Not that most of them seemed the type to care about the gods. Who could blame them? Autumnstar couldn't think of a single god who would lower himself to take goblins as followers.

And the one goblin who might have cared, who might have actually made a connection with Tymalous Shadowstar, was now roasting over Golaka's kitchen fires.

But perhaps his child. . . .

"Nice to see you again, Jig Dragonslayer."

Stars filled the sky. The air was dry and dusty, though at least Jig had escaped the eye-watering smell of all those leaves and flowers. He sat up and touched his face. His spectacles were gone, but he could see perfectly well. The only time that had ever happened was in the temple of Tymalous Shadowstar. His *real* temple, not the little cave back at the goblin lair.

Jig turned toward the voice.

The god stood leaning against a broken wall, his arms folded over his chest. He was unchanged from the last time Jig had seen him. Still short. Still skinny. The wispy silver hair was still thin on the top. He could have passed for human, aside from those freakish eyes. Where eyeballs should have been, Shadowstar's face held two spots of perfect blackness, each one broken by the twinkling of a miniature star.

Jig backed away. "You told Braf to kill me!"

Shadowstar gave a sheepish shrug. "I told him to knock you unconscious. That's not as easy as it sounds, you know. And . . . well, he's Braf. Don't worry, Darnak is doing his best to fix your skull. If it's any consolation, Braf broke his spear in the process."

Oddly, that did make Jig feel a little better. "Does it give you a headache?" he asked. "Having stars for eyes, I mean."

Shadowstar shrugged. "I can see in the dark, which is fun." He wore the same loose-fitting clothes of black silk, with tiny silver bells down the sleeves and trousers. Those bells jingled as he rubbed his eyes. "Though my vision is still a bit fuzzy from seeing the Rod of Creation explode. I may have to borrow your spectacles."

Jig frowned. "It didn't explode."

"That much pent-up magical energy, released with no spells to contain it? It was like watching a tiny universe form and implode in a single heartbeat. Just be grateful you don't have a god's sight," Shadowstar said, chuckling.

"What did it look like?"

"Mostly purple." Shadowstar rubbed his eyes. "Jig, there are things you have to understand. Starting with the reason the Forgotten Gods went to war all those years ago. Haven't you ever asked yourself why I fought alongside Isa and the others?"

Jig shook his head.

"The nameless twins, the two gods of the beginning,

they're all but mindless. Vastly powerful, but dumb as gob— Well, they're dumb."

"So you went to war because they're stupid?" If Jig followed that sort of thinking, he'd have to declare war on half the lair.

"Some did," Shadowstar said. "They thought such power should be given to those wise enough to use it."

"Themselves, you mean?"

"Of course." Shadowstar picked up a fist-size chunk of stone and turned it over in his hands. "Isa was one such goddess."

"Why did you help her?" Jig asked, honestly curious. Also, the longer he kept Shadowstar talking, the longer he could stay here. Broken and depressing as Shadowstar's temple was, it was the one place Jig felt safe. Plus he kind of liked being able to see without his spectacles.

"To understand that, you need to understand how the universe works." He ran one hand over his head, flipping silver hair back from his face. "The universe . . . it has layers."

"Like ogres?" Jig asked.

Shadowstar stopped with his mouth half open. "Excuse me?"

"After we fought the ogres last year, we had lots and lots of leftovers. Golaka made up a dessert that has a layer of ogre meat, mushroom gravy, rat liver, and another layer of ogre. You sprinkle blue fungus flakes on the top, to give it that sweet aftertaste." His mouth watered at the memory.

"The universe is *not* like ogres," Shadowstar said, his voice stern. He set the stone on the floor between them and brushed his fingers over the rough surface. "You mortals see only the upper layer. It's rare that any of you notice the depth between you. Rarer still for one to reach down and touch those depths."

"So you're saying we're like the blue fungus on the top of Golaka's dessert?" Jig asked.

Starburst pupils rolled skyward. "Sure, why not.

And we gods can be the mushrooms. The important thing is to realize that you fungus flakes—" He grinned. "I think I like this metaphor."

"Do you have anything to eat here?" Jig asked, glancing around.

"Nothing that would be safe for you. Sorry."

Jig checked his cloak, but the pockets were empty. Smudge hadn't accompanied him, not that Jig had expected him to. But the leftover rat he had saved was gone too.

"The point is, you fungus flakes live in a universe supported by mushrooms. I mean, by gods. You may not see what happens in the realm of the gods, but what we do affects your world."

"Like if the pan is lopsided and all of the mushrooms slide to one side?" Jig licked his lips. "Then the top layer of meat sinks, and somebody gets stuck eating all mushrooms and no meat."

"If you don't stop obsessing about food, I'm going to throw you into the void," Shadowstar said, his voice light.

Jig swallowed, then nodded.

"The two gods of the beginning have fought one another since the universe began. Imagine living things struggling at the base of your dessert. Think of what that would eventually do to the surface."

Jig nodded. "Sometimes Golaka adds—"

"I don't want to know!" Shadowstar said quickly. "The point is, their battle will one day consume the universe. Your world, ours, all of it will be destroyed." The light in his eyes faded slightly. "I thought . . . I believed we could stop them. That we could save the universe from destruction."

Jig glanced at the sky. "How long do you think it will be before—"

"Nobody knows. The universe is vast and deep. It could survive for millions of years. Billions, even."

"Good." Jig still kept one eye on the stars, though.

"What I learned is that I'm really bad at being a warrior." Shadowstar gave a sheepish shrug. "I'm the

God of the Autumn Star. I help maintain the progress of time, the changing of seasons. I ease the terror of death, and I create the opportunity for new life. I'm a minor god, Jig, but I'm no fighter." He stood and folded his arms. "That's why I need you to be my champion."

Jig gestured at himself. "Have you forgotten I'm a goblin?"

"But you're mortal. I'm a god. What I was is what I am. What I am is what I will forever be."

"Huh?"

Shadowstar sighed. "Mortals can change. Gods can't. I can help you move beyond your fear, Jig. You have the opportunity to become more than just a goblin."

Jig shook his head. "I don't want to be more than a goblin."

"Your people need you," Shadowstar said. "You have the chance to protect them, both from Billa and from the humans. Stop Billa and you save them all. The goblins, my son, everyone."

Jig shook his head. The Rod of Creation was destroyed. If Theodore hadn't been able to stop Billa, how was Jig supposed to?

Shadowstar grabbed Jig by the arms and lifted him into the air. For one terrifying moment, Jig thought he was about to be flung out into the darkness beyond Shadowstar's temple. But the god set Jig down ever so gently by the archway. "Isa is stronger than me, but I have strength of my own, Jig Dragonslayer. For thousands of years I rested, gathering my strength. Rebuilding myself. Rebuilding this place."

Jig glanced at the edge of the floor, where the stone seemed on the verge of crumbling into nothingness.

"I never claimed to be a very good builder," Shadowstar admitted. "But what strength I have is yours. I can't fight Billa for you, but I can protect you."

Jig's ears perked up. He liked the sound of that. But Shadowstar had already said Isa was stronger. "What if I say no?"

"You're mortal," Shadowstar said. "Your fate is yours to choose."

"Good. I choose—"

"Though I'm not sure you'd appreciate the consequences." Shadowstar patted Jig's shoulder and stepped away, dragging his fingers over the broken walls and humming "The Song of Jig."

"What consequences?" Jig asked. He knew he shouldn't ask, but he couldn't help it.

"Reject me, and you reject all I've given you." Shadowstar still didn't look at him. "It would be as though you had never felt my power. Including all of that nice healing magic."

Slowly, Jig realized what Shadowstar was saying. Without that magic, any number of his wounds would have killed him. The worst was when another goblin stabbed him in the back last year, during their battle with the fairies. And that didn't begin to count all of the scrapes and cuts and burns—

"You're lying," Jig said. "You just told me you're a god of comfort and protection. You can't kill your own follower!"

Shadowstar shrugged, ringing the bells on his sleeves. "You wouldn't be my follower anymore, would you?"

Jig shook his head. "But you still can't—"

"Maybe not." Shadowstar turned around, and Jig could see him struggling to keep from laughing. His lower lip twitched, and his eyes literally sparkled. "But that's one of the wonderful things about you goblins. You're cowards. I don't mean that as an insult. Cowardice is a far better survival trait than heroism. But it means even if you're almost certain I'm bluffing, you're still not going to risk it."

Jig stared at him for a long time. "Please don't do this to me." Strange, to be so afraid of losing his fear. But fear kept goblins alive.

"I'm sorry, Jig." Shadowstar's amusement had vanished. He actually sounded like he meant it. He reached out to press one hand over Jig's chest. "Your people need you. I need you."

Jig tried to sit up and immediately regretted it. Shadowstar might have taken away his fear, but Jig would have preferred to lose his nausea. His head throbbed like a drum, and when he touched his scalp, his hand came away bloody.

"He's alive!" That was Trok, his voice sending new cracks through Jig's skull. Other goblins formed a loose circle in the road.

"Of course he's alive, Earthmaker's not failed me yet." Darnak's meaty hand pushed Jig flat. "This was a stubborn wound, but I'll have him up and about in no time."

"Good." That was Princess Genevieve, standing beside Trok and looking annoyed.

Jig squinted at the sky. Hadn't the sun been on the other side of town? And why was Darnak the one healing him? "Where's Braf?"

"I'll be healing him next, so we can ask him a few questions," Darnak said.

Healing Braf? Jig tried a second time to push himself up, but Darnak held him in place. Jig might as well have tried to move a mountain. He settled for twisting his head and squinting. His spectacles were covered in snow and blood, but he could still make out Braf sprawled in the snow a short distance away. "What happened?"

Trok started to snicker. "Relka nearly killed him. Big, bad Braf, knocked senseless by a little kitchen drudge."

"You should have let me kill that coward!" Relka shouted. Several other goblins held her by the arms as she kicked and struggled. Her face was wet. Had she fallen in the snow while she was fighting with Braf? And why had she attacked Braf in the first place?

You goblins are truly dense, you know that?

Fortunately, Jig had long ago learned to ignore his god's snider comments.

"There we go," Darnak said. The pounding in Jig's head eased. Darnak hauled him upright. "Any idea what led him to try to split your skull like that? I'm thinking he's one of Billa's men, myself."

"You mean a spy? Braf?" Jig grinned despite his pain. "He was just confused, that's all. It happens a lot. Relka, you don't have to kill him."

"But he—" She squirmed and wiped her nose. She was calmer now, but the other goblins still kept firm hold of her upper arms. Twisting to face Darnak, she said, "He's really going to be all right?"

"Good as new," Darnak said. He patted Jig's head hard enough to knock him down again. "So tell me, Jig, when have you been finding the time to get yourself a new cloak?"

"A new what?" Jig tugged his cloak out so he could see. The material was still torn and stained, with the same ugly vines along the edges. Only there was a new design over the chest, right where Shadowstar had touched him. A starburst and lightning bolt were embroidered in black and silver thread.

"Looks a bit like her pendant," Darnak said, cocking a thumb at Relka.

"It does, doesn't it?" Jig ran his fingers over the design.

I like her work, Shadowstar said.

Jig turned to Genevieve. "Why are you here? I thought you were busy reading that message from your father."

"That was six hours ago," she said.

Darnak tugged his beard. "Fixing your skull was easy enough, but waking you was a bit of a trick."

Six hours. That would explain the sun's movement. Jig shivered. The air always felt colder in the evening.

Genevieve rubbed her forehead and said, "There's been a lot of snowfall in the mountains. My father's army won't arrive until late tomorrow. When he does . . . he means to attack."

"What?" The revelation didn't frighten him one bit,

thanks to Shadowstar's power. But the loss of Jig's fear meant there was plenty of room for other emotions. Dismay, anger, even a bit of despair. "Didn't you tell him about Billa's plan? That's what she wants!"

"He didn't believe me," Genevieve said. "He's ordered me to secure Avery and do nothing until he arrives. I've sent a second hawk to my mother, hoping she'll be able to talk some sense into him. But even if she could reach him in time, I doubt he'd listen."

"Wendel's a stubborn one, even for a king. He'll hear nothing of any plan that allows Billa's army to live." Darnak shook his head. "I'm sorry, Jig. I never should have told him of Theodore's death. He might have listened had I not—"

"My father? Listen?" Genevieve laughed. "You've been a bird too long, Darnak. He's never listened to me, and your counsel has been less than welcome since you returned bearing news of Ryslind and Barius."

"What about Billa?" Jig asked. "You said one of her kobolds had come with a message. Why would she do that?"

"She offered to let me and my soldiers go free," Genevieve said. She took a deep breath. "All I have to do is turn you over to her."

That made sense. Why waste her own soldiers coming after Jig when she could get the humans to do it for her? Jig checked to see if he was armed. He still had the knife he had taken from that elf, but Shadowstar hadn't given him any divine weapons.

I'm not that good at weapons, Shadowstar said.

Naturally. Embroidery he could do. Weapons, no. Resting one hand on his knife, Jig asked, "What did you tell her?"

Genevieve raised an eyebrow and touched her own sword, as if daring him to attack her. "That you were a sneaky, conniving little coward who had managed to escape. I asked that she give us until tomorrow night to capture you, at which time I would hand you over."

"And Billa agreed to this?"

"Aye." Darnak had wound his hands into his beard, presumably for warmth. It made him look like he was wearing snarly black mittens. "From what you said, Billa doesn't care about Avery. She'd rather preserve her forces for King Wendel. She'll want as much death as possible. Taking the town would cost her a few hundred soldiers, and every monster she loses is one less death to attract Noc's attention."

Before Jig could ask anything more, Relka shouted, "Watch out!"

Jig spun. A single goblin leaped from behind one of the houses and ran toward him. Jig squinted and lowered his head, trying to find a clear spot on his lenses. Through the smeared blood and snow, he thought he recognized Gratz.

"Traitor!" Gratz shouted. He pointed a crossbow at Jig as he ran. "Regulations require me to arrest you for treason. You are ordered to—" Gratz slipped on a patch of ice, and the crossbow discharged.

The impact as the bolt thudded into Jig's shoulder wasn't as bad as, say, being struck by a dragon. But it was enough to knock Jig backward several steps. He waved his arms to keep from falling.

Gratz was already drawing a sword from his belt. Where had he gotten all of these weapons? He was supposed to be locked up, not—

"Why am I still standing?" Jig whispered. He looked down. The crossbow bolt lay in the snow a few steps away. His cloak was unmarked, though Jig could feel a bruise forming on his chest . . . right below the symbol Shadowstar had created on his cloak.

I do make good armor, though, Shadowstar said smugly.

That won't do me much good if he stabs me in the face. Jig drew his knife and started toward Gratz. Maybe Gratz would stumble again and impale himself, but Jig doubted it. Gratz was a trained soldier. As trained as goblins got, at any rate.

Jig glanced around. The other goblins were already

making wagers and grinning with anticipation, as goblins did. But these were supposed to be soldiers too. *Jig's* soldiers.

He sheathed his knife and stopped walking. "Why are you all standing about, you lazy bastards?"

He did his best to mimic Silverfang's disgusted anger. From the shocked expressions on the goblins' faces, it worked. Before they could respond, Jig pointed at Gratz and yelled, "Get him!"

The goblins roared as they charged. Soldier or not, Gratz was still a goblin at heart. He threw down his sword and fled.

Jig smiled. He kind of liked being a general.

The dining hall in the barracks had the largest tables, which made them the ideal choice for spreading out all Darnak's maps. Unfortunately, the barracks was also one of the original elf buildings, and the table was in dire need of a trimming. Budding twigs sprouted from the edges, tickling Jig's wrists as he leaned in to study the maps. He wiped his eyes and tried not to sneeze.

Candles burned in holders formed of living vines. The too-sweet smell of perfumed beeswax did nothing to help Jig's nose.

Darnak had placed the bulk of his figurines on one side of Avery to represent Billa's army. Others were scattered through the woods to either side. "Billa's sent scouts through the woods, probably to make sure you don't try to flee."

He set another group of blocks at the top of the valley. "Once Wendel arrives, he'll send his cavalry down, hoping to ride right over Billa's monsters."

A third line marked the elves on the opposite side of the valley. "If we could somehow drive Billa's forces across the border, the elves would help—"

"Billa's monsters won't retreat," Jig said. "It's probably against regulations."

"It doesn't matter," said Genevieve. "We have to stop Billa before my father arrives."

"Wendel ordered you to sit tight," Darnak said.

"I know." She picked up several of the figurines from within Avery, setting them in a line outside the walls.

Jig studied the map. Darnak didn't appear to have a figurine for Billa, so he had used a large gray pebble instead. That pebble was currently guarded by several thousand monsters, most represented by larger metal blocks.

Jig frowned and looked closer. The figurines Genevieve had moved outside the wall were all goblins, though there was something odd about the frontmost one. He picked it up and peered more closely. Darnak had painted amethyst spectacles onto the goblin's face.

"You promised to kill Billa for me, remember?" asked Genevieve.

"Your goblins will pretend you're a prisoner." Darnak split a path through Billa's forces, then moved the goblins through. "Once you're within range, you charge. It's a desperate plan, but you'll have the advantage of surprise. Theodore's mistake was to attack in plain sight. Might as well have sent a note telling Billa exactly when he'd be dropping by."

"*One* of his mistakes, anyway," Genevieve said.

"He was overconfident, and it killed him." Darnak's voice was tight.

Jig studied the map. Overconfidence wouldn't be a problem for goblins. He moved the figurines into the center of the army, near the pebble that was Billa. "Say we somehow manage to catch Billa by surprise and kill her. What happens then?"

Darnak fiddled with his quill. Genevieve stared at the map.

Jig reached out and pushed the blocks of Billa's army until they surrounded the goblins. "We're all going to die."

"I told you this one was clever," Darnak said quietly.

This was the point where any reasonable goblin would have fled for his miserable life. Yet Jig didn't move.

"The orcs will be closest," he said. "They'll probably be the ones to kill us. And then they'll turn toward Avery."

"Not necessarily," said Genevieve. "For those who do, the walls will hold until my father arrives."

"We're hoping there will be some squabbling," Darnak added. "The death of their leader will be an enormous blow to morale. Not to mention they'll have to sort out who's in charge, with Billa gone."

Jig tried to imagine the chaos. Whenever a goblin chief died, the smarter goblins made themselves scarce for the next few days, emerging to see who had survived long enough to seize control. Given the size of Billa's army, Jig wouldn't want to be anywhere near that power struggle. Though that likely wouldn't be a problem, since he would be dead before it began.

Genevieve plucked the blocks from Darnak's map. "With luck, they'll give up and go home. Can you imagine my father's face? Him and his army arriving to an empty field." Her expression was wistful. She frowned as she studied the map. "What if Jig's goblins betray him? If he's smart enough to realize what could happen, maybe they will, too. They'll rejoin Billa to save themselves."

"Not Relka," Darnak said. "I get the sense that one would walk into a dragon's maw for him. A few of the others, too. As for the rest, well, Jig's already told them what Billa has in mind."

"We should do this soon." Jig turned the tiny, spectacled goblin over in his hand. He wondered if Darnak could sculpt a little spider to go with it. "Before they have time to think about it."

"Sunrise would be best," Genevieve said. "The sun rises almost directly behind Avery. It will work in your favor."

Jig nodded. There were a few things he needed to take care of, if he was to lead the goblins into battle. He stood to go.

"Jig, wait." Genevieve hesitated, then reached down to grab a long, cloth-wrapped bundle from the floor. "I promised you a sword."

Jig took the bundle. It was lighter than he had expected.

"This was my brother's short sword," she said. "Companion to the blade he carried when he fell. The elves gave them to him as a gift, the first time he snuck into their woods."

"You really think he'd want you giving that to a goblin?" Darnak asked.

Genevieve grinned. "No." She reached out to grab Jig's arm. "My father passed the law ordering us to kill goblins on sight. The worst thing you could do to him is to succeed where his son failed."

Jig's answering smile made his jaw ache. He had been clenching it so long it hurt to do anything else. Whatever flaws Genevieve might possess, she certainly knew how to motivate a goblin.

CHAPTER 14

*T*he son was born a twisted blue runt with comically
oversized ears.

"Are you sure that thing came from Golaka?" One
of the nursery workers hobbled over. She was a
hunched, wrinkled thing, leaning heavily on a yellow
cane. "I've seen rats with more meat."

The goblin holding the baby jabbed her claw into
his belly. He batted weakly at her finger. "He's a pasty
little mouse. He hasn't even cried."

"Nothing wrong with a bit of quiet." The older goblin tucked a bit of hard candy into her cheek. "Maybe
he can teach you how to keep your mouth shut."

"Careful, Grell." The younger worker balanced the
baby in one hand and drew a short sword with her
other. She jabbed the sword in Grell's direction. The
baby turned his head, eyes wide as he followed the
tarnished steel. He was an observant thing, and if that
goblin wasn't careful, she was going to drop him on
his head. If that happened, Shadowstar intended to give
her a smiting like the world had never seen.

"Put that away," Grell said, rapping the sword with
her cane. "Kill me, and you're on your own come
diaper-changing time." She grinned. "Remember those
dried fruits I swiped from that last group of adventurers? Well, a few of the brats found them. It's going to
make diaper duty pretty exciting for the next few days.

But by all means, run me through with your little sword and wipe their arses all by yourself."

The other goblin stared at her sword. She looked as though she was half tempted to fall on it. With a sigh, she rammed it back into her sheath. *"Why don't you check diapers, and I'll take the runt outside for the wolves."*

Tymalous Shadowstar shook his head. That runt had potential, for a goblin. Besides, it was kind of cute the way those ears kept flopping down into his eyes. Shadowstar couldn't simply let him die.

He concentrated on Grell, but she mentally swatted him away like a bug. So he turned to the younger goblin. Aggressive and angry, she was a true goblin, willing to do anything to get her way.

"Wait," she said. *"I have a better idea."*

"You have an idea?" Grell snorted. *"And here I thought I'd seen everything."*

Shadowstar whispered, and the goblin said, *"I'll bet you a week's worth of diaper-changing duty that you can't keep the runt alive long enough to see his first full moon."*

Grell's cane clicked against the obsidian floor as she limped over to take the baby. *"A month,"* she said.

"A month it is." The other goblin touched the hilt of her sword.

"Try it, and I'll make you eat those diapers."

Shadowstar grinned. He was starting to like these goblins.

Jig scowled at his new sword. The blade was light as air, and stronger than any human steel. Had any goblin ever possessed so fine a weapon?

If they had, Jig suspected they would have soon thrown it away. For Jig had learned the true nature of the elves' magical weapons. In addition to being so strong and sharp and light, the sword glowed orange in the presence of orcs and ogres . . . and goblins. Every time Jig looked at his own sword, it burned an image of itself onto his eyelids.

"Stupid elves," Jig muttered. He turned to Darnak. "Can't you turn it off?"

Darnak chuckled. "The steel remembers the light of the forge. Be thankful it doesn't recall the heat as well." He closed the box of figurines and crammed it into his pack.

Actually, a heated sword would have been nice. At least he would have been able to feel his fingers.

Genevieve had already gone off to prepare her soldiers, leaving Jig and Darnak alone in the barracks. Jig bent to pick up the goblin figurine, which had fallen onto the floor beneath the table.

"Keep it," Darnak said. "As for the sword, the magic will wear off in time. Most elven blades lose their power after a thousand years or so. Two thousand at the most."

The sword cast about as much light as a muck lantern or torch. Still, it was a far cry better than the old kitchen knife he used to carry. Not that he expected it to make much difference. Sure, Jig's sword could help him avoid stubbing his toe in the darkness. Billa's could kill a god.

A tugging on his cloak drew Jig's attention. Smudge crept slowly up the hem, toward Jig's neck. He took slow, careful steps, as he did when he was hunting. Just beneath Jig's chin, the fire-spider stopped. One leg at a time, he turned to face the sword.

"Odd pets you goblins keep," Darnak said.

Smudge pounced. The move was so sudden Jig nearly dropped the sword. Smudge landed on the blade, slipped, and fell into the snow.

Instantly, Smudge was scrambling for Jig's leg. He climbed up again and crouched, waiting.

Jig started to smile. Smudge probably thought he had discovered the world's largest glow-fly. He waited until Smudge pounced, then flicked the blade out of the way.

Next time, Smudge was smarter. He simply ran down Jig's arm and onto the blade. He steadied himself on the crossguard and tried to take a bite out of the edge. After a few such attempts, he turned around, all eight eyes glaring up at Jig.

"Don't get mad at me. I never said you could eat it." Jig ran a finger over the bristly fur on Smudge's back. "Darnak, I have to ask you for something."

"Genevieve's in charge," Darnak said. "Not me."

Jig shook his head. "No, it's nothing like that. Will you take care of Smudge for me?"

Darnak cocked his head. "That's Smudge? I thought that little guy got himself squished back when you and Barius fought."

"He . . . he survived." Had he ever thanked Shadowstar for that miracle?

No.

Jig sheathed his sword and held Smudge out to Darnak. "He doesn't deserve to die out there."

Slowly Darnak opened his hand. Jig poked Smudge, gently at first, then harder. Smudge lowered his body, his feet heating Jig's palm. Finally Jig grabbed him with his other hand and pulled him free. "Don't let him get near your beard unless you want to lose it. And try to keep him out of the cold, if you can. When this is all over you can take him back to our lair. There's a fire-spider nest in the tunnels below our cavern. If you put him into the garbage crevasse, he should remember how to find it."

Darnak held the fire-spider at arm's length. "Wouldn't it be making more sense to give this beastie to another goblin?"

Jig shook his head. "Most goblins don't like them very much. Fire-spiders sneak into the distillery and the muck pits. They like to eat the muck. When I was young, a distillery worker startled a fire-spider that was hiding in one of the pans. The explosion killed four goblins and deafened nine more."

From the look on Darnak's face, Jig might as well have given him a pile of wolf scat. With his free hand, Darnak twisted his beard into a rope and tucked it down the front of his shirt. "You sure it's me you're wanting to look after him?"

"If you say you'll protect him, you will. You're like that." Jig glanced at the map. "And he's safer with you than with me."

Slowly Darnak nodded. "True enough. I'll do my best to care for the beast—for Smudge—and to get him back home where he belongs. My word on it."

Jig searched his pockets for something to give to Smudge. He found one tiny troll toe, covered in purple lint, but Smudge wasn't interested.

Jig's throat felt as though *he* had tried to swallow a toe. A big one. He blinked and turned toward the door.

"Jig!" Trok burst inside and stomped snow from his boots. "We caught Gratz. He's outside. Nobody knew where you had gotten to."

"Oh." That was good. Maybe he could give pieces of Gratz to Smudge as a final present.

"Well?" Trok said. "Aren't you going to come kill him?"

Jig blinked. "He's still alive?"

"He said that as an officer, regulations required us to turn him over to our superior for questioning."

"Trok, those are *Billa's* regulations." Jig heard Darnak chuckling behind him. With a sigh, Jig pulled up his hood and adjusted his sheath. This sword was wider than his last, and the end kept catching on his cloak. "Forget it. I'll deal with Gratz. There's something else I need you to take care of."

"What's that?" Trok sounded wary.

"I'm down to a single troll toe, and I doubt the other goblins have enough to control the wolves when we attack." Jig pointed to Trok's sword. "Why don't you take some of the goblins and introduce them to Toe Stub?"

Slowly Trok grinned. "Yes, sir!"

"What's Toe Stub?" Darnak asked after he left.

"You probably don't want to know." Jig pushed open the door and stepped into the cold.

*   *   *

About half the goblins followed Trok to learn about Toe Stub. The rest surrounded Gratz, who was bloody and bruised, but still alive. That he had convinced them not to kill him was quite the trick, particularly given the way Relka kept playing with her torch. Jig got the feeling she would happily cook him right here in the street if Jig gave the word.

Braf stood on the opposite side of the mob, keeping a wary eye on Gratz. Or maybe he was watching Relka. His clothes were still torn and bloody from the beating Relka had given him.

The goblins quieted as Jig approached. Gratz straightened. "As a prisoner of war, regulations require me to—"

Relka cleared her throat. Gratz glanced at her, and his mouth snapped shut.

"How did you escape?" Jig asked.

"The humans don't have a proper dungeon," Gratz said. "So they tied me up in the bakery, surrounded by stale bread."

Jig grimaced at the thought.

"I tried to bite through the ropes. These weren't those blasted elf ropes you told me about, but they were still too tough to chew. I thought I was done for. And then I remembered Billa's regulations."

Jig groaned. He wasn't the only one.

"Regulations say you're supposed to dislocate your own thumbs to escape the bonds of the enemy."

Jig studied him with a bit more respect. "You did that?"

Gratz shook his head. "I tried. Screamed and passed out from the pain. When I came to, one of the humans was staring down at me, so I kicked him in the giblets and took his weapons. That's in the regs too, you know."

Jig really needed to read those regulations. He gestured at the other goblins. "And then you attacked me in front of everyone. What do your regulations say about that?"

"It's a bit unclear," Gratz admitted. "Audacity is one of the keys to victory. But it also tends to get you killed."

Audacity. So be it. Jig stepped back and raised his voice so all the goblins would hear. "We're going to attack Billa in the morning." Several of the goblins cheered. The smarter ones looked worried. Jig tried to ignore them all. "And you're going to lead that attack," he said to Gratz.

That took care of the cheering.

"Are you sure Darnak finished healing your head?" Braf asked. "I hit you pretty hard."

Jig turned and walked toward the wall. "Bring Gratz. The rest of you get some sleep." He swiveled his ear, tracking their footsteps in the snow and waiting for one of them to try to kill him. It's what he would have done, had someone told him he had to attack Billa's army. But apparently the goblins were too stunned to act.

Jig climbed to the top of the wall, stepping onto the walkway without any hesitation. He found Genevieve and Darnak standing there, watching Billa's army.

"Bring Gratz," Jig shouted.

Relka sank her claws into Gratz's arm and dragged him to the ladder. Jig waited until they reached the top. There were no lanterns or torches, probably so that Billa's monsters would have a harder time targeting anyone.

"What are you doing?" Genevieve asked, lowering her elf scope.

"Planning tomorrow's attack."

Gratz clung to the railing as he stepped onto the wall. Jig didn't bother. He had no fear of falling. He had no fear of anything. That was the only reason he could walk up to Gratz and grab him by his lone ear.

He tugged Gratz to the opposite railing, yanking his head around so he was looking out at Billa's army.

"You mean to attack *that*?" Gratz shook his head. "You should have let me kill you. It would have been faster."

"What do Billa's regulations say about attacking a town?" Jig asked. Scattered campfires burned as far back as Jig could see. They had taken over the farmhouses too. At least one was on fire, though Jig wasn't sure that had been deliberate. Goblins swarmed around the burning building in a panic. "Billa has thousands of monsters. We have—"

"Eighty-seven soldiers and twenty-nine goblins," Genevieve said.

"And one dwarf," added Darnak.

"Given the weather, Billa's best choice would be to strike hard and fast," Gratz said. "Audacity, like I said. Surround the town and hit it from all sides at once. Use ladders and siege towers to—"

"What ladders?" Jig pointed. "Do you see any ladders? Or siege towers?" Not that he knew what a siege tower was.

"We left the siege equipment back in Pottersville," Gratz said. "It got pretty beat up in the attack, and—"

"So why aren't they building more?" Jig asked. "All those trees, but they're just sitting there. Waiting. Billa gave Genevieve until tomorrow to surrender."

Gratz shook his head. "That doesn't make sense. Giving humans time is always a mistake. They'll find a secret way out of the city, or some unassuming farm boy will sneak away to summon help, then before you know it a wizard shows up out of nowhere with reinforcements, and everything goes straight into the privy."

Jig shrugged and leaned against the railing, his back to Billa's army. "So this must be some sort of trick," he said. "Billa's secretly moving her forces into an attack formation."

Gratz shook his head. "That's no formation I've ever seen. Most of them seem to be sleeping!"

"You said the casualty ratio against a walled town was ten-to-one," Jig said.

"Billa has goblins and kobolds out in front," Gratz mumbled. "Make it fifteen-to-one."

"She has plenty of monsters," Jig said. "She could

take Avery by noon tomorrow if she wanted. Then her forces would be safe behind the walls. Doesn't that make sense?"

Slowly Gratz nodded. "I don't understand it. No siege equipment. No sappers."

"That wouldn't work anyway," said Genevieve. "Steelthorn roots spread wide and deep."

Jig frowned, trying to understand what sap had to do with anything. He knew sap came from trees, and the walls were made of steelthorn trees, but why—? It didn't matter. He could see Gratz's confusion. Now it was only a matter of pushing.

"Her formation does make sense," Jig said. "Her lines are spread to face the north. She's waiting for Wendel's army to arrive."

"Why would she do that?" Gratz's fingers dug into the railing.

"Because I was telling you the truth before. She doesn't want to beat the humans. She wants to kill them. Them and us, all at once."

"No!"

Relka started forward, but Jig waved her away.

Gratz turned to Jig. His tone was pleading "That's not possible. Billa the Bloody is a liberator." He rubbed his arm, the one with the scar of rank.

That gave Jig an idea. "If you're still not convinced, I could try to trigger the spell she carved onto your arm."

Gratz stared at his arm.

"We should probably lower you down outside the wall, first," Jig said. "Genevieve, do you have ropes? I don't know exactly how much damage this is going to do."

"No!" Gratz blinked, and cocked his head, as if he wasn't sure who had shouted. In a softer voice, he said, "No."

Genevieve was staring at Jig just as intently as the goblins. "You could do that? Trigger the spell? That could destroy Billa's army!"

It wouldn't work, Shadowstar said. *Every spell in-*

cludes a rune binding the magic to Isa. You'd have to rip each one away from her, and neither of us are strong enough to wrest control from Isa. I doubt you could even trigger Gratz's spell.

I don't have to. Out loud, he said, "No, I can't," Jig said. "Billa created those spells. She's the only one who can use them."

Gratz's face turned a darker shade of blue. He grabbed the front of Jig's cloak. "But you said—"

Jig kicked him in the shin. "And you believed me! Deep down, you know that scar isn't just a sign of rank." He bit Gratz's arm until he let go of Jig's cloak. And then Relka slammed into Gratz from the side, knocking him down hard enough to make the branches tremble beneath them.

Jig knelt and grabbed the sheaf of paper sticking out from Gratz's shirt. The corners were wrinkled and filthy, speckled with dirt and Gratz's blood. He waved them in Gratz's face. "Doesn't Billa's plan to kill everyone qualify as treason?"

"Technically, since it's her army, she can't commit treason," Gratz said.

Jig fought the urge to try out his brand new elf sword. "At sunrise the other goblins are going to pretend to take me prisoner. We're going to get as close as we possibly can, and then I'm going to kill Billa." At least that was the plan. So far, his plans had been falling apart with annoying regularity. "It would be much more believable if you were the one leading that group. Billa knows you. Everyone knows you. Even the kobolds said you were a stuck-up, rule-bound arse-kisser."

"That's true," Gratz muttered. Then, to Jig's confusion, he began to laugh. He hugged himself, shaking so hard Jig worried he would fall down. Tears dripped from his cheeks.

"Goblins have the strangest sense of humor," Genevieve said.

"She could have done it," Gratz said, gasping for breath. He wiped his face on his sleeve. "Billa raised an army. She could have beaten the humans. She could have won, Jig."

Somewhere toward the middle of town, a goblin screamed. Genevieve had her sword drawn in an instant, her eyes wide. Her men raised crossbows, searching for a target.

"That's probably just Trok," Jig said. He turned his head, perking his ears. As the screaming quieted, he could hear other goblins jeering. Hopefully he would have time to heal the losers before it was time to leave. He reached out to grab Gratz's arm. "The princess gave me her word. If I stop Billa, she'll make sure the humans leave us alone."

Gratz grabbed the railing with one hand and pulled himself up. "Billa played us all for fools, Jig." His hand shook as he pulled out his battered regulations. "Always wash between your toes," he whispered.

"What?" Jig asked.

"First regulation I ever learned." Gratz stared out at Billa's army. "If you don't keep clean, you get fungus and rot and all sorts of nastiness."

"Good advice," Darnak agreed. "And it's not just toes, either. My cousin Dinla spent too much time in the mines one summer and got herself the worst case of armpit mold you'll ever see."

Behind him, Genevieve looked faintly nauseated.

"You'll want to hide that sword," Gratz said. "Regulations require all prisoners to be disarmed. If anyone sees it, they'll know something's wrong." He stretched his arms, then laced his fingers together to crack the joints in his hands. "I never liked those stinking orcs anyway. Always strutting about like they're better than us."

"So you'll help us?" Jig asked.

Gratz nodded.

To Darnak, Jig asked, "Is he telling the truth?"

"What's that?"

"When I first told you about Billa, Genevieve had you cast a spell to figure out if I was lying." Jig pointed at Gratz. "Is he telling the truth? If he means to turn me over to Billa, we should throw him off the wall and I'll have Trok lead us instead."

"Betraying your commanding officer gives your superiors the right to . . . hold on." Gratz flipped through his pages. "Ah. The right to use your skin as a blanket." He shoved the manual back into his shirt. "You're my commanding officer, General Jig. I have no interest in becoming a blanket."

"He means it," Darnak said, shaking his head. He looked both surprised and sad.

Jig wasn't surprised. Gratz was as bad as Relka. Without Billa to believe in, Gratz had latched on to Jig instead. Relka would have him wearing his very own starburst if he wasn't careful. Goblins were fools.

Their faith gives them courage, said Shadowstar. *Neither of them needed divine intervention to help them overcome their fear. They'll stand beside you and die with you.*

Jig nodded. *Exactly.*

Jig didn't sleep much that night. Maybe being a champion of Tymalous Shadowstar meant he didn't need as much sleep. Or maybe the idea of leading an attack against Billa the Bloody was enough to keep him awake, even without his fear. He kept thinking about all the things that could go wrong, and wondering which would be the one to kill him. Falling off of his wolf and breaking his neck would be embarrassing, but at least it would be quick. Slipping in the snow right as he reached Billa would be worse.

When he could lie there no longer, he got up and tiptoed out of the stables, past a heap of snoring goblins. Wrapping an extra blanket tight around his body, he hurried to the wall.

To his surprise, Genevieve was still there, staring out at the campfires of Billa's army.

Jig announced his arrival with a wet sneeze. At least tomorrow would see him free of all these plants.

Several of her guards moved toward him, but Genevieve waved them back. She started to speak, then wrinkled her nose. "What is that smell?"

"What smell? Oh, wait." Jig tugged a pouch from one of his cloak pockets and handed it to her. Genevieve's face went pale as she opened the bag.

"We were almost out of troll toes," Jig said. "Trok says the hardest part was convincing everyone to take off their shoes. I guess that makes it easier to score a full sever. I healed them the best I could. The wolf-riders will still be able to ride, and the rest . . . well, they can limp along behind us."

"Goblins." She tossed the sack at Jig's feet. One toe rolled free and disappeared into the cracks of the woven walkway. "For years, my brothers fought to earn our father's attention and respect. All they accomplished was to get themselves killed." She sighed and rested her arms on the railing. "I never blamed the goblins for killing Barius and Ryslind. I blamed him."

"Your father didn't kill them. I'm the one who turned them into trout." And that was why goblins needed their fear. Fear would have stopped him from saying something so incredibly stupid. He braced himself for Genevieve's response. At the very least, he expected a quick punch to the face. If he was unlucky, Genevieve would just run him through.

She did neither. "My mother says I'm too harsh. He's fought for this kingdom his whole life. I remember watching him teach my brothers how to fight. He was *laughing*." She shook her head. "He never laughs when he wears that stupid crown."

"Maybe he should give it to someone else," Jig said.

"My mother has said the same thing, in private. She even used to joke about changing the law so that the youngest daughter could inherit the crown. Then she and my father could retire to Silver Lake and spend their time fishing and watching the griffins on the cliffs. When I told her I'd use that crown to bludgeon the first person who tried to put it on my head, she smiled and said that only proved I was smarter than my brothers."

"That's not saying much." There he went again. But Genevieve only smiled.

"This coming from the goblin who tried to attack an entire city."

"We won!" Jig said, trying not to sound defensive.

"Only because I wasn't smart enough to come inside the walls when Darnak told me to." She yawned again, then fumbled through her cloak until she found a long wooden pipe. She walked to the closest lantern and lit a taper, which she used to start the tobacco burning. "Dwarven tobacco. It helps my nerves, and it's nice to be able to breathe without feeling like my lungs are about to freeze. Please don't tell my father, though. He'd kill me."

Jig managed to keep from rolling his eyes. "I'll try to keep it to myself."

She blew a puff of smoke, which quickly disappeared into the cold wind. "You deserve better than this, you know."

"Tell that to Tymalous Shadowstar."

"Who?"

Jig sighed. "Never mind." He tried to count the campfires, but quickly gave up.

"I can't imagine what my father would say if he saw me up here talking to a goblin." Her grin appeared strained. She tugged a leaf from the railing and pulled it apart. "I don't blame you for hating us, you know."

Jig shook his head. "We don't hate you. At least not any more than we hate the lizard-fish and the tunnel cats and the hobgoblins and everything else that kills us."

"Oh."

Jig had a hard time reading her expression.

"You should try to sleep," Genevieve said. "Nobody dies faster than a tired soldier."

"What about a goblin?" Jig asked.

That earned a soft chuckle. She blew another stream of smoke into the wind and stared up at the moon.

Jig turned to go, then hesitated. "Aren't you going to get some sleep too?"

"Eventually." She sucked another breath through the pipe. "Darnak used to tell us stories about the great dwarf commanders, and how they would walk among their men the night before the battle." She ducked her head and added, "Besides, I get nightmares."

Jig started down the ladder. He had just lowered himself down so his hands clutched the top disk of lichen when Genevieve said, "For what it's worth, I'm sorry, Jig."

She sounded almost drunk, but her breath didn't have the stink of alcohol. Humans were weird.

It's time, Jig.

Shadowstar's voice yanked Jig from a dream in which Billa and her orcs had been pelting him with potatoes. He blinked and rubbed his eyes, then hooked his spectacles over his ears. The sight of all those snoring, drooling goblins was anything but pretty.

The stable door slid open, and Gratz peeked inside.

"You're awake." Gratz sounded surprised.

"What are you doing?" The idea of Gratz out and moving around on his own made Jig nervous.

"Checking on the wolves, sir. I thought it best to make sure they were fed before we attack. Not too much, of course. Hunger gives a wolf his edge, right?"

"Sure." Jig staggered toward the door. He stopped long enough to nudge Trok awake. "Get the wolf-riders ready," Jig said, fighting a yawn.

"Get them yourself, you scrawny little—" Trok rubbed his eyes. "Er. Sorry." He leaned over and punched the closest goblin in the gut. "Get everyone awake, and be quick about it."

That wasn't exactly what Jig had intended, but it worked. Soon his entire command was gathered outside the stables, shivering in the wind. The sky overhead was a dark blue color. Most of the stars had faded, and the moon was gone from sight. Over the far wall, Jig could see a faint trace of red.

"Beautiful morning, eh?" Darnak shouted as he jogged toward them, followed by Genevieve and several other humans. "Nothing like the chill of the pre-dawn air to get the blood pumping."

Darnak was the closest thing Jig had to a friend here, but if the dwarf kept grinning like that, Jig was going to stab him.

Dark smudges beneath Genevieve's eyes made her look a bit like a raccoon. Her expression was one of complete understanding. "It could be worse," she muttered. "When he woke me up, he was *singing*."

Jig grinned and checked his sword. Orange light spilled from the end of the scabbard. Jig hurried back into the stable and grabbed a blanket. He pulled it over himself, wrapping one corner around the sword to hide it. "Gratz, Trok, take some of the goblins and go get the wolves."

"What about food?" Relka asked.

"Billa's troops will be breaking their fast soon," Darnak said. "Attack now, and we catch them in the middle of their meal. They'll be reluctant to abandon their food, and that gives you the advantage."

"Here," said Relka. She handed Jig a strip of meat so dry it crunched. "I swiped it from the humans last night."

"What is it?" Jig asked warily.

"They called it bacon." Relka glared at Darnak. "It's quick, and we can eat it while we prepare. No goblin should die hungry."

Jig took a bite, and the smoky, spicy taste caused his mouth to fill with drool. He stuffed the rest into his mouth and grinned. "You're sure this is human food? It's *good*!"

Relka handed him another greasy strip of bacon, then turned to the other goblins. Soon all of Jig's troops were wiping greasy fingers on their clothes, their hair, and each other.

Snarls and growls signaled the arrival of the wolves.

Gratz, Trok, and a few other goblins strained at the ropes. The wolves tugged and fought, but Gratz and Trok had tied them well. The ropes circling the wolves' necks were knotted in front of the throat. The more the wolves pulled, the deeper that knot pressed into their windpipes.

Of course, if you were Bastard, you could simply double back and bite the arm of the goblin holding your leash. With blue blood dripping from his jaws, Bastard bounded down the road toward Jig, his rope bouncing along the road behind him.

Darnak drew his club and stepped in front of Genevieve, shoving her out of Bastard's path. Several of the humans fumbled with their weapons. The goblins, being smarter, fought to get out of the way. Jig grabbed the sack Trok had given him. By the time his cold fingers closed around a toe, Bastard was almost on top of him.

"Bastard, down!" Jig squealed, throwing the toe.

Bastard twisted, snapped the toe out of the air, and crashed into Jig. Still chewing, Bastard bent down to sniff Jig's face.

"Argh," Jig gasped. "Toe breath!"

Relka grabbed Bastard's leash and tugged. Bastard barely noticed, but then Darnak added his weight to Relka's, dragging the wolf back enough for Jig to wiggle free.

Thirteen wolves in total, including Bastard. Fourteen if you counted Fungus, who was still limping from an arrow wound. Jig had already tried to get close enough to heal Fungus' wound. The attempt had almost cost him a hand.

He stood and brushed wolf fur from his cloak. Amazing how much these animals could shed.

"Do you have riders picked out?" Genevieve asked.

Jig nodded. Keeping his voice low, he said, "A mix of our goblins and the ones from Billa's army. Mostly goblins who are too dumb to realize what's going to happen to them. Gratz and I will be on Bastard."

It was a good thing Shadowstar was still muffling

Jig's fear. Bad enough he would be riding with the goblin who had tried to kill him yesterday. Without Shadowstar's help, the idea of riding Bastard again would have sent Jig running from town.

Jig handed out the toes Trok had collected and watched as his goblins climbed onto the wolves. Seeing them knot themselves into place made him think about the way Silverfang had died. "Everyone make sure you have a knife as well as a sword. If something happens, you'll want to cut yourselves free before your wolf falls on you."

Darnak cleared his throat. "Not that I'm one to tell goblins how to ride a wolf, but I'm thinking you might want to use a slipknot for those harnesses."

"A what?" Gratz asked.

Darnak walked up to one of the wolves, apparently unworried by the huge, growling jaws. Maybe his god took away his fear, too. Or maybe dwarves just didn't know how to be afraid. He twisted and tugged the rope, forming a small loop. A few more twists gave him a second, larger loop.

"This will hold you tight as a babe," Darnak said, tugging the loop. He switched his grip and grabbed one of the ends. "Something goes wrong, pull here." A swift jerk, and the loop fell apart.

Jig waited while the other goblins climbed onto their wolves. Trok was riding Smelly again, and looked as happy as Jig had ever seen him. Relka was on Ugly, and Braf was feeding Fungus a few extra toes, distracting the wolf long enough to heal his leg.

"Sir?" Gratz said. "I . . . I don't think Bastard will let me ride him without you."

Jig nodded and stepped past Gratz. Bastard licked his face, nearly knocking him into the snow. Jig shoved the wolf's muzzle aside and climbed onto his back. His legs and groin were already aching from the memory of his last ride.

He raised his hands while Darnak tied him into place. A second slipknot secured Jig's wrists. Anyone looking would assume he was a helpless prisoner. He pulled his cloak and blanket so they covered his sword.

Gratz climbed up behind him and reached around to grab Bastard's reins.

"Wait!" Jig shouted suddenly. He yanked the release ropes and hopped down.

"What is it, sir?" Gratz asked. "What's wrong?"

Relka leaped from her own wolf. "Is it an omen from Shadowstar?"

"Not exactly." Jig's face was burning. "I just . . . if I'm going to ride Bastard, I really need to use the privy first."

CHAPTER 15

*J*ig was marvelous! Selfish and cowardly and completely untrustworthy, but also clever and resourceful
and desperate to be something more than he was. Unfortunately, he was also so busy staying alive that he
rarely thought about things beyond his little world in
the caves . . . until now.

Did the adventurers who had captured him realize
how Jig was studying them, how he drank in every
word, every action, trying to learn how he too could
be such a hero?

And did Jig realize what he had already accomplished? He had survived the ambush of his patrol and
single-handedly helped the adventurers survive a hobgoblin trap. He had even played a part in overcoming
the various surprises the Necromancer had scattered
through his tunnels. They were currently resting, having
explored much of those tunnels to no avail.

This was Shadowstar's chance. He had seen how
keenly Jig watched the dwarf, fascinated by Darnak's
healing abilities. Shadowstar reached out, subtly nudg-
ing Jig until the goblin's curiosity overpowered his fear.

"Tell me of the gods," Jig said.

Shadowstar gathered his power. With no worshipers,
he had to forge and maintain his own connection to

the mortal realm. He would have to wait for the perfect moment.

Darnak started talking. And talking. The other adventurers retreated to the far side of the room. Jig's eyes began to glaze. Still the dwarf talked.

Was he even stopping long enough to breathe? Jig hadn't asked for a lecture on the romantic preferences of Olin Birch, one of the woodland gods, let alone the resulting diseases that had followed him through succeeding centuries.

Shadowstar grinned at the memories. Old Olin Knottytwig, they had called him.

On and on the dwarf talked. Despite himself, Shadowstar was impressed. Darnak knew the gods' histories better than most gods.

Finally, Darnak paused for a drink. Shadowstar reached out, channeling his power into a single seed of thought and praying it would take root in the dwarf's mind.

He chuckled when he realized Darnak's earlier tale had gotten him thinking in tree metaphors.

Darnak belched. "Then you had the Forgotten Gods." He frowned, apparently confused, and took another sip of wine.

Jig stared, hardly hearing a word of it. A bit of drool trickled from one side of his mouth. He was exhausted and bored out of his mind. Shadowstar gathered himself and poked Jig as hard as he could.

"What was that?" Jig asked.

Shadowstar turned his power back onto Darnak, who blinked. "Eh? Oh, the Fifteen Forgotten Gods of the War of Shadows?"

"Who were they?"

Shadowstar could already feel his connection to the dwarf fading. "Remember," he begged. The curse had been laid by a god, so a god should be strong enough to break it, even if only for a brief time. "Remember, blast you!"

"Take the Shadowstar," Darnak said. "They stripped

*his mind, flayed his body with blades of lightning, and
cast him loose in the desert."*

*Shadowstar's grip on the dwarf slipped. Had it
been enough?*

*Darnak babbled a few moments longer, and then his
voice trailed off. He glanced about in confusion. "What
was I saying just then?"*

*It didn't matter. Shadowstar could already feel Jig
reaching out, searching.*

*For the first time in thousands of years, Tymalous
Shadowstar had a follower.*

Jig kept one hand on his rope, ready to loosen his
bonds at the first hint of trouble. The fingers of his
other hand twisted into his cloak, holding it shut to
hide his sword. He grimaced and hunched his head.
He wished he could have put up his hood, but they
needed his face to be visible so everyone would see
he was a prisoner. But that meant Gratz's breath kept
tickling his neck as they rode.

The gates of Avery swung shut behind them. Given
the size of the gates, he expected a loud clang, or at
least a heavy thud. Anything to mark the drama of
the moment as the small goblin force set out to get
themselves killed. The only sound the elf-grown doors
made was an annoying squeak.

Jig wouldn't have thought it possible, but Billa's
army appeared even bigger from the ground. Goblins
and kobolds huddled around feebly burning campfires.
The monsters had camped on the road as well as in
the fields, so there was no clear path to Billa.

Gratz guided Bastard toward the goblin ranks,
avoiding the kobolds. Hopefully the goblins would be
less suspicious of their own kind. Even so, goblins everywhere stopped what they were doing to stare.

Gratz tugged the reins as they passed the first few
goblins, trying to keep the wolf from investigating the
rabbit turning over a fire, or the particularly smelly
goblin who scampered past.

Familiar odors surrounded them. Smoke from the

damp wood of the campfires. Burning meat. Filthy soldiers. Sheep droppings. Jig hadn't realized how accustomed he had grown to the smells in his short time with Billa. Then the wind shifted, and the stench of Smelly the wolf overpowered it all.

An armored goblin approached, a spear clutched in his hands. "Gratz, is that you? What happened to Silverfang?"

Jig held his breath. It wasn't that he was afraid of Gratz's response. Fear had nothing to do with it. The simple fact was that Gratz was a goblin, and this was the best chance he would have to betray Jig.

"The runt killed him." Gratz slapped the back of Jig's head. "Billa has plans for this one." He leaned his head down and whispered, "Sorry, sir. I know regulations say I'm not allowed to hit a superior officer, but if I act like you're my superior officer, nobody's going to believe—"

"Shut up," Jig said.

The guard grinned at Jig. "Try not to scream too loudly when she kills you. Some of the troops are still sleeping."

Jig did his best to look afraid. Strange, to have to force his features into an expression of terror. He hoped it wasn't too fake.

Goblins whispered and pointed as they rode, but none moved to stop them. Word spread quickly in the army. Jig could hear Gratz muttering, sounding more and more annoyed with every step.

"Regulations require them to challenge everyone who passes. They should have stopped us before we ever reached the perimeter." He glared back at the goblin with the spear. "He doesn't even have his spear in a proper grip. With thirteen wolves, he should have brought reinforcements. He should have insisted on searching the prisoner, to make sure you're not smuggling anything in."

"I am," Jig said. "I'm smuggling a sword, remember?"

"I know. That doesn't make it any less shameful. Silverfang would have—"

The creaking of branches interrupted whatever Gratz was saying. Snow shivered from Oakbottom's branches as he waded through the goblin camp, moving to intercept the wolf-riders. Several of the drowsy goblins were too slow to move out of his way. Their screams made Jig wince.

"What's this?" Oakbottom asked, stopping directly in front of Jig.

"That's more like it," Gratz said. "Though by rights, he never should have allowed us this deep into—"

Jig jabbed an elbow into his ribs.

Gratz coughed, then said, "The humans decided to surrender Jig to Billa the Bloody, and to let us go free!"

As planned, the other wolf-riders cheered and waved their weapons in the air. Jig studied Oakbottom, waiting to see whether he believed their story. How was Jig supposed to read the facial expressions of a tree?

How did Oakbottom even see? He had no eyes, as far as Jig could tell. It had to be even worse during the summer, when all his leaves grew in. Did he have someone trim his branches?

"Billa will be interested in hearing what took you so long," Oakbottom said.

"I'll give her my full report when I turn over the prisoner," Gratz answered, snapping off a quick salute.

"Bring your wolves to the pen." Oakbottom pointed his branches toward a small farmhouse. "Billa said I was to take the prisoner, if they turned him over. Apparently this one's tricky, for a goblin."

Jig waited, but Gratz didn't answer. Oakbottom stood unmoving, like . . . well, like a tree.

"Gratz?" Jig whispered. Hopefully Oakbottom's hearing wasn't as acute as a goblin's.

"Yes, sir?" Gratz's voice was equally low.

"Answer the tree!"

"What do I say?"

Jig groaned. Of course Gratz didn't know what to

do. Regulations didn't say how to handle it when your plan fell apart and your superior officer couldn't bark out new orders because he was pretending to be a prisoner.

Jig glanced around. They were roughly halfway through the goblins. Too far to turn back, but not close enough to have any hope of reaching Billa.

Jig was used to his plans not working. All goblins were. But he had hoped to make a bit more progress before everything fell apart.

"Is there a problem, goblin?"

Was it Jig's imagination, or did Oakbottom sound hopeful? Maybe he hadn't been able to toss a goblin in a few days.

Before Jig or Gratz could respond, another wolf bounded past. Relka pointed her sword at Oakbottom and shouted, "For Jig and Shadowstar!"

Why had Jig insisted on bringing the stupid goblins along? He tugged the release rope, freeing his hands and giving himself a nasty rope burn on his wrists. "Split into two lines," he shouted. "Run past him and make for Billa!"

Gratz was already tugging Bastard's reins, leading him to the right. The other wolves began to charge, like a river flowing around a rock. Or around a big, angry tree who liked to throw goblins. Nobody wanted to come within reach of those branches.

Nobody except Relka. She and Ugly rode straight for Oakbottom. He reached out, and she slammed her sword into his branch.

The blade stuck. Oakbottom raised the branch. Relka tugged her rope, slipping free of the wolf as she rose into the air. Oakbottom plucked her free with another branch and grabbed her wolf with a third. He spun in a circle and threw both Relka and Ugly at Jig.

"Faster!" Jig yelled, kicking Bastard in the sides. He ducked as Relka passed overhead. With Ugly, Oakbottom actually did them a favor. The yelping wolf crashed into the charging goblins, knocking them back and clearing a bit of space for Bastard.

Jig drew his sword and waved it overhead. With this many goblins around, the elven blade shone like a beacon. Hopefully it would help the other wolf-riders to follow him through the chaos.

The goblins in front of them leaped away. Bastard's snapping jaws probably had more to do with their fear than Jig's sword, but he liked to think the glowing blade helped.

"For Jig and Shadowstar!" Gratz shouted, all but deafening him.

Jig's face burned as the other goblins picked up the cry.

"The orcs are fearless," Gratz warned him. "They won't budge." Up ahead, the orcs were already racing into formation, raising shields and spears to break Jig's charge.

Yes, they will, said Shadowstar.

A wash of heat was Jig's only warning before red light flashed from his body. When he fought the elf scout days before, he had lit up like a little goblin bonfire. Now it was as if the Autumn Star rode Bastard into battle. Though the sun wasn't fully risen, the land around him was bright as daylight. Red-tinged daylight, sure. But daylight nonetheless. The orcs staggered back, raising their hands and shields to protect their eyes.

Jig twisted to look at his riders. They seemed unaffected by the light, but Billa's army fell away as though they were blind.

One of the perks of being a champion of Tymalous Shadowstar. There's a chance Noc or another god will notice, but it's a bit late for worrying about that, eh? Shadowstar sounded ridiculously cheerful, not to mention smug.

Jig grinned and clung to Bastard's fur as the wolf leaped past the first line of orcs. Jig kept his ears flat. The tips were ice cold from the wind. *I don't suppose you could provide the heat of the Autumn Star as well as the light?*

Only if you want to be burned to ashes before your wolf takes another step, said Shadowstar.

Where was Billa? Tents and wagons marked the orc camp. Billa had to be here, probably near the center, but which tent was hers?

Gratz waved his sword in the air. "Spearpoint formation!"

Most of the wolves closed into a single line with Bastard at the head. Two of the goblins—Braf and another warrior from Jig's lair—looked at one another in confusion then went back to laying about with their weapons. They had no idea what a spearpoint formation was, but the chaos and confusion they caused helped protect the main line.

With Billa's troops blind and confused, it was easy for the wolf-riders to hit goblins, kobolds, and anyone else who got in the way. But that led to a new danger, as Jig's goblins grew intoxicated by their momentary advantage. The formation wavered as individual riders laid about with their weapons. One goblin even swerved to attack a goat that had wandered too close. The blow killed the goat and dislocated the goblin's shoulder when he tried to hold on to his weapon, which had lodged in the goat's back.

Jig groaned as he counted his wolves. He was down to eight, counting Bastard.

"There!" Trok pulled alongside, grinning as he pointed his sword at one of the tents.

Billa stood barefoot in a heavy nightgown, her sword strapped over her shoulder. She looked as if she had just climbed out of bed. Did she sleep with that sword?

"Everyone, follow me!" Gratz shouted. "Sorry. I mean, follow Jig!"

Jig and Gratz both tugged Bastard's harness, guiding him toward Billa. Billa and the crowd of heavily armed and armored orcs who stood before her.

Why aren't they blind like the rest of her troops? Jig asked.

Isa is protecting them, just as I'm protecting your goblins and your wolves.

Trok kicked his wolf into the lead. "Left flank, help me hit the ugly one there!"

"Which one is the ugly one?" Braf yelled.

And then they were crashing through orcs. Jig saw one goblin go down, but the weight of the charging wolf still knocked the orc to the ground. Trok ducked and hamstrung a second.

Bastard trampled a third, which slowed them down enough for more orcs to close in. Jig gripped his sword with both hands, holding it at arm's length to block a much bigger sword that would have taken his head clean off and probably killed Gratz as well. The impact knocked Jig's sword back and numbed his arms.

"Parry at an angle," Gratz yelled. "You don't have to stop the weapon. Just knock it out of the way."

Blood trickled down Jig's face. Apparently he had cut his scalp with the back edge of his own sword. He hadn't even felt it.

A glancing blow bruised his ribs but failed to penetrate his cloak. He would definitely have to remember to thank Shadowstar for that.

Jig gave up trying to follow everything that was happening. The noise was worse than the lair back home on the nights Golaka brewed up a fresh batch of klak beer. The bloodshed was about the same, though.

Up ahead, Billa was waving her sword and shouting orders. Only a few orcs still stood between her and the goblins.

They were winning! The realization nearly made Jig drop his sword. Gratz had been right. Audacity was the key to victory.

"Get the leader," Billa shouted.

One of the orcs hesitated. "Which one is that?"

Jig stabbed that orc in the leg as he rode past. His sword cut through the orc's heavy furs and armor as if they were cobwebs.

Maybe elf swords weren't so bad after all.

Billa shook her head. "The one who's glowing, you idiot!"

There was only one more orc between Jig and Billa. Jig reached into his cloak and pulled out one of his last goblin toes. He threw it to the orc, who automatically reached to catch it with his free hand.

Bastard snapped up both the toe and the hand in one bite.

Billa sprang forward and swung her sword with both hands. Bastard yelped and staggered to the side, one leg cleanly severed.

Jig barely managed to yank the release line as Bastard fell. The world tilted, and Jig found himself sitting in the snow with a sore rump.

Gratz wasn't so lucky. He covered his head with both hands, trying to protect himself from Bastard's flailing. The poor wolf was completely panicked. He wasn't bleeding, thanks to the cold of Billa's sword. Not yet, anyway. But he was biting and snarling at everything that moved, including Gratz.

The remaining goblins and wolves circled around Billa, who took a cautious step back. Her face was still blistered and scabbed from Jig's torch, back in the lair.

With Bastard down, Jig had five wolves, one of which was carrying a dead goblin. Braf was holding a bloody gash in his side, and Jig could sense the pulsing warmth of Shadowstar's magic as he healed himself. Convenient, that magic. Trok's sword was broken and his leg was soaked in blood, but he was grinning like a madman.

Most of the orcs lay dead or wounded in the snow. For goblins, they had done exceptionally well.

"Orders, general?" Trok asked.

Jig pointed at Billa. There was probably an appropriate formation for something like this, but Jig had no idea what it might be. "Get her!"

Jig managed two steps before the wind slammed him to his knees. His cloak flapped behind him, tugging him onto his back. That would be just his luck, to choke to death on his own cloak. He fumbled at the clasp, but his numb fingers were all but useless.

At least Jig's spectacles provided some small protection. He could see the other goblins covering their faces as they huddled in the snow.

Several wolves toppled over, trapping their riders. The surviving orcs bent into the wind, but they were as helpless as Jig. Only Billa the Bloody appeared untouched by the frigid wind. Her gown fluttered about her legs, and her hair danced in all directions. Her expression reminded him of a tunnel cat toying with its prey.

Help? Jig asked.

I'm trying. Isa is stronger than I am.

Jig lifted his sword into a guard position. The wind caught the flat of his blade, and he nearly cut off his own arm before he managed to turn the sword so the edge pointed into the wind. He tried to climb to his feet, but the instant he stood, the wind tossed him onto his back. He actually slid a short distance.

"For Shadowstar!" The wind nearly swallowed Relka's defiant cry as she limped into the wind, using her sword as a walking stick to pull herself along. Apparently the wind lost strength the farther you were from Billa. Which meant the smart thing was to get as far from Billa as possible.

Relka stepped closer. One of the orcs near Jig turned around and took a cautious step toward her. With his second step, the wind pushed him into an uncontrolled run. He raised his ax and bellowed, his great leaps quickly closing the distance between him and Relka.

Relka raised her weapon, lost her balance, and fell over. She would never get up in time to protect herself. Even if she did. . . .

Jig switched his sword to his left hand, nearly losing it to the wind. More carefully, he pulled out his dagger to throw, then hesitated.

Warriors could throw their weapons. The last few

times Jig had tried, the results had been laughable. He could imagine himself stretching his arm back to throw, only to have the wind rip the knife from his hand. Knowing his luck, the blade would jab him in his own backside.

Instead, Jig gently tossed the knife into the air.

Billa's wind caught the knife, flinging it with far greater force than he could ever have managed. It flipped through the air, buzzing like an angry insect. The hilt smashed into the orc's skull. He tripped over Relka and skidded face-first in the snow. Jig grinned and turned back around to face Billa.

Well done, said Shadowstar.

You told me once that when I die, I'll come before you, Jig said, watching as Billa advanced. *Is that true?*

It is.

Good. Because any minute now, I plan to walk right up to you and bite you in the—

Have faith, Jig Dragonslayer. Shadowstar's voice was firm. *Hold your strike until I give the word.*

What strike? Did Shadowstar actually think Jig would get the chance to attack before Billa ran him through?

I can't blind the orcs and protect you from the wind at the same time. Be ready.

"Isa spent centuries preparing for this," Billa shouted. "Do you believe she'd allow a goblin to interfere?"

"Not really," Jig said.

Now.

The blinding red faded, returning the world to its dreary palate of snow and mud. At the same time, the wind seemed to vanish. Jig could still hear it roaring past, but he couldn't feel a thing. It was like when he had turned his sword sideways, so the blade cut through the wind instead of fighting it.

Less introspection and more attacking!

What's introspection? Oh—right. Jig leaped forward, thrusting the tip of his sword at Billa's stomach.

Billa's sword was in the wrong position to parry,

but she managed to twist out of the way. Jig's sword grazed a line on her nightgown, but nothing more. Off balance, Jig had to jump aside as Billa spun around and tried to decapitate him.

Jig tumbled into the snow. He glanced down to see a long section of cloak hanging down around his feet. Any closer, and she would have taken his leg as well.

Billa stepped back. She scowled as she studied Jig. "Isa wants you dead, goblin. I've never heard her so angry. What did you do?"

"I melted her head with my fire-spider," Jig said.

Billa snorted. For a heartbeat, genuine mirth peeked through Billa's anger. She wiped her nose on the sleeve of her nightgown, then raised her sword so the blade angled up across her body.

Jig stepped sideways, searching for an opening. Billa's sword was longer than his. So were her arms, for that matter. By the time he got close enough to strike, Billa could run him through.

He would have to be quick. A feint to distract her, causing her to overextend in one direction, and then he could dash around and stab her in the belly. Once he was close, Billa's larger weapon could be a disadvantage. She wouldn't have room for a great, sweeping blow. Though with that sword, even a tiny cut might be enough to kill.

Jig cocked his head. "Your nose is bleeding again."

Billa reached up to touch her nostrils. As she did, her sword dipped lower. Jig screamed, doing his best to mimic the panicked fury of a goblin war cry, and stabbed at her foot.

Even as Billa lurched to parry, Jig pushed off hard, bringing his sword up to her stomach and—

Billa jumped back, sucking in her gut. Once again Jig scored a small cut, and then Billa's fist caught him in the side of the head.

His sword flew away. Jig hit the ground, then rolled away from Billa's huge feet as she tried to stomp on his face. He spat snow and blood. *You should have given me a helmet too.*

Sorry.

The light from his sword made it easy to spot. Unfortunately, Billa spotted it too. She kicked it out of Jig's reach.

Jig glanced around. The surviving goblins and wolves were ringed by orcs. And Oakbottom. The orcs appeared to be waiting for Billa to finish him off. Letting her prove how tough and scary she was, no doubt.

Jig started to grab his dagger, then remembered he had thrown it away to protect Relka. Relka, who had once again begun to sing.

> *"I looked upon the glory of the glowing blade of Jig.*
> *He fought the ugly orc who had a nose just like a fig.*
> *And though his light has faded and the orcs are*
>   *drawing near,*
> *With him I have no fear."*

Billa shook her head. "Is she always like this?"

"Pretty much," said Jig as he struggled to stand. "Sorry." He knew it couldn't be fear making his legs tremble. Therefore it must be an aftereffect of Billa's punch.

I'm sorry, he said silently. *Did you really believe I could beat Billa?*

Would he feel the blow that killed him? Billa was fast, and her sword was magically sharp. Any pain would be over in the blink of an eye. Unless she deliberately tried to prolong his suffering.

Billa thrust the point of her sword straight at Jig's throat.

The impact was lower than he expected, like a punch to the chest. He flew back, hitting the ground hard enough to make his ears ring.

The wind died. Nobody spoke. Unnerved by the silence, Jig reached down to touch his stomach.

The shirt was whole. But Shadowstar's cloak wasn't strong enough to block Isa's weapon. And why could he still hear ringing?

Jig jumped to his feet and stared.

Tymalous Shadowstar stood facing him, his hands still extended. He must have pushed Jig out of the way. The bells on Shadowstar's sleeves shivered as he reached down to touch the icy blade protruding from his stomach.

"Doesn't that hurt?" Jig asked.

Shadowstar nodded. "Very much, yes." He tightened his fingers around the blade and grunted as Billa tried to pull it free.

"You saved me."

"It's what I am." He winced. "I kind of hoped it wouldn't come to this, though."

There was no blood. Did gods even have blood? But as Jig watched, water began to drip from between Shadowstar's fingers where he held the sword.

"No!" Billa shouted. She grabbed the hilt with both hands, but it wouldn't budge. Rivulets of water dripped down to the tip to splash into the snow.

"Would you mind?" Shadowstar asked. He turned his head, and the starbursts in his eyes flitted toward Billa.

Jig moved toward his sword. Two orcs stepped in front of him, brandishing a club and an ax. Before Jig could react, they raised their own weapons . . . and then toppled over, asleep.

Jig glanced back at Shadowstar, who winked. "I am a god of protection, of peace and rest," he said. His voice was tight with pain. "They looked like they could use a nap."

"Stop him!" Billa shrieked. With a grunt, she stumbled back, nearly falling. She still held Isa's sword, but the blade was broken a short distance from the hilt. Shadowstar's grip had melted right through it. The broken blade continued to shrink away, dripping water over her hands. She flung it away and ran toward Jig's sword.

Jig didn't bother. He bent down, picked up a club one of the orcs had dropped, and slammed it into Billa's leg. She dropped and clutched her knee.

As Jig struggled to get the oversize weapon into

position for a second blow, another goblin shoved him aside.

Gratz's clothes were a bloody mess. Shallow wolf bites covered his forearms. He clutched his sword with both hands. The blade trembled as he pointed it at Billa.

He and Billa stared at one another for several breaths, and then Gratz said, "The penalty for treason is death." He rammed his sword into her chest, and added, "Sir."

Nobody spoke as Billa toppled backward, Gratz's sword still protruding from her chest. Only the heavy snores of two sleeping orcs disturbed the silence.

"Is Isa's sword destroyed?" Shadowstar asked.

Jig picked up the hilt. It was cold to the touch, but not unbearably so. The blade was completely gone. He brought it over to Shadowstar, who turned it over in his hands. A few drops of water fell to the ground.

Shadowstar smiled and sat down in the snow, one hand holding the hilt, the other clutching his stomach. There was no visible wound, but Shadowstar was clearly in pain. Without thinking, Jig reached out and put his hand over Shadowstar's, trying to heal the damage, but nothing happened.

"You're drawing—" Shadowstar coughed. *You're drawing on my power to heal me. It doesn't work that way.*

The monsters crowded around had begun to whisper. Very soon now the shock would pass, and then things would get messy indeed. Already the goblins were backing away from the orcs. The orcs were eyeing the goblins. The few kobolds who had come were still jumping up and down to try to see what was going on.

The only one who didn't appear to notice the tension was Relka. She seemed to see nothing but Shadowstar as she limped closer.

"Who is that?" she whispered. Her voice shook. She clutched her amulet so tightly her hands bled.

"He's the one who got me into this mess," Jig said.

Shadowstar chuckled. "It's one of my gifts."

Relka stopped just beyond arm's reach. For the first time that Jig could remember, she appeared unsure. She glanced at Jig, then back at Shadowstar, like a rat trying to decide which way to flee. "You're him, aren't you? Tymalous Shadowstar."

Shadowstar bowed his head.

"Billa was going to kill me," Jig said. "You pushed me out of the way. Why?"

Because you didn't think to duck. And because it was the only way to get my hands on Isa's sword long enough to destroy it. His bells rang as he coughed again, an odd combination of sounds. *I did say I'd try to protect you.*

"The runt killed Billa!" shouted one of the orcs.

Good job, said Jig. He drew a deep breath, pointed at Gratz, and said, "He did the actual killing."

Braf frowned. "Does that mean he's in charge of Billa's army now?"

Before Jig could answer, another orc snarled and raised an ax. "I'm not taking orders from some scrawny goblin."

The goblins began readying their own weapons. "Better than following another stinking orc!" someone shouted.

One of the kobolds chimed in, saying, "Orcs and goblins both stink."

Jig guessed it would be the orcs who killed him. They were closest, and they had the best weapons and armor. But instead of sheer, skin-chilling terror, Jig mostly felt sad. All of Billa's work was melting away with her death. The monsters would turn on one another, decimating their own ranks. The survivors would scatter, to be hunted by humans and other adventurers.

I never thought I'd say this to you, but I think you're being optimistic.

Jig turned to look at Shadowstar, who pointed to the northern side of the valley.

Maybe Shadowstar's wounds had sapped too much

of his strength for him to continue stealing Jig's fear. Or maybe there was only so much terror a god could take away.

Regardless, the cloud of arrows arching from the upper edge of the valley was enough to shatter Jig's divine courage.

"Oh, dung." His voice was little more than a whisper.

"What is it?" Relka asked.

"Wendel's army."

CHAPTER 16

*The manifestation of Tymalous Shadowstar, cur-
rently resting in the snow as Jig panicked, showed
no wound from Billa's attack. Unfortunately, things in
his temple were quite different.*

*All that blood, dripping onto his temple floor. How
messy.*

*"You've looked better." Isa stood in the doorway.
Snow swirled around her white gown, and her breath
turned to frost. "Really, Tymalous. Sacrificing yourself
for a goblin?"*

He coughed and said, "I like that goblin."

*"He's going to die anyway. If my orcs don't kill
him, the humans will." Isa ran one hand through her
windswept hair, almost as if she were checking for spiders. "This isn't what I wanted, you know."*

*Shadowstar pushed himself higher, propping his
back against the wall. "I know."*

*She stomped across the temple. "What were you
thinking, throwing yourself between Billa and that goblin? Aren't you taking this whole protection thing a bit
too far?"*

*"It's what I am." Shadowstar smiled. Her eyes were
the color of the northern glaciers, and they shone when
she was angry.*

*"I would have spared your pet goblin," she said. "If
you'd—"*

"If I'd helped you kill my son?"

Isa spun away, and Shadowstar chuckled. For thousands of years, mortal poets had associated passion and rage with the element of fire. That might have changed, if Noc's curse hadn't robbed their memories of Isa and her temper.

"Shortsighted as always, Tymalous." She kept her back turned, but Shadowstar could hear the pain in her voice. *"Who will stop me next time? I'll raise a new army, recreate my sword—"*

"That sword took years to make."

Isa laughed. *"That's the beauty of Noc's curse, love. They've forgotten us. I have all the time in the universe."*

Shadowstar closed his eyes, remembering the last time Isa had spoken to him of the inevitability of victory. That war had almost destroyed them, but Isa had learned nothing. She couldn't. She was the winter wind, returning each year without fail. Unstoppable and inevitable.

"Isa, what do you think will happen when this wound kills me?"

Isa turned to face him. *"I'm sorry, Tymalous. I would save you if I could, but healing has never been my strength."*

"That's not what I meant." He coughed, then grimaced as more blood seeped through his fingers. *"Who comes to oversee the death of the gods?"*

Isa went still. *"There are several gods of death,"* she whispered. *"It might not be—"*

"He's my son, Isa. He will come for me, and he will remember."

"You planned this." She stepped toward him, hands balled into fists, then caught herself. Throttling him would only speed Noc's arrival. *"I'm not ready! Without my sword—"*

"You should leave now," Shadowstar said. *"Get a head start. If you elude him long enough, he might even forget you again. But I'm told it's very difficult to escape death once he adds your name to his list."*

"You let Billa kill you, all so you could destroy my sword and send your traitor son after me."

"I was hoping to avoid the part where Billa killed me, but otherwise, yes." Shadowstar shrugged and spread his hands. *"He's my son."*

Snow blinded him, and then Isa was gone. Frost covered the stones.

"I'm sorry about your orc!" Shadowstar called out. He chuckled to himself. *"Maybe you should have gotten yourself a goblin instead."*

The arrows fell like rain, landing mostly among the kobolds—either deliberately or because that was the limit of their range. The attack sent the kobolds into a panic. The injured howled and yipped. The healthy trampled the injured.

"I thought the humans weren't supposed to arrive for another day or so," Trok said.

"Brilliant tactical move on their part," said Gratz. "Using Jig to take out Billa the Bloody, throwing our forces into chaos."

Except that if Jig had failed, Wendel's strategy would have gotten his entire army killed when Billa triggered her spell.

"The goblins betrayed us to the humans," shouted an enormous, bare-chested orc with muscles like a mountain range. A scar on his arm showed him to be one of Billa's high-ranking orcs. Either that, or a wolf had gnawed on his shoulder for a while.

"No, the humans betrayed us to the other humans," Braf argued.

The orcs didn't listen. "Kill them all," said another, a cry which quickly spread through the ranks. The bare-chested orc snarled and stomped toward Trok and the goblins, waving an enormous ax overhead. Halfway there, a ball of snow and mud exploded against the side of his head.

Everyone turned to look at Jig. Jig wiped his hand on his cloak to dry it. He wasn't sure what surprised him more, that he had thrown the muddy snow at the orc, or that he had actually hit what he was aiming at. *Did you take away my fear again?*

Not this time, said Shadowstar. *You did that all by yourself.*

Right. Jig wouldn't be shaking so hard if Shadowstar was still stealing his fear.

The orc pointed his ax. "Pound that one into the mud."

"Pound me yourself," Jig yelled. He hugged himself to hide his trembling. *You said you'd have to wrest control from Billa and Isa in order to use the spells in those scars. Are you strong enough—*

Shadowstar smiled and leaned back, closing his eyes. *Billa is dead, and Isa is . . . busy. I can guide you, but you'll have to trigger the spell.*

The orc was laughing as he readied himself, but at least the others had drawn back to see what happened. He swung his ax through the air, stretching the muscles in his arms. He managed to kill a goblin on the backswing. He blinked in surprise, then shrugged and wiped the edge of his ax on his trousers.

"Wait," Jig squeaked. "Let me get my sword." He scrambled away from the orc. Ten paces ought to be enough distance.

Make it twenty.

Jig kept backing away. Behind the orc, Jig saw Braf tugging the other goblins and dragging them back. Shadowstar must have warned him what Jig was about to do.

"Hey, you forgot your sword!" Another orc grabbed Jig's weapon and tossed it.

Jig dove out of the way, barely avoiding being impaled by his own weapon.

Focus on the scar, said Shadowstar.

Jig began to shiver. His skin pimpled from cold that seemed to come from within, as if the blood had frozen in his veins. His fangs were the worst. This cold had come on so quickly that they actually froze to his lips.

Concentrate, Shadowstar snapped.

Jig nodded and turned toward the orc. Even at this distance, he could feel the scar on the orc's shoulder, the bitter cold that threatened to freeze Jig's eyeballs in his skull. Those spots of cold were everywhere, scattered throughout Billa's army, but Jig concentrated on the orc.

Imagine yourself melting the ice within that scar to release the spell.

Jig closed his eyes. He could still see the scar, a blur of blue cold jostling about in the darkness. All he had to do was—

Limping footsteps crunched through the snow. Jig stepped back, his eyes snapping open. Relka stood between Jig and the orc, holding a bloody sword in both hands. "I'll kill you all before I let you hurt Jig Dragonslayer."

"Fair enough," said the orc.

Now, Jig. Melt the ice.

Jig held his breath and imagined a fire-spider in his hand. He could almost feel Smudge's terror burning his palm. Praying Shadowstar knew what he was doing, Jig visualized himself throwing the spider.

His imagination was a bit too true to life. In his mind, Smudge flew wide and landed in the snow, where he turned to glare back at Jig.

The spider is in your mind, Jig! Shadowstar shouted. *How could you possibly miss?*

Jig concentrated, imagining a nest of whiteworms on the orc's arm. Plump, delicious whiteworms, one of Smudge's favorites.

His vision blurred. Was the cold freezing his eyeballs? He hoped Shadowstar would be able to heal them. He closed his eyes and concentrated on Smudge.

In his mind, Smudge raced up the orc's body and settled directly onto the scar to feast.

Hurry, Jig.

Jig could hear the orc approaching. Clenching his fists, he imagined Golaka the chef coming up to Smudge with a pot and spoon. Jig wasn't terribly fond

of fire-spider soup, but many of the goblins loved it.
The risk of biting down on a flame gland and burning
through your lip was part of the fun.

The imaginary Smudge looked up from his
whiteworms and reacted with the same terror anyone
would feel when faced with a hungry Golaka. Heat
seared the scar on the orc's arm, and Jig cried out as
a wind colder than any Jig had known passed *through*
his body.

The wind passed in an instant. Jig didn't know how
much was in his mind, but the cold had been real
enough to freeze Jig's fangs to his cheeks. He
wrenched his lower jaw, tearing his fangs free as he
looked around.

The lenses of his spectacles had fogged over, so he
lowered his head and peered over the top of the
frames.

A group of orcs lay unmoving in the snow. Jig's
would-be executioner stood in the center, his ax still
raised overhead.

A kobold ran up to kick the closest orc. The orc's
hand snapped off.

With a triumphant howl, the kobold snatched up
the hand and raced back to his fellows.

In the distance, arrows continued to pour into the
far edge of Billa's army, but the screams seemed far
away, like echoes from a distant tunnel. Jig sheathed
his sword and hugged himself to try to control his
shivering.

"Who did that?" asked an orc.

Trok was the first to respond. "Jig Dragonslayer."
He pointed to Jig. "The new commander of Billa's
army."

"Unless anyone else wants to end up like this lot?"
Relka added. She folded her arms and contemplated
the frozen orcs. "I wonder how long the meat will
keep, frozen like that."

"Orders, sir?" asked Gratz. Billa's blood still covered his sword. The orcs kept staring at Jig and muttering to themselves.

How long before they decided to try again? Between Shadowstar's weakness and the horrible chill of the magic, Jig doubted he could freeze another orc if he tried. He needed to take control before they all killed one another and saved the humans the trouble.

"Tell the kobolds to pull back out of range," he said.

"Why?" One of the orcs laughed. "So they kill a few dogs. Why should we care?"

"Stupid orc!" A kobold darted past two of the orcs and plunged a knife into the taunter's leg.

"No!" How had Billa done it? All the monsters wanted to do was kill one another, even with an entire army ready to ride down and destroy them.

Relka tugged his arm and pointed. Slowly Jig started to smile.

"What's the penalty for brawling on duty?" he shouted. He wasn't loud enough for the orc or the kobold to hear him over their angry cries. If they had, they might have heard Oakbottom's approach.

The orc grabbed the kobold, and then Oakbottom grabbed them both. Moments later both the orc and the kobold were soaring over the fields.

"Oakbottom, you have permission to toss anyone else who disobeys," Jig said.

"Hey, you're not—" That was as far as the orc got before Oakbottom launched her after the others.

Oakbottom didn't care about rank or loyalty, so long as he had the chance to throw people. Jig wouldn't be able to keep control for long, but he doubted anyone would survive long enough for that to matter.

"They're going to charge right over us." Jig stood on his toes, trying to see. The orcs blocked his view of Billa's army, but he could see movement atop the far side of the valley as the human archers advanced through the trees.

Gratz shook his head. "The valley's too steep and snowy for a true charge. Horses can't handle it, and the men will have to march slow and careful. But they'll be thorough. The king will probably send hunting parties out with dogs once he's broken our forces."

And the king wouldn't stop with the valley. They knew where the goblin lair was, and they knew it was once again open to the world. Wendel had lost yet another son. He wouldn't rest until every last goblin was dead.

"Billa the Bloody would have marched this army to victory."

Even Jig's ears couldn't pick out the speaker. "Billa's dead." He turned to Gratz. "How many wolves do we have?"

"Only a few of ours survived that attack," Gratz said. "The other goblin regiments have a few more squads of wolf-riders, though. We've probably got about eighty or so all total."

Good. "Trok, go get everyone mounted up and ready to retreat."

"Typical goblin," muttered one of the orcs. "Running away like a coward."

Jig nodded to himself. That described goblins pretty well. He thought about the tunnels and caves back home, the smell of the muck lanterns, the firm feel of obsidian beneath his feet, the taste of Golaka's cooking. . . .

Angry roars shook Jig free of his stupor.

"The trolls have gotten loose," Relka commented. Jig couldn't see the former slaves, but he could hear them rampaging through the ranks. From the screams, it sounded as though they were more interested in escape than revenge.

If he was going to do anything, it had to be now, before things got any more out of control. He turned to the orcs. "You're going to take Avery for us."

"How?" asked Gratz. "We have no siege equipment, remember?"

"Sure we do," Jig said, grinning. He pointed toward Oakbottom. "We've got him. Oakbottom, how would you like to toss an entire army of orcs?"

Oakbottom's branches quivered. Presumably that

was a good thing, a sign of anticipation. Or maybe it was the wind.

"Do you think you're good enough to land them on top of the wall?" Jig asked.

"Let's find out." Oakbottom reached for the nearest orc.

"Not from here!" Jig shouted.

The orcs backed away. "I'm not about to let some walking tree throw me about," said one.

Jig folded his arms. "I understand if you're afraid. I jumped from the top of that wall and survived, but it was a little frightening. If you don't think you're tough enough—"

You jumped? Shadowstar asked.

Jumped. Fell. What's the difference?

The difference is that you had Darnak there to fix you.

The orcs were already charging toward Avery. Oakbottom scooped up a few orcs for practice, flinging them toward the walls as he followed. Jig tried to imagine what it would be like to be a human atop the wall, to see orc after orc hurtling through the air, screaming and waving their weapons. Even if most of the orcs died from the impact, Oakbottom would still be able to knock the humans off the wall. And it only took a few survivors to open the gates from inside.

He turned to the goblins and kobolds. The kobolds had already drawn back past the road, safely out of range for now. They really were quick.

"When Wendel's forces see what we're doing, they'll speed up the attack, sending more men to defend Avery." Jig wished he had thought to swipe a few of Darnak's maps. This would be much easier to plan if he could see everything.

"Is that when we attack?" asked Gratz.

Jig shook his head. "We're goblins. That's when we run away."

Goblin drums were bad enough. Combined with the braying of orcish horns and the shrill yowls the kobolds used to relay commands, the noise was enough to set Jig's teeth grinding. He flattened his ears and tugged the cloak off a fallen orc. The material was bloody, but tough. He wrapped it around two spears, tying the sleeves in a tight knot. He did the same with the bottom corners. "Help me."

Braf and Relka gently lifted Tymalous Shadowstar onto Jig's cloak. Each grabbed the spears and started to lift. Then Braf cursed and dropped his end.

Jig tried not to weep. "Maybe you should grab the spears *behind* the points."

"Sorry." Braf tried a second time. "Shouldn't gods be heavier?"

Loud howls made Jig jump, even though he had been expecting it. He turned to see Trok leading the wolf-riders past Avery. The kobolds fled in the opposite direction, scampering at top speed in the general direction of Pottersville. Just let Wendel's army try to catch them all.

Promise me something, Jig.

"What?"

Shadowstar managed a smile. *Don't let them eat me.*

Jig stared at Tymalous Shadowstar. There was no blood, but he looked like . . . well, like someone who had been run through with a big sword. His face was even paler than usual, and his eyes had dimmed.

Despite everything he had seen, Jig still couldn't accept the idea of a god dying. Gods didn't do that. Humans and orcs and kobolds and goblins, sure. Especially goblins. But not gods. Part of being a god was that you didn't die.

You could run away faster if you weren't carrying me, Shadowstar pointed out.

That's why I had Braf and Relka carry you instead of doing it myself, Jig answered. "We need to get to the edge of the woods. Make sure nobody crosses the boundary into elf lands."

"How will we know?" asked Braf.

"If everyone starts getting shot with arrows, we've gone too far."

The sharp scream of an elfhawk nearly made them drop Shadowstar. Everyone turned to stare at the two enormous birds flying from Avery. Jig squinted through his spectacles, trying to discern whether the hawks carried riders.

As the birds reached the edge of the army, a few goblins and kobolds hurled spears. Most missed, and those that hit didn't appear to do any damage. Prince Theodore must have hardened his hawks' skins against attack, the same as he had done to his men.

One of the goblins leaped and swung his sword. The hawk swerved, and its talons dug into the goblin's arm. Powerful wings pounded the air. The goblin screamed and kicked as the hawk hauled him higher, then dropped him.

To a bird that size, Jig was nothing more than a rat. A scrawny rat. So hopefully the hawks would go after plumper prey.

As usual, luck was not on Jig's side. The lead hawk banked sharply, then dove.

"They look like they're coming right at us," said Braf.

Jig dropped to the ground and crawled beneath Shadowstar. Braf and Relka promptly dropped the god on top of Jig and pulled out their weapons.

None of it made any difference. The hawk drew up sharply, and one of the enormous wings knocked Braf backward. The other batted Relka to the ground. Huge talons curled around Jig's neck and chest.

"Jig!" Relka pushed to her feet and leaped. Wrapping one arm around the hawk's other leg, she tried to drive her knife into the chest. And then they were airborne.

"Easy down there." Windswept black hair all but obscured Darnak's face as he peered down from atop the hawk. "Aha! No wonder she's having trouble climbing. If your friend was so eager to come along, she should have grabbed Genevieve's bird."

Jig tried to answer, but whatever faint squeak he might have managed was lost in the beating of wings.

They were already far above the treetops. He could see Braf still standing there, a confused look on his tiny face. Behind them, Genevieve clung tightly to her hawk. Her black cloak flapped behind her.

"Let us go!" Relka shouted. She clung with her arm and both legs as she tried to stab the bird in the foot.

"Hey there, none of that. What are you planning to do if you actually hurt the beast, eh? Last I knew, you goblins couldn't exactly sprout wings." Darnak had abandoned his bulky pack, as well as his armor. He carried nothing more than his war club, no doubt to minimize the burden on his mount.

"What do you want?" Jig shouted.

Genevieve guided her hawk alongside. "My father sent orders to my men to confine me for 'collaborating with the enemy.' He lied about when he would arrive, because he didn't want to spur me into doing anything rash."

"Like breaking out and escaping on your brother's elfhawks?" Darnak asked, chuckling.

"Why are you here?" Jig asked. "I mean, why am *I* here?"

"I gave my word I'd try to protect you," said Genevieve. "There's nothing we can do to help your army, but we can at least get you back to your lair. I'm sorry, Jig. It's the best I can do for you."

Darnak leaned out to rub the hawk's neck, ruffling the wide blue feathers. This close, Jig could see the leather harness and stirrups Darnak used to ride the hawk. If he leaned any farther, he would tumble right off.

"Be careful!" Jig yelled.

"Nothing to worry about, lad," said Darnak. "You know, if you'd told me two years ago that I'd miss this, I'd have called you mad. Flying through the air, not a care in the world. There's nothing like it."

Jig craned his head, trying to pick out Braf and Shadowstar, but he was too high. The goblins were little more than panicked blue dots on the ground.

He hoped the wind wouldn't knock off his spectacles. The frames hooked pretty securely around his ears, but still. . . .

There was Wendel's army, moving out of the trees. Lines of foot soldiers marched in unison, their shields and spearheads gleaming in the sun. Behind them, archers continued to loose their arrows. There were horses as well, but as Gratz had predicted, they weren't galloping after the monsters.

Wendel's army had broken into two distinct groups. One attacked the orcs, who were busy assaulting Avery. The other spread out to pursue the retreating goblins and kobolds.

From up here, it reminded him of a tunnel-sweep, where goblins would line up and march through the caverns and tunnels to drive out the rats and other pests. Usually a second row of goblins waited in front to catch the rats for Golaka's stewpot. In this case, the elves at the top of the valley would provide the second line, killing anyone who retreated a step too far.

Trying to move as little as possible, Jig turned to look up at Darnak. "I'm not very good at directions, but isn't our lair that way?"

"Er." Darnak scowled. The hawk was flying them to the opposite side of the valley, directly toward King Wendel's army. "Like any intelligent beast, they sometimes get ideas into their heads."

Without warning, Darnak threw his weight to the right. The hawk tilted.

Jig closed his eyes, but that only made things worse. He could feel his bacon from this morning fighting to escape. Thankfully, the hawk soon leveled back out. Once again it flew straight toward the humans.

"Your cloak!" Genevieve swore. "Jig, get rid of your cloak!"

"Oh, no." The hawks were trained by color. Genevieve had used a strip of his cloak to send one of the smaller hawks to her father. Jig tried to squirm free, but the hawk's claws circling his body made it impossible.

"Does this mean we're going to your father's palace?" Relka asked.

"They're not trained to deliver messages to the palace," said Darnak. "They're trained to fly to the king. Elfhawks have senses that go beyond ours. They know exactly where Wendel is, and once they've accepted a message, nothing short of death will divert them."

Killing the hawk was hardly an option, even if Jig had a weapon that would penetrate the bird's skin.

"I'm not afraid," Relka said. "Shadowstar will—"

"Shadowstar is dying, Relka." It came out far angrier than Jig had intended. For all he knew, Shadowstar might already be dead. The thought made his stomach hurt.

I'm not dead yet, said Shadowstar. *This isn't how I'd choose to spend my last moments in this realm, though. Bouncing through the snow, staring up at Braf's backside. You'd think he could at least pull me headfirst.*

"Father's going to kill me," Genevieve said.

"He's going to kill *you*?" Jig yelled. As they reached the top of the valley, Jig saw bright green circles scattered throughout the woods. Tents, he realized. From the look of things, most of the camp's inhabitants were off chasing orcs and goblins and kobolds.

The hawk circled lower, giving Jig a better view. The humans had made their camp along a frozen stream. The tents appeared to be arranged in rings with the largest, fanciest tents near the center.

Jig spotted any number of horses, as well as other animals. Squat gray things, like miniature horses. Larger, dark-furred animals with curved horns, tied next to oversize carts. They reminded him of goats, only fluffier. Heavy tarps hid the contents of the carts, though Jig could see men unloading barrels from one. Closer to the middle of the camp, men and women melted pots of snow over the fires.

Darnak's hawk appeared to be flying toward one of the largest tents, near the center of camp. Genevieve followed, even though she probably could have flown elsewhere. Her hawk wasn't carrying a "message," after all.

A green and white banner hung limply from the center pole of the tent. The horses and other animals spooked and pulled away as the hawks swooped down. Jig did his best to keep from throwing up.

With a loud flapping, the hawk hovered lightly in the air, so Jig was roughly level with the top of the tents. The claws relaxed, and Jig dropped into the snow. Relka landed beside him.

By the time the hawks landed, Jig and Relka were surrounded by humans with spears. The king had kept at least some of his soldiers here. Why they needed so many weapons to capture two goblins was beyond Jig. After that ride, he could hardly stand, let alone fight.

"Sorry about this," Darnak muttered, dropping to the ground. He kept one hand on his war club.

Genevieve went a step farther, drawing her own sword and stepping in front of Jig. "We've come to speak with my father," she said. "You're welcome to try to stop us."

Darnak clucked his tongue. "I wouldn't envy you the job of explaining why you had to stick Wendel's daughter with your spears."

One of the guards lowered his spear. "But Your Highness, the goblins—"

"Have come to beg for mercy." Genevieve glanced at Jig, an apologetic expression on her face.

"The champion of Tymalous Shadowstar doesn't beg," said Relka.

Jig cleared his throat. "Actually—"

"He fought Billa the Bloody and single-handedly saved your father's army." Relka folded her arms. "Your king should be on his knees to thank Jig."

Genevieve rolled her eyes. "When you beg, don't let her say anything."

"The goblins will have to surrender their weapons," said another of the guards.

Jig handed his sword over to Darnak. Relka did the same with her own weapons.

"Darnak, what happened to Smudge?" Jig whispered.

The dwarf turned to show a metal box hanging from the side of his belt. Darnak had fashioned a light wire cage with a hinged top. Inside, Smudge sat happily munching the charred remains of an enormous moth.

"I used a bit of Earthmaker's magic to forge the bars," Darnak said. "Your pet's not the prettiest beast in the world, but he grows on you after a while. I imagine you could hang his cage by a lantern at night, and he'd do a nice job of clearing the insects from your tent."

Jig smiled and poked a finger through the bars to scratch Smudge's back. He squeezed his thumb against one of the bars, testing its strength. The cage was sturdier than it appeared. Not that this should have come as a surprise, given its creator. Dwarves probably even made their socks from plates of reinforced iron.

"You'd better hold on to him," Jig said.

"Aye." Darnak clapped Jig's shoulder. "Don't be giving up hope just yet, though."

Jig cocked his head, trying to hear the sounds of battle. By now Wendel's army had to be most of the way across the valley. The monsters would be fleeing in both directions, pinned between the elven forest and the charging soldiers. Which meant that any moment now—

The goblin drums changed from the panicked chaos of retreat to an even, three-beat rhythm. At the same time, the kobolds howled as one. The wolves joined in, their cries deeper and louder than the kobolds'.

"Sounds like they're rallying for one last attack," said one of the guards.

Darnak frowned and turned to Jig. Before he could say anything, Genevieve grabbed Jig by the arm and shoved him into the tent. "Say nothing until I signal," she whispered.

Large as the tent was, it felt as crowded as the goblin dining tables a year or so back, when Golaka was making ogre chitterlings. King Wendel practically had his own army crammed within these flapping walls. Jig could barely move without bumping into angry-looking men with big swords and heavy armor.

Grudgingly, the guards stepped back to clear a path.

The canvas walls turned the sun to twilight. In the center of the room, a long table sat to one side of a crackling fire. Smoke rose through a hole in the top of the tent.

Jig recognized more of Darnak's maps spread across the table. A heavyset man with short gray hair and a heavy cloak of black fur sat studying the maps. He wore a gold crown around his forehead. It looked terribly uncomfortable. The weight pushed his ears outward, making him look a bit like a goblin child.

Genevieve and Darnak pulled Jig toward the fire. He stumbled, nearly toppling headfirst into the flames before regaining his balance.

Genevieve sighed and said, "Father, I present to you the goblin who slew Billa the Bloody."

Where your son failed. The words were unspoken, but Jig suspected everyone heard them just the same.

King Wendel's pale, leathery face tightened. Jig heard unhappy mutters from the guards as well.

"He comes now to beg for mercy in exchange for that boon," Genevieve continued. "To throw himself before you, a broken and—"

"Can I surrender yet?" Jig asked. He perked his ears, straining to follow the sounds of battle in the valley. He glanced over his shoulder, but the guards had closed their circle, blocking any escape.

"Cowards, all of them," the king muttered. His voice was like a rusty sword being drawn from a too tight sheath. He stood, resting his hands on the edge of the table as he stared down at Jig. "What would you have me do, goblin? Allow thousands of monsters to roam freely through my land, slaughtering and eating my people? Turn Avery over to the orcs who even now assault its walls?"

"Your land?" Relka stepped up to stand beside Jig.

One blue finger jabbed in Genevieve's direction. "She and her brother came into *our* mountain, killing our warriors and dragging the rest off to serve as slaves! You're lucky Jig doesn't slay you all!"

Genevieve grabbed Relka's ear and yanked her back. Darnak sighed and shook his head.

The king's face turned dark. Jig remembered Barius' face doing the same thing, generally right before he punched Jig. Would the king punch the goblins himself, or did kings order others to do their punching?

"We owe him, Father," Genevieve said. The corner of her mouth quirked up. "Besides, he's kind of cute, with those big spectacles and—"

"Cute?" The king stared at Jig, as if he wanted nothing more than to shove the table out of the way and snap Jig's neck with his bare hands.

"Oh, Genevieve," Darnak murmured. "Always having to tug the griffin's tail."

"They murdered your brothers," the king said.

"And they saved your daughter," Genevieve snapped. "Is that worth nothing to you?"

On the bright side, at least Wendel's fury was no longer directed at Jig. Were kings allowed to punch their own daughters? If they were anything like goblin leaders, they could probably do whatever they liked. Though Genevieve looked fully prepared to strike him in return.

"Tell me, Father," said Genevieve. "What do you think Mother will do if she learns you ordered her only daughter arrested?"

The king glanced away. "I meant only to keep you safe."

"*Safe?* If I hadn't escaped, I would be locked away in Avery, a city currently under siege by orcs." Genevieve bit her lip, and when she spoke again, her voice was cool. "You meant to keep me from interfering with your little war."

What were the chances of Jig sneaking away in the confusion, he wondered.

Outside the tent someone shouted, "The monsters are attacking!"

So much for sneaking away.

The guards moved aside as a panting soldier shoved through the door flaps. "Sire, the goblins charge through the valley, toward our camp."

"A move of desperation," said the king. He glanced at the map, adjusting several blocks with one hand. "Order the lancers to intercept."

"They're *past* the lancers."

The king froze. "How?"

Before anyone could answer, a second guard followed the first. "The kobolds. They've circled around our lines, and they're running this way."

Jig shrunk back. He knew exactly how it had happened. The wolf-riders had fled around to the far side of Avery before turning back. Wolves were faster than anything in Wendel's army. They would have raced past the lines, never slowing as they charged the camp. Then, as Wendel's army tried to pursue, the kobolds would have done the same from the opposite end of the monster line. Kobolds weren't as fast as wolves, but they were quick, and none of the monsters were stopping to fight Wendel's soldiers. No doubt some would be cut down by human archers, but most should reach the camp. A perfect flanking maneuver. Gratz should be thrilled.

Genevieve turned to stare at Jig. Her father followed her gaze.

The king's face got even wrinklier when he was angry. He drew a gleaming sword and stepped around the table. "Treachery! You beg for mercy in order to buy time for your army."

"I didn't mean to!" Jig squeaked.

"And you! You *helped* these creatures?" He pointed his sword at Genevieve. "Arrest my daughter. Darnak as well. And kill the goblins!"

Clearly stunned, Darnak didn't react fast enough as Relka snatched her sword from him. She leaped toward the king. "For Shadowstar!"

She made it only a single step before a crossbow bolt knocked her to the ground. The king walked forward and shoved his sword through her belly.

It happened so fast. Jig ran toward Relka, barely noticing the other guards closing in around him. The crossbow bolt had struck Relka in the shoulder. She could survive that wound. But as the king yanked his sword free, blood spurted from her stomach.

Jig covered the wound with both hands. *Help me.*

I don't have a lot of power to spare right now, Jig. I'm sorry.

Jig tightened his fingers, trying to hold the wound shut to slow the bleeding. The king's sword had pierced Relka's stomach just below the scar left by Jig's own blade the year before. *She's dying because she believed in you. Because she wanted to protect the goblins, like* you *told us to do. Now help her!*

Slowly, magic filled Jig's fingers. Always before, Shadowstar's power had heated Jig's hands like a fire. Now only his fingertips felt anything at all.

"Father, no!"

Jig glanced back, then yelped and dove out of the way. The king's sword tore through his cloak and sliced a shallow gash along his back. Jig rolled and crawled as fast as he could, nearly burning his hand in the fire.

He reached back to touch the cut, and his fingers came away bloody. Shadowstar must not be strong enough to keep Jig's cloak swordproof. That wasn't a good sign.

The king followed, stabbing at Jig's legs. At least none of the guards appeared willing to shoot their crossbows, not with the king so close to Jig. So all Jig had to do was stay close to the king without getting killed. Also, he had to finish healing Relka. And find a way out of here.

The guards moved to block his escape. Everywhere he looked, boots crowded together like trees.

Jig tried to crawl beneath the table, but Wendel stabbed his sword through the end of Jig's cloak, pinning him in place. Jig gagged and rolled over. A sharp tug tore the cloak free, but Wendel was already standing over him.

"Wait!" Jig said. "If you want to fight me, do it with honor. A duel."

The king was going to kill Jig anyway. At least this way he wouldn't have to worry about the guards interfering. If Wendel was as stupid about honor as his sons had been . . .

"Stabbing an unarmed prisoner is the sort of treacherous, dishonorable thing a goblin would do," Jig added.

Wendel's jaw clenched. "True."

Darnak grabbed the king's arm. "Wendel, don't be an—" He clenched his jaw. "Sorry, sire. What I was meaning to say is, that's an ill-advised choice. We need you leading our defense against their counterattack, not wasting your time with this goblin."

Wendel's sword shook. It was a large weapon, with ornate engravings all along the blade. The pommel held a ring of emeralds and diamonds, surrounding a carved animal head. "They murdered my boys, Darnak."

"And we've killed more goblin sons than I can count," Darnak said. "Both before and after they killed the princes. Your daughter promised to put an end to the slaughter in exchange for this goblin's help against Billa."

"Genevieve exceeded her authority."

"Aye," said Darnak. "And you'd have done the same thing in your youth."

"Enough, Darnak." Wendel picked up Relka's sword and threw it to Jig. Jig barely managed to grab the hilt, and then Wendel swung.

Jig rolled out of the way. Unfortunately, he rolled right into the fire pit. The searing pain in his hand was annoying, but his years with Smudge had accustomed him to such things. He scrambled back, brushing embers from his skin. The edges of his cloak began to burn. Some of the guards snickered.

He patted himself out, and something jabbed him in the side. He checked his pocket as he backed away. Perhaps Shadowstar had slipped an extra weapon into the cloak.

His fingers found the tiny goblin figurine Darnak had given him. Having no better ideas, he flung it at the king.

The metal goblin bounced off of the king's forehead, right beneath the crown. Wendel stepped back. A dot of blood formed on his skin, then dripped down over his nose.

Jig lunged.

Wendel was faster than he looked. He parried Jig's thrust down and to one side. The blade barely scratched the side of his leg. Then the king punched Jig's face with his other hand.

The sword slipped away, and Jig found himself on the dirt, staring up at the top of the tent. His mouth tasted like blood. Wendel punched *hard*. Jig tried to sit up, but movement made him want to vomit.

King Wendel filled his vision. Two of them, actually. Two Wendels and two big swords. As if one wasn't enough. Jig blinked, trying to clear his eyes and reconcile the two kings. Which sword should Jig try to avoid?

Wendel swung. Jig's panicked scream almost blocked out the simultaneous thud and clang that followed.

A slender sword blade crossed with a battered war club over Jig's head. Both weapons held the king's sword away from Jig. "You dare to raise arms against your king?" Wendel asked.

"I raise arms to support your daughter," Darnak said. "To support the future queen of Adenkar."

"You swore an oath to me."

"To you and Jeneve, aye," Darnak said, showing no sign of strain as he held the king's sword at bay. None of the guards so much as breathed. "She's the one who'll be cursing my shade if I let the two of you get killed, and she'd have the right of it. I've been helping to raise your children from the time they were in diapers, and I've watched too many of them die. I'll not see Ginny lost to the same foolishness. We're about to be overrun. They've already reached the edge of our encampment. That goblin you're about to murder is the only one who might be able to stop them from slaughtering every last one of us."

Wendel turned toward Genevieve, who used her own sword to shove the king's weapon to the side. "Besides," she said, her voice light, "if you kill him, you'll never find out what poison he used."

He blinked. "Poison?"

Genevieve pointed to the cut on the king's leg. "When we attacked the goblin lair, I learned that goblins poison their blades."

"Pah. Darnak can heal the wound." Wendel shoved Genevieve back, then raised his sword again.

"Begging Your Majesty's pardon, but goblins have been known to use some nasty toxins," Darnak said. "Without knowing the actual poison, well, I might be able to save your life, but the side effects could be unpleasant."

Jig stared from Darnak to Genevieve and back, trying to understand. They both knew perfectly well that goblins didn't use poison on their weapons. Given the number of self-inflicted injuries Jig had healed over the years, poison would have wiped out half the lair.

They were bluffing. Like Grell had done. Only they were doing it to protect him.

Wendel spun to face Jig. "Was the blade poisoned?"

Jig managed to sit up without losing his last meal. "Well, I *am* a goblin."

"Tell Darnak what toxin you used, or—"

"You'll kill me?" Jig glanced at Relka. She was pale, but still breathing. "You'll do that anyway. And how many goblins can die knowing they killed a king?"

Slowly Wendel lowered his sword. "What do you want, goblin?"

"A treaty," Jig said. "Like you have with the elves." His lip was puffy and split, making his voice sound funny. "I want you to stop killing us."

Which was stronger, Jig wondered, the king's hatred of goblins or his desire to survive? From the fury on his face, it was a close thing.

More and more guards were glancing around, their expressions tense. Even Darnak jumped as a wolf howled nearby.

"As if these beasts would listen to you," Wendel said.

"They'll listen to him." Relka's voice was weak as a child's, and she drooled blood as she spoke. "He's Jig Dragonslayer."

Jig prayed she was right. *Have Braf get to the drummers and the orcs. Tell them to order a halt. Don't retreat, but wait for my signal.*

There was no answer. *Shadowstar?* Jig's chest tightened.

Then in the distance, the drumbeats changed to a slow, steady rhythm, like a heartbeat. The horns blew a moment later.

Jig was already moving toward Relka. He could barely feel Shadowstar's magic anymore, but he pressed what power he could into her wound.

"Sire, the goblins—" One of the guards stood in the open flap of the tent, gasping for breath. "They've stopped."

"How?" For the first time, the hatred had faded slightly from Wendel's voice, replaced by genuine curiosity.

"The power of Tymalous Shadowstar," Relka said, holding her necklace.

"Who?" asked Wendel.

Shadowstar, god of idiot goblins. Jig pinched the skin together, trying to physically force the wound to seal. *What had Relka been thinking? Every time Jig thought he had seen the limits of her madness, she proved him wrong. Leaping onto a hawk, attacking a king, all in the name of a god who—*

Shadowstar's laughter, soft and strained, made Jig jump. *You think she did that for me?*

Ever since I stabbed her, she hasn't been able to shut up about the glory of Tymalous Shadowstar.

You're a smart one, Jig. For a goblin. Silence followed, long enough that Jig started to wonder if something had happened. Then Shadowstar said, *She could have stayed behind with her dying god. Instead she went with you. Why do you think she did that?*

Because she's crazy!

Another quiet chuckle. *Probably.*

"Order the men to withdraw, Father," said Genevieve. "Sign the goblin's treaty."

"Your sons are gone," Darnak said softly. "This won't bring them back. And losing you and Genevieve will destroy the queen."

Wendel's shoulders slumped. He wiped blood from his face and nodded. "The cure, goblin."

What cure? Oh, right. The poison.

"You *do* have an antidote, don't you?" Genevieve's glare rivaled Grell's.

Keeping one hand on Relka's wound, Jig used his other to fish through his cloak. "Swallow this, and you should be fine."

The king backed away. Rarely had Jig seen such an expression of horror from anyone, goblin or human. "It's a toe."

"It's been soaked in lizard-fish blood," Jig lied. "Something about their blood counters the poison."

"It's a *toe*," Wendel repeated.

Darnak handed a flask to the king. "Drink deep, sire. Dwarven ale's strong enough to mask most any taste."

Jig ignored them. He could feel Relka's muscle repairing itself one strand at a time as Shadowstar's magic trickled from Jig's fingertips. He hadn't even tried to pull the crossbow bolt from her shoulder yet, but if he could heal the worst of the damage to her stomach, she should survive.

Angry voices outside the tent made him cringe. At

least one belonged to a goblin. What were they doing here? Hadn't they heard the drums? If they attacked now, everything would fall apart.

Several of the humans readied their weapons. Both Genevieve and Darnak looked at Jig. He shook his head. This wasn't anything of his planning.

The voices drew closer, and then the tent flap was flung open. Two figures stood in the blinding sunlight.

"Jig?" Trok's voice.

The smaller figure shoved him aside. "See? Hessafa told you smelly goblin was here! Always trust scent!"

CHAPTER 17

Jig had never realized how many people could fit onto the mountainside. He tried not to shiver as he glanced around. Kobolds and a few orcs covered the rocky ground. Many of the kobolds watched from the branches, shoved aside by a small delegation of orcs. Most of the orcs had already left, claiming the colder, treeless land higher up the mountainside. Apparently they *liked* the snow and wind. It gave them more opportunity to prove how tough they were. Rumor had it that a few of them had even taken to diving naked into the icy lake.

Orcs were weird. Or maybe the cold helped with the itching. During the attack at Avery, some of the orcs had circled around the town, searching for another way in that didn't involve being flung by a tree. In the process they had trampled through the vines the humans called poison ivy. They said regular poison ivy was bad enough, but these vines grew on elven soil. . . .

The hobgoblins were already discussing how best to bring the vines back and incorporate them into their traps.

Goblins crowded by the cave, packed together like pickles in a barrel. Jig grimaced and tried to force that image from his mind.

A smaller group of hobgoblins stood nearby, scowling and testing their weapons. Apparently, with Jig gone and the goblin warriors all dragged away to Avery, the hobgoblins had run wild, looting the lair and slaughtering anyone who dared to challenge them. They had tried to do the same thing to Jig and his companions when they finally returned.

Oakbottom had tossed nine hobgoblins down the mountainside before the rest retreated. They retaliated by loosing some of their tunnel cats.

Bastard and the other wolves had solved that problem. Fortunately, Braf had managed to heal the stump of Bastard's leg, and the three-legged wolf was still as mean as ever. Jig just hoped they hadn't developed a taste for tunnel cats.

For now, the wolves were being kept at a smaller cave farther up the mountain. Jig still needed to figure out how to feed the beasts. Maybe the hobgoblin chief would donate a few of the warriors who had mocked Jig in the past.

Jig cocked his head, automatically silencing his thoughts while he waited for Tymalous Shadowstar to rebuke him for such a vindictive, goblinlike thought. There was no response. Jig had heard nothing from his god since leaving the king's tent four days ago.

With a sigh, he reached down to stroke Smudge, who sat happily in his cage on Jig's belt. At least the weather had improved since the battle the humans were calling "Billa's Fall." The snow was gone, and Jig could stand outside without shivering. Without shivering from the cold, at any rate. He pulled his cloak tighter, trying not to think about what was about to happen.

"They're coming," said Relka.

Directly ahead, Princess Genevieve approached on foot, followed by Darnak and her retinue of human soldiers. Her face was flushed from the hike, but she was grinning.

Beside Relka, Gratz was frantically paging through his notes. Dark blue scabs covered his face and arms from being trapped beneath Bastard. He was lucky the wolf hadn't killed him. Jig had worried that Gratz would try to punish Bastard for his injuries, but Gratz had been delighted. These days, the trick was to get him to stop showing off his "war scars."

"Do you remember your lines, sir?" Gratz asked. "Protocol dictates that you speak first."

Jig glanced at Trok, who made a half-hearted grab for his sword, as if offering to shut Gratz up. Jig shook his head, then turned his attention to Genevieve and Darnak.

The princess wore a new black tabard, this one trimmed with gold. A thin silver band circled her forehead. Jig could hear some of the kobolds admiring the crown.

Darnak had brushed his beard into twin braids. He carried a new war club of gleaming black wood. If the kobolds liked Genevieve's crown, they were practically falling out of the trees at the sight of Darnak's armor. Gleaming steel covered his chest, thighs, and shoulders. Heavy links of mail protected his arms and legs. Combined with the bulging pack on his back, Jig was amazed the dwarf could walk at all.

Genevieve stopped. Goblins, orcs, and kobolds all began to whisper.

Oh, right. Jig took a step forward. "Welcome, Princess Genevieve, to—" He swallowed. The other monsters weren't going to like this. "To Goblinshire."

Behind him, Braf whispered, "To where?"

There was a sharp thud, like a wooden cane smacking a goblin skull. Jig relaxed slightly. He had worried Grell wouldn't be able to make it.

"Well met, goblin," said Genevieve. With one hand, she slowly pulled her sword from its sheath.

Every monster went silent. Jig could see them reaching for their own weapons. Others searched the mountainside. Genevieve hadn't brought enough soldiers to fight, unless this was some sort of trap.

Indeed, looking at the stern expression on the princess' face, Jig was half tempted to draw his own weapon, even though they had warned him that this was coming.

Now was the part where Jig was supposed to kneel and let Genevieve finish a brief ceremony to seal the treaty. A ceremony that involved Genevieve resting her sword on Jig's shoulder. Right beside his neck. Where a slight tug would slit his throat.

Gratz coughed and waved his hand, urging Jig forward.

Jig stared at the sword. "Grell's the chief. Maybe she should be the one to—"

"Finish that sentence, and I'll have Golaka feed you to your wolves," Grell snapped.

Right. Jig dropped to one knee and held his breath. Genevieve had saved his life, back in the king's tent. She wouldn't kill him now.

The flat of the sword landed on his shoulder, hard enough to bruise.

"In the name of Wendel, King of Adenkar, in recognition for your—" Genevieve coughed. Her mouth was quivering, as if she were trying not to laugh. "Your service to the throne, I hereby grant thee the title of baron, Lord of Goblinshire and all who dwell in that land. Rise, Baron Jig of Goblinshire."

Jig waited until her sword was back in its scabbard to stand. As he did, Darnak stepped forward, holding a green ribbon with a silver medallion. As many times as he had mocked Relka's necklace, this one was worse. The medallion had the same ridiculous crest as Genevieve's armor. Darnak looped it over Jig's head like a noose.

In the silence that followed, everyone heard Grell's muttered, "If he thinks he can take my room, I'll strangle him with his own ribbon."

Jig turned the medallion over in his hand, studying the boar on the crest. Well, it had nice fangs, if nothing else.

A few of the human guards clapped their hands together. The noise startled the closest monsters into drawing weapons.

"They were applauding," Darnak said hastily. "To congratulate you. Genevieve ordered them to applaud, or else she'd be leaving them here to serve you."

From the look on the humans' faces, they were as unhappy about the whole process as Jig. In order for this treaty to be valid, apparently there had to be a baron to oversee the goblins' lands. Jig didn't know who had been more horrified, himself or the king. But according to the humans' laws, this was the only way.

Even now, Jig suspected the king was hard at work rewriting those laws. Just as, from the sound of it, the other goblins were hard at work fighting not to laugh.

Darnak unrolled a heavy scroll of lambskin. Wax seals and ribbons decorated the bottom beside the king's signature. Darnak pulled out a blue quill and dipped it into the pot of ink lashed to the strap of his backpack, then handed the quill to Jig.

Ink splattered the bottom of the treaty as Jig scrawled his name. He returned the quill to Darnak, then turned to face the other monsters.

"That's it?" Braf asked.

"I think so," Jig said. He glanced at Genevieve, then added, "They've officially given us our own mountain."

Genevieve was clearly losing her struggle to avoid laughing in Jig's face. "I've convinced my father to forgo your first tax payment, so you won't have to worry about that until midsummer."

And Jig had thought his stomach couldn't hurt any worse. "Tax payment?"

"I'll let you explain that one to the hobgoblin chief," Grell said. She didn't bother to hide her amusement.

"You're also responsible for maintaining order here in . . . Goblinshire," Genevieve continued. "In the case of war, you can be summoned to lead your warriors to assist in the protection of Adenkar. A representative of my father's court will be by in the next few days to review your other obligations and duties."

From her wicked grin, she was already selecting which human to punish with goblin duty.

Darnak squeezed Jig's arm. "Good luck to you, Jig. Goblinshire has a fine protector. An unusual one, to be certain. But you've proven yourself a resourceful lad. Don't let your newfound title worry you. Having lived among goblins and their backstabbing, treacherous ways, you're far better prepared for politics than most."

Apparently that was the end of it. Genevieve pulled out her pipe as she turned to go.

Wheezing laughter turned to coughs behind him. Poor Grell was laughing so hard her canes barely supported her. Before Jig could say anything, Trok tugged his sleeve.

"Grell doesn't sound so good," he said, his voice eager. He sounded like a child about to get his first taste of Golaka's elf soufflé. "Remember what you promised me."

"I remember," Jig snapped. Already other monsters were closing in. Goblins, mostly. But there were hobgoblins, kobolds, even an orc, all shoving to be the first to talk to him. Jig had a sinking feeling that this would be his life for some time to come.

"Gratz!"

Gratz snapped to attention. "Yes, Lord General, sir?"

Jig rolled his eyes. "Deal with them." Before Gratz could answer, Jig scurried after Genevieve and Darnak. "Princess, wait!"

Genevieve stopped a short distance down the trail.

Jig moved uncomfortably close to the human and lowered his voice. "You haven't told your father the truth about Barius and Ryslind, have you?"

Genevieve shook her head. "What truth? That they were idiots who never should have come here? Even if I wanted to tell him, it's going to be a long time before he's willing to listen to me again."

"Don't worry yourself too much," said Darnak.

"Once your mother goes to work, she'll bring him around. She got him to rescind my banishment, didn't she? The way I spoke to him, I half expected he'd be declaring war on all dwarfkind."

"There are those who would say yours was a harsher punishment," Genevieve said, pulling out her pipe. "Removed from the king's service and given to his daughter."

"A cruel sentence, to be sure," Darnak said, grinning.

She turned her attention back to Jig and smiled. "Besides, as long as I'm the only human who knows the truth, it means I have you as a friend."

"What do you mean?" Jig asked.

"My brothers are dead. That puts me directly in line for the throne, once my father passes on." Her fingers tightened. "If the people learn that the Baron of Goblinshire murdered two human princes, they'll go right back to hunting you goblins down. And that means you and I are going to be friends for a long time." She flashed a smile. "My family isn't terribly popular these days. I'll need a few friends."

That was reasoning a goblin could understand. Jig smiled back. "Thanks!"

Sure, she was manipulating him. But if she wanted to *keep* manipulating him, she also had to help keep him alive. What more could Jig ask?

He turned to Darnak and said, "Thanks for healing my tooth."

"Thank Earthmaker," Darnak said, touching his amulet.

Jig had tried and failed to heal the broken tooth himself, following his fight with the king. He was still adjusting to the everyday scrapes and cuts of life in the mountain. He hadn't realized how spoiled he had become over the past few years.

Darnak poked a finger through Smudge's cage. "You take care of your master now, you hear?"

Genevieve shuddered. Apparently humans simply couldn't appreciate a good spider. "Come, Darnak. We've a long ride home."

Jig waited among the trees and watched them leave. Partly he wanted to make sure none of the monsters tried to ambush them as they left. Mostly he simply wasn't ready to go back and be a baron. This was worse than being chief.

"You arranged all of this, didn't you?" he asked, staring at the sky. He took off his spectacles and wiped them on his shirt. "I don't know how, but this is all your fault."

"Is he speaking to you again?"

Jig yelled and fumbled for his sword. "Relka?"

She bent to retrieve his spectacles from the mud. "He's not dead, you know."

"Billa the Bloody stabbed him with a god-killing sword," Jig snapped, grabbing his spectacles. "And unlike you, Shadowstar didn't have a dwarf priest around to finish healing him."

According to Braf, Shadowstar had simply . . . disappeared. Braf wasn't sure, but he thought Shadowstar had said something like "It's good to see you again," before he died. Whatever that meant. Between the drums and the horns and the shouts, Jig suspected Braf had simply misheard.

"Tymalous Shadowstar was one of the Forgotten Gods," said Relka. "You saw how the humans and elves and other 'civilized' races couldn't even remember his name."

"So what?"

Relka pointed back toward the lair. "Kobolds and hobgoblins and orcs and goblins, all living together without killing each other. Not much, at any rate. A treaty with the humans. A goblin baron." She spread her arms. "Jig, Shadowstar was civilizing us. That's why he stopped talking to you. It's not enough that we've forgotten him. Not yet, anyway. But it's enough that we can't see or hear him anymore."

That was the dumbest theory Jig had ever heard. Though it did sound like something Shadowstar might do.

Could Shadowstar have somehow survived being

run through with Isa's sword? "You really believe that?"

"I know it."

Relka was an idiot. Yet the knots in Jig's stomach eased a little. Shadowstar was a god, after all. Jig was only a goblin. Who was he to say what could or couldn't have happened?

"Relka, when Shadowstar was dying . . . or not dying. When he was back there in the valley. You could have stayed with him. Instead you came with me. Why—?" He hesitated, then decided he would need a few mugs of klak beer before he was ready to ask *that* question. "Never mind."

Jig stared at the medallion Genevieve had given him. Strange, to think that such an ugly little thing could stop the humans from killing them. From doing it openly, at least. This and his name on a piece of paper were all it took.

"Where is this so-called baron?" That sounded like the hobgoblin chief. Jig turned to see him making his way down the path, followed by a clearly agitated Gratz. "Your idiot goblins have ruined three of our hunting traps!"

"I'm sorry, Lord," Gratz shouted. "He didn't want to stand in line, and—"

The hobgoblin drew his sword, and Gratz shut up.

"What did they do to your traps?" Jig asked.

The hobgoblin's scarred, wrinkled face was a deep yellow, flushed with anger. "Well, one of them fell into our pit and broke his leg. Another tripped a rockslide Charak had been working on. The third . . . well, that wasn't a trap, exactly. By that time, my hobgoblins were a bit annoyed. Your goblin kind of stumbled onto Renlok's spear. Eleven times."

Before Jig could figure out how to respond, Trok came running down to join them. A hobgoblin with a scar along his face was with him. Jig recognized Charak, a trapmaker better known to the goblins by his nickname, Slash.

Trok stepped so close to the hobgoblin chief that

their chests nearly touched. "One of your tunnel cats got into the wolf pens again! Killed two of my goblins in the process."

Gratz cleared his throat.

"Right." Trok jabbed a thumb at Jig. "Two of *his* goblins."

Jig groaned. His stomach was bad enough, but now his head was beginning to hurt as well. If there was one thing the hobgoblins wouldn't tolerate, it was an attack against their trained tunnel cats. "Was there anything left of the cat?"

Slash grinned. "What makes you think they were fighting?"

Oh. Could tunnel cats and wolves interbreed? That was just what Jig needed, a litter of cross-breeds running loose in the mountain, eating anyone who got too close.

Jig grabbed Trok by the arm and shoved him toward Slash. "Go help the hobgoblins retrieve their tunnel cat." If he was lucky, maybe the wolf would eat Trok, and he would have one less problem to worry about. "Gratz, sit down with the hobgoblin chief and come up with some regulations about hunting and traps."

As Jig had hoped, the goblins and hobgoblins immediately began to argue with one another, instead of with him. Only after they had gone did he realize the rest of the monsters had disappeared. The mountainside was actually quiet! He turned back to Relka. "Where did everybody go?"

"Golaka and I were working in the kitchens earlier, preparing a few roast hobgoblins. I guess they must have finished roasting."

Jig's stomach rumbled at the thought. The hobgoblins might not be too happy about their dead warriors, but even they couldn't turn down Golaka's cooking. He wondered if barons were entitled to extra helpings.

He turned to head back, then hesitated.

"What is it?"

Jig perked his ears. The trees were empty. He heard

nothing but the wind in the branches and the very distant sound of Trok and the hobgoblin chief shouting at one another.

"Nothing," he said. "I thought . . . nothing." He must have imagined the faint sound of bells in the distance.

He shook his head. "Come on, Relka. Let's go eat some hobgoblins."

Civilized, indeed.

Jim Hines

The **Jig the Goblin** series

"Clever satire… Reminiscent of Terry Pratchett
and Robert Asprin at their best."
Romantic Times

"If you've always kinda rooted for the little guy,
even maybe had a bit of a place in your heart for
Gollum, rather than the Boromirs and Gandalfs
of the world, pick up *Goblin Quest.*"
—*The SF Site*

"This exciting adult fairy tale is filled with
adventure and action, but the keys to the fantasy
are Jig and the belief that the mythological creatures are real in the realm of Jim C. Hines."
—*Midwest Book Review*

"A rollicking ride, enjoyable from beginning to
end… Jim Hines has just become one of my
must-read authors." -—Julie E. Czerneda

GOBLIN QUEST   978-07564-0400-0
GOBLIN HERO   978-07564-0442-0
GOBLIN WAR   978-07564-0493-2

To Order Call: 1-800-788-6262
www.dawbooks.com

Tanya Huff
The *Smoke* Series

Featuring Henry Fitzroy, Vampire

"Fans of *Buffy* and *The X-Files* will cheer the latest exploits of Tony Foster, wizard-in-training.... This spin-off from Huff's popular Blood series stands alone as an entertaining supernatural adventure with plenty of sex, violence, and sarcastic humor."

—*Publishers Weekly*

SMOKE AND SHADOWS
0-7564-0263-8
978-0-7564-0263-1

SMOKE AND MIRRORS
0-7564-0348-0
978-0-7564-0348-5

SMOKE AND ASHES
978-0-7564-0415-4

To Order Call: 1-800-788-6262
www.dawbooks.com

Kristen Britain

The **GREEN RIDER** series

"Wonderfully captivating...a truly
enjoyable read." —Terry Goodkind

"A fresh, well-organized fantasy debut,
with a spirited heroine and a reliable
supporting cast." —*Kirkus*

"The author's skill at world building and her feel
for dramatic storytelling make this first-rate
fantasy a good choice." —*Library Journal*

"Britain keeps the excitement high from beginning to end, balancing epic magical battles with
the humor and camaraderie of Karigan and her
fellow Riders." —*Publishers Weekly*

GREEN RIDER   0-88677-858-1
FIRST RIDER'S CALL   0-7564-0209-3

and now available in hardcover:
THE HIGH KING'S TOMB 0-7564-0209-3

To Order Call: 1-800-788-6262
www.dawbooks.com